Dear Readers,

I'm so honored and delighted to have you holding this edition in your hands. Between these covers is nearly two years worth of brainstorming, researching, drafting, editing, and polishing—three books that I've infused with as much fun and filth as I possibly could. *Misadventures with a Professor, Misadventures of a Curvy Girl,* and *Misadventures in Blue* are all products of my wandering (and depraved) mind, and I hope you'll join me for the sexy, swoony ride from the lush English countryside through the sprawling prairie to the waiting arms of a rugged police officer... A journey through some of my absolute favorite tropes in romance.

In fact, writing these tropes helped me cement why I love writing this genre so much.

See, when I first started baking up ideas for the Misadventures series, I had the opportunity for the first time since I started writing romance to ask myself *why* I loved it. I already knew why I loved telling the kinds of stories I did—stories about history and mythology and spirituality—but why was I drawn to tell those stories through the lens of romance, and erotic romance in particular? Why does it make so much internal sense to me?

Another way of asking that question is what do a professor, a farmer, and a cop all have in common?

To answer, I'll need to back up a little bit to when I started writing as Sierra several years ago. And when I started the Sierra name with the Markham Hall series (eagle-eyed readers will spot Oliver's connection to the Markham family in *Misadventures with a Professor*), I made myself a promise. And that promise was that I was only going to write the books that I wanted to write; I was only going to chase after ideas if they lit me on fire with excitement. And sometimes that's been its own struggle—when you have an idea you're passionate about, you tend to push yourself harder. Higher, further, faster, as Captain Marvel says. There's no mentally checking out on a project you're dedicated to, and there's no time for fooling around. There's also no pulling back from the edge with a story that needs to be told daringly.

Sometimes, people will tell me that I'm fearless, and I don't always know what to say to that, because I don't *feel* fearless. When I'm writing, when I'm neck-deep in the sludge of characters making bad decisions and encountering all their shames, big and small, I am the opposite of fearless. I'm filled with doubt. I'm terrified of creating a story that will hurt or harm readers. I'm convinced that any lack of moral clarity on my part is going to rip open a hole in the integrity universe and end the world.

(My mind is a pretty intense place to be, if you haven't already guessed.)

But I realized after a while that when people say the word *fearless*, they mean *brave*, which has nothing to do with the presence of fear and everything to do with the actions one takes independent of fear. And when people mean that *I'm* brave, I think what they really mean is that my characters are brave.

Which brings me back to why I love romance.

In romance, we only have one real guarantee, and that's the Happily Ever After, the Holy Grail ending where our couple (or thruple, in the case of *Misadventures of a Curvy Girl*) has found a place of sustainable peace and growth and love. Which means no matter how deep the wound, no matter how gloomy the dark night of the soul, there will be justice and redemption and love at the end.

Which means that all bravery is rewarded in romance. Courage is ultimately honored.

I love romance because it infuses struggle and vulnerability with optimism and hope. And I love erotic romance in particular because sexuality has a way of cracking open every shell we put around ourselves for pride and protection. Sex has a way of making us exposed and human, of getting to the deepest, rawest parts of us that we might not even have words for.

Whether it's shame or curiosity about kink, as in *Misadventures with a Professor*, or internalized fatphobia in *Misadventures with a Curvy Girl*, or falling in love with a man younger than you like in *Misadventures in Blue*, sexuality becomes the locus of the brave and hard conversations we have to have with ourselves about who we are and who we want to become. It also becomes a space where we see characters mirroring growth and struggle as it happens in real life—with mistakes, with pain, with progress that can slide sideways and careen backward. Sex positivity and body positivity and anti-ageism doesn't happen all at once, and it doesn't happen in a straight line.

The beauty of romance is that we can witness growth in all its messy, tormented glory— and know that at the end, all that mess and torment is rewarded. All the vulnerability, all the stripped-down, chaotic humanity—it's all acknowledged, honored, and loved at the end. And those are the only kinds of stories I want to write.

So what do a professor, a farmer, and a cop all have in common? (Other than being absolutely *filthy* in bed, of course?)

All of them—and the people they love—make mistakes, feel shame, feel fear—and yet they are brave and chase love anyway. They find the Happily Ever Afters they deserve not because they're perfect, but because they're *human* and therefore enough.

What I love about romance and the Misadventures series as a whole is that it shows us over and over again that a sexy, sweet, tender HEA belongs to all of us, no matter our backgrounds, our jobs, our fears, or our mistakes. A Misadventures book is a journey that belongs to all of us, and so I hope you'll be brave with me today and turn the page. I hope you'll find as much fun reading my spanky professor and stoic country boys and hunky cop as I did writing them. And I hope Zandy and Ireland and Cat will inspire you to chase bravely after your own Happily Ever Afters long after you read the last page.

A Collection of Misadventures

FORBIDDEN TRINITY

A Collection of Misadventures

FORBIDDEN TRINITY

USA TODAY BESTSELLING AUTHOR

SIERRA SIMONE

WATERHOUSE PRESS

TABLE OF CONTENTS

MISADVENTURES

WITH A

PROFESSOR

To Ashley Brown Morris and Kate Fasse—
Our friendship uses only the good notes.

CHAPTER ONE

ZANDY

I forgot the umbrella.

I remembered a backup battery charger, lipstick, condoms, my passport, a disposable toothbrush, and an appropriate amount of petty cash in case of emergency. I spent hours perfecting my hair and makeup into a look that proclaimed the perfect blend of sexual and social experience. I researched my route and destination and reviewed my notes for the plan.

I was prepared for every single contingency—except the most obvious one, which is that it rains in England sometimes.

Okay, a lot of times. It rains in England *a lot of times*.

And I forgot the damn umbrella in my hotel room.

I squint up at the street sign on the building next to me and then back down to my phone, trying to get my bearings. Unfortunately, the rain has made it nearly impossible to view the app on my screen, and even more unfortunately, I'm certain I've never come across this street in all my planning and preparation, which means I'm definitely lost—although it's hard to tell, given how London streets rename themselves at bafflingly random intervals.

And it's while I'm standing there trying to rub my rain-spattered screen on my equally rain-spattered dress that the silver drizzle decides to become a downpour, darkening the already dim evening and soaking through my dress and hair in a matter of seconds.

"Shit!" I mutter, cupping a hand over my eyes, trying to peer through the chilling curtain of rain. I can't even see across the street, much less try to get my bearings.

"Shit, shit, shit."

A black cab hisses by, sending a wave of water up and over my only pair of high heels—bought specially for tonight and the plan—and it's the last straw. Screw getting my bearings. I want to get *dry*. I start walking, heels *squelch-squelching* as I go, and in a fit of pique, I yank them off my feet and start jogging barefoot down the slick sidewalk, wondering how my perfectly orchestrated agenda got so off-kilter.

When my father arranged for me to spend the summer with an old friend of his as a research assistant, I was beyond excited. An entire summer in the English countryside cataloging old books and annotating metadata? Basically paradise for me.

But my real excitement came when I realized I'd have a night alone in London before I went to Professor Graeme's house. A single night in one of the best cities in the world to fix a very serious problem of mine:

I, Zandy Lynch, twenty-two years old and soon-to-be-graduate student, am a virgin. And that is no longer acceptable.

I'm tired of ending my nights with a skinny margarita and a vibrator. I'm tired of dates that go nowhere, tired of coming home alone, tired of lying in bed with a hollow *ache* that no amount of battery power can massage away. And it was as I was poring over my acceptance letter for library school that I realized I've become that silly old stereotype: the spinster librarian. The virgin nerd.

Ugh.

It's not *fair*. I never asked to be a virgin at twenty-two! I never asked to be a spinster! All I ever asked for was a cute guy with a willing penis.

Okay, well, and a college education—preferably graduate level or higher.

And a good job—preferably in academia or a related field.

And an extensive shared list of common interests—including, but not limited to, modern literature, premodern literature, postmodern literature, Tolkien marginalia, crossword puzzles, animals, coffee, travel to places where druids sacrificed virgins, and variations of fruit pie.

So maybe my standards were a little high.

I started the plan the way I start everything—with a trip to the library. I outlined my objectives, decided on my research methodology, and created a timeline. I devoured books, articles, studies, and anecdotal data about how to get over my hymen-hurdle, and after all that, I came to a very certain conclusion.

I'd been going about this all wrong.

Sex is supposed to be spontaneous, unforced, mutually initiated. I can't plan my way into someone's pants...but I *can* plan the perfect environment to facilitate depantsing. So when Dad surprised me with the research vacation, I knew this night in London was my chance to find the perfect depantsing environment.

Except now it's raining and I'm lost and barefoot and the plan has quickly unraveled into a wet, chilly disaster.

Okay, Zandy, focus.

There was a tube station marked on my phone's map before the water made it totally impossible to navigate—maybe it's just past the next cross street? I'll duck inside, out of the rain, get my phone working again, and think of my next steps. And check my makeup.

I only have tonight, after all, and I'm not ready to give up, umbrella or not.

I pick up my jog, my head bent down to shield my eyes from the worst of the rain, the sopping-wet hem of my dress slapping and sticking around my thighs, when I collide with a firm chest and wheeze out an *oof*. Something resembling a grunt comes from the chest.

From him.

Warm hands come up to my elbows to steady me, and I look up into a pale face marked by darkly slashed eyebrows, high cheekbones, and a squared, clean-shaven jaw. His eyes in the rainy night seem like every kind of color, light and dark, brown and blue and green, and they're framed by the longest, sultriest lashes I've ever seen on a man.

But it's his mouth that fascinates me—slightly too wide and slightly too thin but hauntingly pretty, with perfectly formed peaks at his upper lip and a tantalizing hint of fullness to his lower one. Rain drips from his cheeks and the longish ends of his dark hair to catch along the sharp edges of his lips and gather in the tempting bow of his philtrum.

And with a sudden illicit thrill, I realize I want to lick the rainwater off those lips. I want to kiss them until they're warm and soft under my own. I want to feel the shape of his mouth under mine, murmuring my name—except...

That perfect, rain-slicked mouth is currently creased in a harsh, unhappy scowl.

CHAPTER TWO

OLIVER

She's shivering.

It takes me a moment to notice, as I'm still processing how someone emerged out of this tempest right in front of me. I'm also still processing how this someone in question is a creature made of pale skin, dark hair, and a sinfully red and lush mouth. Like a vampiress straight from a storybook but with the most incongruously innocent eyes I've ever seen.

She's also young, drenched to the bone, and utterly, utterly inappropriately dressed for a night like this.

"Why aren't you wearing a coat?" I demand over the roar of the rain, and her gaze blinks up at me—which is when I realize she's been staring at my mouth. A kick of heat goes straight to my cock.

I ignore it.

"And why are you barefoot?"

Her eyes flick back to my frowning mouth, and her own mouth parts ever so slightly, as if my bad-tempered scowl fascinates her. Her tongue darts over her lower lip, licking away a bead of rainwater that settled over her fire-engine-red

lipstick, and I find I want her to do it again. And again. And again.

I could watch her licking rain off her lips for the rest of my life.

"I'm looking for the Goose and Gander," she finally offers. It's hard to hear her over the rain, and yet even with the *whoosh* and *churr* of the torrent, I can hear her accent. Broad and wide and a little flat, American television style.

I know where the Goose and Gander is. I just came from there, actually, having endured a meal deconstructed into various mason jars and served on a wooden plank for the sake of seeing some old friends. But I'd drawn the line at overpriced cocktails decanted into chemistry beakers and opted to go back to my hotel instead.

Which is where I want to be—in my dry bed, with dry clothes and dry blankets and a dry book—not in the drenching rain with a barefoot little American. No matter how red her lips are. Or how enticingly her wet dress clings to her frame.

I scowl again.

"It's back that way," I say, pointing behind me. "Just around the corner."

"What?" she asks, clearly unable to hear me.

"It's back that— Oh, fuck it," I mutter, taking her by the elbow and yanking her into the deep doorway of a closed shop. The absence of the rain is almost as shocking as the presence of it, although it still rushes down next to us in a dull, silver roar.

"It's just past the corner there," I say again, and in the sheltered cove of the doorway, she can finally hear my words. "Left at the lights, then just a street down."

"Oh, good," she says, looking genuinely pleased. And also genuinely cold. Goosebumps pebble her bare arms and chest, and I make a valiant effort not to notice her nipples bunched tight under her dress.

A very valiant effort.

I fail, of course.

Her teeth chatter as she says, "Th-Thank you! My phone wouldn't work in the rain, and I thought I memorized the way, but it all looked different once I actually got here, and then the rain made it so hard to see—" Her own shivers break apart her words, and for some reason this makes me unaccountably annoyed.

"Here," I say gruffly, shrugging out of my jacket and putting it over her shoulders. She's flapping a hand in protest, but her hand stills as soon as the dry, warm interior of the jacket touches her shoulders. She practically folds herself into the jacket then, doing this thing where she rubs her cheek against the collar, and I know it's to get dry—*I know that*—but fuck if it doesn't look like she's nuzzling into it. Like a kitten against the warm palm of its owner.

"Thank you," says the girl, her eyes wide pools of deep blue. I notice with a strange curl of satisfaction that she's not shivering as hard now.

"Why don't you have a jacket?" I demand again, knowing I sound surly but refusing to care. Everyone else in my life has written me off as a miserable bastard and they ignore me as such—this girl might as well learn too.

At that, her mouth forms into a defensive little moue. "It's *June*," she says. "I shouldn't need a jacket in *June*."

I stare at her like she's insane, which maybe she is.

"And the bare feet?"

"My feet got wet," she says, as if this is an entirely adequate explanation.

"I didn't like it."

"You realize they've gotten even wetter without shoes."

"It's better this way," she insists, waving her shoes at me. Once I see them, I have to agree. I don't see how anyone could walk in those across the width of the shoe shop, much less along slippery, uneven pavement.

"I hope whoever you're meeting sends you home in a taxi," I mutter.

"Oh, I'm not meeting anyone," she says.

"What?"

She reaches up to brush a wet strand of hair off her cheek, but I beat her to it. I don't know why, but it's instinctive, like breathing, like blinking. Touching her.

My fingertips linger on her cheek after I brush the hair aside, and she stares up at me with something too close to trust. I drop my hand.

"I only have one night in London," she says, all that trust and big-eyed nuzzling replaced by something matter-of-fact and utterly practical. "And I spent days researching where to go for a drink tonight. It had to be within walking distance of my hotel, it had to have several five-star reviews on multiple restaurant rating sites, and it had to be established enough to have regulars but new enough to be trendy. The Goose and Gander met all of those requirements."

Well, that's where research will get you. An obnoxious hipster cave of Edison bulbs and reclaimed wood.

"And why that specific criteria?" I ask, but I'm already peering back out into the rain, wondering if it's let up enough that I can send this crazy, shivering girl on her way. Get back to my night. My night in a dry bed with my book, alone.

Somehow it doesn't sound as appetizing as it did just a few minutes ago.

"Oh," she chirps, like she's pleased I asked. "I wanted to find a man to sleep with."

It takes a moment for her words to unfold in my brain, and I'm still staring at the rain when her meaning becomes clear. An unpleasant bolt of *something* hits me with a muffled thud.

My head swivels slowly back so I can look at her. "Excuse me?"

Her face is animated now, all red lips and high brows and dark lashes in the shadowed, rainy night. "Well, I have a plan, and I think it's a very good plan, but unfortunately my circumstances are narrowed to this one night in particular—"

"A *plan*."

She nods, that pleased look again, like I'm her star pupil.

Fuck that. *I'm* the professor here, and I have the sudden urge to tell her so. To press her against the wall and put my lips to her ear and murmur all the ways she'll respect my authority and experience.

My cock responds to the image, straining full and heavy at the thought of touching her. Teaching her. Punishing her.

"You see," she says, totally oblivious to the deviant lust pounding through me, "I really need a man with a willing penis—or I suppose I should say a willing man with a penis, but when I say it like that, it sounds very dismissive of non— You're scowling again."

She's right. "So what you're saying is that you have a plan to go to a place you've never been, in a city you've never visited, to find a man you've never met to fuck you?" My voice is frigid, bordering on cruel, and I see her blanch.

"That's very judgmental," she scolds, but I'm not to be scolded. Not right now, because I do the scolding, I make the rules, and the sooner she learns that—

Wait, no, what am I thinking? She's not going to learn anything from me. I'm not going to teach her anything. I'm not even going to spend another ten minutes with this deranged, bedraggled girl.

Even if she has the kind of long, thick hair that begs to be wrapped around a fist. Even if she has a rain-chilled body just crying to be loved warm again.

Even if she has the kind of plush red lips designed to drive men mad.

But I've been down this road before, and I know what lies at the other end of it. Bitter memories and a life left in pieces.

Never again.

"I'm judgmental because it's an idiotic idea," I reply in a sharp voice. "Do you have any idea how unsafe that is? How foolish?"

Even in the dark, I see how heat glints in her eyes, and she sticks a finger in my chest as if she's about to deliver me a scathing lecture. As she does, her arm leaves the warm confines of my jacket and reveals a delicate wrist circled with a thin band of leather.

A watch.

I don't know why that's the thing that does it, but something shears off inside my mind, sending my control bumping and careening off the tracks.

"Where's your hotel?" I ask before she can start in on whatever she was about to say.

Her brows pull together and her mouth closes. Opens again. "Why?" she asks suspiciously.

"Because I'm taking you back there."

"Why?" she asks, genuinely confused now.

"Because there's no way in hell I'm letting you prance off to a bar to find some stranger to fuck you," I say. And I give her a brief once-over, my eyes tracing where the fabric of her dress clings to her breasts and her soft belly and her achingly shaped hips. There are no secrets through that wet fabric, and those shockingly abundant curves are on clear display for anyone with eyes. For the undoubtedly many willing penises back at the pub.

The thought makes my chest tighten with something uncivilized and jealous.

"Especially not looking like *that*," I add.

Her cheeks flush dark enough that it's visible even in the night shadows, and I realize too late she thinks I'm mocking her, not warning her.

Fine. So be it. If that's what it takes to save her from the greedy arseholes at the Goose and Gander, then I'll pay the price. "What hotel?" I repeat.

She worries her bottom lip between her teeth, and that simple act has my erection throbbing against the damp fabric of my trousers, begging to be let free, begging out to play. And oh, how it could play along the soft lines of her mouth and over the wet pink of her tongue. How rude and rough it would look against the overflowing handfuls of her tits...

"The Douglass," she says finally.

"I'm staying at the Douglass too," I say before I can stop myself, and then horror curls through my chest.

She's too close.

Too real.

Too...*possible.*

Would it be so bad? a tiny voice whispers in my mind. *Just one night with a girl you'll never see again?*

Yes, goddammit. Yes, it would.

Meanwhile, the girl seems to be having some sort of insight. Some sort of wild epiphany. "You," she says slowly.

"What?"

"You!" Her entire face lights up. "You could be the one!"

I stare at her. "You're joking."

She's too excited to catch on to the rhetorical nature of my statement, already bouncing on the balls of her feet. She's so short that even on her tiptoes, the top of her head barely clears my chin. "I'm not joking! It's perfect, don't you see? We're even staying at the same hotel! You can have sex with me and then just go right back to your room!" She beams up at me, as if expecting some kind of approbation for working out this problem of hers.

"You cannot be serious," I say in something very close to a stammer, which pisses me off. I'm *not* uncertain, I know how I feel about everything always, and I know how I feel about this: the girl is mad and I'm leaving.

"I *am* serious," she says, brow furrowed, as if puzzled as to why that would even occur to me. "I would just like to have sex with someone tonight, and you're handsome and you're here."

And that's when I realize she's not mad. She's something much, much worse—she's innocent. And willing.

I turn to go, and she catches my arm, her little watch flashing in the shimmering glow of the streetlights. A stupid little watch that I bet she puts on every morning so she won't be late for whatever burlesque antics she has devised for that day. I bet she's on time for everything. I bet she's early to every class or meeting or shift, sitting with a straight back and with a pencil caught between her teeth, a spare pencil speared through a bun of soft, glossy hair...

Fuck.

I pull free of her arm. "Keep the jacket," I mutter, ducking back into the rain and away from this creature who seems to be built out of my most shameful temptations, every inch of me protesting at the distance between us, at pulling away from her.

But there's no other way. For the sake of her soul and mine, I should stay far away from her and her little watch and her wanton body with its big, soft curves and needy nipples.

The chilly rain sluicing down is a relief, soaking me straight through without my jacket and quelling the heat inside my blood just enough so I can think again. So I can remember the life I built, free of temptation, free of chaos, free of sin.

I take a deep, rainy breath. It's going to be okay. I was tested and came up with full marks. And now to my reward, which is a chaos-free night. Alone.

Fuck, what cold comfort. Comfort even colder than the rain soaking me through.

But the cost of giving in to my urges would make my life even colder still.

"You're not married, are you?" a voice comes from beside me.

I look over at the girl following me. She peers closely at me through the rain. "Girlfriend? Boyfriend?"

"I'm not married, and I'm not seeing anyone. *Not that it matters.*"

I try to walk faster, shoving my hands in my pockets and ducking my head from the rain, but she keeps up, nearly jogging now. My jacket hangs open enough that I can see what effect jogging has on the glistening rounds of her breasts peeking up over her bodice.

Christ.

"I'm not either," she says. "Married or dating, that is."

"It doesn't matter."

"Do you think I'm pretty enough to have sex with?" she says, her voice growing louder as a bus sloshes by.

"What?"

"I mean, if you're not attracted to me, I totally understand." She hops over a puddle in an expedient, unself-conscious move that almost makes me smile.

"Most men aren't attracted to me. That's why I had to come all the way to London to..." She trails off, clutching the jacket tighter around her. "Anyway," she continues in a defeated voice. "I'd understand if you weren't."

The lonely note in her voice draws me up short, even though the safety of our hotel shimmers mirage-sweet just across the road.

I turn to her in the rain. "You think I'm not attracted to you?"

"Well, most guys—"

"I'm not most *guys*," I growl, and her lower lip goes between her teeth again. But not in fear like it should.

In interest. In desire.

She's too innocent by far.

"You think men don't want you?" I ask in a low voice, taking a step forward. She watches me with an eager trepidation, and it makes me harder than I thought possible. "Everything about your body reminds a man of fucking. Your tits, your mouth, those ridiculous hips. Even those big blue eyes of yours make a man wonder what they'd look like peering up at him with you on your knees. Looking at him from over your shoulder as he bends you over his desk." I stop abruptly, my words getting too personal, too tailored to my own fucked-up needs.

She releases that lower lip, and I'm nearly undone by how open she looks, how vulnerable. I want to sweep her into my arms and cover all that vulnerability with my body—protect her from the world even as I refuse to protect her from myself.

Get a fucking grip, Oliver.

This can't happen.

But what if it could? I won't ever have to see this girl again. She's not my student.

She's not Rosie, the little voice reminds me. *She can't hurt you.*

"Well, then it's simple," the girl says, as if she can read my thoughts. "If you're attracted to my body and you're unattached—"

"It's complicated," I say, pushing past her to splash my way to the hotel. She has no idea how complicated.

She has no idea how *wrong*.

Like before, she follows me. "Please. I promise I'm not crazy. I'm just tired of—" She stops, seems to change her words. "Tired of not having sex. Please."

"It's for your own good," I mutter, even though my entire body is swirling with the need to give her what's *actually* for her own good, which is her over my lap, legs kicking adorably, as I redden her ass with my palm.

I'm so hard now. Hard enough that it must be obvious. Hard enough to be past caring. Hard enough that the minute I slip inside my hotel room, I'm going to have a hand braced on the door while my other fists my cock.

"How do you know what's for my own good?" the girl asks, and it's the way she asks that makes my steps falter. She doesn't demand it like most women would, and she doesn't deny that I *might*. That I might know what's for her own good and that I might know it well enough to tell her.

No.

No.

"We're not doing this," I tell her as we reach the doors of the Douglass, and I recognize how ridiculous it is that I'm holding the door open for this woman even as I'm trying to push her away. "You're just going to have to trust me."

She steps inside, and it's so bright that my eyes take a moment to adjust. When they do, I see that she's shoving my jacket at me.

"Here. Thank you for this, and take it back. And for the record, I *don't* trust you, and why should I? I'm a grown woman and I don't know you—and also I've done a lot of research about sex, so I'm pretty sure I know what I'm talking about."

She's gesturing now, the hand still clutching her shoes waving them around, but I'm not watching the shoes, I'm watching *her*—the almost embarrassingly generous curves of her. Not embarrassing because of the generosity but because of the near-wantonness of them. The illicit thoughts those curves conjure even fully clothed as she is.

Of course, *fully clothed* is a misleading term at the moment, because yes, that little waist and those lavish tits and hips are covered with fabric, but the wet dress clings to every contour and swerve of her body. I can even make out the gentle dip of her navel, the place where her thighs meet her body. The sweet bullets of her nipples.

Even the rest of her body is wanton: the long arch of her neck, still slicked with rain, the exposed square of her shoulders, the long wet hair that waves in dark webs down her back and over the elegant line of her collarbone.

Even her innocent anger feels tempting. Even the cocoon of inexperience around her drives me crazy.

Even that goddamn watch is irresistible.

I take my jacket and start walking to the lift. I have to put some space between us or my skin's going to catch on fire.

"Please?" she asks one last time. "*Please?*"

"No." I'm almost to the lift doors now, I'm almost safe.

Or rather, *she's* almost safe.

"Then I'm going to the Goose and Gander," she says, frustrated. "Or *anywhere*. But I'm not giving up, not when I only have one night here."

I've already hit the button for the lift by the time she's uttered the words, but it's not too late to spin around and glare at her. "What did you just say?" I ask in a low voice.

She's already turning around, and I realize with some mixture of fury, horror, and lust that she *means it*. She's going to go back out into that gale. To find another man.

My hand finds her elbow, and I pull her into me with a growl. "You're not going anywhere."

She gives me a glare as turbulently aroused as my own, pressing her wet curves against me in something between a challenge and a request.

"What exactly are you going to do about it?" she dares.

My cock is a hot bar of steel between us, fussing at the seam of my trousers, and I can't help but press it into her belly. And my mouth is dry, so fucking dry, with wanting her. "Girls who disobey get punished," I warn.

"By you?"

"By me."

Suddenly, I find that I'm not holding her to me so much as she's holding herself to me, her high heels dropping to the floor in a dull clatter as her fingers find the flats of my chest under my thin sweater.

"Punishing bad girls... Is this you being kinky or a serial killer?" she asks, that red mouth curved in what could only be called impertinence.

I can barely breathe. And I can't even fathom saying the word *kinky* like she's just said it, like she would say *tall* or *English*. Like it's nothing. Like it's no big deal.

Like she might want it.

All I choke out is a husky, "I'm not a killer."

She has no reason to believe me, no reason to believe that I'm safe, which is exactly why I didn't want her trawling for strange men in the middle of London.

And all thoughts sizzle and melt away in a searing instant because she's hooked her arms behind my neck and pulled herself up to my mouth.

Because she's kissing me with red, rain-spattered lips.

And I am done for.

CHAPTER THREE

ZANDY

He tastes like mint.

Not toothpaste mint, but fresh mint, straight from the garden, herbal and with the tiniest bit of cold sting. I moan the minute I taste it, the minute our tongues slide together, and his answering moan has me throwing all lingering doubts onto the floor along with my dumb shoes.

I don't care that I don't know him. I don't care that he's not the plan. I want it to be him. Him with his testy refusals. Him with his dark threats. Him with those hypnotic eyes that are every color and that mouth shaped somewhere between elegance and cruelty.

His hands are spread big and possessive on my back now, keeping me so tight against him that I can feel every flat, hard plane of his chest and stomach. I can feel the heavy ridge in his pants that tells me how much he meant his words from earlier in the rain.

Everything about your body reminds a man of fucking.

It's the first time I've ever thought of my body that way—of sexy instead of heavy, of desirable instead of softly messy. And I like it. I like how his eyes burned over my curves, as if he were already planning things that would take him straight to hell.

I want it to be him.

And almost like he reads my mind, he turns us and starts walking me backward into the elevator, pausing only to duck down and grab my shoes. Once we go through the elevator doors, he reaches for my thighs and lifts me up as if I weigh nothing, still kissing me with those soft, minty lips all the while.

Well, not kiss, really. *Devour* is more like it, as if he hasn't kissed a woman in years—as if he hasn't even *touched* anyone in years. He seems that hungry for it. But new to sex as I am, I know you don't kiss like him without vast experience, so surely he's not that hard up for it? Surely someone like him, handsome and mysterious and captivating, has someone in his bed every night?

Funny how the observation makes me jealous, given that I don't even know him. I don't even know his name. But even as I'm jealous of all the experience belied by his capable handling of me, I'm also grateful for it.

Grateful for the easy, knowledgeable way his hands work my body, pinning me between his leanly muscled frame and the wall of the elevator.

Grateful for the expert way he matches our bodies together, sliding me so that my lace-covered pussy grinds over the thick part of him that throbs for me.

Grateful for the smooth way he deepens our kiss, exploring my mouth, biting at my lips and my jaw, and leaving me a wriggling, wet mess.

"Which floor?" he growls into my mouth.

"Wh-What?"

"We're doing this in your room," he says, and it was always my plan to bring someone to my room for safety reasons, so I tell him.

"Nine."

He slams a fist against the wall of buttons, and then he's back to plundering my mouth, not so much coaxing me open as taking what he wants, and God, it's like nothing I ever could have dreamed. I've known lust myself. I've known what it feels like to have my body aching with the need for friction and fullness, but I've never, ever imagined *this*. The rush of power and pure biological frenzy of feeling someone *else's* lust. The way it threads through my own desire like a hot copper wire. The way it makes me want more, more, more.

And more.

I have almost no control over myself in this moment, grinding my needy core against him, rubbing my breasts against his chest, yanking everywhere at his sweater and his firm arms and shoulders and at the wet lengths of his hair—too short to be long but too long to be anything other than unkempt.

He lets me pluck and paw at him, and it seems to drive him madder and madder—his kisses growing more savage, his grip more merciless, until the elevator doors open and he drops me to my feet, yanking me into the hallway before I can find my balance.

"Nine thirteen," I manage, fumbling with my purse for my phone as I'm pulled down the hallway and then surfacing with it right before I'm crushed against my door and kissed within an inch of my life.

"Take a picture of me," he says breathlessly against my lips.

"I— What?"

He pulls back just enough so I can see he's serious. Those blue-green-brown eyes swirl with something stormy and pained. "Take a picture of me and send it to someone you trust." And then he rattles off a string of numbers. His birthday.

26

"Why?" I ask again, even though I suspect why.

"Surely," he says, raising one warm hand to grip my jaw and hold me close for another hard kiss, "with all your research, you know why."

"So someone knows I'm with you."

"So you'll be safe," he corrects gently, nipping at my neck and then meeting my gaze. "I don't know if I can ever forgive you for being so careless with yourself."

I laugh—half from his bossy words and half from the new flicker of his tongue along the shell of my ear. "My body is my own to be careless with."

"Not tonight, it isn't," he whispers. "Tonight it's mine."

☉

I text his picture to a friend of mine, along with his birthday and name—*Oliver Markham*—and then I use the hotel app on my phone to unlock the door.

"What's your name?" he asks as we kiss our way into the room. I left a light on when I went out earlier, so I reach to turn it off because sex happens in the dark, I know that much, but he catches my wrist before I can do it. "Lights stay on," he rasps. "And I want your name. I told you mine."

That he did, and hell if Oliver Markham doesn't sound so fancy and English-y that I can hardly stand it. Suddenly I'm embarrassed of my own name, which seems to make me all the younger than the ten years I now know separate us.

"Amanda," I say, telling him my real name. No one calls me that—I've been Zandy since basically the moment I was born—but I file taxes as Amanda, and it does sound a lot more grown-up. Like the kind of name an Oliver would be paired with.

Oliver and Amanda sounds perfect.

Oliver and Zandy sounds like a joke.

"Amanda," he murmurs as his hands cup my face, his thumbs tracing soft lines along the rises of my cheekbones. "What do you want tonight?"

"I want you to have sex with me."

And that's all he needs.

His hands drop to my skirt, and they ruck up the wet fabric easily, hitching it all to my waist, and then he cups my pussy with one elegant hand. "You need to be fucked here? Hmm?"

"Yes," I sigh, trying to press into his hand. It feels so good, so fucking good, and I've never gotten this far...never had only a scrap of lace between my aching emptiness and a man's possessive touch.

But then his touch leaves my pussy, and I whimper. He reaches for the zipper of my dress and, with a practiced move, tugs it down. Before I can fully process what's happening, I'm bared to the waist, with only the thin silk of my bra between my body's secrets and his hungry eyes.

"But these need me too, don't they?" he says, his hands smoothing over the rounds of my breasts, shaping to their weight and ample size. Despite the cold and sharp cast of his mouth and the equally cold and aristocratic cut of his features, there's something almost boyish in his gaze as he cups and fondles me. Something awed and greedy. He slides the straps of my bra over my shoulders and then peels the damp silk cups from my skin.

"Christ," he mutters to himself as my nipples peek free and my breasts spill over the rest of the cups. "Jesus Christ."

And before I can say anything or even cover myself, like my instincts demand, his mouth is closing warm and wet over the needy tip of one breast, and I let out a noise that's nearly embarrassing in its shocked honesty. It's not the rehearsed coo of a woman in a porn video—it's a noise that comes straight from my belly, a low moan of unfiltered need.

I had no idea it could feel so good.

No idea.

His mouth is slick and warm, sucking every secret dirty wish of mine right to the surface of my skin as he works me and worries my nipple with rough nips and pulls.

I feel the wet response between my legs like nothing I've ever felt before. I mean, wet after a few minutes with battery power, sure, but wet from a stranger's mouth moving hungrily over my breasts? Wet from the flashing multicolored gaze of a man I don't know as he tears my dress down my hips and then scowls at my exposed form?

"You're so much," he says accusingly. "You're so fucking much."

I've always known that. I've always been so much. I'm the girl who raises her hand at the end of class because she can't bear for it to end. The girl who does every extra-credit assignment and then asks for more because she wants the teacher to like her. I'm curvy and eager and relentlessly energetic, and I've been those things ever since I can remember.

And yet never has being *too much* sounded like he's making it sound right now.

As if I'm a treasure and a curse all at once. As if he both loves and hates me.

As if I'm killing him simply by being myself and he wouldn't have it any other way.

Oliver circles me now, like a predator, like a wolf, and when I move to shift and put my arms over myself in a surge of self-consciousness, his hands are on me again, folding my wrists at the small of my back and locking them there with strong fingers.

"Bad girl," he murmurs into my ear, standing behind me so that all I have of him is that deliciously refined English voice and the warm grip of his hand. "Very bad girl."

"I'm not a bad girl," I protest, because his words are hooking somewhere deep inside me, somewhere deep inside the eager teacher's pet that is Zandy Lynch. Too late I remember I'm supposed to be Amanda, someone older and more sophisticated, someone who's been around the block and isn't as eager to please.

But it doesn't seem to matter. My eagerness to be a good girl for him seems to gratify, because he bites at my shoulder with a pleased noise.

"You want to be a good girl for me?" he asks. "You want to make me happy?"

"I do," I breathe. "I do, I do."

An approving growl at my ear.

I'm bent over the bed without so much as a warning; the only concession to my comfort is the pause he gives me to turn my head so I can breathe easily. And then my panties are ripped to my ankles and done away with.

"Red means stop," he says and kicks my legs apart.

I hold my breath, waiting for it...for something...for fingers or spanking or for him just to shove his cock right inside me. And oh shit, if he's going to do that, he needs a condom. But just as I'm about to tell him that, something utterly unexpected and utterly magical happens.

He runs his tongue soft and slick through the split between my legs, and I nearly jump up from the bed. A stinging slap to my ass makes me freeze.

"Good girls hold *still*," Oliver warns from behind me. I can feel the warm breath of his words against my pussy, a lurid reminder that he's able to see and smell and taste a part of me that no one has ever seen or smelled or tasted before, and I can't handle it. I can't even pretend to handle it. I squirm against the bed.

"Oliver," I moan, and it happens again. His tongue. His tongue and his lips and the intimate press of his nose into me, and I could peel apart with embarrassment, but he puts a hand on the small of my back and keeps me bent over the bed as he samples me.

I'm trapped. Trapped between his hands, which hold me down or spread me open depending on his whim. Trapped between the bed and his hungry mouth. Trapped between my embarrassment and just how insanely delicious it feels. Delicious because he thinks I'm delicious. Delicious because it's intimate and wet and hot.

Delicious because it's nothing like the familiar massage of my hands or the plastic hum of a vibrator. It's human and messy and dirty. It's not the tame thing I thought it was at all.

It's wild. It's primal. Like a lioness being pinned and bitten by her male. Like a cavewoman being slung over the shoulder of a lusty caveman. I thought I knew the boundaries of it. I thought my research would make the act planned and civilized...

There's nothing civilized about this. And despite his expensive sweater and even more expensive accent, there's nothing civilized about Oliver at all.

"I love the way you taste," he tells me, pulling back to bite at my ass. "Like summer. Fresh and tart and rich."

"I—" I have no words for this. Never in a thousand years when I made my plans and fantasized about finally having sex did I imagine what this would feel like—not just his mouth on my clit, but hearing him talk about my body with such raw pleasure, knowing that my secrets were secret no longer.

And never could I have imagined that he'd sit on the bed and then haul me over his lap like a child, his hand smoothing over the curve of my ass.

I look back at him, and he looks back at me with those uncannily colored eyes.

"Red means stop," he repeats.

And then he brings his palm down against my ass, and I buck over his lap.

"That is for going out alone in a strange city," he says as he tucks me even harder against his lap.

And spanks me again. "That is for looking for a strange man to fuck you."

And again. "And that is for being so fucking delicious that I couldn't say no when you asked."

I'm breathing hard into the blanket, the skin along my ass and thighs nearly dancing with sparks. There's heat everywhere—heat on my skin, heat deep in my muscles, heat in my belly, and heat between my legs.

I...I had no idea.

This definitely was not the plan. The plan never involved *spanking*. It never involved pain or punishment, and yet...when he soothes the skin with his hand, rubbing gently...when he croons that I'm a *good girl*, I'm more alive than I've ever felt. I'm dizzy with it and drunk with it, and I feel giddy and heady and wild. Like I can do anything and have anything.

Have anyone.

"I liked that," I murmur in disbelief. "I *liked* that."

His hand stops over my ass. "You did?" he asks in nearly as much disbelief.

I realize he's trembling where he touches me. His hands are shaking, and I can feel minute shudders chasing up and down his solid body.

I suddenly panic that I've done something wrong, that I've accidentally been disgusting by admitting that I liked it, but then he bends over me, pressing his lips to my back.

"Amanda," he groans and then bites me. "Where the hell did you come from?"

I don't know, but I'm suddenly encouraged. He's shaking because of *me*. Because I liked what he did to me. I can't separate my enjoyment of it from his enjoyment of it, but maybe I'm not supposed to. Maybe that's the point.

And for once in my life, I'm happy not to overanalyze. Happy just to be in the moment and do something that feels good.

"More?" I ask, batting my eyelashes for good measure. "I know you've already spanked me for being a bad girl, but maybe some more just for fun?"

I don't have to ask twice.

A pleased noise rumbles deep in Oliver's chest, and he resumes his work—a bit lighter this time, I notice. Hard enough to sting but not so hard that it truly hurts. Soon I'm arching and squeaking with each strike, rocking back into his touch and also trying to press my pussy into the firm length of his thigh. His erection burns at my belly even through his pants, and he's breathing harder than I am—breathing like he's run a race, like he's pushed himself to the point of collapse.

And when the collapse comes, it's not his body but his control that fails. He scoops me up and tosses me back onto the bed, slouching over me like a lion in truth.

"Tell me you're wet," he says, lowering his body over mine and taking a nipple into his mouth. "Tell me you need it," he murmurs around my skin, leaving my nipple to kiss at the soft skin between my breasts and down the even softer contours of my belly. "Tell me you can't wait another minute." His mouth reaches my pussy, and it's like all the fire he's laid into my backside is now kindling here, here, *here*. And when he slides one long finger inside me, his lips and tongue and teeth all working to worship my clit, I'm done for.

Battery power has nothing on this.

My back bows off the bed as I cry out and grab for him, my fingers threading through his hair as I quiver and shake against his mouth, as my first ever non-solo orgasm tears through me with tidal, elemental power. I feel it everywhere—to the roots of my hair and in the balls of my feet—and as I'm racked with the gorgeous agony of it, he still pleasures me, still kisses and feasts on me like he can't bear to stop.

And when I finally, finally still against his lips, going from wire-tight to limp and happy, he gives my pussy a final kiss and rises up to his knees, tugging off his sweater and kicking off his shoes and trousers. He should look clumsy, pulling off damp clothes, but in that mysterious Oliver way, it all looks graceful. Powerful. And inch by inch, his body appears. His handsomely squared shoulders and deceptively wide chest and a torso ridged with lean muscle and marked with a single line of dark hair trailing down from his navel.

And then those hips, trim and narrow, the spread of dark hair low, low on his belly, the tops of firm thighs, and then—

Jesus, Mary, and Joseph.

His cock.

It flexes as I trace it with my gaze, the veined thickness, the blunt swell of the head, and the proud jut of its hardness. There's something so potent and arresting about this part of him; it's so very male and handsome, and even just looking at it makes my belly churn low with new longing.

"You want it," Oliver says, drawing my gaze up to his. It's not a question, but I answer anyway.

"Yes."

He looks down at my pussy, spread and wet, and then up to my face. I can't read his expression, but there's something twisting the sharp corners of his lips, and I realize it's excitement. I realize it's glazed fervor.

He wants me as much as I want him.

And God, how that punches me in the gut.

"I wear condoms," he informs me, reaching for his wallet.

"Okay."

"Every time."

"Okay."

He tears the wrapper open with long fingers, nimble and dexterous in the way that brings to mind writing or piano playing, and then rolls the latex sheath over himself with an ease that both fascinates and frustrates me.

"And I'm on top this time."

"Okay by me." And it really is because I'd have no idea what the hell to do if I were on top. And being so exposed—not just with my braless breasts and my soft thighs but with my inexperience, with my unpracticed movements... I don't think I'm ready for that yet. Especially not with someone as wickedly sophisticated as Oliver.

"Any other rules?" I tease, even though I like the rules. I've always liked rules, and from him, there's nothing sexier.

"Yes," he says, crawling back between my legs. "Red still means stop."

And then he lays his body over mine, matches the wide crest of himself to my cunt's opening, and begins to push inside.

I arch in a slow writhe, the pressure too much, the bite of pain too real, and for a substantial moment, I think about pushing him away. I think about saying *red*. It's one thing to read about the discomfort some women face in their inaugural encounters with penetration, but it's an entirely different thing to feel it. It's so unfamiliar, this discomfort. It's so intimate, right at the heart of me, as if I'm being split open by the coolly vicious man above me.

Except not vicious.

Not really.

Even as he spanked me, he soothed me and played with my pussy, and even as he wedges inside me now, he strokes the hair from my face and sucks at my neck. And the noises he makes as he grits his teeth and pushes in—guttural noises, animal noises, words uttered in the most filthy tone possible: *tight, Jesus, tight* and *goddammit, you feel so good* and *so fucking much, so fucking much.*

"Going to fuck you," he whispers into my neck as his head drops to the pillow next to mine. He's still only halfway in. "Going to fuck you until you're a good girl again."

All of it, all of it, but especially those last words, take the pinch of pain and turn it into something new. Something as good as the good girl I want to be for him, and instead of pushing him away, my hands wander down to the tight clench of his ass and coax him in farther. Deeper. Until he's seated as deep as a man can go in a woman.

"Oliver," I gasp, because he's filling me where I've never been filled, heating me and stretching me and stroking me, and the tip of him is kissing against a part of me I never even knew was there. "Oh, Oliver. It feels— I can't believe how it feels."

He pulls up and stares down at me, that sharp-tipped mouth pressed into a line and his eyebrows furrowed. "I can't believe how *you* feel," he corrects. And then he shakes his head slightly, his mouth twisting in some conversation with himself. "You're not at all what I expected," he says. "You're not at all how you look."

"How do I look?" I whisper.

He gives a dark smile and reaches up to run a thumb over my fire-engine red lips and then down over a plump breast. "Like you know everything there is about fucking."

"I don't know anything," I admit. It was never the plan to reveal my virginity to my would-be paramour, and it seems strange to tell Oliver about it now, when he's already inside me. But a big part of me wants to tell him, wants him to know how much I'm trusting him with, how much I need him to continue being his mixture of safe and dangerous. But then I add, "You have to show me. Have to teach me," and his eyes go so dark, so feral, that I decide the conversation can wait until later.

I want him ferocious now. I want him looking like this, all possessed and desperate.

"You want me to teach you?" he rasps, moving between my legs again. "You want to be my little student? My little whore?"

Holy shit. I nearly come from his words alone—from this teacher game, this good-girl game. And still he moves, long and sweet strokes that have my toes curling and my back arching.

"Good girls come on the cocks their teachers give them," Oliver says as he fucks me. "You want to be a good girl, don't you?"

I nod vehemently. It's all I want, it's all I'll ever want, and I need to be his good girl. I need it like I need air and water and breath. "Please," I whimper. "Help me be a good girl, please, please."

He moves the wide pad of his thumb to my clit between us, rubbing in time to his deep, rolling thrusts, and the orgasm builds like nothing I've ever felt. A runaway train bearing down on me, a wall of sweaty, dirty pleasure—it's so much that I try to move away from it, try to squirm away from under him.

I can't bear it. I know I can't. I'll die if I orgasm, because it's too strong, too fucking strong, it will shake the bones right out of my body.

"Oh no, you don't," Oliver murmurs, his body easily chasing mine, his thumb on my swollen pearl all the while. "You give it to me first. You let me have it."

And I can't resist him—not the thick bar of needy male inside me, not his polished accent, not his still-damp hair tousled around his face. Not his savage mouth or his kaleidoscopic eyes. He stills me just enough for the climax to nip at my heels, to tackle me down, and with a panicked moan, I'm felled by it.

I'm slayed by it.

It starts in the deepest pit of my belly, right around the wide tip of him, crushing in and then exploding out like an atom bomb, crumpling through me like I'm nothing but paper in a strong fist. I can feel myself clenching—my belly and my thighs and the inner parts of me—squeezing and clutching at his erection, and he hisses, long and wounded, his hands fisting hard enough in the pillows around my head that I can hear the stress of the fabric. And I can't speak, I can't ask if his reaction is good or bad, but there's something in the rigid tension of his torso, in the strained cords of his neck, that make me think it's good, that he's getting pleasure from my pleasure just as I did from his when he spanked me.

"Dammit," he says through gritted teeth. "God*dammit*. I'm going to— you're making me—Amanda—"

The last comes out as a jagged groan, and then he's up on his knees, his hands curling hard over my hips as he fucks his way through his own climax. His eyes flutter closed, so I can watch him in my state of limp stupefaction as he uses my body to his own ends. As he uses my happy pussy to send himself over the edge. And then with a grunt and the impossible tightening of all those delicious muscles in his arms and chest and belly, he stills, buried to the hilt, as he pulses in fast, flexing throbs.

"Fuck," he mumbles, his head dropping down to hang between his shoulders. His eyes are still closed, and I shamelessly drink him in: the tightly carved body and the wide root of his cock just barely visible below the rise of my cunt. The furrowed pull of those dark eyebrows, as if his own pleasure is a problem he's trying to mentally work out, and the soft part of his lips, as if something about this has rendered him unexpectedly vulnerable. The nearly too-square jaw and the high cheekbones—giving his face a geometric cast normally only seen in marble busts—and the vaguely unkempt hair that waves over his neck and temples.

I'm curious about his hair, which is gorgeous but obviously neglected. I'm curious about his hands, strong but pale, as if they rarely see the sun. And I'm curious about his lean body and his earlier self-denial and his obvious kinky side.

I'm curious about *him*. I want more of *him*.

Oh.

Oh no.

I've read about this. I've researched this. This is the inevitable rush of connection that comes from all the oxytocin Oliver's stoked in my blood. He's flooded me with hormones, and now those hormones are insisting that I form a human bond with him, and that's why people get snuggly and all clingy after sex.

Well, that's not going to happen with me. That's not the plan. And given what I know about Oliver, I doubt it's his plan either.

I'm not going to be curious.

I'm not going to want him.

He solved my problem, and that's that.

I'm so busy reminding myself that all this affection and vulnerability is hormone-based and therefore not real that I don't notice he's opened his eyes and is staring back down at me.

"Amanda," he says huskily.

I don't know what to say back because the research didn't cover this.

Do I say his name back? Do I offer him my shower? Do I tell him I don't expect him to stay?

But before I can decide, he circles himself with a finger and thumb and makes to pull out of me, and I bite my lip at the sudden sting.

He freezes, and I realize that he's looking with some worry at the pain on my face, and then with slow horror, his gaze goes to his cock.

Even from here, I can see the remnants of my innocence smeared on the condom.

"Oliver," I say quickly. "I can explain."

CHAPTER FOUR

OLIVER

I have to get her blood off me, and I have to—I don't even know what I have to do. Clean her. Clean myself. Offer to lash my own back. Whatever it is you do when you've accidentally fucked a virgin.

Shit.

Shit.

It makes so much sense now. Her little gasps of surprise let out at the smallest things. Her expression of wonder as I serviced her cunt. Her wide, vulnerable gaze as I slowly stretched her open. Stretched her open for the first time.

And I'm going to hell because guilt is not the first thing that races through me.

It's excitement.

It's more lust, stiffening my spent cock.

It's a dark possession, growling and flexing claws in my chest, telling me she's mine mine *mine.*

I ignore these though, holding up a hand to stay her words as I climb off the bed and rid myself of the condom. I've forgotten how wet sex is, how messy, although given how long it's been, I'm shocked I remember anything.

I walk back to the bed, tracing the lines of her body with my eyes because I can't help it. She's some kind of vision like this, her dark hair tangled everywhere in lovers' knots and her body a topography of pure adolescent fantasy—lush tits, a nipped-in waist, and hips in a decadently feminine spread.

And then there's the blood on the inside of her thighs. The questions in her deep blue eyes. The lingering redness around the sides of her hips reminding me of how she felt over my lap, squealing and writhing as she took her punishment.

I spanked a *virgin.* Oh God.

"I'm getting a cloth for you," I say. "Stay here." It comes out sterner than I mean it to—sterner than it should have, given what I've just robbed from her—but the immediate acquiescence in her gaze whisks the follow-up apology right off my lips. And replaces it with a noise of approval.

She is such a good student.

I quickly clean myself in the bathroom and then bring out a fresh warm cloth for her, thinking I'll hand it to her and let her clean herself, but as I approach, she parts her legs for me, as if it's the most natural thing in the world. As if it's my due.

My cock jolts again, bobbing at visions of a future that will never happen: of this girl spreading her legs for me whenever I ask, offering up her sweet body like it's mine to take. Sucking my cock under my desk while I work. Writing lines at her own desk, naked and ashamed. Crawling over my lap whenever I need it, letting me pet and tease and spank that round ass until she's begging for relief.

No, Oliver. It's a miracle she didn't run away screaming the moment I bent her over the bed. There's no way a nice girl like her—a barely non-virgin, a girl with a watch—would ever want to play my sick games.

But I let myself have this moment where I clean her myself. Where I spread her even more, carefully, see to her tender skin. Roll her over and check her bottom, even though I took it fairly easy on her. The funny thing is that after all these years, "fairly easy" was still enough to nearly make me come in my pants. And it was her who made it that way. Her gratifying little moans and tempting little wriggles. The way she said *I liked that* with such pleased surprise. With such innocent abandon.

Fuck.

It's not a good thing the way it makes me feel. As if I'm not so lonely. As if I can have...this.

She sighs as I clean her, and after I put the washcloth over the towel bar in the bathroom to dry, I wonder what comes next. The last time I slept with a virgin, I was a fumbling virgin myself, and whatever followed the too-short act is blurred by enough awkwardness and time that I can barely remember it. I have no idea what to do as a man. As a polite and—dubiously—civilized man.

And so I debate whether I should apologize or get dressed or what, and then she holds out her arms.

"I know it's just the oxytocin," she says sleepily. "But I'd like you to hold me for a minute. You don't have to stay long, just—" She yawns, those red lips stretching hypnotically, her tongue so temptingly wet and pink. "Just for a few minutes until I can metabolize these hormones."

I should hesitate. I *would* hesitate with any other woman. I don't do holding, I don't do postcoital anything except shame and regret, and yet somehow I'm climbing into the bed with her. Somehow I'm sliding under the covers and folding her into my arms, and somehow I'm not balking at the familiar way she nestles into me, as if she belongs there.

Somehow I'm relaxing around her. Somehow I'm enjoying the way she feels like this, with her head pillowed on my chest, her curves smashed against me, and her cheek rubbing against me like a needy cat's.

I should leave.

I should say I'm sorry—for the spanking and for the barbaric way I fucked her—and then I should leave. And I'm going to.

In just a minute.

After I've enjoyed the sated warmth of her for a little longer. After I've gotten my fill of her scent, all deep floral and spice.

After I've rested my eyes and given in to the strange peace she's infected me with.

I really am going to leave.

I really am...

The sunshine breaks through the room with a sheepish kind of warmth, as if embarrassed to wake me up, and it's pure instinct that makes me reach for the woman in bed with me. Well, pure instinct and a painfully erect cock, aching from a night of dreams about an American girl who likes spanking and spreading her legs for me.

But my fingers encounter nothing but cool sheets, and when I open my eyes, I see groggily that I'm alone.

Suddenly, I'm not so groggy. The entire shameful night floods back into my memories. What I did to Amanda, what I took from her. Falling asleep uninvited like an idiot.

What a cretin she must think I am...what a monster.

And she's not wrong. I am a monster.

I sit up, and it should relieve any person to see what I see next, which is a hotel room bereft of the effects of its occupant. No more suitcase on the stand. No laptop situated neatly on the desk. When I go to the bathroom, the space is as clean as it must have been when she rented it, a still-wet shower and sink the only evidence that she was here.

That and a note propped against the mirror.

Oliver, it reads in a neatly printed hand.

*I'm sorry if last night caused you any worry, but I wanted you to know
it was better than I ever could have dreamed. We won't see each other again, but I'll never
forget how good you made me feel. I'm proud to have been your good and bad girl, even if
only for one night.*

—*Amanda*

My chest feels heavy with something unfamiliar, and I find myself rubbing idly at it as I set the note down. Pick it up and read it again.

Fold it and put it in my jacket pocket—so the hotel staff won't find it, I tell myself—but after I dress and leave the room, I find myself touching it. Rereading it as I ride the lift down to my own floor to change clothes and shower. Running my fingers along the edges as I walk to the British Museum to meet a friend helping me with some research at one of the libraries there.

I'll never forget how good you made me feel.

I'm proud to have been your good and bad girl.

Even if only for one night.

This should be a good morning. I blew off some steam with a girl who let me practice all manner of depravities upon her, and then when I woke up, she was gone. No dangling expectations; no awkward send-off. Just a sweet note that was meant to assuage me of my guilt and firmly close the door on the possibility of more.

Which—excellent, right? The last thing I need is some curvy, blunt American invading my thoughts while I have important work to do. Invading my space with her wanting to be spanked and her mumbling about oxytocin and her fucking *watch*.

Last thing I need.

All for the best.

Right.

CHAPTER FIVE

ZANDY

The oxytocin isn't wearing off. Or at least it's not wearing off the way I thought it would.

I'm frowning at the glass of my train window as the countryside swishes by—flattish fields studded with animals and telephone poles, just like in Kansas—and I'm feeling an inconvenient restlessness, like I've left something important back in London. Something back in bed with Oliver.

Stop it.

It's not like he's a phone charger or a passport. I don't need him for anything else while I'm in the country, and this...this...*mooning* over him is immature. And if there's any advantage to losing my virginity at the ripe old age of twenty-two, it should be that I know better.

But it's weird, this feeling. It's immune to logic; it defies knowing better. I find myself smiling whenever I shift in my seat and the secret aches inside me declare Oliver's touch. I find myself biting my lip as I replay the fire and frenzy of his hand on my ass. And I squirm when I remember his words.

Good girls hold still.

Good girls come on the cocks their teachers give them.

Jesus.

But I do manage to stop myself from searching for Oliver Markham on social media. There's no point. Even with all these infatuated thoughts pinging around my brain, I know I'd never be so crazy as to track him down and reach out. My research indicated those things are unwanted. Considered clingy.

So I put my phone away and watch as the fields outside London slowly fold into rich, slow worlds of green trees and far-off church spires, and there's nothing Kansas-like about the view anymore. And with no homework and my job for Professor Graeme not yet started, I find myself in the luxurious position of having nothing to do.

I doze off to the gorgeous green view and the slow shake of the train.

And when I do, I dream of Oliver.

The rain is making it hard to hear my dad's voice. I press the phone closer to my ear and squint through my clear umbrella at the house in front of me—a white, thatched affair with deep windows and riots of flowers crowding the front.

"I said, did you make it to Graeme's house okay?" Dad repeats. "I should have done a better job with the timing or had him pick you up in London."

He sounds nervous, which is always how my father sounds. He teaches Victorian social history at the University of Kansas, and he's more comfortable in his cluttered office or in front of a whiteboard than he is in the real world, and these kinds of situations, even secondhand, tend to stress him out.

"The timing is fine, Dad. I wanted to have a night in London, remember?"

He makes a fretting noise. "I just wish he were there now to help you get settled in."

Professor Graeme scheduled an impromptu research trip to London after I'd already booked my flight, and I assured Dad—and told him to tell the professor—that I honestly didn't mind being by myself for the weekend. I mean, a chance to rattle around an adorable old cottage and explore the gorgeous sights of the Peak District? I'd *pay* to do that, so the opportunity to do so for free is not a hardship.

"I'll be fine," I soothe. "I can find my way to the kitchen and the bathroom, and that's all I need."

"Well, okay," Dad says in a worried tone. "You call me if you need anything. Graeme is a good man, but he's always been a bit reserved and not a little distracted. I can't imagine he'll be a very attentive host."

"Dad, you didn't set this up so I could sample English hospitality. You set it up so I could have hands-on experience with a private collection before I start library school." I walk up the flagged path to the front door, looking for the bright-blue flowerpot that should be hiding the key. "And if I can handle you, I'm sure I can handle him."

Whether man or woman, fussy old scholars are all the same. And I should know, because after my mom died, my father's fellow professors basically became my second family. I've spent my entire life around the species, and I'm incredibly grateful my dad's extensive network of academic colleagues yielded the chance to spend my summer in one of the most beautiful corners of the world.

However, I *have* adjusted my expectations to include all the things that living with an old person working on a book will mean.

Terrible television shows.

Stale store-bought cookies.

Finicky and exacting demands on my time.

But it will be worth it.

I say goodbye to Dad and let myself inside the house, parking my suitcase and wet umbrella carefully by the door so I don't drip water all over the clean flagstone floor. And then I step through the narrow hallway into the house of my dreams.

The flagged hallway is lined by bookshelf after bookshelf, each one crowded with a combination of well-worn paperbacks and sleek leather volumes and colorful modern hardcovers. The librarian's itch I feel to sort them is pure joy, pure brain-lust. I could spend hours poring over these shelves...and I will, I decide right then. I'll ask Professor Graeme if I can shelve these in my spare time, while I'm not helping him catalogue research. It would take me several delicious days to decide on a method, weighing my options between the traditional Dewey or a contemporary, more intuitive scheme...

I force myself on, past the sitting room overlooking the front garden full of flowers, past the snug with its cozy fireplace, and into the kitchen. It's massive and rambling and beamed and flagged and vaguely cluttered in a way that speaks to home and hearth rather than true untidiness.

I follow the stairs up to find three bedrooms—two of which are clearly guest rooms, with narrow beds and nondescript furnishings, and the last is obviously Professor Graeme's. I feel a little guilty peeking inside, but I tell myself it's simply for orientation's sake as I get to know the house. In any case, there's not much to see. A large bed with an IKEA-looking duvet. An end table stacked with books. Sheepskin slippers tucked by the bed.

Slippers.

Well, if that's not a marker of advanced age, I don't know what is.

It's only as I leave his room and walk back down the hall that I realize I haven't seen any pictures anywhere. There are *paintings*—small landscape-ish things that have that unmistakable "acquired by a grandmother" look—and a bust of Charles Dickens with untold years of dust caught in the bronze curls of his beard, but no pictures of Professor Graeme himself. No long-dead wife or kids or grandkids, no obligatory picture frames with nieces and nephews.

Nothing.

That's a little strange, right?

Mulling over this, I hop down the stairs and find my way to the back of the house, which is dominated by his study. Where I imagine most of the working and cataloging will be. Like the curious cat I am, I push the already cracked door open farther and step inside.

It's a mistake.

The opening door sends a pile of books and pamphlets scattering across the rug—not that there's much room to scatter, given that there are piles and piles of books and paper *everywhere*.

Old books. New books. Rare books. Pamphlets that should be in clear archival envelopes or at least under glass. Folders upon folders of what appear to be photocopies. And a cat. Who opens her eyes at my appearance, stretches all her paws out to the same point, and then rolls over so her belly's in the air.

And goes back to sleep.

There is a small desk off to the side—mine, I should think...or it will be mine—and a large desk that's no less cluttered than the floor but at least shows signs of rudimentary organization. An old-fashioned ink pen lies across a closed leather notebook, a blotting paper and inkwell nearby, which does nothing to revise my assessment of his age. And behind the desk, there's a wide line of windows, stretching nearly the width of the room, showing nothing but silver rain at the moment.

I sigh at the room, at the rare books left carelessly on the floor and the Victorian documents moldering among photocopies and a sleepy cat, and I feel a librarian itch that's not so pleasant. None of these things will last if they're not properly taken care of, and between organizing, cataloging, and—now, I can see—preservation efforts, I don't think I'm going to have any time at all for the books in the hallway.

Or anything else.

I leave the books and the cat and finally walk through a glassed-in conservatory to the back of the house, where a jewel-green lawn studded with wildflowers leads down to the shallow River Wye. Even in the rain, the colorful stones under the water seem to sparkle and flash, and I think of Oliver's eyes. Green and blue and brown.

And after I remember his eyes, it's impossible not to remember his hand sowing fire along my backside, his lips on my mouth and my neck and my breasts.

His lips lower down.

The sounds he made as he came.

With an abrupt turn, I leave the river and trudge back to the house through the rain.

Soon there will be too much work to do to think of Oliver Markham and his every-color eyes.

I spend the weekend busily, if not entirely happily. I walk the mile or so to Bakewell and enjoy my first Bakewell tart—or pudding, as I am briskly informed it's called here. I visit Haddon Hall and enjoy the massive blooming roses with the fat bees doddering around them, and then I have tea at Chatsworth with only myself and a book. I walk the rambling paths around the vales of the Peak District, challenging in the kind of way that makes you grateful to have a drink at the end of the day but easy enough to walk in a dress like the ones I usually wear.

The cat has been left with plenty of food, but I treat her to bits and pieces of chicken from the sandwiches I get in town, and she sleeps on my lap in the evening as I read in the snug.

I absolutely, positively don't think of Oliver.

Not whenever I catch a glimpse of the river that reminds me of his eyes. Not when I peel off my damp clothes and remember how it felt to be undressed by him. Not in bed, where my curious fingers explore my secret soreness and try to mimic the feel of a haughty man's mouth.

Not at all, not at all, not at all, until finally on Sunday night, I kick off my covers and climb out of bed. It's late—close to eleven—but I don't care. I'm sick of masturbating in an old man's guest room. Sick of remembering Oliver's cool, cultivated voice. Sick of pretending I'm too sophisticated to care that the man I coaxed into bed is also mysterious, English, and handsome beyond belief.

It's like Oliver was some kind of vampire, and now I'm bitten. Now I'm doomed to crave his touch for eternity.

Ugh. And now he's turning me into the kind of girl who makes stupid metaphors!

I'm stopping this shit right now. I'm going to put so many things inside my brain that there won't even be room for Oliver Markham and his perfect body.

Dad said Professor Graeme wouldn't get in until tomorrow morning at the earliest, so I don't bother to change out of my camisole and sleep shorts. Instead, I walk downstairs huffing to myself, doing a little dance across the cold flagstone floors until I get to the study and its many cozy rugs. That cat comes with me, oblivious to the cold floors, walks up to a pile of yellowing newsprint and kneads it pointlessly for a minute, and then lies down.

I walk around the room, hugging my arms around myself to ward off the clammy night chill. I poke at some of the stacks with my toes, trying to get a feel for what the professor's research seems to encompass. I know he probably won't want me to start on anything in earnest until he arrives, but I can at least start sorting some of it and making lists of things to do and archival materials to order. But I have to be doing *something.* I have to keep my thoughts occupied. Otherwise Oliver will creep into them again, and I can't have that.

The thing is that I've never had any trouble achieving something I've set my mind to. Honor roll, valedictorian, grad school of my choice—everything has boiled down to research and focus and discipline. I'm excellent at those things. I'm an excellent student.

So it was easy to promise myself that I'd be the perfect virgin. I'd be honest but not too honest, enthusiastic but not needy. I'd be able to shelve away the experience like a book and be able to revisit it with fond, wise memories. There was no reason to think I wouldn't be excellent at this either. But I'm not.

The thought makes me shuffle papers and books around a little harder than I should, sending dust clouding up into the air and stacks slumping sideways, much to the irritation of the cat, who looks at me over her shoulder and flicks her tail in a very deliberately unimpressed way.

"Oh sure," I tell her. "It's so easy to judge a girl when all you have to do is nap and eat."

Another tail flick. I glare at her.

"You know, this wouldn't be such a mess if your owner would clean up after himself," I grumble. "Why would anyone keep an office in this state? Or their research?"

"Because I like it that way," a cold voice says from behind me.

And I spin around to see the furious face of Oliver Markham.

CHAPTER SIX

OLIVER

It was a hard trip home.

Literally.

I spent my time on the train with crossed legs and gritted teeth, and then it took some artful draping of my jacket over my arm to cover my, ah, situation as I climbed onto the late bus from Matlock. And it isn't until right now, at my front door—tired and frustrated, a heavy bag full of photocopies and clothes slung over my shoulder—that I remember.

That I fucking remember.

The girl. Michael Lynch's girl.

Shit.

Lynch is an old acquaintance of mine. First my professor, when I spent a year studying abroad in America during my undergraduate degree, and then later a colleague and peer as we corresponded back and forth about various topics within our closely related fields. In one exchange, I made passing mention of needing an assistant simply to wade through all the material and make sense of it. It was a throwaway comment, bordering on a joke. Until Lynch wrote me back, offering up his librarian daughter for the cost of room and board.

He talked about the girl frequently—the fond asides of a proud father but not much more. To be honest, I forgot she existed until he mentioned her.

Zandy.

I pictured a girl looking like Michael—beanpole thin and bespectacled—poking around my research and asking all sorts of nosy questions about my methods, and I almost immediately said no. I enjoyed Michael's correspondence and his company, but I took this damn sabbatical from teaching precisely so I *wouldn't* have to talk to strangers. And that included any timid, mousy Lynch offspring inside my home. Inside my sanctuary.

But I owe Michael. He's been a good friend all these years, even after Rosie happened, even after I took a break from teaching—and, well, I really *do* need the help, if I am being honest. What started as a small stack of research beside my laptop has now become a behemoth of paper and ink that is happily swallowing up the rest of my study. Walking inside it is starting to put me in a bad mood—fine, a *worse* mood—and even my cat, Beatrix, seems to be losing patience with the unstable stacks of books, which have the tendency to slide and collapse under her feet when she tries to climb them.

Michael deserves the favor, and I deserve the help.

So I said *yes* and steeled myself to the thought of the summer with a girl bound to be as awkward and fretful as her father. It's only two months, and surely Michael would prepare his daughter for what a cold, miserable bastard I am. Surely she wouldn't take it personally.

I'd made my peace with Zandy's presence before I left for London, but now...

Now there's been Amanda.

And there's no peace left inside me. None at all.

In the moonless summer night, the lights inside the cottage burn a merry, welcoming yellow, although I can't help but rather grimly think of what I'll find inside. I repeatedly charge myself to be *nice*—or polite at the very least—and I remind myself that none of this is her fault. Not that I met a woman. Not that the woman let me play wicked games with her. Not that the woman let me deflower her and then somehow lulled me to sleep with soft curves and a faintly spicy smell.

It's certainly not her fault that I can't get this woman out of my head and that I'm strangely upset she left me that morning. Strangely bothered by the finality in her note.

We won't see each other again.

Why does that sting so much?

At least my lingering hard-on has settled down. It's a small comfort as I unlock the front door, unshoulder my bag, and step inside. I expect Beatrix to come whining for food as she usually does, but the front hall remains empty as I shut the door and shuck off my jacket.

She must be with the girl.

It's late, near midnight, and the girl should be in bed. Given all the lights, however, I assume she's in the snug or the kitchen, reading perhaps. Michael's always said he's a night owl himself, so perhaps it's fair to assume Zandy is the same.

When I get to the snug, though, she's not there. Nor is she in the kitchen. Maybe she went to bed and left the lights on for me?

But then I see it from the back hall off the kitchen—the light coming from under the study door. Suddenly all of the dread about this arrangement comes roaring back. All of the frustration about Amanda. And I hate that someone's in my study while I'm not in there, touching my things without my permission.

I stalk to the study door, ready to kick it down and roar like a true Bluebeard, when I hear a low voice talking. A woman's alto, with a hint of rasp around the edges. I wonder if she's talking on the phone, but then I hear her pause to wait for a response, and Beatrix meows.

The girl is talking to the damn cat.

It shouldn't be so irritating, really, this familiarity with my cat, but it is. She's already in my study. She's already touching things she shouldn't be. And for my only companion to be drawn into this flagrant violation of hospitality? It's infuriating.

I'm going to eviscerate her for this. I'm going to make her regret ever setting foot in my private space and making friends with my cat. I don't care how ridiculous that sounds. It's still forbidden!

I start to open the door. And freeze.

I'm not greeted with the sight of some scrawny, owlish bookworm. No, I'm greeted with a heart-shaped bottom that begs to be pulled over my lap. And a narrow waist and lush breasts and—bloody Nora—no bra. She's only in a thin camisole and some very short sleeping shorts, moving on all fours at an angle away from me, her long dark hair spilling in luscious waves and breaking over her shoulders.

No, not scrawny at all. She's a siren. She's...she's...

She turns as she chatters to the cat and I see her face for the first time. No lipstick, but I'd remember those plush, sinful lips anywhere.

The girl inside is not Michael Lynch's daughter.

She can't be.

Because she's Amanda.

My Amanda.

"Why would anyone keep an office in this state? Or their research?"

My voice is harsh. "Because I like it that way."

She spins with a gasp, dropping the book she was holding. I don't trust myself to take another step inside, not sure if I'd take her over my knee or fuck her senseless. But I do know one thing. I thought I was furious before?

It's nothing compared to now.

"What the fuck are you doing here?" I demand. "Are you stalking me?"

Her face goes from confused to stung in an instant. Then to angry. "I think the real question is what are *you* doing here?" she asks. And then she reaches for one of the pokers still hanging by the disused fireplace. She waves it at me. "I'll— I'll call the police. And the professor. He's supposed to be back any minute now. He just went out to the...the store...and if he comes back and finds an intruder, he'll get the police for sure!" Her voice is warbling higher in her hysteria, and I'm so bemused by the poker situation and the way she's talking about me like I'm in the third person and all the *lies* she's telling and has told, that it takes me a moment to realize she doesn't know I'm Professor Graeme.

She thinks I'm the intruder. She thinks I might hurt her.

Which—no. Never. I would never raise a hand against her.

Except if you've got her over your knee, a silky voice reminds me. Visions of her rump under my palm fill my head, and I know the voice is right.

"I fucking live here," I say. "This is my fucking house. Now do you want to explain what the bloody hell you're doing inside of it? After that little note? 'We'll never see each other again'? Did you steal my credit card information too?"

"You do *not* fucking live here. Professor Graeme does, and Professor Graeme is an old man. He's friends with my father and has slippers and everything!"

Well, now I think she's gone truly insane.

Except...

"Friends with your father," I repeat. I stare at her. "Your father is Michael Lynch?"

The tip of the fire poker lowers the slightest amount. "Yes," she answers, her eyes narrowing. It has the unfortunate—for me—effect of making her eyelashes sweep lower, long and sooty against her cheeks.

"Are you Zandy Lynch?"

The poker lowers a bit more. "Yes," she says.

"You told me your name was Amanda."

She drops the poker all the way down but still holds on to it, as if she's ready to strike me at any moment. "It is Amanda. Zandy's my nickname."

"It's still a lie."

"It's not," she fires back. "And you said your name was Oliver Markham!"

I hesitate because she's got a point. It's not entirely a lie either, but it wasn't the whole truth. "Oliver Markham Graeme," I say. "Markham is a family name. I knew...I knew it would be enough for anyone to locate me, coupled with my birthday and picture, if that alleviates any retroactive safety concerns of yours."

"Graeme," she mumbles. "You're Professor Graeme. But...but you're not old at all." Her cheeks go pink in the most tempting way, and then I notice—oh Christ—her nipples have pulled tight under the criminally thin fabric of her camisole.

Fuck. How dare she be so delicious now? When I'm so furious with her?

She drops the poker, and it bounces off a pile of books. "But you have slippers and everything," she whispers.

Why is she so fixated on my damn slippers? And how does she know I even have them unless she's been in my bedroom?

She's been in my bedroom.

A desperate, lust-filled rage floods me anew. "Tell me one thing," I demand. "Did you really not know? Did you really not know it was me?"

She shakes her head vehemently. "That was the whole plan," she says, gesturing in front of her as if *the plan* is something she can trace the shape of. "That's why it had to be London. It had to be a stranger. I wanted to get rid of it and then go on with my life."

I study her. Years of fibbing and malingering students have given me a keen ability to detect the truth, and there's nothing but honesty glowing from her blue eyes and flushed cheeks.

She didn't know.

A realization comes, jagged with relief and something that's too close to disappointment. "You should leave."

"Right," she says, smoothing down her hair. Her tits move under her camisole with mouthwatering heaviness. "I should go to bed, and then we'll discuss this after we've had some sleep."

"No," I interrupt. "I mean you should *leave*. Go back home."

I'm not prepared for the sudden hurt and unhappiness that floods her face. "Oliver," she says.

"It's Professor Graeme."

"Professor," she says. "Please."

The proximity of those two words together, coming out of a mouth like hers, lances heat right to my groin.

Professor, please.

Fuck.

"I really, really want this," she continues. "Not just for the work, although it will be invaluable to have on my résumé, but to have a summer that's somewhere new and different. If you send me home, I'll just be bored and alone with nothing to do, and I promise to be good if you let me stay. I'll be so, so good, Professor. Please."

I have to swallow.

Remember again that I'm a man and not a monster. "It's impossible, Zandy. Surely you see that. It's wildly inappropriate for us to work together now."

Her tongue peeps out to wet her lower lip. "I won't be inappropriate," she whispers. "I promise."

Does she not understand? She is inappropriate without even trying. Her earnestness. Her extravagant body. Everything about Zandy Lynch is fiercely unseemly, and it makes me crave very unseemly things. I can't have her in this house—her spiced and flowery scent in my nose, her dark hair catching the sunlight in my study—and not want to bend her over a desk. Not want her on her knees with her mouth open and those blue eyes trained up at me as she waits for the crumbs of my approval.

And I've vowed not to be that man anymore. Whatever happened in London be damned, I'll control myself starting now.

I ignore the tear-shine in her eyes when I say, "You'll leave tomorrow. We'll make the arrangements in the morning."

I mean to leave her there, with the finality of my decision hanging around her, but I have to stop. I don't turn to look at her. I simply make sure she hears me. "I don't like how you talk about your virginity like it's a burden. Something you had to coax a stranger into doing away with. It was a gift to me."

Then I leave her among the books and the papers, and when I reach my bedroom, I pull out my cock with embarrassingly frantic hands and stroke myself, thinking of those tits under her camisole. And after I come all over my fist and clean up, I kick my slippers under my bed with a growl, crawl into bed, and lie awake for untold hours, Zandy Lynch haunting my thoughts like a spirit haunts a house.

&

I barely sleep. And around five, when the sun is beginning to paint the sky on the other side of my little valley, I climb out of bed. Frustrated and hard, even after two more rounds with my fist. Quiet rounds, so that she wouldn't hear, although I almost wanted her to. I wanted her to creep by the door and listen to what she did to me. I wanted her to push her way in as boldly as she pushed her way into my night three days ago and demand to be fucked.

Beg to be fucked.

Promise to be her professor's good girl.

Of course it didn't happen, and I came into a T-shirt like a fucking adolescent, furious all the while. I'd done so well after Rosie—so well for *years*—and now here's Zandy Lynch with her mouth just made for my cock, with her backside just begging to be spanked.

Grumbling, I fish out my slippers from under the bed, yank some drawstring pants up over my hips, and pull on a clean T-shirt. If I can't sleep, I may as well work.

Beatrix joins me as I make a cup of tea and set out some of the latest texts I've been reading, along with my notebook and pen. She curls up on the table next to my notebook, oblivious to how many times I nudge at her to make writing room for my hand, and together we work until the kitchen slowly fills with light and the sun decides to peer directly into my house. I flip over the latest sheet of what I've been reading—a selection from a Victorian ladies' magazine—and move it to the edge of my workspace, which happens to be a nearly perfect square of sunlight coming in through the window.

"You really shouldn't expose it to the light like that," comes a voice from behind me, and it takes everything I have not to flinch at the sudden intrusion.

Zandy appears at the edge of my vision, her body in some kind of knit dress that looks nearly pornographic on her curves, her hair woven into a long, messy braid—the kind of braid that makes a man think of pulling on it. Her mouth is curved into a small smile as she sits at the kitchen table, but there's a flat sheen of defeat in her eyes.

I look away from her and rub at my chest again. "I suppose next you'll chide me for not using gloves."

"Actually, you shouldn't use gloves with paper," she says. "The fibers of the glove might catch on the document, and it's also important to have a feel for the page itself as you handle it. It's a delicate thing, handling something that rare, and you need every tiny, minute sensation to help you feel for whether it's brittle or supple. Whether it might break or bend."

I'm hard.

From her talking about paper.

"Duly noted," I say shortly, hoping she doesn't see how she's affected me. I tug the page out of the sunlight. A moment passes, when I pretend to go back to my reading and ignore her—as if I could ignore her. My body definitely can't.

She endures the silence for an admirably long time. And then, "Are you really going to send me home?"

She asks it in a soft voice, and when I look up, I see that defeat in her gaze again. I can't say why it bothers me, only that it does. Only that in the bizarre and short circumstances of our acquaintance, I've come to expect that blue gaze to bubble over with confidence and eager energy.

I set my pen down and run a hand over my face. "You have to see why it's impossible."

"But I don't. I already told you I'd be good. I'd be better—"

"Your father sent you to me with the tacit implication that I'd keep you reasonably safe during your stay. Do you honestly think he'd be comfortable with you staying in my house if he knew what happened in London?"

"I'm twenty-two," Zandy insists, leaning forward. "He knows I'm an adult. And besides, it was one time. *One time.* And we didn't know who the other really was. It's an outlier, not even a real data point, and it should be thrown out."

I scowl at her. I scowl because there's a part of her argument that's logical and because I don't even care about the parts that aren't. As much as I know she needs to go, as much as I want her to go—dammit, *I do*—my thoughts keep crowding with plans and ideas and all the moments we'd have together if she stayed.

"And," she says, sensing my weakness and gaining momentum now, "you really do need someone to fix this mess of yours."

"It's not a mess," I say coldly, but we both know I'm lying. Mess is possibly the kindest word for it.

"I can organize it, index it all, and store it safely. And you won't even know I'm in the room."

I have the vision of Zandy brushing sweaty tendrils of hair off her forehead as she carries books around, bending over often. Scratching away at her desk like a good little girl.

I have to swallow again.

"Please, Professor?" she asks, leaning forward so much now that her breasts press against the table. But that's not what I chiefly notice this time. No, it's her eyes, sparkling like sunlight dancing off ocean waves, even as she braces herself for my rejection.

I abruptly want that look out of her eyes. I want to see her eyes as they were that night we spent together, awed and worshipful and happy. That's the only reason I can think of for why I say it.

"Fine."

"Fine?" Her entire face lights up, a happy flush high on her cheeks and her eyes like blue fires. She looks like she wants to kiss me.

I wonder how I look.

"Yes. Fine. You can stay."

CHAPTER SEVEN

ZANDY

Oliver stands up, the sunlight catching on the waves of his hair. He impatiently shakes it out of his eyes, just as he did earlier when I stood behind him and watched him work. He'd been too absorbed to hear me as I walked in, too absorbed to notice me staring at his long fingers as they gripped his pen and made notes in an endearingly untidy scrawl. His too-pale skin and disheveled hair make sense to me now, fitted into the context of his work. He's an obsessed scholar, subsumed by his projects, and it's easy to see how the everyday details of life have become unimportant. My father is the same way, and so are most of his friends. They'd forget to eat if someone didn't remind them.

"I'm going to change," Oliver says in that short, clipped way of his, "and then I'll be back downstairs and we can begin." He still doesn't sound pleased, but I'm so relieved I get to stay that I ignore his grouchiness.

"Is there anything I can do while you get ready? Make you some coffee?" I think for a minute, remembering where I'm at. "Tea?"

He narrows his eyes. "Just don't touch anything while I'm not around."

"Whatever you say," I reply, fast enough that it nearly sounds sarcastic. "Professor," I add, hoping that will ameliorate any unintentional offense.

His eyes darken at my last word, and he stalks from the room as if I've enraged him.

I sigh the moment I think it's safe. While I'm used to grumpy scholars, Oliver has to be the grumpiest I've ever encountered. Well, not grumpy, exactly. *Cold* is a better word. Glacial, even.

Unfeeling.

Stony.

I stand up and stretch, deciding *don't touch anything* surely doesn't extend to coffee or tea and needing the familiar act to steady myself, because holy fuck, Oliver Markham is Professor Graeme.

The man I'm spending the summer with is the man who ended my virginity, and if I was worried about my ability to be wise and sophisticated about this before, it's nothing compared to now.

Because even with as cool and distant as he is, I still yearn for his touch. Even with his gaze flashing displeasure, I crave the trace of it over my body. Even in its cruelty, his perfect mouth begs for my own mouth, my fingertips. And even covered with a T-shirt and loose pants, his leanly muscled body calls to mine, bringing me memories of how he looked moving between my legs, memories of how taut and rigid he went as he filled my pussy with his own ecstasy.

I take a deep, steadying breath, trying to stop my body's response to the visions of that night, to the presence of him in the house. I can't work next to him like this, all wet and nipples hard, not when I need to prove to him how professional I can be. I'll save it for bedtime, when I'm alone in the dark, one hand clapped over my own mouth so he can't hear me come.

Like I did last night.

Oliver doesn't have any coffee, so I decide to make a cup of tea. I find a mug, fill it with water, and pop it in the microwave for a couple of minutes. When it's done, I carefully take it out, and I'm about to drop in the bag when Oliver says in a horrified voice, "What on earth are you doing?"

I whirl to see him looking unfairly sexy in a thin sweater and belted trousers that hang low on his narrow hips. He's leaning against the kitchen doorway, his arms crossed and a frown on that sharp-edged mouth.

"I'm making tea?" I say, the last part lifting up like a question because I'm feeling suddenly unsure. Maybe I grabbed his favorite mug, or maybe I'm using some precious store of teabags that visitors aren't allowed to touch—or maybe visitors aren't allowed to touch anything at all, and he's provoked that I didn't listen to his edict about touching things.

"That's not how you make tea," he says. "You use the *kettle* for tea, not the microwave as barbarians do."

The disgust in his voice is so pronounced that I can't help but giggle. This only deepens his frown.

"We have work to do," he bites out. "Follow me. Bring that cup of atrocity if you must."

I do bring my cup of atrocity, following him down the hall and trying very hard not to notice how his ass and hips look in his pants—tight and trim. Powerful in a subtle, spare way. Powerful in the kind of way that makes a girl think of how they'd feel under her hands. How they'd look bunching and flexing between her thighs.

I give a little shiver. *Down, girl.*

I've got to be good today. I've got to prove that he doesn't need to send me home.

The cat winds between our feet as we walk into the study, plopping down on the first pile of papers she sees, and I set my mug on my desk and wait for Oliver to give me instructions.

He stands behind his own desk now, gazing at me with a haughty expression. "You'll do as I say in here," he says flatly. "That's without question. Understood?"

"Understood."

His hands are flexing by his sides as he looks at me, and for a moment, all I can remember is the way they felt as he spanked me. One palm setting fire to my skin as the other hand held me steady over his lap.

I have to press my legs together at the sudden throb my clit gives at the memory. Who would have thought I'd like being spanked so much? So much that not only had I become a wet, squirming mess at the time, but that I longed for it again?

He swallows, and I realize that his beautiful eyes are no longer on my face but on my body. On the place where I'm pressing my thighs together.

"Sit," he commands hoarsely. "Get something to take notes with."

I sit, finding a notepad and a pen that have been shoved into one of the drawers. "Ready when you are, Professor," I say, and he makes a noise, tearing his eyes away from where I sit with my legs crossed and pen poised in the air.

He sits as well, keeping his gaze away from me. "I'm writing a book about Victorian courtship narratives," he says to the William Holman Hunt painting on his wall. "Not necessarily the rituals themselves but the morality tales given to young people in order to illustrate how they *should* behave. As well as the satirical tales that illustrate how they *did* behave."

"And how did they behave?" I ask as I write.

"As youth everywhere and in every time behaves," he says grimly. "Improperly."

I look up at him with a smile. He doesn't smile back, glancing away from me as soon as our eyes meet. "Surely that's kind of heartwarming," I say. "Kind of fun? To think even Victorians couldn't help being naughty?"

Oliver presses his eyes closed. "I think," he says slowly, "it proves that we never learn from the mistakes of the past."

There's a deep bitterness in his words that takes me by surprise; whatever he's thinking of at the moment, it's viciously unhappy. It has teeth, and it's chewing at his mind—I can see it playing out across his beautiful face.

And then he opens his eyes with a long inhale, speaking to the painting once more. "I've only been through a third of the things I've collected, perhaps less, and so as part of any organization scheme, we need to index if I've seen it before."

"Of course," I say, jotting that down. "What else do you need? Digitization?"

He makes a face—it's very similar to the face he made at my cup of tea. "I prefer paper."

"Victorian paper is very cheap and very acidic," I inform him. "Even in the best of conditions, which..." I trail off meaningfully, tilting my head at the room of decaying paper sitting in the sunlight.

"And?" Oliver prompts testily.

"And some of these paper works are not going to be around much longer. By the time you get to them, they may crumble in your hands. Digitizing what you can isn't just helpful for your research, it's the responsible thing to do as potentially the sole owner of some of these texts."

He gives a put-upon sigh. "If you think it necessary...then I suppose."

"I'll only mark the most at-risk items for photographing or scanning," I promise. I make a few more notes and give the room an assessing look. "We'll need to order some archival supplies—is there room in the budget for that?"

"The budget," he echoes, sounding puzzled.

"Dad said you were working with grant money."

"Oh yes, the grant." He gives a shrug that conveys something close to discomfort, and I watch curiously, as I've never seen him truly uncomfortable before—only annoyed. "Money is not a concern," he says, and he actually looks embarrassed by this. Maybe it was an exceptionally large grant and he feels strange about accepting it? Who knows.

"Okay, then," I say, standing up. "Shall we get started?"

An imperious look. "You shall get started. *I* shall work."

"Yes, Professor." I say it perhaps too mockingly, earning myself a glare, and I scuttle over to the far corner of the room and get to work before he scolds me again.

It becomes clear that Oliver's system, if that word can even be used, has been to stack the most promising texts closest to his desk and the least promising in the corners and along the far wall. I work steadily through the morning, building up a light sweat as I shift through stacks of material, trying to get a handle on what I'll need to know to build a comprehensive database for Oliver.

Several times I peek up over my work to watch him at his desk, unable to stop myself from staring at the chiseled jaw flexing in concentration and the long eyelashes sweeping against his cheeks as he studies his papers and types on his laptop.

It should be illegal for a man to be that handsome *and* English. It just isn't fair.

I suspect he doesn't want to be bothered, so around lunchtime I wander into his kitchen and make us simple sandwiches, bringing his plate back and wordlessly setting it at the edge of his desk. He reaches for the food automatically, eyes pinned to his laptop screen, and it isn't until he's finished his sandwich that he seems to realize he's eaten it at all.

"Thank you," he says after a minute, and I notice that his voice has thawed the tiniest bit. Not much. But a bit. I'm already back to work, and I look up to see him staring at me with an expression I can't decipher.

"You're welcome, Professor," I say, and he grunts in response. I take it as progress and fight a smile as I lean back down to my stacks of books.

The day passes much the same as this. I finally get my laptop from my room and start on the database. Oliver sighs a lot at the frequent tapping of my keyboard, but when I offer to go work in the kitchen, he merely scowls and mutters, "Stay."

So I stay.

Around six, I bring up the subject of dinner and ask if he'd like me to make it. He seems to fight some inner war with himself. "I'll order takeaway," he says, which is how we end up eating delicious Indian food at the kitchen table with his cat complaining loudly at our feet.

"How did the writing go today?" I ask innocently enough, and he stabs at his butter chicken with a fierce frown.

"You should know better than to ask any writer that question."

"So it went well?"

He directs the frown at me. "You're teasing me." He says it incredulously, as if no one has ever dared do it before. In fact, I'm suddenly quite certain no one ever has dared to tease him before this. He's very un-teasable, with that haughty face and icy gaze. But I'm feeling energetic and playful from my own productive day, and it's so very hard not to provoke him when he makes such handsome provoked faces.

"I won't tease you any more if it hurts your feelings," I poke.

He glares at me. "It doesn't hurt my feelings."

"You seem a little hurt."

"I'm not hurt."

"In fact, I think I need to make it up to you," I banter back. "Maybe you can make me write an essay on my bad behavior."

His pupils dilate at the same instant that my own words filter back through my mind, along with their subtext. Which is punishment.

Which of course makes me think of the night we were together, which of course makes me want to be bent over that strong knee again. And with the way Oliver's fingers are clenched around his fork, I wonder if he's wanting the same thing.

"Excuse me," he says abruptly, standing up and setting his dishes by the sink. He leaves to go to his study, and I hear the door close firmly behind him. The message is clear.

Do not follow.

Feeling a little flushed from my body's immediate response to the idea of punishment from Oliver, I clean up after dinner and go upstairs. I mean to read for a while or maybe watch a movie on my tablet, but by the time I shower and get in bed, I'm more worked up than ever. I make sure my door is locked, and then I quietly climb into bed. I reach into my panties and let my mind fill with everything Oliver—his ferocious hands and his wicked mouth and his cock so heavy and so thick with wanting me.

It doesn't take long, the climax, because it's been building all day. All day like a slow fire inside me, and at the first touch of my hand, my body is already quivering and tense, ready to snap like a rubber band. The orgasm is fast and furious and ultimately unsatisfying, and when I come down from it, I come down with an itchy feeling of disappointment.

Of unabated longing.

And then as I sigh and pull my hand away from myself, I hear it—the creak of a floorboard outside my room. I go completely still, flooded with embarrassment and something else that's harder to name.

Anticipation?

Hope?

Do I want Oliver to kick down the door, pin me to the bed, and finally go all professor on me?

Yes. Yes, I do.

God, I want it more than anything.

The floorboard creaks again, and I can't breathe. I can't move. I'm ready for him to force his way in here and relieve the still-aching need deep in my core.

But he doesn't.

Hushed silence fills the corners and crevices of the room, and I'm left alone. Empty. Unfulfilled.

Sleep takes a long time to find me after that.

☋

A week goes by like this. During the day, Oliver is uncommunicative and distant. I work and he works, and I steal glimpses of him working, his light-brown hair burnished in a near-gold by the June sunlight and his jaw ticking in that particular way of his as he thinks. I feed him lunch, which he barely notices, and then at some point I tentatively bring up dinner, which is almost always some kind of carryout and also an excuse for him to jab angrily at his food until he finds a reason to leave the table.

And then I go up to my room and read or work until I can't stand it anymore, and I rub myself to climax. I never do hear that floorboard again, but every single time I hope I do.

I hope Oliver comes in and claims me. I want it more than I want anything, even more than I wanted to stay. Or maybe I wanted to stay because I wanted him to claim me more than anything. *So much for being sophisticated, Zandy.*

By my seventh day, the air in the study is thick with tension.

The sun is hot through the window, and I'm a very dismayed American when I realize that a box fan is the closest thing Oliver has to air conditioning. We crack open the windows and angle the fan so it doesn't blow century-old paper everywhere, but it barely helps. Even the cat escapes the house with a cantankerous meow, jumping out the open window and loping into the back garden in search of shade.

My sleeveless dress is too hot, and I'm tugging constantly at the neckline, feeling warm and flushed even with my hair fastened up on top of my head. I'm jealous of the cat, jealous of her shade, but all of my work is here in the study, and I can't leave either my work or Professor Grouch, who is even grouchier than usual today.

The second time I trip over a stack of books, making a ton of mess and noise, Oliver slams his laptop shut. "You," he says darkly.

Just that.

Just *you.*

And then he glares at me.

"I'm sorry," I say. "It's just messy and hot and...what is it?"

"Do you even care that you're making it impossible for me to work?"

Normally, I find his arrogant coolness sexy or amusing, but not today. It's too hot for one thing, and I'm eyeballs deep in fixing *his* mess, and so I snap back, "Not in the slightest."

I know instantly that I've fucked up. Oliver is a man of little patience, and the kind of lippy insolence I just displayed is absolutely one of his pet peeves. I feel a quick dart of fear that I've just managed to get myself fired.

Get myself sent home.

Shit.

Oliver's face could be cut from stone right now, and his words are made of ice when he finally speaks. "Come here."

"Oliver—"

"You call me professor in here or nothing at all," he interrupts coolly.

"Professor—"

"Come. *Here.*"

With some trepidation, I straighten my dress and walk toward him, bracing myself for the inevitable words. *You're fired. Get out of my sight.* And I hate the way tears burn at the back of my eyes, the way my throat balls up, because it's stupid that I have grown so attached in such a short amount of time. Not just to this beautiful cottage in this beautiful place but to *him*, the most beautiful thing of all. If I had to leave him, I wouldn't be able to bear the disappointment.

Disappointment. What a stupid word.

I'd be heartbroken.

Oliver regards me from across his desk, his arms folded over his chest, his mouth pressed in a flat line. "Come *here*," he repeats, and I realize what he wants. He wants me close to him, on the other side of his desk.

My heartbeat kicks up a thousand paces. My mouth goes dry. He wants me close so that there's no mistaking his angry dismissal. He wants me close so that he can make it very, very clear that I have to leave. And maybe I deserve it. Not for knocking over books but because I haven't been a very good girl at all this week, what with all the silent, pining looks I've been throwing his way and the equally silent masturbating in his guest bed.

Tears threaten to spill out of my eyes, and crazy promises threaten to spill out of my mouth: that I really will be good this time, that I'll be the best assistant a professor could have, that I'll happily endure all of his moods and cutting remarks if only he'd let me stay close to him.

But I swallow both the tears and the words. I need to keep my dignity, I know at least that much about myself. That when I'm back home in my tiny apartment, curled around an empty bottle of wine, I'll be able to hold on to the memory of me being composed and resilient, to the knowledge that I didn't humiliate myself.

As I walk around the desk, Oliver pushes his chair back as if he'll stand, but he stays seated, keeping his body angled to the front. I take a deep breath, willing myself to be as cool and untouchable as he is, waiting for him to say the words that will send me home.

But those aren't the words he says.

"Red means stop," he tells me, and then I'm seized and thrown over his lap.

Blood rushes to my head as my hands find the floor in pure instinct, and his hands easily catch and arrange me, one of his long legs hooking over mine when they kick up in the air.

And I'm wet.

Instantly, shamefully wet.

It's like all the silent orgasms and all the daylight fantasies and muffled desire, they are all concentrated into longing for this one thing, this one act. I don't need a kiss or a murmured compliment—I need *this*. To be bent over Oliver's knee like a disobedient schoolgirl.

And *he* needs it too. That much is clear from the way his hands tremble as they shape over my backside, smoothing over the fabric of my dress with a slowness that feels very much like desperation in disguise. A thick shape nudges into my hip, solid and blunt, and the tangible proof that he wants me is enough to make me whimper.

The whole thing is enough to make me whimper.

He's not going to be hearing any safe words out of my mouth. Not today.

"You make it impossible for me to work," he breathes. "You make it impossible to concentrate. To eat. To sleep."

"Because I made a mess?" I ask tremulously.

His hand slips under the hem of my dress and palms my backside. "Because you made a mess," he says in a growl, squeezing my ass hard enough for me to yelp. "And because you distract me with your dresses and your fucking hair and your fucking watch." He flips the skirt of the dress up over my waist, baring my ass and thighs to the warm air of the room.

"What are these?" he asks dangerously, a finger tracing along the lacy edge of my panties.

"Um, underwear," I answer, my face burning and my core clenching. I want so very badly for him to stroke along my center, to slip a finger inside of the lace and rub me where I'm swollen and wet, but he doesn't. He just continues with that maddening tease.

"These are the kinds of things bad girls wear," he says sternly. "Are you a bad girl?"

"Yes," I exhale. "Yes, I am."

The first spank. I squeal, my body arching away from the force, but there's nowhere to go, nowhere to be except against his hot, firm body.

"You know what else makes it impossible?" he asks.

"What?" I manage.

"Listening to you come on your own hand, night after night."

I suck in a guilty breath, grateful he can't see my face. "I—that's not—I mean—"

"Don't lie to me, Miss Lynch."

Not Zandy.

Not even Amanda.

Miss Lynch, like I'm a misbehaving student of his. The thought turns me on beyond all belief, and I squirm in his lap. "I didn't mean to—"

"You're lying," he accuses. "You think I don't know what you do at night, dirty girl? You think I don't know how you slip your fingers between your legs and wish it were my fingers? My mouth? My cock?"

I'm so far gone with lust at this point that all I can do is moan.

"Did you do it to drive me mad? Hmm?" Another spank. "Did you do it hoping I would break down the door and fuck you like your fingers couldn't?"

"Yes," I whisper as another spank lands hard. "Yes, I wanted that."

"Naughty girl," he admonishes. "Very naughty girl." Several more rain down on my backside, and I am past struggling now, past anything but the need for friction against my clit, the need to be filled deep inside.

"Please," I beg wildly. My hair is tumbling down around my face, and my nose is starting to run, and it feels like I've been spanked within an inch of my life, and I need *something*, something only he can give me. "Please, Oliver."

He gives me an almighty spank. "Try again."

"*Please, Professor.*"

"Much better," he rumbles, and then his fingers are right where I need him, pressing against the fabric covering my pussy. He tugs the panties aside, studying his prize for a long moment before fingering me in rough exploration. He makes a noise of approval at what he finds.

"So wet," he says with crude pleasure. "So wet for me."

His hand grips my hair and turns my head so I can look at him—his other hand keeps working at my sopping-wet pussy, teasing my entrance and working inside my channel so slowly that my toes curl.

"What do you want, Miss Lynch?" he asks, and he's as scornfully proud as ever, but there's something in the way he asks and in the way his hand pauses inside me...

He's waiting for me to carry this kinky game of his further. He's waiting for me to choose. And it's not even a choice. It hasn't been a choice since I clung to him in the London rain.

I will never choose *red*.

"I want to be your good girl, Professor Graeme. Please let me be your good girl again."

CHAPTER EIGHT

OLIVER

I knew this morning that I was near my breaking point.

All week it's been building, stoked by every fire imaginable. Her adorable and distracting habit of running the top of her pen over her lip as she worked. The thoughtful feeding and bringing of fresh mugs of tea, once she figured out the kettle. The unknowing way she flashed me her panties as she crawled on all fours around my office, shifting through stacks of research.

And at night...*fuck*.

It was purely an accident the first time. I was passing down the hallway to get a glass of water when I heard her. It was only a quiet *mmm* of feminine relief, but it went through me like an electric shock. I froze to the spot, instantly picking up on the rustle of sheets and the quickening of breath and—God have mercy on my soul—a sound that could be nothing other than a slender finger moving through a wet pussy.

I listened, hard and throbbing, until the very end with her sweet gasp of pleasure, and then I stole back to my room to toss off fast and vicious, coming so quickly that I could barely catch my breath.

I've repeated the voyeurism every night since.

How could I not?

I burned with wanting her, I ached with being so near and yet holding myself back, and by today, I was near mad with it. Her lewd curves and even lewder mouth, both combined with those still-innocent eyes. And then she had to go and put her hair up, with only a few damp tendrils escaping, as if to taunt me by caressing all the places along her neck and shoulders that I could not.

I didn't care that she knocked over a stack of books. I *cared* that she made me a madman. A wild thing, a beast, a hunter.

A monster.

I cared that I wanted her beyond all sense and propriety, and I cared that she was too fucking smart and helpful for me to find any fault with.

I cared, in other words, that she was perfect, and that by being perfect, she made me the most imperfect version of myself.

So as I hold her over my lap, one hand twisted in that luscious hair and the other still wet from her cunt, I ask her one last time. "Are you sure you want to be my good girl? It will take a lot of work."

She pulls her plump lower lip between her teeth. "Red means stop, right? So I say *red* when I need a time-out?"

"That's correct, Miss Lynch."

She blinks up at me. "Then that's all I need to know. Do what you like with me, Professor."

Christ, but she's dangerous. Some kind of siren sent to lure me off my path. I push her to her knees in front of me, spreading my legs on either side of her, enjoying the view of her big blue eyes all sultry as she looks up at me. I enjoy it almost as much as I enjoyed the glowing skin of her ass. Almost as much as examining the tight entrance to her body, all pink and wet, and remembering how unthinkably tight she'd been around my penis that night. How I had to wedge my way in.

Hell, I enjoy it all. I drink it all in like a man who hasn't tasted a drop of water in years.

"You've made me hard, like a bad girl," I drawl, loving how her eyes widen at the word *hard*. "And a good girl would fix it."

"Fix..." she asks, and then her cheeks go very pink. "*Oh.*"

"Yes. Take it out, Miss Lynch. I'm getting impatient."

Her hands are nervous and unpracticed as she works my belt open. "I've never..." Her voice comes out in a faltering murmur that's unlike her usual confident alto. She clears her throat. "I've never done this."

"Then just do as I say," I inform her.

She nods, squaring her shoulders a bit, and sets her attention to the task, like any good student would. There's something deeply erotic about her inexperience, something that makes it more than the playacting this kind of roleplay usually is.

A part of this is real—so real that it might be wrong—and I can't bring myself to stop it. I let the wrongness of it wash over me, opening to it, letting it inside a cold, sleeping heart that's been dead to real pleasure for far too long.

I hiss as her hands seek me out, drawing my naked and ruddy flesh into the air.

She stares at it with just as much awe and panic and excitement as she did that night in London—as if she can't wait to have me inside her even as she knows I'll be too big—and that makes me want to pound my chest like a caveman. Makes me want to pull her up onto the chair and thrust into her wet opening. I want her impaled on me. I want her writhing from the stretch of me. I want her coming so hard her body tries to curl into a ball because she can't stand it, she just can't stand it.

But for now, I settle for this: "Put your mouth there, Miss Lynch."

Her eyelashes flutter as she looks up at me. "But what if I'm not any good at it?"

Frankly, it's a miracle I haven't erupted all over her already, but I don't break character to tell her that. "Then you'll have to practice. Best to start now."

The lower lip gets bitten, and one eyebrow arches slightly in a movement I know means she's deep in thought. And then she leans forward and presses a chaste kiss to the underside of my cock.

"Like that?" she asks, peering up at me. Her mouth is still close enough to my flesh that I feel the sweet puffs of her breath.

My belly clenches. "Almost, Miss Lynch. Use your tongue. Lick me."

"Lick," she murmurs to herself. "I can do that." And she does, setting that plush mouth to me once again, this time parting her lips, allowing her tongue to slip out.

The second it touches me, I let out a ragged breath; it's heaven, pure heaven, and the look she gives me is nothing short of vixenish—which, despite everything, despite how lurid and depraved this moment is, almost makes me smile with a grudging kind of respect. I can say many things about Zandy Lynch, and most of them are grievances—that she's too bold, too eager, too *happy*—but those are also the same things I can't ever imagine changing about her. They are the same things that reassure me that, while I might be a monster, I'm still a monster with a conscience, because the girl between my legs knows exactly what she's doing. She'll survive this.

Even if I don't.

She licks me again, less tentative this time and more certain, a long steady motion that has my blood heating and freezing in fitful starts. And then her natural eagerness spills over and she starts licking at my crown as if it's a lollipop, like she can't get enough of it. I thread my hands through her hair, but I don't push her down. Not yet. I simply flex and twist my fingers in the silky strands and guide her mouth to where I need it. From my taut, swollen tip to the turgid base, from the root to the velvety underside, rewarding her with my groans whenever she does well.

"Suck it," I say hoarsely. "Put it in your mouth and suck."

She does.

· The flood of heat and soft wet is almost too much, and I'm gritting my teeth against the urge to come. "God, you suck me so good," I groan, my head falling back against my chair. I keep my hands in her hair, pushing her down just far enough to get that squeeze at the head of my prick. "Fuck."

I look down at her, and she's a vision like this, her dark hair tumbling everywhere around my hands and her perfect mouth wrapped around my cock. Her cheeks are hollowed and her eyes are wet and blue, and I think I could look at this for the rest of my life. Except there's something I want to see more.

"On your feet," I tell her, wincing as her hot mouth leaves my cock to throb wet and alone in the air of the room. I stand as she stands, and then I bend her over the desk, ignoring the papers and notes that go flying as I do.

"Stay here," I command, and I go up to my bedroom to find a condom. The box in my end table is depressingly old, and it would be funny to think that I've seen more sex in the past week than I have in the past three years if it weren't so painfully true. I find myself taking the steps back downstairs faster than I should, not only excited to get back down to Zandy and her willing body, but also crawling with this odd fear that I'd return to the study and find her gone. That she'd come to her senses and leave and take her forthright sweetness elsewhere.

The fear is astonishingly pervasive, and I find myself rubbing at the tight spot in my chest as I push open the study door.

And find her still stretched over my desk, like the good listener she is.

The relief at seeing her nearly makes me stumble, nearly makes me drunk, and I'm on her with a fast desperation I don't care to identify. I bend over her body, covering her with mine. We're both still fully clothed, still sweaty in the June heat, and it makes it dirtier somehow. Coarser.

Obscene.

"Oliver," she pleads, voice breaking, and I don't correct her this time. The game is melting away—into what, though, I'm not certain.

"I know what you need, girl. Hold still."

I straighten up and roll on the condom as fast as I've ever done it in my life, peeling her panties off her skin and kicking them away. I cup her pussy in my hand with a hard, possessive grip, and she wriggles against it, trying to get the friction against her clit, and she's so wet, so fucking wet, that my palm comes back slicked with her.

I use that hand to stroke my swollen cock once, twice, before nudging the shiny latex tip at her small opening. I remind myself that this is only her second time being fucked, to take it easy on her, and it's with all the unraveling self-control left in me that I refrain from slamming into that tight cunt with one savage thrust.

I settle for two savage thrusts instead.

The thick, heavy crown stretches her, and I get to halfway in, holding her hips down as she whimpers and tosses underneath me. And then I shove the rest of the way in, wishing I could listen to her noises forever. Her long, low cry as I fully seat myself inside her. Her pants and mewls as I roll my hips to feel the wet silk of her around my root. And then her eye-rolling moan as I slide my hand around her hip and start massaging the swollen pearl of her clit.

She is amazing like this, bent over my desk like some kind of academic sacrifice, her sweet ass filling one hand while my other hand works her into a frenzy. Her hair is a tumbled mess, and her eyes, when they flutter back at me, are lost and dazed and adoring. And her body around mine, even through the condom, is everything—soft and hot and tight beyond belief. A spark of wonder kindles in my chest that she's letting a miserable bastard like me fuck her again. That she's still happy and willing to play any kind of game with me after how I've acted the past week.

Christ, what a gift.

The spark kindles into a real fire now, something possessive and primal and as certain as the sun and the wind and the sparkling river glinting behind me as I fuck her.

She's mine.

Maybe it's just for this moment, as she starts quivering and fluttering around my cock, or maybe it's only for today. But she's mine, and I want to roar my pleasure at the knowledge.

I want more of her. More of this. This raw fucking with my hips plowing into her spank-reddened bottom, this sweet clenching around my cock as she comes. And after my own release tears through me, filling the condom with hot and heavy spurts, I barely give her a minute to breathe. I tear off the condom, scoop her limp and sweaty into my arms, and carry her up to my bedroom.

I'm ravenous tonight. Insatiable. Because, selfish man that I am, if I'm going to break my rules and break the trust I have with her father, then I may as well do it thoroughly.

And I am very, very thorough.

I peel off her clothes and explore every exposed contour of her with my mouth. I feast on those abundant tits like I've been fantasizing about, like I've been stroking myself to the thought of all week, and I turn her into a wriggling, gasping mess.

"I forgot," she breathes out, her eyes glowing in the fading light of my bedroom.

"You forgot what?"

"That your mouth could feel so good there," she whispers as I kiss and lick at the softly curved underside of her breast. "That it would make me want you so much again."

"Then let me make it so you remember forever."

I move my lips from the underside to her nipple, tugging gently at the straining tip with my teeth and then drawing it into my mouth for a long, swirling suck. She arches underneath me, a movement that matches us together down below, and before I can do anything about it, she's rubbing her empty pussy against me, lifting her hips and grinding against my hardness.

The feel of her wet and soft against my bare cock is like a nightmare and dream wrapped into one, and for the first time in years, I find I want to fuck a woman bare. I want to push into Zandy with nothing between us, and I want her to see how raw she makes me, how vulnerable. I want her to feel every inch of what she does to me. I want her to feel it when I come in her, marking her.

Mine.

And then I duck my head down to kiss along her stomach, terrified of my own thoughts, terrified she'll see them. Terrified she'll see them and she won't be scared and I won't be scared either and we'll do something regrettable.

There's a good reason I fuck with condoms every time. There's a good reason I fuck with condoms always.

I work my way down the gentle curves of her stomach and then over the rise of her pubic bone, kissing and licking all the way.

"Stop," she gasps. "I'm sweaty, and I should clean myself if you're going to do that again and—"

"Is this a *red* stop, or is this you trying to hide yourself from me?"

"It's not a red stop," she clarifies. She has no idea how tantalizing she looks like this, her head propped on a pillow, near-black waves of hair everywhere, her nipples standing to attention and her wet cunt spread before me. "But I have been sweaty all day—"

"I make the rules," I inform her in a clipped voice. "In this bed, I'm the professor and you're my student, and I'm going to taste you. And then I'm going to fuck you."

She wiggles a little, color in her cheeks. "But..."

"Those are the rules, Miss Lynch. You want to follow my rules, don't you? Be a good girl for me?"

God, how she responds to me when I talk to her like this. Like she was made to fit me. Her mouth parts, and her tongue licks out at her lower lip. Her eyes are huge, dark pools of needy blue when she answers, "Yes, Professor."

I make a noise of satisfaction and resume my kissing, using my hands to spread her wide so she's completely on display for me. That night in London, I'd been too impatient, too fast—years of celibacy chasing me down and making me weak, and when she broke open my control, she broke open all of it. The restraint. The time I normally took with a woman in bed.

Not now. Not tonight.

Tonight, I'm in full control, and I take my time staring at her, using my thumbs to make it so she hides nothing. There's no wet secret of hers that I don't want to taste and learn. There's no hollow of her body that I don't want to know my touch.

Mine.

I trace every fold with my tongue, I suckle on the firm berry of her clit until she's moaning, and then right before she comes, I sheathe my cock in latex and drive home, kissing her aggressive and deep with a mouth still wet from her pussy.

"Zandy," I grind out, my hips changing from slow rolls to heavy, fast thrusts. "Fuck, Zandy, you feel so fucking good."

She is lost to the drive of me between her legs, her head tossing. "It's too much, Oliver," she mumbles, her eyes closed. "I can't—it's too—"

She comes so hard she screams, and I feel it all around my cock, a grip so tight that it almost feels like she's trying to push me out. It's work to fuck through all that—the most delicious kind of work—and when I come, it feels like something rips open inside me. Something that's been held back for far too long. The throbs are so sudden and strong that I find myself slumping over her, unable to keep my own body upright as I fill the condom and something rearranges itself deep in my chest.

After I clean us up, she looks like she thinks she should leave, and I climb into bed and anchor her to me with one arm around her stomach, pulling her back to my chest and her perfect rump into my hips. My knees tuck behind her knees, and her long hair is everywhere like a sea of floral-smelling shadows.

"Oliver?" she asks after a moment.

"It's the oxytocin," I mumble against her neck, and that seems to settle her.

But it takes a long time for me to fall asleep, and the reason why is that I know something she doesn't.

It's not the oxytocin.

It's because I'm not ready to let her go.

CHAPTER NINE

ZANDY

I wake up sore between the legs and happy. The kind of happy that has no real reason to it. The kind of happy that suffuses your blood before you even open your eyes. And when I do finally open my eyes to summer sunshine and Oliver's neatly furnished room, I'm smiling.

Before I'm even all the way conscious, I know he's gone. But I'm not upset by it—I've noticed that he takes himself on punishingly long runs most mornings; and anyway, I'm glad I get to have this very, very girlish moment to myself. The moment where I roll over and smell the sheets and squeal inwardly to myself.

Oliver fucked me again.

And more than that—he's been wanting me as much as I've been wanting him. Every glimpse I stole of his eyes and aristocratic mouth, he was stealing similar glimpses of me. He was wanting me, craving me...listening to me finger myself night after night in vivid torment.

The thought makes me curl and blush with agony—agonized shame and agonized delight. To be caught doing such things is beyond humiliating, and yet to know that those same things aroused and haunted him fills me with a smug feminine pride. To know that the person you want wants you back?

It's like a pure life arrowing right through the middle of me. Like I'm entirely new. An entirely new Zandy— not one who's too much but one who's just the right amount.

Just right for a man like Oliver.

The thought makes me blush anew with how stupidly juvenile it is, with how many unspoken hopes are woven through it, and I push myself out of bed to get away from it. From the wanting more, from the wanting things that Oliver almost certainly won't want to give. *Sophisticated*—I still need to be sophisticated.

So I have my best sophisticated face on as I go downstairs after I shower and dress. I enter the kitchen looking the perfect mix of cool and sultry, prepared to have a cool and sultry breakfast and...

Oliver's not here.

Probably still on a run, I think, but I deflate a little bit. Which is dumb.

Why am I acting so dumb?

Chiding myself, I make a cup of tea with the kettle—see, I'm learning—and then decide to get to work. That will please him, I think, to come back and find me at my desk. Maybe it will please him enough to let me have his cock again...

But then I go into the study, and he's there, and his very presence reverberates through my bones like a gong's been struck. The bent head, still proud, still haughty, even craned over his work. The long, strong fingers and the carved swells of muscle pressing against his shirt as he breathes. Those eyelashes so long on his cheeks and the prismatic eyes themselves.

Eyes like I've never seen before I met him. Eyes as complicated and mysterious as the man they belong to.

I offer up a shy smile, my heart going a million miles a minute. I'm not sure what to say or what to do; all of this is completely uncharted for me. What do all these sophisticated, sexual women say to their lover-slash-bosses the morning after a tryst? *Hello?* Or perhaps *I'm wet just from looking at you. Can we do it again?*

But I can't be a sophisticated, sexual woman. I can only be Zandy. So I beam at him. "Hi," I say, giddily and somewhat lamely.

His mouth tugs down in a scowl. "Glad to see you're ready to start your work for the day."

"I didn't have my alarm set. I was..."

I was sleeping in bed with you, I want to say, but something stops me. His expression maybe, growing colder by the second, or the way his beautiful hands have gone still over his notebook.

Zandy that I am, I can't help but try again. "I slept so well, though. Last night was—"

"Last night was a mistake," he cuts me off. His voice is glacial, the words sharp enough to cut me with their corners. "And it won't happen again."

It takes too long for his words and their meaning to make sense in my mind, but once they do, I think I'd rather be drawn and quartered. I hate being so expressive, I *hate* it, and I hate that he can probably see the whip-cut of his words across my face. I duck my head so he can't see the shame, the hurt, the confusion.

Keep your dignity, Zandy, because it's the only comfort you'll be able to hang on to.

"Of course," I mumble, making my way over to my desk while trying not to let my tears fall. Trying not to let my mind race with the inevitable questions. The *whys*.

Am I not pretty enough? Thin enough? Cool enough? Was I bad in bed? Was it terrible sex and I had no idea because I'm so inexperienced? Or, oh God, what if I did something embarrassing in my sleep? Clung to him or drooled on him—or worse?

"You'll find a credit card on your desk," Oliver says to the side of my face once I'm seated. "For archival materials. Like I said before, there's no budget. Use what you need."

And those are the last words he says to me all morning.

My first jobs were as research assistants to my father's friends and of course to my father himself. Since the age of fourteen, I've spent summers and winter breaks running photocopies and flagging promising entries in annotated bibliographies. I'm used to working in rooms with humans so deep in thought that they forget I'm there. I'm used to working in silence.

This is different.

Every moment feels amplified, as if it's under a jeweler's glass, and every noise seems to quake through the room with geologic force. Even the burble of the river outside the open window is deafening. When I set down a handful of books and one drops on the floor, it's as if I've knocked the house over.

The air between us thrums with unhappy electricity, and it takes all morning for me to get to a point where I think I might not cry. How can he be so cold? How can he be so cruel?

And how—*how*—after all that I've scolded myself, could I have still gotten attached? Gotten all happy and hopeful and...I don't know...oxytocin-y?

Stupid, stupid, stupid.

I make him lunch as usual, and he eats it blindly as usual, and I hate how I still crave something from him in this moment—a compliment or a grunt of approval or anything. I hate how I still want to be his good girl. His teacher's pet.

It's after lunch that I find the note.

It's in a pile of books under an ottoman, and despite the entire terrible morning, I can't help but give a cluck of librarian censure when I find them. The books have been shoved under the ottoman so haphazardly that a few pages are bent up, and one of the leather-bound volumes has a permanent dent in the spine. With a sigh, I gather the neglected babies to my chest and carry them over to my desk, where I'll catalog them for the database.

Which is when the note slips out.

I set the books on my desk and go back to retrieve it, painfully aware of how Oliver's eyes are not on me, aware of how studiously he ignores me. It burns, that rebuffing, burns like I'm being dipped in scalding water, and I know I have the red cheeks and swollen, tender heart to prove it. I try to ignore him back, pretend I don't care that the only man I've ever had sex with seems to hate me, and I scan over the piece of paper as I walk back to my desk.

Usually these loose bits of paper are receipts, if not from Oliver's purchase, then a previous owner's purchase from years back. Other times, it might be one of Oliver's own notes—a quick scrawl about why he bought the book or a more detailed write-up outlining the contents.

But instead of Oliver's messy, spiky hand, I see words in pretty and symmetrical loops, written in the kind of pen that leaves little flourishes at the end of every word.

Oliver,

You hardly ever remember the things you say in bed, but I do. I hope this is proof.

Your girl,

Rosie

My stomach twists, hiking itself up into my chest.

There's no mistaking the subtext to that note. There's no miscategorization. No shelving this on the wrong shelf. This Rosie, whoever she was, was Oliver's lover.

Or is still his lover, a quiet voice warns me. *How would you know?*

There's no date on the note, although it is the tiniest bit yellowed in one corner, which is to be expected if it's been stuck in a decaying book for any length of time. There's also no real way of telling which book the note fell out of, although I do notice that all the books from this pile deal with the subculture of Victorian erotica.

I flip through one of them and find my breath tangling around the twists in my stomach.

Lots of spanking in here. Lots of it. Drawings and photographs of women bent over, their petticoats all rucked up in heaps around their waists. Stories of wives and debutantes and schoolgirls getting disciplined, sometimes in very erotic circumstances and sometimes in simple morality tales.

What had Oliver told this Rosie in bed that prompted her to buy these things for him? Had he been talking about research as they nodded off toward sleep? Or had it been something more intimate? Did he play the same bedroom games with Rosie that he played with me?

Of course he did, that voice says. *You think he just decided to spank a stranger without ever having done it before?*

The whole thing—the professor and his good-girl game—is obviously Oliver's kink, and I might have been a virgin until just a week ago, but I was a very well-read virgin, and even I know that kinks don't just pop up overnight. Oliver must have done it with other women, which somehow nettles me more than thinking of him merely fucking another woman.

A bitter envy poisons my blood, and I walk over to his desk and drop the note onto the page he's reading.

"I found this," I say. "Looks important."

It's almost worth my own pain to see the flash of anguish in his eyes.

"Can I expect to find more things from Rosie?" I ask, too upset to care that I've finally succeeded in sounding very aloof and reserved right now. "Would you like me to set them aside or save them for you to look through?"

Oliver picks up the note, his jaw working to the side, his hands so still that he might be a statue of himself. Then he gives the note a vicious crumble and drops it in the small trash can by his desk. "Don't bother," he says shortly. "I don't want to see them."

And then he goes back to pretending I don't exist.

Perverse satisfaction buoys me for a moment or two. Whoever this Rosie is, she's not a lover of Oliver's any longer, it seems. But soon I'm weighed down with razor-sharp anguish again. At least he *talked* to Rosie in bed. I was only ravished within an inch of my life—not that I'm complaining—and then summarily scorned the next day...and I *am* complaining about that. He won't even look at me now, as if I'm beneath his attention, and yet I never feel like he's not aware of me. Of where I move and when I move, of how I sit and how I write. I just can't tell if his awareness is one of cold annoyance or of burning dislike. It can't be anything else.

It's the slowest afternoon of my life, and as it drones on, too warm and narrated by the drone of a bee that gets stuck inside the study and bumbles about while Beatrix watches, I begin to wonder if I can really do this for the rest of the summer. Can I sit in a room with a man I want, a man I gave my body to, and have him treat me like this?

No.

I'd rather be spanked every day, because an entire summer of Oliver treating me the way he's treated me today—that would be the real masochism.

After six o'clock rolls over, I close my laptop, coming to a decision. Dinner with Oliver would be an exercise in heartache and misery, and I can't bear it. I won't do it to myself.

If he wants to ignore me, fine. I'll make myself very easy to ignore.

"May I sit here?" a warm voice asks, and I look up to see a very good-looking man in a button-down shirt and trousers standing next to me at the bar inside the Slaughtered Lamb pub.

"Of course," I say with a smile, and his face opens up with an answering grin.

"You're American."

I give a sheepish smile as I pat the stool next to me. "Take a seat, and I'll tell you all about it."

"That's an invitation no man can refuse." He chuckles, and there's a little bit of heat to his gaze as his eyes make a surreptitious flick over my body.

We both order drinks, and we start chatting—he does some type of accounting for a local quarrying company, and I explain why I'm spending my summer before grad school helping a scholar with research.

He seems charmed by me, and I can't help but wonder if this is how it would have happened if I'd made it to the Goose and Gander that night. If I'd met any other handsome Englishman, anyone other than Oliver. If it would've been as easy as I'd planned on it being—just two adults sharing a night together and then going their separate ways. Not whatever it is that Oliver and I have going on.

But at least I scored a point for my dignity tonight. I stood up and left the study as if I were simply going to get another mug of tea, and then I got my wallet and left the house, walking the short, pleasant route up to Bakewell and indulging in some Indian food before I decided to stop by the Slaughtered Lamb for a much-needed drink.

I hope Oliver enjoyed his dinner alone.

I hope he enjoys the rest of his summer alone, because I've made up my mind. I'm not going to stay. It stings and it rankles, having to give this up just because he's a colossal dick, but nothing's worth being this miserable. I'll go back tonight, announce that I'm leaving, and then tomorrow I'll be on my way home, away from him and his perfect eyes and his perfect mouth and his perfect everything that even now sets my body on fire just thinking about it.

"Have you been enjoying your stay?" Matthew the Quarry Guy says, and I feel a stab of guilt when I realize this isn't the first time Matthew's asked the question.

"I have been." I give him my renewed focus and another smile, which he seems to enjoy very much. "It's so beautiful here, so much more beautiful than I could have ever imagined."

"I'd be happy to show you around sometime," Matthew says, his voice going lower. "I'd hate for you to miss anything."

I'm about to tell him I appreciate it but I can't because an arrogant professor broke my heart and now I have to go home early, but I'm stopped by the sudden appearance of a man right behind Matthew.

A man with blue-green-brown eyes who's practically vibrating with rage.

"Oliver?" I ask as he takes my elbow.

"We're going home, Miss Lynch," Oliver says through clenched teeth, and oh, it's terrible, but hearing him call me Miss Lynch again makes me want to squirm in the best kind of way.

"May I help you?" Matthew asks, looking a bit alarmed for my sake, but Oliver cuts him a glare so ferocious that Matthew withers immediately, and I can't blame him.

"Only Miss Lynch can help me by coming home, which she's doing now, so any help from you is quite unnecessary," Oliver pronounces stonily. "If you'll excuse us."

I don't have to go with him. Not only could I struggle free if I wanted, but I think if I said *red*, he'd relinquish me right away. He'd let me go.

But I do go with him, flashing an apologetic smile at Matthew and letting Oliver guide me out the door of the pub, grateful that I've already paid my tab.

"What were you doing in there?" he demands the minute we're in the open air.

"Getting a drink."

"No. What were you doing with that man?"

I roll my eyes and start to pull away, but Oliver pins me against the outside wall of the pub, one hand on either side of my head and his body a shield of angry male in front of me.

"Were you going to let him kiss you?" he asks in a dangerous voice. "Were you going to let him fuck you?"

I want to say *yes*. I want to make Oliver angry and miserable, just as he's made me. I want to prove that I *am* sophisticated, that I do have dignity, and that I'm just as good at ignoring him as he is at ignoring me.

But like earlier today, I find I can only be Zandy. Honest, embarrassing Zandy.

"No," I admit, looking away.

"Fuck right, you weren't," Oliver growls. "He's not allowed to touch you."

"Why do you care?" I ask, searching his face. It's near-dusk, still light enough to be warm but dark enough for shadows to dance in his eyes. "You made it very clear today how you feel about me."

"That's what you think?"

"Yes," I shoot back hotly. "Yes, that's what I think. What else?"

"What else?" he breathes. "Not that you drive me mad? Not that I can't work, I can't focus, I can't even *think* when you're around me?"

We stare at each other, chests rising and falling with jagged breaths, our mouths nearly close enough to touch. To kiss.

My lips part and my eyes hood low, ready for him to lay waste to me with his skilled mouth and tongue. Ready for those hard, greedy kisses he delivered with such furious conviction for a man normally so cold.

He doesn't kiss me.

When I open my eyes all the way in confused disappointment, he's glaring at me like I've taken a match to his rare books. "We're going home *now*, Miss Lynch," he seethes, and I don't argue, because the minute I get back to his house, I'm packing my suitcase and *leaving*. I don't care if I sleep in some open-air train station. I am not staying.

I'm fuming as I climb into Oliver's car for the short ride to his house. Fuming and rehearsing my grand speech about leaving and how Oliver can go fuck himself. But when we pull up to the cottage and I get out of the car, Oliver meets me at my side, crowding me against the car door.

I expect more of his anger, or maybe that we'd go back to the cutting chill of earlier, but the man in front of me is neither angry nor cold. He's breathing hard, and there's something in his eyes that looks bruised and tender and young.

"I want you, Zandy, and I can't tell you how much that terrifies me."

Terrifies *him*? It's so hard to imagine this marble-cut man being terrified of anything, much less *me*.

"I don't understand."

He gives a bleak kind of laugh at that. "No. You wouldn't, because you're still happy and ready for the world. You're still unhurt. And I— I woke up this morning horrified at the thought that I may have stolen that from you."

I stare at him, beyond baffled. "What? By sleeping with me?"

He runs an agitated hand through his hair. "By sleeping with you and...all the other things."

The front garden is a dark haven of flowers and rich grass, lit only by the faint kitchen light coming out of the cottage, so it's hard to be sure—but I think I see color in Oliver's cheeks.

He's ashamed, I realize, and the thought is so bizarre to me, so foreign, that it takes a minute to absorb it. *He's ashamed of what he likes in bed.*

And abruptly, everything else—his behavior today, my leaving—is set aside. Or, rather, filtered through the light of this new information.

"Oliver," I say, catching his eyes. "I *liked* what we did. Both times. It's sexy to me, and..." I search for the right word. "It's not any more complicated than that. I like it. Who cares if I like it because I was raised by professors or because I've worked for professors before or because I'm an incurable teacher's pet? It's fun, and I consented wholeheartedly. What more can there be to it than that?"

It's Oliver's turn to stare, and he's staring at me like he can't believe I'm real.

"What?" I ask, suddenly self-conscious.

"You," he says, like he said yesterday afternoon, except this time it's not dark or tortured. It's wondering.

Possessive.

The way he says *you* might as well be *mine.*

"Me?" I ask, and it's ridiculous, but I think I've been waiting to hear that word my entire life.

You.

"You," he repeats, and then his mouth slants over mine, hot and greedy, just like I've come to crave, and within an instant, I'm against the car, my legs around his waist and his arms crushing me tight to him. I have so much more to ask him, so much more to wonder about, but it's like everything shrinks to the points of contact between us: his mouth so searingly thorough and his lean hips between my thighs and his wide hands splayed over my ass. And where his erection pushes, thick and heavy, between my legs.

"Professor," I whimper into his mouth, and he shudders underneath my touch.

"You don't...you don't have to," he says. "I want you any way you'll let me have you. Even without the games."

"I'll call you whatever I like," I shoot back stubbornly, biting at his lip. "It's my game too. My fun too, whether I want you as Oliver or as my professor."

And again he shudders, but this time it's not only with lust. The wonder is back in his eyes, the awe. "How are you real?" he says, biting at my neck. "How can you possibly be real?"

Suddenly, I'm being carried, and I think it's inside, I think it's to his bed, but we end up tumbling over right in the lush grass below a cottage window, blown summer flowers bobbing all around us. His strong arms and hands protect me as we collapse onto the lawn, and above me is only the shape of a beautiful man outlined by stars.

"I want you," he manages in between searing kisses. "Now."

"Yes," I say eagerly, tugging at his clothes. "You won't hear any *red*s from me."

And it's the first time I hear a laugh from him that's real and open, not bleak at all.

"And please tell me you have a condom," I say, biting at his earlobe. "I can't wait a moment longer."

"You won't," he vows, pulling up. "You're mine now."

There are no houses around, and even if there were, we'd be completely surrounded by flowers and shrubs, but it's still insanely exhilarating to be like this, tumbled and tousled onto the lawn with my skirt bunched up around my thighs and Oliver on his knees between my legs, rolling on a condom. The feeling of being exposed, of being *filthy*, is enough to have me ready before Oliver even touches me.

"Oh, good girl," he murmurs when he tests my pussy to see if I'm wet and finds out exactly how wet I am. "Such a good girl."

I squirm under his touch. "Oliver..."

"I know, girl. Hold still." With a thick, urgent stretch, he fills me, and together we fuck under the stars until I cry out and he joins me in long, jerking pulses, and we roll giggling and grass-stained off the lawn and into the house.

CHAPTER TEN

OLIVER

I'm insatiable again, but I don't care. Maybe I'm making up for lost time, or maybe it's the heady pleasure of finding a woman who loves the way I am in bed.

Or maybe it's her.

Maybe it's this enthusiastic and boldly vulnerable girl who disarms me at every turn. This girl who warms my chest just with her smiles and with the way she holds her pen and her fucking adorable watch, who approaches dusty books with a zeal usually reserved for sex and religion. She gets under my skin, and I hate it and I love it all at once. And for a man who makes his living from words—studying them, analyzing them, writing them—I can't find the right words now to explain all this to her. That I want her, that she's mine, and that if she wanted, she could pluck out what's left of my heart and eat it, and I'd let her.

So I settle for telling her with my body. With my face between her legs, with my lips running along her thighs and stomach, with my mouth on her sweet tits. She begs to be spanked again, and this time I do it with her on all fours and my cock in her mouth, arranging her so that I can easily swat her ass from the side as she pleasures me.

Then we fuck again.

And again.

The early hours of the morning find us showered and sated, with her in my arms as I toy idly with her hair. I don't pretend it's only the oxytocin this time, and she doesn't ask, but I ask myself anyway.

What are you doing with her, Oliver?

What exactly are you doing?

And the answer is that I don't know, and it bothers me.

"Why are you ashamed of what you like?" Zandy asks softly, dreamily, like someone on the cusp of sleep.

I tense around her, the question taking me by surprise. Once again I'm struck by how *easy* this is for her, by how she can just ask and talk about these things like they're not...like they're not taboo. Like they're not twisted.

She senses my reticence and turns toward me, tilting her head up so she can see my face. "Oliver?"

I open my mouth and close it, the words just as elusive as they were earlier tonight.

"Was it Rosie?" Zandy asks, and she's so fearless, so brave, and it suddenly seems important to tell her so.

"You have so much courage," I murmur, stroking her cheek. "In your shoes, I'd never be able to ask about a lover's former flame."

Zandy blinks up at me in a very endearing manner. "I'm very plucky."

"I was going to say pugnacious. Or perhaps pesky."

She laughs, as always, at my surliness, and I melt a little. I want to be brave and happy like her; I want to—I don't know—reward her, I suppose. Not like a professor rewards a student but how a lover rewards his lover. Vulnerability for vulnerability. Strength for strength.

Honesty for honesty.

"We met at the university I work for," I say finally. "We met, and it seemed like, oh, I don't know, all those stereotypes about falling in love. Like the world grew a thousand times bigger." I successfully keep most of the old bitterness from my voice, but there's enough that Zandy still notices, a little line appearing between her eyebrows. I reach over and smooth it with my thumb.

"Was she the first person you ever got kinky with?" Zandy asks, and again that word *kinky*, like it's just a word and not a rebuke. Not something I've tortured myself with in the years since Rosie left me.

"She was."

Zandy runs her hand in lazy circles over the muscles of my chest, playing slowly over the lean ridges of my abs. It feels impossibly nice. "Did she like it? The kinky stuff?"

"At first," I say, and the words leave me heavily. "At first. It was new to me— all of it was new. I was only just realizing what I liked and what I needed, and I think it became too real in the end."

"Because you were her professor?"

"I wasn't her professor," I reply. "She was mine."

Zandy's fingers still on my skin, and I can tell I've surprised her. "She was?"

"We met as I was studying for my PhD. I'd like to say that we restrained ourselves until such a time when a liaison was ethical, but that would be a lie."

"You wouldn't be the first couple to start that way," Zandy says, and it warms me a little bit to see this young thing trying to comfort me. "So were the roles reversed? Did she do the spanking?"

There's a hint of a tease in her voice, and I give her a mock-stern tweak to the chin. "I always do the spanking, Miss Lynch. And I think the reversal of our power dynamic in the classroom is what excited her at first. For her, it was novel. To me, it became necessary."

I find that I miss Zandy's hand moving over my skin, and I wish she'd keep stroking me as I talked. Even with her, the first person I've felt a desire to open up to in years, it's not an easy story to tell. "We had about a year together. And then she got pregnant."

Zandy stiffens in my arms. "You have a child?"

"Miss Lynch, listen when your professor is talking." It's the closest I've come to a joke around her, and the answering smile on her face is worth everything. I resolve to do and say whatever I have to in order to make her smile more often.

"I was dazed when she told first told me she was pregnant," I continue. "Too dazed to be either elated or terrified, I think, but I offered her everything I could. I offered all of my support. I offered to quit my PhD program or transfer to another university so that I could marry her. I was ready to give up any part of my life I had to in order to make it work."

"And what did she say?"

"That she wanted a paternity test," I say, and in my mind, I can still see us arguing in that dimly lit flat, the rain pouring outside and the blank expression on Rosie's face.

"What?" Zandy asks.

"The baby wasn't mine," I explain.

"But then—*oh*." I can see as she puts it together. The timelines, the evidence of infidelity. "Oh."

"She didn't want it to be mine. She was very blunt about that. She was very blunt about...well, lots of things. She'd been unhappy for some time, hence the cheating."

"That bitch," Zandy mutters, and her ferocious loyalty makes something in my chest impossibly light but tight too, like a balloon.

"Well, it was partially my fault. We'd grown into our bedroom games together, you see, and sometimes when something happens organically, you forget to communicate about it. And that's what happened with Rosie. I was happy, so I thought she was happy."

"Would she have been happy without the kink, you think?"

A fair question and one I've asked myself every day since that fight. All the names she called me, all the reasons she didn't want to raise a child with me, they've rattled around my mind for so long that they've become part of me, like a tree growing around a fence.

Degenerate.

Deviant.

Pervert.

"It's hard to say. I offered that too, to give up the professor games, but she refused... I think she resented me too much by then. The last time she spoke to me was an email informing me the test had proved the baby was his."

"Did you want the baby to be yours?"

I sigh. "I don't know. Yes...and no. I think the idea of a child with a woman you love always seems thrilling, but in retrospect, she didn't love me and I'm not even sure I loved her. Not in a lasting way, at least."

She moves her head, nodding against my shoulder in understanding, her hair sliding all silky and sweet smelling over my skin.

Either the memory's teeth have blunted over the years or something about Zandy eases the ache, but I find that I feel okay about the past. About Rosie. It's hard to feel upset about anything that led to this moment, with Zandy's soft curves tucked against my side and her hands on my body like it belongs to her.

"What happened after you broke up? Did you do the kink with anyone else?"

I think back to the intervening years between Rosie and now. I was a mess, both personally and professionally, and I owe a lot to the friends who saw me through, like Zandy's father, who helped me in every way he could. "I saw a few people, nothing serious. The kind of hookups you arrange online, that kind of thing. It got old after a while because it wasn't the same without someone I also liked and respected on an intellectual level."

She grins up at me. "Does this mean you like me, Professor Graeme?"

I give her a playful scowl and tug on her hair. "Don't push your luck, Miss Lynch."

She nestles back into me with a little yawn. "That explains why you're such a stickler about the condoms," she says. "The baby thing."

"Precisely so."

"Do you want babies someday? Or has that all been ruined?"

"So blunt, Miss Lynch."

But she's not asking in a fishing way—rather like she genuinely wants to know, and I think about it. About how Rosie was recently promoted to department head at my university and how there was no avoiding her then. No avoiding the very pregnant belly with her third child inside and her giant wedding ring. I took this sabbatical right after.

Deviant.

Degenerate.

"No," I finally answer. "I think that door has shut for me."

"That's sad," Zandy says sleepily.

I suppose it is sad, but I can't imagine going through all that again. The hope and the joy, and then the shame and the disgust...the heartbreak. Better just to avoid it entirely.

After a few minutes, I say, "I don't think kinky professors get to have babies and wives," and I'm rather proud of myself for saying the word *kinky* out loud... until I realize the girl next to me is fast asleep and snoring against my chest.

CHAPTER ELEVEN

ZANDY

When I wake up the next morning, Oliver is across the pillow from me, his beautiful river-colored eyes all soft and gentle on my face.

"Good morning, Miss Lynch," he says with a smile that's small but open and real, and I feel my heart dipping low inside me, like it's weighed down with happiness and is going to sink right through the mattress.

"Good morning," I answer in a sleep-croak, and then I make a face. My breath must be awful, not to mention the makeup I surely have smeared around my face. Of course he looks gorgeous right now, with that perfect, haughty face and his even more perfect hair. I try to roll away, and he catches me. "No," I moan, ducking my head into my pillow to try to hide my morning self. "I need to clean up."

"And you may, but I have to know, Zandy, were you planning on leaving last night?"

His voice is husky from sleep too, but it's also more vulnerable than I've ever heard him. Gentler. As if he's already bracing himself for the answer.

"Yes," I say honestly, because I do like to be honest. "But not anymore."

His brows furrow the slightest bit, and it's just so unfairly handsome on him that I can't stand it. I kiss him with my terrible morning mouth and get out of bed.

"So you're staying?" he asks, and the vulnerability is louder than ever, filling in the spaces between the words and lighting something very young and sad-looking in his face.

"Yes, Oliver. I'm staying."

Relief illuminates his face, and I'm rewarded with another one of those massive smiles, so big there are lines around his mouth and eyes when he makes it.

"Even with the"—I see him struggle to say the word, but he manages it with only a little bit of a blush—"the kinky stuff?"

"Especially because of the kinky stuff," I assure him with a wink, and then I go find a shower and a toothbrush, a big smile on my own face.

After I'm all cleaned up and ready to work, I find myself strangely slow to go down to the office. Which Oliver will I find there? It seemed like we connected last night and this morning, but I thought that the first time we made love here at the cottage, and I was wrong. I don't think I can bear it if I open the door to find another cold Oliver again. Not after what we've shared together.

So it's with a deep breath and a lot of bravery—and a pat on Beatrix's head for good luck—that I open the door to Oliver's study and walk inside.

He's already behind the desk and bent over his work, all tousled hair and long fingers and wide shoulders. That old-fashioned ink pen winks in the sunlight as it moves in deft motions across the page. He finishes penning something in his notebook, ends it with an efficient little flourish, and then deigns to notice my presence. When he looks up, his mouth is in that sharp frown I normally find so irresistible, although it terrifies me right now.

"Miss Lynch," he says brusquely, and my heart plummets to my feet. Is that what this is going to be? Is today going to be a repeat of yesterday?

Am I being rejected again?

But then Oliver leans back in his chair and studies me in a way that I recognize, with his pulse jumping in his throat and his eyes gleaming with hunger.

"Come here. I need a word."

I don't have to pretend to be shy or uncertain as I walk to the desk. My chest is being hammered at with a heartbeat that's out of control, pumping every kind of hormone every which way through my body, and my mind is racing through every possibility. Is this a game? Or is this real? Did he come down to the office and find something I'd done wrong? Did he come down here and suddenly realize he wanted me to leave after all?

When I get to his desk, he impatiently gestures for me to come around the other side, and so I do with some worry, biting my lip.

"We need to talk about your work," he says, pointing to a paper on the desk.

I'm already puzzled because this isn't my work. My work is all databases and bookshelves, and this is just a paper with a single line written across it in ink pen. When I get closer, however, I see what's written on the paper, and then I'm biting my lip for an entirely different reason.

Red means stop.

I look up at him, and while he's still frowning, there's a palpable thrum of excited lust around him.

This is a game, I realize. And he wants to make sure it's okay with me if we play. He wants to check, and I love how careful he is for a man who seems so aloof.

How can he think he's twisted inside when he's so clearly concerned about my safety and emotional comfort? And has been even since our first night together in the rain?

He's a good man, I think, *and he doesn't even know it.* This Rosie hurt him too much for him to see that his kinks don't make him some kind of depraved freak. They might make him dirty, yes, unique maybe—but dirty and unique in a way that fit me perfectly, and I'm going to prove it to him.

I'm going to show him how much the filthy whorls and loops of his personality fascinate me. How well they feed me and please my inner teacher's pet.

"I don't see the problem with my assignment, Professor," I say, giving him my best innocent face. "I thought I followed all the instructions you gave me."

He gives me a dazzling smile and reaches out to squeeze my hand once before settling back into his flinty look from earlier.

"You didn't," he says shortly. "And I'm afraid there's no time for you to rework the assignment."

"Please," I say, putting my hands in front of me and twisting them. I'm a little surprised at how easily it comes to me, my role, but it's because I do really want to please him and it's so easy to imagine how unhappily desperate I'd feel in these circumstances. "Please, I'll do anything. Just don't give me a bad grade."

He studies me, propping his head against his fingers and letting his eyes roam over my body with predatory leisure. "Anything?" he murmurs. "Do you need the grade so badly?"

"I do. Please, you know I do." I cast around for what I might really say if I were in some kind of academic trouble, letting the sharp judgment in his gaze affect me. I feel ashamed, as if I really have messed up an assignment, and I also feel so fucking turned on I can't think straight. "I'll do an extra assignment. Two extra assignments!" I add when he starts to shake his head.

"That won't work, unfortunately," he says. "Unless..."

I don't even have to pretend to light up, that's how real this all feels. "Yes? I'll do it. I promise I will."

"Fine," he sighs, "but it's highly unusual. I daresay you won't be making the same mistakes with your paper after this."

"Yes, sir."

His pulse jumps above the collar of his button-down. He likes that.

"Are you wearing knickers beneath that dress, Miss Lynch?"

"Professor?"

"Take them off. You won't need them for this."

"B-But, sir—" I pretend to protest, even though inside I'm already squirming with delight. Already thinking of his palm on my backside and his long, thick cock pumping inside me.

He cuts me a look that brooks no argument. "This is *your* grade. If you want to fix it, this is how."

I give my best impression of a timid pout, although I think he can see the grin threatening to break through as I shimmy out of my panties. He holds out an imperious hand, taking them expressionlessly and putting them in a desk drawer.

"My bra too?"

"Bra too."

I take off my bra from under my dress, a little clumsily, wondering if I should just peel the whole dress off but deciding I should follow his instructions literally for now. It does feel quite lewd after I hand him the bra, standing there in a thin dress with nothing underneath. The soft jersey against my sensitive nipples only pulls them tighter and tighter, and my breasts feel obscene like this, heavy and loose and hard-tipped. Oliver seems to agree, his eyes darkening as he takes in my curves under my dress.

"You have a filthy little body, Miss Lynch. It's fucking profane. It makes me think shameful thoughts, and do you know what happens to a man when he thinks thoughts like I'm thinking?"

I shake my head, even though my eyes drop down to his lap.

"That's right," he says. "My cock gets hard and it needs to come."

I lick my lips instinctively at the thought, and he growls.

"Up on the desk."

I'd expected to go over his lap, so my hesitation is real. "Sir?"

"You heard me, Amanda." The use of my full name isn't lost on me—he means business now, and I'd better listen.

And I wouldn't have it any other way...although the punishment for not listening might be kind of fun too.

I sit on the edge of the desk facing him, keeping my skirt primly around my knees, which of course he doesn't allow for long. He grabs at the hem and pushes it up to my waist, separating my knees with an impatient hand. The kiss of coolish morning air against my wet and swollen cunt is nearly unbearable—almost as unbearable as his wicked gaze taking in my most feminine place.

He wastes no time in inspecting my pussy, rubbing me with his long fingers and then spreading me open to see if I glisten for him yet. I do. I can hear it as he moves his fingers over me, and I take a strange kind of pride in showing off how wet I get for him, how needy and slutty he makes me. I don't want him to doubt ever that his needs are also my needs—that they get me off as surely as they do him.

"You are so fucking filthy," he swears, and I can see how fast his chest heaves under his button-down. "You like this, don't you? You wanted it."

"Yes," I breathe, my head lolling to the side as one finger probes inside. "I wanted it."

"I knew it. I've seen the way you watch me in class, Miss Lynch. It's improper. It's very wrong."

"I can't help it," I whimper, lost to our game and to the skilled massage of his finger inside my pussy.

"I bet you even failed your assignment on purpose, just to provoke me into punishing you."

"I had to," I gasp. The heel of his palm is rolling against my clit now, and my legs are spread as wide as they'll go as I shamelessly fuck his entire hand. "I didn't know how else to get you to notice me."

"You think I didn't notice you? Those eyes, so innocent, with that mouth that just begs for a cock? You think I didn't notice those wanton tits? How they spill over your bra when you bend over? How they jiggle when you move?" He breaks off on his own groan now, and I can see the painful-looking outline of his dick in his trousers, pressing so hard against the fabric that the shape of the flared crown is visible.

"I think you need to be taught a lesson, filthy girl," he growls. "I think you need to fix the mess you've made."

"Anything," I say, bucking wildly against his hand. I'm so close, so very close. "Anything you want."

He removes his hand so suddenly that I curl around its absence, whining at the loss. He ignores me, unfastening his belt and trousers and pulling out his penis. It's dark and thick, so hard that the skin at the top shines and I can make out every ridge of muscle and vein under the thin, velvety skin of it.

"Suck," he orders, and I comply eagerly, scrambling to my knees between his legs and taking the delicious organ into my mouth.

His answering moan is worth every discomfort I feel as he gently gags the back of my throat, as he winds his hands through my hair and guides me faster and deeper over him. I'm grateful for the guidance, as I'm still so new to this, and I let Oliver's tensing thighs and hitched breaths teach me where he likes my tongue, how deep he likes to linger.

"I should keep you as my pet," he mutters viciously to the top of my head. "Keep you under my desk sucking me all day. Keep you tied up and bent over my desk so I can fuck that pretty cunt whenever I get bored. What do you think?"

I make an assenting noise around his shaft, and he grunts his approval.

"Enough." He pulls me off his cock with a faint popping sound and then rolls on a condom he grabs from a drawer. He spreads his legs, using his thumb to press his erection away from his belly. The message is clear.

"Come fix your grade, Miss Lynch," he says huskily, and I crawl up into his lap as quickly as humanly possible, aching for that thick part of him to fill me up and ease the ache that's been there ever since we fell asleep last night.

"I've never..." I trail off as I pause over him, catching his gaze. I'm suddenly apprehensive about this, about being on top. Everything else we've done, he's taken total control of, he's guided me and taught me, but if we do it like this...my inexperience will be on display. All of my clumsy attempts will be right there for him to see.

"I like that you've never," he says in a low voice. "But you're a smart girl, aren't you? You'll figure it out."

Determination settles through me. I want to show him what a smart and good girl I am, even if I look foolish doing it. I lower myself until I feel the wide latex kiss of his tip at my opening, having to squirm and circle to get him worked inside.

"You feel bigger like this," I say as he stretches me. "Fuck."

"Language, Amanda," he chides. Other than holding himself up straight at the base, he makes no move to help me as I pant and shiver my way down his cock, impaling myself inch by thick inch, until I'm fully seated against him, so filled up with him that I can barely breathe.

My head drops to his shoulder, and he lets me sit there for a moment, quivering and misted with sweat. "Oh God," I mumble into his neck. "Oh my God."

His hands run appreciatively over the round swell of my bottom, up to my hips, and back down to my ass again. "Let's see you fix that grade, girl," he murmurs into my ear. "Get to work."

With my arms wrapped around his neck and my face still in his shoulder, I start to move, moaning as I do. I'm stretched so wide, crammed full of him, and every movement I make sends agonies of sensation all over me. Good agonies, bad agonies, I don't even know which anymore—just that this colossal erection is going to split me open and also that I'm about to come from the pressure of it alone.

It only takes the tiniest of movements—a rocking forward so that my weight grinds the bead of my clit against him—and then I shudder out a deep, soul-shaking climax, clinging to him and crying my pleasure into his neck. He holds completely still underneath me, allowing me to quiver my way through and use his hard body how I need, and then he cups my bottom again with his hands as I collapse against his chest, utterly exhausted.

"That was very nice," he says crisply, as if I've just finished a violin solo and not wrung out a delicious orgasm on his perfect cock. "But I'm afraid it's not enough to fix your grade."

"Do you need to come, Professor?" I ask, sitting up and letting my hands fall to his chest. Even through the fabric of his button-down, I can feel the tattoo of his heart beating against my palm.

"Yes," he says, and he can use that precisely clipped voice all he wants, because his need is stamped all over his face. It burns inside his eyes and carves itself around the sharp lines of his sculpted mouth. "I need to come now."

It's both easier and harder to move along him—easier because of how wet and slippery I am and harder because the orgasm has made me exquisitely sensitive—and Oliver is riveted by my face as I begin to rock against him. His fingertips trace the fleeting furrows in my brow, the little pouts of pleasure and quick smiles I make. There's feeling everywhere, everywhere, chasing all over my skin; my nipples are so taut they ache, and my thighs are warm with his hips between them, and even the soles of my feet are tickled by the gentle breeze coming through the open window. I'm going to come again, and I don't think I'll live through it when I do.

Luckily, Oliver is close, and with something between a growl and a roar, he surges off his chair with me in his arms and lays me out across his desk. Papers go everywhere, the inkwell smashes over and spatters us with dark ink, and he's so mindless with his lust that he doesn't care. I watch a drop of ink trace down his neck like onyx-colored blood as he fucks me with a clenched jaw and powerful hips, and that line of ink is all that anchors me to reality as I come for an explosive, final time, too tired and wrung out to do anything other than whimper my way through it, my hands curling weakly around his straining biceps.

"You make me come so good," he grunts, his eyes closing as his body goes rigid over mine. "Fuck...Zandy...oh my fucking God."

He fills the condom with a series of hard, jerking throbs, slumping over my body as he drains inside me. Our hearts pound together, ink and sweat smears between us, and I'm pretty sure everyone from Bakewell to Berlin heard me screaming and grunting, but I don't even care. I don't ever want to move. I don't ever want to get clean. I don't ever want Oliver's body anywhere but right here, inside mine and pressed against mine and dripping ink everywhere.

And I look into his eyes where they peer down at me in their dappled blue-brown-green, and I can almost imagine he feels the same way.

I can almost imagine that we're falling in love.

CHAPTER TWELVE

OLIVER

Ten Days Later...

"I still don't understand what it is about slippers that you associate with advanced age."

Zandy and I are down by the river behind the house, and I'm meant to still be working, but I've given up. I thought by moving us out of the office that I wouldn't be tempted to fuck her, but as it turns out, I want to fuck her everywhere, and I very nearly have.

In the past two weeks, I've fucked her uncountable times over my desk, on my study floor, in my bed, in my shower, and on my kitchen table. I've spanked her until she's been a wet, whimpering mess. I've made her write essays naked at her desk. I've had her service me with her mouth under my desk while I finished taking notes on a Victorian pamphlet about marriage proposals. We've spent nearly every hour together, working and talking and fucking and sometimes just with her curled in my lap kissing me until we're both breathless and beyond speech. Every meal, every shower, every mug of passable tea in the last two weeks has happened with her by my side.

And I haven't hated it.

I haven't hated it at all.

Somehow, someway, Zandy has made my life sweeter, and a callous, terrible part of me wants to dismiss it as a natural result of all the fucking, but the rest of me knows better. This thing I have with Zandy is remarkably different than whatever I had with Rosie—better and more honest and more real—but there's enough of the same for me to recognize what's happening.

I care for Zandy.

Although as I watch her pick her way around the riverbank, looking for stones and ignoring my comment about slippers, I know I can do better than *I care for her.*

I'm falling in love with her.

And it makes me angry and terrified and excited, and I'm not sure what to do about it. I'm not sure I *should* do anything about it. After all, she's young and vibrant and has an entire life waiting for her at the end of the summer. The last thing she wants is some surly bastard making claims to her life.

It stings though, thinking that these days of splashing in the river and wandering up to town after a long day of work are numbered. Listening to the quiet rustle of her writing on the other side of the room, looking forward to tangling my limbs around hers at night.

But it would be ridiculous to want more than the summer. In fact, I can't believe I'm even thinking about it. Of course she needs to leave—her life is in the States and my life is here, and my life doesn't include another person, no matter how sexy or warm or open she is. Never mind how much she looks at me like I matter, like my needs matter, like I'm not a deviant but someone she adores.

She won't adore you for long. Rosie couldn't.

With that depressing reminder, I look up to see Zandy climbing the riverbank toward me, green blades of wet grass sticking to her feet. She flops onto the blanket next to my pile of books with a sigh.

"I won't apologize for the slippers," she says, finally addressing my comment from earlier. "Only old people wear them."

"Objectively not true, as I wear them."

She wrinkles her nose at me. "But why?"

"The floors get cold," I say defensively. "I have cold floors."

"And then there's the old man pen."

"It has character."

"And the old landscape paintings."

I bristle a little. "Those are tasteful."

Those soft lips are creased in a teasing smile, and I realize she's poking fun at me. I crawl over her body and pin her to the blanket.

"I believe," I whisper against her lips, "that you're being very impertinent at the moment, Miss Lynch."

She wriggles happily underneath me, her dark-blue eyes glowing with her smug little smile. "And I suppose impertinent girls have to be punished, Professor?"

"How right you are," I growl before sealing my mouth over hers in a fierce kiss, licking against her tongue until she moans up into me. But I decide I can't wait, and I start shoving up the skirt of her dress right then and there.

"Do you have a condom?" she asks breathlessly, her hands already at work to shimmy out of her panties.

I've been obsessive about having one—or three—with me at all times, but I'd genuinely thought I'd be able to control myself this afternoon. "Fuck, darling," I say, giving her a quick kiss. "I'll run in and get one."

"Hurry." She pouts as I get off the blanket, and it's a true test of my strength to leave her like this, with her gleaming hair in a dark halo around her head and her bare pussy already wet and waiting for me.

"I will," I vow, and I stride quickly inside. When I get to my bed table, I realize we've already gone through Zandy's condoms and the new package she bought at the store last week. With a sigh, I dig out the old box at the back of my drawer—the one I've had for an embarrassingly long time—and grab a condom, briefly checking the expiry date as I do. With a sigh of relief that we're still, only just, inside the date, I am downstairs and behind the house as quickly as my legs will carry me. I fall over Zandy like a hungry wolf, eating up her giggles and sighs as if they'll feed me through the winter.

And before long, I'm sheathed and pushing between her legs, relishing the velvet, tight grip of her as I pierce her deep. Fuck, she feels so good. She always feels so good. She's always so soft and tight, always pure heaven to fuck into.

I angle my hips the way I know she likes, pumping into her with strokes that drag along her most sensitive spots, and she's a wild thing beneath me, being both a very good and a very bad girl at the same time, as only she can. I steal another aggressive kiss, wishing I could steal everything of hers and keep it forever—not just her beauty and her extravagant body but her laugh and her intellect and her fearlessness. All the things that make her so perfectly Zandy are the same things that flay me open and make me want to be a better Oliver, a man kind and smart and brave enough to deserve her.

"Oliver," she whispers against my lips, and I feel the telltale flutters in her belly and inner thighs and around my cock—she's going to come. I add my thumb to her clit as I brace myself on a forearm over her, but right as she goes over the edge, I feel something I can't recall feeling before. It feels like a pop, a tiny pop, and then all of a sudden there's a new feeling of warmth and wet.

"Shit," I gasp, pulling out as fast as I can.

"What?" the girl under me says dazedly, still coming down from her climax. "What is it?"

"I think the condom broke."

That's sufficient information to alarm her, and she props herself up on her arms as I peel off the condom and examine it. "But it's okay, right?" she asks worriedly. "Since you haven't come yet?"

"I think so," I say, still peering at the condom in the afternoon sun. It's definitely broken. "It's probably because it's old..."

And then I have a real chill when I remember that old box was the source of my condom in London. Did that condom break without me realizing it? I'm nearly lost to panic at the idea, until something very warm and wet closes over my bare cock, and I look down to see those devilishly soft lips closing around my shaft. Her tongue is everywhere, flickering and soft beyond imagination, and she takes me deep like I prefer, deep enough that her throat squeezes the head of my cock.

I groan.

And as she fucks me with her mouth, I forget all about old condoms and terrifying possibilities and lose myself to Zandy and the warming feeling of coming in the afternoon sun with the river rushing sweetly beside us.

The next day, I propose a work break, and Zandy and I go to Haddon Hall for a lunch of sandwiches and a stroll through the medieval manor.

"Why library school?" I ask as we walk through room after room and she chatters at me about all the architectural details and historical oddities tied to them. "It's clear that you love history. And," I say, a little shyly because I'm strangely unused to giving compliments, "you're damned knowledgeable about it, and you're a fucking good researcher to boot."

She has to hide a beaming little smile at my praise, and it does something to my chest. A puffing thing. I have the power to do that—I have the power to make her happy. I want to make her beam all the time; though as soon as I realize that, I remember that I can only make her beam until the summer is through.

"I could never decide on just one thing that fascinated me," she says, stepping into the long gallery and then spinning in a slow circle to take it in. "Like this building. It's a medieval manor house with a Tudor-style gallery and Victorian monuments in the chapel. I like the idea of my mind being full of layers and chambers and niches and naves, each one filled with different things. As a historian, you have to pick, but as a librarian...you get to have it all."

Her speech is rather charming, even if I feel slightly specious in its reasoning, but it's *her* I am truly held captive by—the way her eyes glow as she speaks, the way her body animates with enthusiasm. "Fine," I concede. "But why school in Kansas? You could go anywhere you'd like—why not somewhere more prestigious?" If she wants libraries, she deserves the best libraries in the world. She deserves everything.

"I'll have you know that there are some very good library schools in Kansas," she sniffs. And then after a moment, she adds quietly, "And I didn't want to leave my dad."

"Why not?" I live less than fifty miles away from my parents, and I still only see them twice a year, and that's more than fine by me. "He's not unwell... or anything?"

She rolls her eyes. "He's perfectly fine, health wise. I just think family is important, don't you?"

I suppose the time it takes for me to reply is answer enough. She examines me for a moment. "Does this have anything to do with why you're so weird about money?" she asks.

"I'm not *weird* about money," I protest, but even as I protest, I lower my voice so no one around us can hear.

She makes a *you're proving my point* face, and I sigh.

"Okay, yes, my family has some money." Even that vague admission feels unclean. "And there's no trauma, no division, but the way they are about what they have is very old-fashioned to me. I try to avoid it and I think they try to avoid me."

And then I let out a breath. It didn't kill me to say it out loud, and it actually felt nice, a little bit, telling someone about how unpleasant my family can be.

"That wasn't so hard, was it?" she asks, taking my hand and pulling me to a cove of mullioned windows to admire the green expanse outside. "Maybe you just need the right family, you know? One that fits you."

And the strange thing is that I'm looking at her as she says that, as she gazes through the diamond patterns of glass out onto the verdant expanse of grass and hills, and I'm thinking of *her*. I'm thinking of her as my family.

It tempts me more than I can bear.

But I force myself to remember the ticking clock of summer. Force myself to remember Rosie's cruel words all those years ago.

Degenerate.

Deviant.

Even if we didn't have that date in August demarcating our time, how could I ever expect someone as full of promise and innocence to want to tie herself to a monstrous recluse like me? Zandy might think these kinds of games are fun for a summer, but how could she ever want someone like me for longer? Someone as contorted and sexually corrupt as me?

At the end of the day, Zandy will be the same as Rosie, and she'll be sick of me. It's better to prepare myself for that now and plan for a clean break, no matter how much it burns to think of it.

No matter how much it hurts.

CHAPTER THIRTEEN

ZANDY

It occurs to me the next day.

I'm at the kitchen table making a shopping list, and then I have to double check the date on my phone. I run upstairs and riffle through my things and see that I've only got a handful of travel-worn tampons to call my own, and my period is due to start any day now. I trot back downstairs and add tampons to the list, along with the various foodstuffs and household supplies Oliver needs. If I didn't shop for him, I think he'd probably survive on canned soup and tea. It's a little charming in a bachelor kind of way, if it isn't also a little stupefying.

The day proceeds as normal—I work, Oliver fucks me, I shop, Oliver fucks me again—and it's as I'm snuggling to sleep in Oliver's arms that I wonder how we'll navigate my period. I've never done this before, the whole lover thing, and I'm not sure what the protocol is. Do I give him a warning that it's coming, or do I just wait until it's arrived and apologize? Will he still be okay fooling around on my period?

And what if he still wants to have sex? Am I comfortable with that?

It's a lot to digest, and so I'm still thinking over it as I fall asleep, and again as I wake up to Oliver stroking my flanks in a way that lets me know he's thinking about spanking me.

We do a morning spanking and a morning fuck, and then it's time for the day to get on, except there's a little niggle of unease at the back of my mind.

No period yet.

I shower and go downstairs, and he gets in from his run and showers too, and we work together for most of the day, my sense of unease growing. But I have no idea how to vocalize it to him, no idea how to express my worries, because what if his first thought is of Rosie? What if he's so triggered by his bad pregnancy experience with her that he gets angry with me?

Or worse, what if he thinks I'm the clingy girl who's tried to trap him into something by getting pregnant?

Oh God. Just the thought itself is enough to make me nauseous...except, was I already nauseous? Am I truly nauseous now? No. I'm overreacting, I'm just queasy from nerves and worry, that's all. Nothing to do with *that*.

Except the next morning when I wake up in Oliver's arms, I am *definitely* nauseous. For real nauseous. I slide free of him and make my way to the bathroom, where I splash my face with cold water and force myself to get *un*-nauseous.

He said the condom broke that day by the river.

But that was just two days ago. I've done enough research to know that conception could have only happened two weeks or so ago, and that would have been in London, and I'd bought all of those condoms brand new. But...

We used one of his condoms in London.

Oh God.

No.

"No," I say out loud, just to make extra certain my brain processed the word. "No. This is not happening."

This can't be happening.

I go downstairs in only my thin cotton robe and make my way down the flagged path to the river. It's still very early morning, with only a faint-pink sun and river fog like a shroud over everything, and more than life itself, I want to go crawl back in bed with the handsome, snobby professor I've come to love.

Oh shit. *Do* I love him? Because this is a hell of a time to decide. But even with my lingering nausea and fear, I think I know the answer.

Yes.

Yes, of course, I love Professor Graeme. His dirty games and his sharp words and his brilliant intellect. His rare flashes of warmth and kindness, his hidden passion and fire just waiting for the right person to patiently uncover them...

I love him.

And I may be pregnant with his child, and somehow I just *know* he'd never forgive me if that were true, no matter how innocent of it I may be. No matter how accidental, no matter how not my fault, the one wound he bears is so deeply tied to a baby, and how can I, just a silly little student, ever hope to heal him of it?

First thing's first, I order myself. No sense in worrying about something that might not even be true. I'll get dressed and find a pharmacy and get a pregnancy test. And then I can decide what comes next and what it means for my professor and me.

I'm to the pharmacy and back to the cottage before Oliver is finished with his run, and I have a plan. I'll go to the bathroom—the small water closet by the snug, the one we hardly ever use—and I'll use the tests. Yes, *tests* plural, because I couldn't decide on a brand, and despite having everything from the best nursing bras to the best infant formula, *Consumer Reports* doesn't have a buying guide for pregnancy tests. So I bought three different brands of pregnancy tests, just to be safe.

But when I lock myself inside the bathroom, I'm gripped by a slow, creeping hesitation. Like I'm being gradually, gradually frozen in ice, until I'm sitting on the floor across from the sink with my head between my legs just staring at the tile. The nausea from the early morning has faded, leaving only a tingling kind of displacement in its place, like my stomach and my heart have traded places.

Just go pee on that stick. Just do it.

But even standing up right now feels like a herculean feat—like if I stand up, I'm accepting whatever happens next, and I'm not sure I can do that.

I'm not sure I'm strong enough to do that.

But as romantic as it would be to spend the rest of the day on the floor in a state of languishing gloom, I'm not immune to the ticking clock of Oliver's run. And my ass is cold from the tile. And my own despair is getting a bit boring—it's not like me to despond over a problem. It's like me to tackle the problem head-on, with research and enthusiasm and a big Zandy Lynch grin, and dammit, that's what I'm going to do now.

So I get up and perform the oddly ignoble ritual of peeing on the different sticks and then lining them up according to size and waiting and watching.

It's strange to think that my entire future is concentrated in these little plastic rectangles full of urine and chemical dyes. Strange to think that whatever these rectangles reveal in the next minute or two is going to completely redirect the course of my life for better or for worse, and oh my God, they're finally starting to turn colors, they're finally starting to stripe over with weak washes of blue and—

I sit back down on the floor, except this time I don't stare at the tile, I stare at my hands, as if I expect them to be different. As if I expect my entire body to be different.

Nothing's different.

But everything is. Everything has to be.

Because I'm pregnant, and I'm pregnant with a baby I know Oliver won't want.

I set a timer on my phone and give myself five minutes. Five minutes to freak out—to scream or to cry or whatever I need to do—and then when the timer beeps, I wipe away my tears, sweep the tests with their condemning plus signs into the trash, and go find my laptop to make a plan.

Oliver comes into the study with shower-damp hair and rolled-up sleeves that show off the strong lines of his forearms and wrists. He's scrubbing at the wet hair with his fingertips and frowning in that way that tells me he's already several layers deep into some new insight of his, but he stops when he sees me at my desk and he smiles.

God, that smile.

It's so wide, with lines bracketing those sculpted lips, and it changes his entire face from scornfully distant to sincere and boyish.

"Good morning, Miss Lynch," he says, and I slam my laptop shut so he won't see all the incriminating tabs I have open, and I smile back at him, hoping he won't see how forced it is.

"Good morning, Professor," I say, and then he bends in to kiss my neck. He didn't shave this morning, and his stubble leaves the most delicious burn wherever his soft lips touch me. It's the best kind of sting, and for a minute I let everything else fade away—the pregnancy, the panic, the plan—and just melt into the feeling of him. My professor. My Oliver.

He withdraws too soon, dropping a kiss on my head before he goes to his desk. "You've nearly finished with all the books, I see."

"I still have a lot of the newer ones to do," I say automatically, and then I stop myself because I don't know that I'll get to the newer books. I don't know that I'll be able to get to anything else at all, because I don't know what's going to happen after I tell Oliver I'm pregnant.

Unless you don't tell him...

The idea is beyond tempting. It snakes around my thoughts and my heart until I feel tied up with it.

"Whenever you have time," Oliver says, not noticing my inner struggle. "I'm already astounded at what you've accomplished in just a couple short weeks."

Despite everything, I allow my gaze to follow his around the study, and I don't bother to tamp down the bubble of pride I feel at the progress I've made. Instead of an unsteady maze made of piles of books and paper, I've got the study organized with new shelves and cabinets of glass-topped drawers for the rarer works. Aside from the books stacked under my desk still awaiting cataloguing, the floor in the study is now completely clear—save for the cat bed I bought on a whim for Beatrix—and a person can actually walk around the room without tripping onto centuries-old manuscripts now.

I *have* done a good job here, and I'll be able to take that with me no matter what. I look over to the unbearably handsome man already bent over his work, and I can't help but think that's possibly all I'll get to take with me: the memory of well-shelved books and nothing else.

The thought punches through my chest with grief, and I have to turn away, lest I risk Oliver seeing all these wild emotions move across my face. No, it's best I approach him as controlled and composed as possible. I need to be cold like him.

By the end of the afternoon, I've done all the surreptitious research I can. I've made a spreadsheet of options, along with their qualitative pros and their quantitative cons. I've found a flight home from Birmingham, and I've begun preparing a small speech to Oliver, with a few salient bullet points.

Namely, that this is not my fault—if it's anyone's fault, it's *his*, for using old-ass condoms—and also, second bullet point, I'm keeping the baby. I've made a *spreadsheet* and I've made a decision, and a spreadsheet decision is a permanent one. Maybe it's insane—maybe I'm insane—but when I sat there looking at all the different paths I could take, my hand kept drifting to my belly and my mind kept drifting to this fantasy of a baby with Oliver's multicolored eyes.

Maybe...maybe he won't be angry? Maybe he won't be terrified? Maybe he's healed enough from what happened with Rosie that he can imagine a little squishy baby with his eyes and my dimples and all will be well?

But what if he doesn't? What if he can't?

What if I tell him and confess to loving him, and he rejects both me and the baby in one fell swoop? What then?

Then you take the flight out of Birmingham and get started on your baby to-do list.

I curl over my desk, bracing my head against my hands, and try not to cry. I don't want to be rejected. I don't want to lose Oliver. And yet, even without the baby, I don't know that he'd want me. He hasn't mentioned anything about an *us*, about this being anything more than a convenient, kinky fling to while away the summer.

I want more than anything to be reasonable, to be logical, but maybe it's the pregnancy hormones or maybe it's the fact that Oliver stirs me up beyond reckoning, but suddenly, the tears are right there, ready to fall. Am I so unlovable? So unlikable? That even something longer than a summer with me is a detestable thought?

"Zandy." A low voice comes from behind me, and I freeze as Oliver's warm hands slide over my shoulders. "Are you okay?"

In my distress, I completely forgot that he could see and hear me. I hoped he was too absorbed in his work to notice my breakdown, but it appears I was wrong.

Like I've been wrong about so much else.

"I'm fine," I say, pressing the heels of my palms against my eyes and swallowing back my emotions. I move my hands and look up at him, giving him my brightest smile. "Just tired."

He frowns. "I've been working you too hard."

"Not at all," I say, grateful that no tears have actually spilled and now only wishing the tremble in my chin would settle. "Really, I'm fine. I probably just need a nap."

And before I can protest—or indeed, even process what's happening—Oliver's scooping me up in his arms and carrying me up the stairs.

"Oliver!" I say, tugging pointlessly at the shirt fabric near his neck and kicking my legs weakly. "Put me down!"

"You're having a nap," he says firmly, carrying me into his bedroom and laying me on the bed. He stands over me, as if torn. Then he climbs onto the bed as well, not to cradle me in his arms but going lower, lower, until his wide shoulders are tucked between my legs.

"This—this isn't a nap," I say breathlessly as he pushes my skirt up to my waist and tugs my panties to the side.

"I'm tucking you in," he says, a single eyebrow arching in mischief. "Making sure you can fall asleep easily."

And I could cry as his mouth descends warm and wet on my intimate flesh, not because I was near to tears before but because I love him so much, because he's made me fall in love with him, because I can hardly stand these rare glimpses of his open, happy soul and I'm terrified I'll have to leave them behind with everything else. I'm terrified of sending him back into his emotionless, cruel shell once I tell him the truth. My mischievous, smiling professor will be gone, and all that will be left is a bitter husk in his place.

You can't know that, I assure myself, although the assurance feels hollow. There's every chance I'll tell Oliver and things will go well. There's every chance this has a happy ending.

But I can't stop the tide of doubt that seeps in along with the tide of pleasure, and as his mouth gently works me toward climax, I find myself clinging on to every single sensation, every single slice of memory. His soft hair under my fingers and his hot mouth and teasing hands pressing and massaging and stroking at all of my most sensitive places, and then finally—sweetest of all—the tender expression on his face as I come undone, pleasure spiraling out from my belly in whorls of ecstasy. I arch and writhe under him, my toes digging at the blankets, my head rolling back, and when I slowly circle back to earth, I see him standing up and getting ready to pull the blankets over me—as if he really means to tuck me in.

"What about you?" I ask, reaching for him.

He pauses, obviously torn. "I don't need—shit, Zandy. Holy shit..."

My hands have found him under his trousers, and I'm giving him a teasing squeeze. He's as hard as a spike.

"I'll just take a minute," I promise, and he growls, already mounting the bed and unfastening his pants.

"The hell you will," he says darkly, and then my lips are being parted by the plump, swollen head of his cock as he feeds it into my mouth.

"Fuck," he hisses as I instinctively suck around him. "Yes, girl, just like that, just like that." And after I've sucked him to his satisfaction, he pulls himself from my mouth and straddles my stomach, yanking down my dress and my bra to expose my tits. I love seeing him like this, feral and quaking with unfiltered lust, and there's something so primal about seeing a man normally as refined as Oliver do something as crude as mark me with his come. But that's what he does, his one hand braced on the headboard above me, and his other hand fucking his cock as if he'll die if he doesn't empty himself immediately. I watch the dusky head disappear and reappear in the ferocious circle of his grip, and then I moan in fascinated lust as his orgasm leaves him in thick, white ropes all over my bare tits.

It's so fucking erotic that I've nearly forgotten about everything that's come before, and I beg him to rub me again, to fix the new empty ache he's made inside me, and by the time we come again and clean up, we're both ready for a nap.

Tomorrow, I think drowsily as I fall asleep. *I'll tell him tomorrow.*

CHAPTER FOURTEEN

OLIVER

Zandy's been acting strange.

I noticed it yesterday before I whisked her up to my bed, and I'm seeing it again today as we start our work for the morning. And I think I know what it's about, which means I'm currently sitting at my desk ruminating not over a photographic illustration of the courtship process, as I should be doing, but over what I should do next.

I mean, it's obvious what I should do next. I should talk to her. But I'm a gelded coward, because even the mere thought of saying what I need to say out loud has me retreating.

A small sigh sifts over to me from Zandy's desk, and I look up to see her running the top of a pen along her mouth, along the seam of those sinful lips. She's got one hand spread low on her belly, and her eyes are distant. She's beautiful. Beautiful and smart, and she's pried open locks inside me that I thought were sealed shut for eternity.

What am I doing with her? Why can't I be as brave and reckless as she can, and why can't I just admit how I feel? Admit that I want her and love her and need her for longer than the summer?

Because that's what she needs, isn't it? That's what this new distance of hers is about? She's finally realized that I've given her nothing more substantial than my cock and the palm of my hand, and even though we promised nothing more between each other, it's catching up with her. She's adjusting her feelings and expectations, and....and I don't want her to. I don't want another morning like the one in London when I woke up alone. I don't want there to be any reason she thinks she has to leave me.

I want her to know how I feel.

"Zandy," I say softly. "Come here."

I've summoned her to my desk countless times since she's arrived at my home, but this is the first time *I* feel nervous as she approaches, the first time I

SIERRA SIMONE

have no idea what happens next. But despite that, my cock hardens as she walks toward me in her little tweed skirt and schoolgirl-ish blouse—exactly the kind of outfit that tempts me to distraction. I'm going to fuck her after we talk, I decide, to reward her for being so perfect.

She's ready to kneel or to bend over my desk, and her eyes flare with pleased surprise as I pull her down into my lap.

"Miss Lynch," I murmur, brushing some of that coffee-dark hair away from her face.

"Professor," she says, the word as always staining her cheeks with an adorable pink. I kiss those cheeks now, then her plush mouth, sliding my tongue against her lips until she opens for me and I can kiss her the way I want. Deep and devouring. Claiming and hungry.

"I love you," I say against her mouth, and the words leave me like my own breath, like water from a spring. As natural as anything, as easy as being alive. And at the sound of them in the gentle summer air of the office, I feel a surge of happiness so real that I can't believe I've waited so long to say them. I should have told her the minute I realized. I should have told her and then told her nothing else for the rest of my life.

Except while I'm smiling against her lips, I realize that Zandy's gone completely rigid in my arms, and when I pull back with a concerned gaze to look at her, I see nothing but pure panic in her face.

Dread sends my stomach plummeting to my feet, and suddenly a horrible thought wedges its way into my mind. What if she doesn't love me? What if she doesn't care for me at all? What if—oh God—all the sighs and the distant looks have been because she wants to be free of me? What if she wants to be free of my deviance? My perversions?

My *kink*, as she so innocently calls it?

It's Rosie all over again, except worse, a thousand times worse, because I didn't love Rosie like I love Zandy. Not even close, not even a little bit. If Zandy doesn't love me, I'm not sure I'll survive it.

But before I can complete my own terror spiral, I see that Zandy's sapphire eyes are brimming with tears, and I reach up to brush them away. She catches my hand with my fingertips on her cheek, nuzzling against my palm like a distressed kitten, and it breaks my heart to see her so upset. And it breaks my heart again to think that she might be upset because she's going to refuse me. Because I confessed to loving her and now she's trying to find the words to tell me that she doesn't love me back.

"Zandy," I say in a choked voice. "You don't have to—I mean, I shouldn't have—please don't—"

She presses her own fingers to my lips now, meeting my eyes with the shining blue of her own.

"I love you too, Oliver," she whispers, but she doesn't sound happy. She sounds anything *but* happy, and her words are like twin swords of joy and pain right to my heart.

Doesn't she feel it? How good and right we are? Doesn't she understand how huge this is for me, how fucking rare and perfect?

"Then why are you crying?" I ask, searching her face. "I don't understand."

She just shakes her head, crying even harder now, and she curls into the tiniest possible ball in my arms, until she's completely nestled into me and the scent of her hair fills my nose. Her legs are pulled up to her chest, which hikes her skirt past her ass, and even though my mind is mostly on soothing her, my body reacts to the rounded flesh now sitting bare on my leg.

And then her lips are on my neck, open and imploring, working their way up to my jaw and my earlobe, her tear-wet face slicking against mine, but I don't deny her. I can't deny her anything, I think, least of all the comfort I'm the most qualified to give.

I meet her mouth with an ardent kiss, tugging her against me so she has no choice but to straddle me, so her hard nipples press through her shirt and drag against my chest, so I can cup her backside in my hands and grind her against my cock for the friction we both crave. Her tongue, when I find it, is eager and needy, chasing mine with a desperation that's underscored by her hands flying everywhere—at my shirt buttons, at the bunched muscles of my arms, at the tensed lines of my neck.

"Oh, Oliver," she mumbles. "Please, please, please."

"Anything, darling," I say, the endearment slipping out of me faster than I can catch it back. But why would I want to catch it back? I love her. She deserves for me to be more than a tight-lipped miser about it.

She's already fumbling with my pants, her small, slender fingers on my cock, and before I can even register how good it feels to have her stroking the hot, thin skin, she's wedging me at her most private place and pushing herself down in wild, frantic thrusts.

It's messy and rough, her skirt bunched around her waist and tears still dripping from her face, but her eyes are completely open and raw on mine and something between us tightens closer than ever, like a knot being cinched shut. I should stop her. I should wipe her tears away. But how can I when the first edge of a smile pulls at her lips and she's chanting, "Yes, Oliver, oh God, yes"?

When she feels like pure fucking ecstasy on my cock, wet and slick and soft, like a tight heaven? It's never felt this good, *ever*. It's never been me clenching every muscle in my belly and ass and thighs so I don't blow too early. It's never been—

I've never been bare with her.

Holy shit.

Holy shit, I'm raw and naked inside her. I'm naked inside her, and it feels better than anything I've ever felt in my entire life. Ever. If I come like this, I don't even know how I'll survive, because I'm barely holding on as it is, and...

But I can't come like this. I *can't*. I've fucked that up before, and I refuse to fuck it up with Zandy. My bold little librarian with her entire life ahead of her; she's far too precious for me to make this mistake a second time.

My hands find her hips, and I try to still the frenzied roll of her body over mine. "Let me get a condom," I say to her. "This isn't safe."

She peers down at me, and for a moment, I treasure just how beautiful she is like this, even with tear tracks shining on her face. Her hair is like the silkiest, sweetest curtain around us, her cheeks are flushed and pink, and her mouth is a study in feminine glory.

"Oliver," she says. Just that. Just my name, and there's an undercurrent of pain in it, like it's the last time she'll ever say it like this, which is ridiculous, of course. If I have it my way, she can say it every day for the rest of her life.

I try to ease her off me. "Let me get prepared, Zandy. It will only take a second, and then you can ride me as long as you want."

She doesn't move yet, her lower lip trembling a little. "It feels so good," she says. "I didn't know it would feel different for me too, but it feels so good."

I give a taut, rough laugh. "Yes, it feels good. Too good, and if we don't fix it, I'm going to be coming inside you."

Her lower lip trembles even more. "What if it didn't matter?"

I stare up at her, my mind spinning even as my cock flexes in happiness at the thought. "But it does matter," I point out. My chest tightens in irritated confusion, because how can she even joke about it not mattering? With her future? With my past?

She closes her eyes. "It doesn't have to. Not now."

"Because we've said I love you?" There's a spiked cynicism to my tone that I don't like, but I can't help it. "I've said those words before, Zandy. They have nothing to do with what will happen if I come inside you."

Her eyes flutter open, and suddenly I know I've said something wrong, something deeply wrong. "Right," she says faintly. "Of course." She tries to climb off my lap, but despite it being what I wanted, it feels wrong now, like if I let her un-join us, something else, something more crucial, will come un-joined as well. I hold her tight to me, catching her eye.

"Zandy?"

"No, it's fine," she says, still trying to move off me, and I have a flash where I realize I'm forcing her to stay on my lap. I let go of her as if I've been burned, horrified at the thought of forcing a woman, but I'm just as horrified at the look on her face when she gets to her feet in front of me. She looks like I've slapped her, and I don't know if it's because I let her go or because of what I said.

She pulls down her skirt, and I have the distinct impression that she's trying to make herself look more dignified, more adult, as if that matters when my cock is still naked and wet between us.

"Do you mean that? What you said about love having nothing to do with fucking bare?"

She's twisted my words, but as much as I work with words for a living, I can't figure out how. It's in the tone, in her giant blue eyes so wounded and the way she wraps her arms around herself, as if to shield her body from me.

"I meant," I say slowly, "that just because I love you doesn't give me permission to be reckless. In fact, *because* I love you, I don't want to be reckless. Not with your future."

Something softens in her face, and her lip quivers again. "What if my future's already changed?" she asks.

"You don't understand what I mean, sweetheart. I mean—"

"I'm pregnant," she blurts out. "I just found out yesterday. I'm pregnant."

There's a kind of static buzzing in my ears, like the air itself has come to life to hiss the truth at me, but it doesn't matter because I find myself groping clumsily for both thoughts and words.

It doesn't make any sense is the first real thought that surfaces, coupled with, *but I was so careful.*

So careful to use protection every single time, so careful to avoid repeating the mistakes of the past. So careful not to ever put myself in that hideous situation again.

I hope it isn't yours.

Pervert.

My silence hasn't gone unnoticed by Zandy, and her face and voice are just on the edge of crumpling when she says, "It must have been in London. I'm not on birth control, and if your condom broke..."

Didn't I think it was all too wet that night when I went to take it off? But who could blame me for not thinking about it when I was still reeling with the fact that she'd *been a virgin*? Yes, the condom was old, but it wasn't so old that I thought twice as I rolled it on, and holy fuck, what were the damn odds? That the night she lost her virginity was also the night she got pregnant?

And it's that more than anything that makes the blood drain from my face, that makes my body cool and grow rigid with self-loathing.

I'm no better than the pervert Rosie thought I was, impregnating some innocent like a fucking caveman, no matter how accidental it was. I pull my pants closed, fumbling for an apology, for anything to convey the sheer fucking horror I feel about what I've done to her, but I'm coming up with nothing, and it's only as I look up at her again that I realize the damage my lack of response has caused.

My silence has cost me something important, although I'm not yet sure what it is.

Because the trembling lip is gone. The tears have dried up. In their place is an expression of blazing determination—not unlike her face the night we met, but there's something heartbreakingly grim in her look now, like she's resigned herself to a future so cold that it's already making her numb.

I sit up, about to say something, anything, just to forestall whatever is about to come out of her mouth, but she speaks first.

"I've already found a flight home," she says clearly, "so I don't want you to worry about me lingering here when I'm unwanted."

Unwanted?

But her reasoning slips by me as I face the reality of what she just said.

She's leaving me.

Not only is she leaving me, but she's already made the plans, which means she's been thinking about leaving me for...bloody Nora, maybe since she found out. Maybe since the moment she realized she was pregnant.

The thought chills me down to my core.

Just like Rosie. She can't stand the idea of carrying my child.

"...a spreadsheet," Zandy is saying, still standing in front of me like she's delivering the bleakest presentation of all time. "And I'm keeping the pregnancy. I've thought about it within both rational and emotional parameters, and it's the decision I feel the happiest with. I know, obviously, you aren't happy and that you won't want anything to do with me or the child, and I promise I won't bother you for anything—"

"You don't know anything," I say, and the cold words cut through her presentation like a sword. It's the first thing I've said since she's revealed this to me, and I'm vaguely aware that my first words should have been kinder, more understanding—but how can she just stand there and announce that she's leaving like it means nothing? Like it's not going to kill me?

Like I don't love her?

And how can she think I wouldn't care that she'd be taking my baby with her?

"I know enough," she says, lifting her chin in that brash assertiveness that I love and that also drives me crazy. "I know you don't want this. I know you don't want us."

Us.

She doesn't mean me and her. She means her and the baby. *My* baby.

My blood pounds hot again, for reasons I don't entirely understand. Anger, hurt, confusion—all of those—but there's something else, something dangerous.

Possession.

"You have no idea what I want," I say, getting to my feet. She takes a step back and then another as I step forward. "You weren't even going to talk to me about this? Before you just up and left?"

Her heel hits the wall behind her and she's trapped, but she refuses to cower. "I won't ask you for anything you're not willing to give," she says proudly. "I didn't do this to trap you. I didn't do this to hurt you."

I know. It's what I should say, what I should tell her, but I'm still thrumming with this *need*, with this *fear*, that she's leaving me and I can't hold on to her, and all I want to do is hold on to her. Her and this baby.

"We can end this healthily, like adults," she says as my arms go to her waist, effectively pinning her against the wall, and her body ripples with response—goose bumps, hard nipples, parted lips.

"No," I say.

"It ended the night we met," she continues but more weakly this time.

"No," I say again, my hands dropping to her pert bottom and lifting her against me. Her legs go to my waist automatically, and she can't help the way she rubs herself against my renewed erection, just as I can't help the way I rub against her still wet and swollen pussy.

"Oliver," she tries, but my mouth is already on hers, kissing her as if I can brand my soul onto her soul, as if I can force her to stay with the heat of my lips alone.

"Red means stop," I say, and when I meet her eyes, I know the word will never leave her lips. And when I reach beneath us to aim my cock at her opening, I'm rewarded with a deep moan. This time, as I thrust into her completely naked, I savor every fucking second of it. Every tight, wet second, every inch of nothing between us.

"You were going to leave me," I grunt, pumping into her. "You were going to leave."

"It's for the best," she gasps, her arms wrapping as tight around my neck as her legs are around my waist.

I don't answer her with words, letting my mouth's actions speak for me instead, blazing hot nips and kisses down her jaw and to her neck, where I keep my face buried as I fuck her. She's so impossibly soft like this, pinned hard against a wall, not just her soft cunt but her breasts pillowing against my chest, her round bottom in my hands, and her velvet thighs around my hips. The orgasm is like a fist at the base of my spine, angry and hot, and I can feel its claws everywhere in my body, tightening in my belly and drawing up my balls and clenching the breath in my chest—but she has to go first, dammit. She's got to come first.

I drop her weight just enough so the friction catches against her clit. I feel it the moment it takes hold in her—the straining, squirming tension of her building climax—and I work it desperately, fan it into flames until she's falling into the fire of her pleasure, fluttering over the edge into release.

"Professor," she gasps, and I freeze, but she doesn't notice. She's still riding out the waves of her orgasm on my cock, and then it doesn't matter how much the word affects me. There's no way any man can hold back now, and I am no exception. With this curvy, dark-haired goddess wet and whimpering and impaled on me, I come like a rubber band snapping, sharp and sudden and nearly painful, grunting into it like a beast.

Spurt after spurt of heat erupts into her, and it's like I can feel it everywhere, from my scalp to my toes, and I never want it to end—the feeling of pouring into her, the feeling of her still coming around me and on me and against me. And she is so perfect.

So perfect.

She deserves better than a twisted man like me.

The world slowly unwinds, slowly brings us back to normal. Normal breath, normal pulse, normal heartbeat—although my heart is still slamming wildly against my chest because I haven't just fucked Zandy the innocent little temptress. I've fucked the mother of my child.

And the responsibility of that is uncomfortably acute.

I carefully set her down and tilt her chin up to meet my face. "How are you?" I ask, abruptly worried that I fucked her too rough, that I was too much and that I've hurt her.

"I'm good," she says, a bit dazed, and then she offers me the first real smile I've seen all day. "Professor."

I flinch, just as I did when she said it a moment ago.

"What?" she asks, her forehead creasing. "What is it?"

"You can't call me that. Not—not anymore."

She keeps her eyes on me as she covers herself. "Why not?"

I'm not as brave as her, not as strong. I look away, using the fastening of my pants and shirt buttons as an excuse not to meet her eyes. "We can't play that game now."

"But I like that game." Her voice is so honest, so clear, and how does she do that? How can she make it all seem so simple? "Not just like it, Oliver, but I think I have to play it too. I need it."

"We can't do it," I repeat, sitting back down at the desk and reaching for a piece of paper. My mind is whirling, spinning, circling faster than I can keep up, as if fucking Zandy has done the opposite of settling me, it's wound me up. "That was all before, don't you see? Everything has to change now."

She goes completely still. "What do you mean?"

"I mean you're pregnant. I can't do the dirty professor routine with you, and we certainly can't keep living like this." I gesture around us to the cottage, with its gentle river noises and ordered bookshelves and sleeping cat. "I have to find a different job—a suitable one for being a father, which isn't whatever the hell I'm doing now—and we need to figure out prenatal care, first and foremost, for you, along with your visa. Ah," I say, my thoughts finally catching up to me. "We'll marry. I think we can get it done as fast as next week. That will solve a few problems fairly easily." I'm already scribbling a list of things to do, things that need to be done to keep Zandy with me, and it takes me a moment to notice that she's put her hand over the top of my paper.

I glance up at her, confused.

"You want to get married?" she asks, her voice layered with something I don't understand.

"I don't see a choice. I have a duty now—*we* have a duty now. To honor the situation."

"This isn't the Victorian ages," she says tightly. "We have more choices than we know what to do with."

But doesn't she get it? I don't want any other choices, I don't want any choice that separates me from her or from the baby. I want her.

I love her and I want her, and I can't let this end in heartbreak. I won't.

"We'll get married, and I'll stop writing and go back to teaching," I say, looking back down at the paper and adding a few more lines on the growing list of things to do.

"Okay," she says faintly, and when I finally look up later, she's left the office. Beatrix hops up on the desk and yowls at me, but I ignore her, just as I ignore the burning feeling in my chest telling me to find Zandy and hold her and tell her I love her again.

There will be time for all that later. But first, I have a duty to her and this baby, and I won't fail and I won't stop.

She'll understand.

CHAPTER FIFTEEN

ZANDY

I have to set another freak-out timer on my phone.

I give myself ten minutes this time, and I lie facedown on my bed, letting the shocked tears leak slowly out of my eyes. Did I think the worst thing that could happen was Oliver rejecting me? Did I dread him turning away in cool anger, ordering me to leave?

I've been a stupid, innocent fool, because there has always been a possibility that is much, much worse, and that is Oliver treating me like some kind of obligation. Like some kind of responsibility he has to shoulder.

I have a duty now. To honor the situation.

Oh God.

Cold rejection is so much less awful than cold acceptance. Cold duty. Talking about marrying me like it's some sort of chore, some kind of burden that has to be carried to the finish line, no matter what.

Feeling like a burden and a chore—why is that so familiar? Oh right, because it's why no one's ever wanted me before. No one's ever wanted me to date and not even to fuck, and it's probably because they could smell the *too much*ness on me. Because they could sense I'd become a *duty* if given half the chance.

When Oliver said he loved me and then fucked me with fierce, unraveling passion against the wall, I thought—well, I didn't think. I hoped.

I hoped that all my fears and worries were misplaced and that somehow and some way, this would have a happily ever after for us. Him, me, and the baby.

But I refuse to be his cold duty. I refuse to sit around waiting for the day when his resignation becomes quiet resentment, because it will. Maybe he'll be able to keep it hidden. Maybe he'll even fool himself into accepting this new, structured life, but eventually he'll hate me for the things he's certain he has to do now.

Giving up his kink.

His research.

His freedom.

He'd hate going back to teaching and giving up on his book, and he'd hate himself for every time he wanted to get kinky with me but would feel like he couldn't. And he'd hate me for marrying him and invading his quiet bubble of a life. I don't know why he thinks he has to give all that up because I'm pregnant, but I know him well enough to tell he won't be moved.

Which only means one thing. It's up to me.

By the time my timer goes off, I've dried my tears and started packing. And by the time Oliver notices I'm missing, it will be far too late.

Two Days Later...

My father's voice is echoing off the kitchen tile in a dry rumble that used to put me to sleep every night as he read to me when I was a child. The familiar sound of it makes me want to cry, but I can't tell if that's lingering jet lag or the baby hormones.

"Yes, she's here," I hear him say, and then there's a long pause. "She's sleeping now. But I can tell her you've called. Again."

I bury my face in my pillow, wishing my bedroom weren't just right up the stairs from the kitchen. Wishing I didn't have to hear the phone ring over and over again with Oliver trying to talk to me.

In a flash of masochism, I lift up my own phone to peek at the screen. Tens, if not hundreds, of notifications, emails, texts, phone calls, everything—all from Oliver.

All from my terrifyingly sexy professor.

It was awful sneaking out of the cottage—more than awful. I thought I was dying as I climbed into the cab waiting outside, as Beatrix sat perched on the stone bench inside the front garden and tilted her little cat head at me. I hated leaving. I hated walking away from the cottage, with its blown flowers and leafy vines and old stone walls. I hated hearing the river nearby, shallow and bright, knowing I'd never hear it again. And I even hated poor little Beatrix for making me love her when she should have known better.

I hated leaving Oliver.

I hated knowing that his polished voice and mysterious eyes wouldn't be mine to hear and to see any longer. I hated how hard it was to sneak away because I also hated how impossible it would be to say goodbye. I would try to leave, and he'd be too handsome, too smart, too magnetic, and I'd stay anyway, even though my staying would wreck his life and ultimately make him loathe me for the part I played in wrecking it.

No, this was the way it was always going to be.

And I hated that most of all.

It only took Oliver an hour or so to realize I was gone, but an hour was all I needed. I was most of the way to Birmingham by then, and I made my way through security and to a flight before he could reach me. Then, like with all the calls and emails today, he was acting out of duty, and I bet even now the relief is starting to creep in. The relief that I won't be ruining his life after all.

I don't read the emails or the texts. I don't let myself. Because as much as I want Oliver to be feeling relief right now, as much as I want to think I've found a way to walk out of this with my head held high, I feel nothing but agony.

Maybe there's a tiny part of me that hopes he'll board a plane to America. That he'll come chasing after me.

It's ridiculous and childish—sheer nonsense given what I've done and how I've refused to talk to him—but maybe I'm too Zandy Lynch *not* to be ridiculous and childish sometimes. Yet another reason Oliver and I would never have worked.

My father appears in my doorway, holding out a mug of coffee for me, which I take even though I won't drink it. I haven't told him about the pregnancy yet—or even that Oliver and I were briefly a thing—although I think he's pieced that together from my unexpected arrival home and Oliver's many phone calls.

"Do you want me to take you to your apartment?" Dad asks softly. "At least to get some fresh clothes?"

I look down at my flannel unicorn pajamas—a relic from my high school years that I found in my old dresser. "I guess I should. But...can I stay here for a few more days?"

He softens, trundling over and sitting on the edge of my bed. "You know I'm always happy to have you here, Zandy. No matter what's going on."

He takes my hand, and I try not to cry in earnest. My dad has always been like this—loyal and quiet and easy. God, how I wish I'd been born the same! Instead of messy and loud and *too much.*

"Dad? Were you ever scared about having me?"

He looks down at my face, and understanding rearranges the smile on his face into something both kinder and sadder.

He knows.

Maybe it's my question or his fatherly intuition, but it's plain that he's just figured it out, and he squeezes my hand.

"When I found out your mother was pregnant, I felt nothing but excitement, because I knew I could do anything with that amazing woman at my side. But when she died..." His eyes grow glassy, and I know he's seeing memories I'm too young to remember. Memories of hospital beds and doctor visits. "I was more than scared. I was paralyzed. Because I didn't think I could do it without her. You were six then and still so young, and every good part of you was because of her. What if I ruined you somehow? What if I stifled all the parts of you that had only flowered because of your mother?"

He's never told me this before, and I sit up a little, curious. "What do you mean, because of her?"

Dad smiles fondly. "I've told you how smart and driven she was, but have I ever told you how funny and friendly she was? How determined? How brave? She could march into a room full of strangers and have them loving her within minutes. She could travel to a country she'd never been to, and within a day, she was already learning the language and having adventures. She was the opposite of me and perfect in every way. And when I saw how like her you were...I wanted to treasure that at all costs. I still do."

I give him a hug, overcome, swelling with pain and pride. "I never knew," I whisper, my eyes leaking tears onto his shoulder.

"I should have told you. But it's hard to talk about for me, and for you...for you, I only wanted you to look forward to your future. Not be stuck with me in a painful past."

"But what do I do now?" I ask tearfully. "What comes next?"

"That, my brave girl, only you can answer. But I will say that I believe fear is part of the process. It's what makes the joy all the more precious in the end."

"That's very wise," I say, sniffling as I pull back.

"Go easy on Oliver," Dad says gently. "Men like us sometimes need longer to become as brave as you and your mom were. He'll find his way."

I shake my head. "He was willing to do so much for me, but it felt all wrong. It felt like he was forcing himself, and I decided at the beginning of the summer that I wouldn't be that girl. That clingy girl who grabbed on to any promise of a future, no matter how emotionally coerced it was."

"So noble," Dad says. "But did you ever consider it's the other way around? That he's trying to cling on to you and just doesn't know how?"

I frown. "It didn't feel like that."

"He's lost someone before, and it sounds to me like the first thing he wanted to make sure of was that he didn't lose you too. Think about it, pumpkin." And with that, Dad drops a kiss on my forehead and leaves me to my thoughts.

Could he be right?

Was Oliver trying to hold on to me, as opposed to grimly shouldering me like some kind of burden?

Did he...*want* me?

And the baby?

And even if he did, would he ever forgive me for running away?

CHAPTER SIXTEEN

OLIVER

I thought I already lived through the worst day of my life. I thought what happened with Rosie was the worst thing I would ever go through, but as I walk through the house calling Zandy's name and realizing with cold, encroaching horror that she is gone, I know I was wrong.

This is the worst day of my life.

This is having my heart broken.

And the shitty thing? I absolutely know why. I know I deserve it.

I walk back into the study where I had her pinned to the wall not an hour before, where I held her curled and crying in my lap.

God, what a fuckup I am. I should have held her until night fell. I should have dropped to my knees and worshiped her. I should have cradled her and murmured how happy I was, how much I loved her, how I would take care of her as long as she'd let me. I should have been honest. I should have just *talked*.

But my God, how could she have expected me to respond right away? Wasn't a man allowed some time to process news like this?

Even as I think a bitter *apparently not*, raking my hand through my hair, I know it doesn't matter. I didn't even *ask* her to marry me, I just told her that we'd do it—God, no wonder she left. I fucked up. Something that becomes more and more apparent as she refuses to answer my calls.

Shit. Where could she have gone? Where does she have to go? I'm the only person she knows here. My cottage is the only place she has that's not in America—

Oh fuck.

The flight from Birmingham. Of course, she even told me about it, but somehow I wasn't able to connect that with her absence now, because, pathetically, I suppose I've been holding out hope that she wouldn't do something so drastic, so...real.

What else is she supposed to do? Stay in a country that's not her own while she carries the child of a man who was grimly planning an emergency wedding?

Good God, I've become my own Victorian morality narrative.

Fuck.

I get in my car and speed to the airport, but I know even as I wince my way through all the speed traps that I'll be too late. Zandy doesn't do anything by half-measures, and she has a plan for everything—whether it's arranging my hallway bookshelves or getting Beatrix to switch to dry cat food. There's no way in hell she doesn't have a concrete plan for escape. She made a spreadsheet to help her decide what to do about this pregnancy, for pity's sake.

And even as I fruitlessly search the public parts of the airport, I can't help but admire her. Even her spreadsheets and escape routes. Even her spine of steel normally hidden behind schoolgirl enthusiasm and lush curves.

How could I have been so foolish as to let a woman like her slip through my fingers?

&

"Zandy, thank fuck."

I'm in my study, warm summer darkness pressing up against the windows and Beatrix lying sideways on my desk, watching me pace the floor. A floor I can only pace because of Zandy's hard work in organizing my research.

"Oliver," Zandy says quietly. I know it's morning in the States—in the last three days of ceaselessly calling and emailing, I've become something of an expert in time zones—but she sounds exhausted. Raspy, like she's been crying.

The thought of it burns in my chest.

"I just—" I stop, searching for the right words to say. I'm still stunned she finally picked up the phone, and I don't want to say anything wrong. I don't want to scare her away. "How are you? And the baby?"

"The baby is currently the size of a pomegranate seed," Zandy says. "So I think it's fine."

She doesn't answer how she is, and she doesn't have to. Her voice says it all.

"Zandy, I—I fucked up. I should have listened. I should have talked. I should have done everything differently."

There's silence on the other end, and somehow I know it wasn't good enough, that she needs more. "I love you," I say. Plead. "I want you. And this baby. And I'll do anything to prove it."

"Are those the things you think you have to say?" she asks softly. Too softly, but I don't see the danger.

"Of course. Aren't they the things you need to hear?"

A sharp breath, like a gasp. From all the way across the Atlantic, it sounds like a gunshot.

"Zandy? What did I say wrong? Tell me, *tell me* and I'll fix it, I swear to God."

"Don't you see?" she whispers. "I don't want this to be about what you think you should do. I don't want you to leave your research. I don't want you to marry me if you are only doing it out of some kind of half-baked obligation of honor."

I sputter a little at that, but she's not done.

"And I especially don't want you to give up the professor games. How could I, when they make me feel more alive than I've ever felt? When they're a part of *you*, and I love every part of you?"

The burning in my chest is a fire now, an inferno, and it's searing my very soul. "I love you too, Zandy. Don't you see that's why I'm willing to give up anything to be with you?"

"And don't you see that's why I can't let you?" Her voice wavers, and I know she's close to tears, if she's not already crying. Damn this distance, this ocean! I tighten my hand around my phone as if I can pull her back to me through the tiny device.

"I want you just as you are," she continues. "And I refuse to be the reason you ruin your life. I'm sorry that Rosie made you feel like you didn't deserve a child or a future because of the things you like in bed, but dammit, Oliver, if you can't see how absurd that is after all these years, then I don't know how to make you."

Defensiveness wells up in my throat. "It's not absurd. It's reality. People like me can't have families; that's why I have to change."

"But money isn't an issue, so you shouldn't need to change jobs, and there's no law that says we have to be married to have a child together. And there's certainly no law that says people can't have playful sex after they have a baby. You're inventing this new version of yourself that's wholly unnecessary, and it's a new version I don't want. I love you how you are, and I refuse to be the excuse for you to hurt yourself." She takes a deep breath, and it trembles enough that I know she's truly crying now. "I love you, but I deserve more than being a duty. I deserve the man I love—*as he is*—choosing me because he's happy to choose me. Not because he feels forced."

She hangs up, and the sudden silence on the other end might kill me, save for one thing.

I understand now.

She isn't upset that I hadn't acted happy enough. She wants to save me from the mire of self-loathing I've been in since Rosie left me. And for the first time in years, I not only want to save myself, but I recognize that I don't have to. I didn't love Rosie in any real measure, and I've been a fool to let her words fester and slowly infect me.

If Zandy will have me as a crabby scholar who delights in taking her over my knee, then that's what she will get.

And to hell with the rest.

CHAPTER SEVENTEEN

ZANDY

Whoosh-whoosh-whoosh-whoosh-whoosh.

I blink at the screen next to me. Everything just looks like a swirl of static, except for the tiny spot at the middle. "Is that sound the heartbeat?" I whisper.

The ultrasound tech smiles at me. "It is. Baby's doing just fine."

I let out a long breath of relief. In the handful of days since Oliver's phone call, I've had light, persistent cramping—nothing too scary, but my new nurse-midwife wanted to make sure everything was progressing well all the same.

I stare at the little bean on the ultrasound monitor, as if it will make the storming thoughts inside my head clearer. As if it will loosen the painful knot in my chest.

It doesn't, but I still feel a spike of mind-boggling awe—as well as a spike of regret. Oliver should be here right now. Oliver should be here to see his child. Even if there's no future for us, he deserves that much at least.

"I'm going to run these images over to your midwife and make sure she doesn't want anything else," the ultrasound tech says, snapping her gloves off and taking some printouts away from the machine. "Stay here."

As if I'm going anywhere naked below the waist and still slicked up with the bluish lube they used for the ultrasound wand. I consider reaching for my phone as the door closes behind the tech, but I decide against it. I'll only be crushed by how blank it is; Oliver hasn't tried to call or contact me at all since we last spoke on the phone.

I close my eyes against the sudden burn, feeling stupid. This is what I wanted, right? Dignity, distance, all of the stuff that sounds so good in theory and *Cosmo* articles.

In real life, however, dignity sucks.

My eyes are still closed as the tech comes back in the room, and I take a deep breath, preparing to act the part of chipper young mom again. It's been a little embarrassing, being here alone, knowing the front desk girls and the clucking, brusque nurses are all forming their own opinions about me, but it's nothing I can't handle, right?

Right.

But before I can open my eyes to greet the tech again, I feel a blunt finger tracing the narrow leather band of my wristwatch. "Always this watch," a wry British voice says. "Even now."

I open my eyes.

He'll never stop being so fucking handsome, will he? The unkempt shadow of a beard on that square jaw matches his tousled hair perfectly, and even the sleepless smudges under his eyes only serve to set off the unfairly long eyelashes and the hypnotically colored eyes. That sensual mouth is currently twisted in a smile so aristocratically and perfectly Oliver Markham Graeme that I could cry.

"You're here," I say pointlessly.

He settles a hand over my lower stomach, but his eyes never leave my face. "I'm here," he affirms.

"But..." I don't have the rest of the words to finish my objection, although it's not really an objection. Even with everything between us, seeing him is like swallowing down pure excitement. A hot flush of happiness starts to creep up my cheeks.

He notices, his smile becoming less dry and more tender. He brushes along my blush-stained cheeks with the back of a finger. "But nothing, darling. You were right. About everything."

"Everything?" I ask, suddenly finding myself uncertain in the trance of his beautiful eyes.

"I wish you hadn't left," he admits. "I wish you would have told me about the baby the moment you found out...but I understand why you didn't. It took you calling me absurd before the truth became clear to me."

"I didn't call *you* absurd," I clarify quickly. "Just your weird self-loathing."

He laughs, the act transforming his expression into that boyish, happy face I love so much. "Okay, fine then. It took you calling my self-loathing absurd for me to understand." He sobers a little, his hand splaying so nice and warm on my belly. "And I think I do understand now. I never wanted you to feel like a duty, Zandy. I want you because I want you. And if you'll have me the way I am"—his eyes meet mine—"then I'm all yours."

I search his expression. "So you aren't going to insist on marriage?"

"I want to marry you, but only if you're willing." The look on his face is fierce and loving. "And I'll be there as long as it takes to make you willing."

"And you're not going to quit your writing and go take a teaching job you hate?"

"No."

"And you'll still be a spanky professor with me?"

He rolls his eyes at the word *spanky*, but a smile tugs at his lips. "And I'll still be a spanky professor with you."

I finally allow myself to grin. "Then that's all I can ask for."

The tech opens the door, making a coo of surprise when she sees Oliver. "Is this Daddy?" she asks, bustling back to the machine.

"Yes," Oliver and I say at the same time.

And we manage to sway the tech into showing us a few more minutes of the baby, even though technically she doesn't need to, and I soak in every moment of Oliver's reserved expression made open and awed with wonder as he watches his baby's heart pulse on the screen.

It's not until we're leaving the office together, several glossy prints of our baby in hand, when I nudge his arm with my shoulder and say, "You're Daddy now."

His gorgeous mouth hooks up at the corner. "Sometimes I'll be, Miss Lynch. But when we're alone, I'm still Professor."

I think I might float away with happiness. "Yes, sir," I say, and I'm rewarded with a kiss that steals my breath right out of my mouth and promises all sorts of dirty, spanky things to come.

As long as I'm a very, very good girl.

EPILOGUE

OLIVER

One Year Later...

Warm summer air blows through the study windows, ruffling my papers. I mumble a frustrated oath, clapping a hand over the pile and trying to ignore Zandy, who is finishing up her assignment using completely digitized materials and is visibly smug about it. Ever since she decided to go to library school in nearby Sheffield, we've been sharing my study, and she's never stopped fussing about my affinity for paper. Or rather, the way the paper I work with tends to clump into piles and stacks and turn our neatly organized study into a warren of discarded books.

The breeze blows again, toying with her hair and fluttering the edges of her blouse, drawing my eyes down to her chest. The baby and nursing have blown out Zandy's buxom shape, transforming her girlishly curvy body to something ripe and irresistible. Looking at her now makes me feel distinctly barbarian-like; I can't catch sight of those lush, milk-heavy breasts or those suggestively wide hips without wanting to throw her over my shoulder and carry her off to some remote tower and mate with her until we both can't move anymore.

I consider doing that right now—sans tower, of course—when a small squeak draws my attention. I look over to the small cot next to my desk, where two chubby waving fists and slowly kicking legs alert me that my little man is awake.

Zandy starts to stand, but I beat her to him, scooping up the squishy bug in my arms and kissing his thick, silky crown of hair. At three months old, Michael—named for her father—looks almost all my child: his eyes so blue at birth now changing into speckles of green and brown as well, his pointed chin, and even his little frowns and scowls. But the hair is all from his mother, and I find myself so fucking enamored sometimes with the idea that he's been created uniquely and solely from me and the woman I love.

The woman who's going to be my wife.

After our conversation and my botched attempt at marrying her the first time, I decided to take no risks with my second approach, and in a very Zandy-ish move, I made a plan. Part of the plan was establishing where we would live and where she would go to school, because I can live anywhere, really, and I knew she'd want to be close to her father. I let her choose every step of the way, reminding her that I'd love her and stay with her no matter what.

She chose England and the cottage and the river and then began a campaign of emotional warfare to convince her father to find a job here near us. A campaign that was successful. He lives a mere ten minutes away from his grandson now.

The other part of the plan was to simply enjoy the process of having Michael. I didn't want to rush her or pressure her when she seemed so happy and alight with his impending arrival, so I decided to wait until after his birth to settle this once and for all.

Zandy's mine.

She's been mine from the moment I covered my body with hers and slid inside her. Hell, she's been mine since the moment she stumbled into me on a rainy London night.

And I have no intention of letting her go.

Zandy finishes up her work while I tend to Michael, and by the time she's finished, he's ready to nurse. I sit at the edge of my desk and watch as she props her feet up on a pile of books and cradles our son to her breast.

I watch appreciatively, happily, because she's a vision like this—her hair in tumble-down waves over her shoulders and her beautiful face bent in tender care...and her perfect breast available to view. As if hearing my thoughts, my son puts a flexing hand over her breast as if to lay claim.

I smile, dropping a kiss on his head as I get up to prepare for this afternoon. *Message received, little sir*, I think with amusement. *She's all yours for now.*

But after he nods off into his habitual milk coma and we lay him down in his nursery upstairs, I lead Zandy back to the study, because for the next hour, she's all mine. And I intend on using that time very well.

The moment I sit back down at my desk and say, "Come here, Miss Lynch," my cock swells against my trousers in Pavlovian response. And it swells even more as I see the rampant evidence of her desire stamped all over her body—nipples like hard little bullets, cheeks stained pink, and her even, white teeth biting into her lower lip.

"Yes, Professor," she murmurs, coming toward me with a smile she can't quite hide.

"I'm afraid you've been a bad girl," I tell her sternly, "and the time has come to do something about it."

"I haven't been a bad girl," she protests as she finally reaches me, and I hear the real umbrage in her voice—my Zandy is someone who always wants to be a good girl, the teacher's pet, and even though she knows it's a game, she still can't stifle the eager schoolgirl inside her who wants to please me entirely. Her puzzled little frown is only half-faked. "I'm a good girl, I promise."

"I don't think so," I say, giving her the steely teacher-ish glare that makes her melt every time. "We need to have a talk about your behavior, Miss Lynch. And about the consequences."

I stand up, and her teeth sink back into her lip in a display of contrition. Heat pools at the base of my spine, and I have to consciously control my breathing and slow it down. *Fuck*, how I need this game. How I need *her* to play it with. Only her, for the rest of my life.

"Do you think I haven't noticed what you've been doing to get my attention, Miss Lynch? The staying after class? The 'extra studying' in my office? And do you think I haven't noticed how you shamelessly display your body to me?"

Deep blue eyes peer up at me through dark, fluttering lashes. "I wasn't doing it on purpose," she breathes. "I promise, sir."

I slide my hand into the loose, silky hair at the nape of her neck. "I think it was on purpose," I say coldly. "I think you are deliberately trying to provoke me. And I think you're about to learn how far you can provoke a man before he acts."

"Acts?" she asks, blinking up at me.

I yank her close enough that she can feel the hot column of my cock against her belly. "That's right, Miss Lynch. It's time for you to face the consequences of your misbehavior."

And then I bend her over the desk.

I'm trembling. I'm almost always trembling by this point, the sheer fucking filthiness of it throbbing deep in my belly and shuddering heat all the way to the tip of my leaking cock. Something about this game rocks me to my core, makes me feel like every time is the first time, and the fact that I can play it with someone who loves it as much as I do is incredible. I'm humbled by it every single fucking time.

She looks up at me over her shoulder, delivering her most innocent pout. "But sir, I won't be bad any longer. I'll be good, I swear."

I flip up her skirt, exposing a round behind and a sweet pussy that are completely bare. No underthings at all. "This doesn't look like you have any plans to be good anytime soon," I say darkly, giving her pussy a hard cup. "I think you're lying. I think you can't help yourself, and you're going to keep this pussy wet and open for me whenever I'm around because you can't stand not having me fuck you, hmm?"

She grinds down against my hand, chasing the pressure and rolling her head along her folded forearms.

"Answer me, girl. Are you going to start behaving now?" I time my question with the dirty, probing slide of one finger deep into her heat, and she mewls at me.

"No, Professor, I'm so sorry. I just can't help it..."

"Then you'll have to face the consequences of your behavior," I say, injecting my voice with as much grimness as I can muster through all the lust currently pounding through my veins. "How do you stop me, Miss Lynch?"

"Red," she moans, whimpering in protest as I remove my finger. "But please don't ever stop."

Thwack.

The first stinging slap across her ass makes her jolt against the desk, one of her bare little feet kicking up reflexively. I move my own feet around hers, enjoying the picture we make very much—the trouser fabric against bare legs and the rumpled plaid waves of her skirt, the expensive leather of my shoes against the adorable red-painted toes and pale skin of her feet. I give her another quick slap and then sit back down in my chair.

"Over my knee, Miss Lynch. I need to make sure you're not getting too comfortable."

The look she cuts me is a prism of all the things I love about our game, about our life. It's fear and arousal and the distinct slice of rueful affection, and it hardens my cock at the same time it softens my heart. I love her, and I love the way we fit together as I pull her over my lap, as she drops a soft kiss on my forearm, and as I give her thigh a quick, reassuring squeeze before we disappear back into the game.

I pull her skirt up to her waist and spank her until she squirms. I spank her until her legs start kicking up and I have to trap them under my leg to keep punishing her. I keep it nice today, my palm working over a liberal area and striking just hard enough to burn but not hard enough to truly hurt. And then once she's nice and pink, I part her legs to inspect her pussy.

"Wet," I declare harshly. "Shamefully wet. I don't think you've learned your lesson at all."

"Maybe not," she gasps as my inspecting hand starts rubbing at her cunt. "I might need more punishment."

"A shame," I say, picking her up and bending her back over the desk. With one hand, I keep her bent over the desk while my other hand fumbles with my trousers to release my aching erection. "I had such hopes I could turn you back into a good girl."

"I can be a good girl starting right now," she begs, lifting up on her tiptoes and bringing her wet, flushed opening level with my cock. I rub my tip against it, enjoying the heat and the slick kiss of her flesh against mine, enjoying her needy moans even more. And finally, finally, after shoving the turgid head into the small seam and lodging myself there, I thrust home.

She's so tight, so hot, that static fuzzes at the edges of my vision. "I've changed my mind," I say breathlessly. "You are a very good girl. Utterly perfect."

She tosses her hair over her shoulder as she sends me the kind of saucy look no actual good girl could ever muster. "I like it when you fuck me, Professor," she says, and she pushes back against me to prove her point. "You make me feel so good."

I give her a stinging spank and then reach in front of her to add my fingers to her pleasure, knowing how she likes the pressure of my touch on her clit as I fuck her tight opening from behind. And it doesn't take her long like this, with me riding her against the desk and my touch on her intimate secrets, and she comes with a surprised wail, clenching so hard around my cock that I very nearly lose it.

But I cling on, by fingernails and teeth, desperate to execute my plan. Because one thing's become clear to me over the past year, and it's how much we need each other like this and how afraid Zandy was of losing this part of me. So I need to prove to her now that she'll never lose it, that it's part of our love now and forever.

After her peak subsides, I reach over and slide a piece of notebook paper in front of her. "I forgot to mention this very important assignment," I say, and I see her glance at it briefly and then back to me, as if she expects it only to have the usual *red means stop* scrawled across, since that's usually how I check in with her during our games.

But this time it says something different.

I see the moment she realizes this, the moment her head dips back to read the paper again, and she freezes underneath my now-leisurely stroking hips.

I love you, the paper says. *Will you marry me? Will you be my wife and let me be your professor?*

"Oliver," she says, and her voice is filled with tears.

I pull out enough that I can turn her around and guide her back onto the desk, on her back this time, and I crawl over her, entering her with a wet, welcome shove.

"I love you. And I want you as you are," I murmur into her mouth, punctuating my words with deep, stroking kisses. "Will you have me? Just as I am?"

"Yes," she says, her tears running off her smiling cheeks. "Yes, I want you. Yes, I'll have you."

"So it's settled, then," I say, feeling like I've swallowed sunshine and grinning like an idiot. "You're mine."

She gives me a challenging look. "And you're mine too."

"Just so."

And when we come together, hot and messy and slick on top of my desk, surrounded by the library she built and with our baby sleeping upstairs, it's not the beginning of something incredible—the beginning happened on a drenching night over a year ago. But it's a confirmation.

A confirmation and a conclusion, and for me being the professor, I have to admit the woman underneath me has taught me more than I ever could have imagined. I couldn't have planned the lesson better myself, although as we start kissing and grinding our way to a second round, I decide there's no way I can ever admit that to her.

I am the professor in this house, after all.

ACKNOWLEDGMENTS

Firstly, thanks go to my beautiful and tireless agent, Rebecca Friedman, whose confidence in my writing is unwavering (and probably undeserved, but I'm taking it anyway!).

To my editor, Scott Saunders, for his sharp eye and flawless observations, and to the rest of the Waterhouse team: Meredith Wild, Robyn Lee, Jennifer Becker, David Grishman, Yvonne Ellis, Haley Byrd, Kurt Vachon, Jonathan Mac, and Jesse Kench. And my undying thanks to Amber Maxwell for a staggeringly good cover!

To Ashley Lindemann, Serena McDonald, Candi Kane, and Melissa Gaston for their help and support with all the back-of-the-house work that comes along with writing a book. To Laurelin Paige, Melanie Harlow, and Kayti McGee, as well as Julie Murphy, Natalie Parker, Tess Gratton, Nana Malone, Sarah MacLean, Carrie Ryan, Jana Aston, and Becca Mysoor—along with everyone else at the Orange Beach and Kiawah retreats for all the support and laughter (and occasionally liquor). And huge and grateful thanks to Karen Cundy, who made sure Oliver sounded more Cambridge than Kansas.

To Doug Hagen, Eddy Bisceglia, Dana Hagen, Kay Hagen, Sandra Whitman, Ed Wells, Lizzie Hagen, and Kathie and Milt Taylor for supporting the brooding author in their lives. And to Josh Taylor, who has to support her most of all.

And lastly to my readers. Thank you for going on yet another dirty, fun journey with me!

MISADVENTURES

OF A

CURVY GIRL

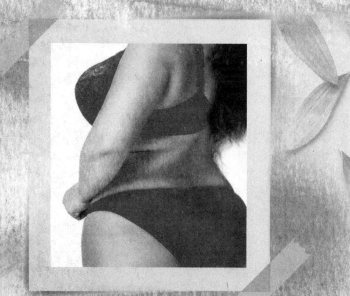

For Julie

CHAPTER ONE

IRELAND

The car was my first mistake.

I can admit that now, sitting here in the mud, my windshield almost too splattered with the stuff to make out the herd of cows chewing curiously at me on the other side of the fence.

With a low curse—and a glare back at the judgmental cows—I fumble for my phone, thinking I'll call someone. Anyone. A friend. A tow truck. An Uber. But when the screen lights up, I realize there's no LTE out here. There's not even 3G.

Not even 3G.

No cell service at all, actually. I throw myself back against my seat and listen to the sporadic drumming of rain on my roof. When my coworkers back at Typeset—the social media strategy firm I work for—heard I was heading out to the Flint Hills in my Prius, they laughed and teased, and a couple even offered me their trucks, but I refused. My little blue car may look like a piece of candy, but it's never let me down in the city. Not once. I didn't see any reason it would let me down just because I was a couple of hours west.

I see the reason now, I assure you. Two words: dirt roads.

I get out of the car again, pushing open my umbrella to shield me from the petulant, spitting rain while I walk around my vehicle to confirm for a final time that yes, all four tires are stuck deeply in the mud. It's rained the past three days straight—something not even worth noticing back in Kansas City except maybe to whine about how it slowed morning traffic—but out here in farm country, the rain definitely makes itself known. The roads are nothing but slicks of rough mud, and the lonely trees look huddled and limp. The long fingers of summer grass crowding up along the side of the road are battered down by the days of rain, and the wet emerald stalks peppered with yellow coneflowers and purple spiderwort look just as sodden and battered.

It *is* beautiful, though. And for a minute, I look up from my mud-bound car and just take it in—the heady abundance of green grass and wildflowers, the brooding sweep of the hills in the near distance. The line of black clouds in the west, promising rain and wind and danger. It's like something that would be printed in a calendar, and the moment I think the thought, I dive back into my car for the expensive Nikon camera in the passenger seat. And then awkwardly crawl back out, abandoning my umbrella so I can capture the moment before it vanishes—the energy, the quietly decadent riot of wildflowers, the promise of abundant prairie summer.

I take as many pictures as I can, trying to pick my way through the mud in my ballet flats, and for a brief moment, I wonder what my life would have been like if I'd taken that photography scholarship out of state instead of staying local and studying marketing all those years ago.

I wanted to see the world once. I wanted to be one of those photographers who tramps all over Patagonia and Punjab, who snaps arresting photos of little Alpine villages and intrepid Antarctic outposts. And maybe if I took enough gorgeous, stirring photos, no one would've cared the woman behind the camera wasn't gorgeous or stirring herself.

Stop it, Ireland.

This is exactly the kind of thought I am done entertaining. I turn to the car, seeing my reflection in the window just as I knew I would. I make myself look at it. Really look. Not the half-sideways glance I used to give, as if my view bounced off any mirrored surface without me actually seeing myself. No. I look, and I take in the pale twenty-four-year-old woman standing there. Ireland Mills.

She has dark hair almost to her waist because she loves having long hair.

A girl of your size really should have shorter hair.

She has wide hips and thighs in a formfitting pencil skirt, and a thin silk blouse that does nothing to hide the shape of her soft, swelling breasts.

Don't you think that's more of a "goal" outfit? For when you lose weight?

A mouth in lavender lipstick, the sweet color visible even in the faint reflection.

I wouldn't draw attention to your face if I were you. I would want to blend in.

Pursing my attention-drawing mouth, I raise the camera and take a picture of myself. It's not a coincidence all the negative thoughts in my head have my sister's voice behind them, and I'm done listening. I'm done listening to her, and I'm done listening to my ex-boyfriend, who dumped me last month when I told him I stopped my eternal diet and dropped my gym membership so I could go to dance classes instead.

"But those classes aren't designed for people to lose weight," Brian explained patiently, as if there was no way I could understand something as complex as a hobby. "They're for fun." Then his expression changed, as if he were about to give me a present. "How about you keep going to the gym, and then if you meet your weight goals, you can take the dance classes as a reward? I bet it's not even too late to reverse your gym cancellation."

He smiled benevolently at me then, like he'd just solved all my problems. Maybe a year ago I would have done anything he asked because I'd been so grateful anyone could want to be with me—because I wanted to be this better, skinnier version of myself that he seemed to envision.

But something shifted deep in my brain, and while I didn't know exactly what it was, I knew I was *over it*. I was over the diets that didn't work. I was over the grueling gym schedule that left no time for fun. I was over hiding behind my friends whenever we took pictures. I was over shopping for print tunics at Blouse Barn.

I want to wear the clothes I want to wear, not the ones I'm supposed to. I want to spend my nights doing what *I* choose, not going to the gym and then listening to Brian's pointed remarks about my body while I pick at my frozen diet entree and stare miserably at the table. I want to live *now*, have fun and do fun things *now*, not wait for some distant, skinnier future that may never come. What if I wake up one day at fifty and realize I spent my youth on diet shakes and broth cleanses for nothing? What if I spent the rest of my years being criticized by Brian and gym trainers and my sister, all while wearing tunics I hated?

So I stopped.

And started wearing the clothes everyone said I shouldn't—crop tops and leggings and short dresses and over-the-knee boots—and I started taking dance classes for the hell of it, because it sounded fun and because I wasn't going to care anymore about being the biggest woman in the room or the one who sweats the most or breathes the loudest. I was going to live in my body *now*.

It was amazing—it *is* amazing. Yes, my sister still keeps sending me links to new diets and making sure my plate is smaller than everyone else's at Sunday dinner. And yes, Brian did dump me after it became clear I wasn't "taking care of myself anymore." But I feel freer than I can ever remember.

And if the price of freedom is being alone, then fine. I'd rather be alone than be with someone who will only love me if I'm skinny.

For good measure, I take another picture of my reflection, feeling a bite of satisfaction when I glance at the digital display on the back of the camera. Dark, loose curls. Cheeky lipstick. All of my curves on display.

I look good. Fuck anyone who says differently.

The wind picks up, reminding me that no matter how confident I'm feeling right now, I'm still stuck in the mud in the middle of nowhere with an angry thunderstorm bearing down on me. And no cell service.

With a sigh, I finally accept I'm going to have to leave the car here and try to walk to better service. I'm not looking forward to plodding back to the last sign of civilization I saw—a tired gas station five miles back when I turned off the small two-lane highway onto the gravel county road that led me to the mess I'm in now. Ugh, and in my cute pencil skirt, which had been perfect for "young professional meets Kansas farmer for a marketing campaign" but is not ideal for "size eighteen girl hikes five muddy miles in the July heat."

My thighs are already wincing, knowing from long experience the chub rub to come.

Why couldn't I have worn jeans?

Because I wanted to look professional, that's why. A grown-up girl with a grown-up job. Instead, I'm going to be the least professional thing of all—a freaking no-show. I was supposed to be at Caleb Carpenter's farm twenty minutes ago, and without a working cell phone, I can't call to explain myself. I'll just have to wait until I get to the gas station and figure it out from there.

If there's one thing Brian made me good at, it was apologizing, so at least I know I'll be able to work up the appropriate amount of remorse when I call the farmer back. So it will just be chub rub *and* professional embarrassment. No big deal. At least the rain seems to have tapered off.

Well, no sense standing here feeling sorry for myself. I grab the weekender bag I packed, throw in the camera, my wallet, and my phone, and then lock the car and start walking. The cows have already moved away in disinterest. This situation is so dull, it bores livestock.

I reach a mud-covered wooden bridge over a swollen creek, and *bang!*— like a gunshot. Close enough to make me duck.

Holy shit.

I know Kansas farmers can be fussy about trespassers, but surely it's fine to walk on the *road*? Or maybe it has nothing to do with me and it's normal farm business to shoot off guns every now and then? Or maybe someone is hunting nearby? Do people hunt in July?

Before I can rationalize away the sound, it happens again, much closer this time, and then up and over the hill behind me comes a rattletrap pickup truck, sluicing through the gloppy mud without a single problem at all, easily shaming my little hybrid—even though my hybrid is barely a year old and the pickup appears to be held together with rust and fond memories.

It comes charging through the mud, heading my way, and for a moment, I almost want to hide. Not only because I'm a woman alone in the middle of nowhere and I have no way to dial 9-1-1 if I need to but also because I'm a bit embarrassed. Okay, a lot embarrassed.

Embarrassed of my car and my clothes and—even though I'm annoyed with myself about it—my body. Sometimes it feels like there's already one strike against me, that whatever happens, no matter what it is, a stranger will look at the situation and then at me and think, *Oh, well, it's because she's overweight.* There's a whole host of things people assume about my intellect and moral compass because I have a bigger body than they do.

That's the old Ireland talking, I remind myself. Potential for being murdered aside, it would be just plain stupid to pass up the chance for help because I'm embarrassed. At the very least, he may be able to give me a ride to the gas station.

So I stand by the side of the road and wait for the creaking truck to come closer, and it thoughtfully slows down long before it reaches me, so as not to splatter me with mud.

Up close, I can see it's an old truck—but not some classic Ford that belongs in a parade. No, this is a brown and white monstrosity from the late eighties with a broken tailgate and rusted wheel wells. The bed is full of an assortment of empty buckets, baling wire, and bungee cords. A tarp, shovel, and a dented toolbox complete the mess.

It rolls to a stop, and the door opens before I can get a good look at the person inside. A three-legged dog jumps nimbly down, barking madly at me but also wagging its tail, as if it can't decide to be happy or distressed about a stranger.

Three-legged dog. Truck that looks like a rolling junkyard. I'm expecting the man climbing out of the truck to be full *Grapes of Wrath*—weather-beaten and gaunt and probably in overalls—and I'm hoping he'll be the kindly sort of old farmer and not the scary American Gothic kind when he walks around the door, and oh—

Oh my God.

Oh my God.

He's not *Grapes of Wrath* at all. He's nearly six and a half feet of muscle and potent masculinity...shoulders stretching a Carhartt T-shirt in the most panty-dampening way, worn jeans clinging to his hard thighs and narrow hips. Big boots, bright-green eyes in a sun-bronzed face, and a close-trimmed beard that would redden the inside of my thighs very nicely...

Oh God, now that would definitely be an upgrade from chub rub.

He looks to be in his early thirties, with the kind of straight nose and full lips that make you think things like *all-American* and *wholesome,* which makes me keenly aware of how *un*wholesome my thoughts are right now. Thoughts about his beard and his hard thighs and his hands, which are big and strong and currently flexing by his sides as if they're itching to do something. I don't see a wedding ring—or even a tan line suggesting he's ever worn one—and the bare finger is practically daring me to imagine sweaty, grunting fantasies.

I manage to drag myself away from my dirty thoughts long enough to realize the farmer is talking to me.

"Ireland Mills?" he's asking. Hearing my name out of this prairie god's mouth is disorienting, and I merely gape at him.

He smiles, revealing even, white teeth and a dimple sent from heaven. "I'm Caleb Carpenter. Thought you might have gotten lost on the way to my farm."

CHAPTER TWO

CALEB

I feel like I've been punched in the chest, and the person doing the punching is a five-foot-two girl with purple lipstick and eyes the color of a spring sky.

I'm suddenly a clumsy country boy all over again, even though this woman is at least ten years younger than me and clearly in need of help. I should feel pretty confident in this situation. Instead, all I feel is a dry mouth and a racing pulse—and an undeniable swelling against the front of my jeans—like I really am a horny teenage boy and not a man in his thirties who should know better.

But it's like that punch in the chest knocked all the sense straight out of me, because suddenly I'm thinking thoughts no gentleman should think. Like how I can see the heaving swells of her breasts under her fancy shirt, how those swells would overflow even my big hands and spill over my fingertips as her nipples harden against my palms.

Like how warm and soft her thighs would be against my hips as I nestled into them, how her ass would feel in my hands as I cupped her bottom and tasted the only woman I want...

The only woman I want.

The thought hits me like a second punch, and I suck in a breath.

This one.

Mine. Ours. Somehow, it's this city girl—the same girl I've been silently cursing all morning.

A friend of mine from my college days called and asked if I'd be willing to let someone from his company come out and take some pictures of the farm. At the time, it seemed dickish to say no. But as the day dawned and I saw how much work I had to do, I began wishing I was more of a dick to my old friend. I didn't have the time to spare to play tour guide, and I felt even surlier about it when the time for her arrival came and went and it became clear she'd stood me up for this thing I was only doing as a favor in the first place.

It took an unkind amount of time to even consider the possibility she might have gotten lost and not stood me up—after all, spotty cell coverage means getting disoriented in these parts happens often enough. After I had that thought, I pinned a note to the door just in case and then climbed into the truck, grumbling the whole time.

But now.

But now.

I owe my old friend an apology and a drink; I owe him everything. Because even though I've just met her, even though I can't explain it, somehow I know something has just changed.

Something I've been waiting years for.

"Oh, thank goodness," Ireland Mills says as I step forward, and she's got one of *those* voices. A slightly throaty alto that sounds like she's been in bed all afternoon.

In bed under me. Over me.

Between Ben and me...

I manage to stop that train of thought before my erection becomes fully visible, and I realize I've been flexing my hands unconsciously at my sides, as if anticipating the feel of her soft curves against them. As if I'm already itching to hike up her tight skirt and mold my hand to the shape of her cunt.

I could make her wet...

I could make her come...

And Ben—

"So then I thought maybe the gas station, because even if they didn't have a signal, they'd probably have a phone, and I could get it sorted from there," Ireland's saying. Greta, my dog, is still barking at her, and Ireland talks over her. "Do you think the car is truly stuck? Should I call a tow truck?"

Before I can answer, Greta decides barking isn't enough and starts trying to jump onto Ireland. "Greta!" I scold, but Greta is determined to smear mud all over Ireland's perfect black skirt.

I expect fear or disgust or at least uncertainty, but Ireland bends down and scratches Greta's ears. "It's okay, puppy," she croons. "We're best friends. You just don't know it yet."

Greta licks her face in agreement, and I'm going to marry this woman.

"No tow truck," I say firmly. "I'll take care of you from here on out."

CHAPTER THREE

IRELAND

Caleb comes forward, takes my bag, and tosses it easily into the cab of the truck, and then he walks back to me. I have to tilt my head to look into his face, and his eyes burn down at me with something that makes my nipples firm up into little pebbles.

"We may just beat the storm if we get a move on," he says in a voice that is all gritty, practical male. I want to wrap myself up in it and live inside it forever. "But I hope you don't mind if we make a quick pit stop first?"

"I—" I'm still trying to absorb the fact that Caleb has eyes like summer itself and they're currently looking at me like I'm the most interesting thing in the world.

He's probably just being polite and attentive, good manners and all that, I tell myself and my fast-beating heart.

I force myself to run through a flowchart of my options, and by far, going with this man I was supposed to meet with anyway is the best choice. If my phone doesn't work at his house, he'll definitely have a landline. And worst-case scenario, I could ask him to ferry me to the interstate motel thirty miles back. I brought a few days' worth of clothes in the event I didn't get all the pictures I'd need for the campaign in one go—and honestly, it might be nice to take a break from the hustle of Typeset and the endless judgmental nagging of my sister back home.

And who am I kidding? I want to be in a truck with the most ruggedly handsome man I've ever seen. I want to go to his house.

"Pit stop's fine," I say, flashing him a smile he doesn't return. If anything, his lingering smile from earlier slowly fades. His hands do the flexing thing by his sides again, and he stares like he's never seen anything like me before. Or, more specifically, he stares at my mouth like he's never seen anything like it before.

With a burst of self-consciousness, I wonder if he hasn't. Chubby girls in lavender lipstick probably don't pop into his life very often, and maybe he thinks I'm ridiculous or trying too hard or something like that, with the big smile and the crazy lipstick and the clothes that suddenly feel a million times tighter than they did a few minutes ago.

Oh God. Of course, it's so like me to meet the best-looking man I've ever seen and then he sees me as some kind of awkward sausage. *I* know I'm not an awkward sausage, but does he know that?

You don't care, remember? It's better to be alone than with someone who doesn't like you with the body you have.

Firmed with resolve, I renew my smile at Caleb. "Should I?" I gesture toward the truck. He starts, as if I've yanked him out of some deep and important reverie.

"Yes, of course." He walks over to the passenger side with me—Greta following us with her hopping three-legged gait—and opens the door. "Careful of the step. It's a big one."

Wanting to seem capable and strong, I ignore his offered hand and make to climb into the truck. Except he was right—the step *is* big—and I forget how tight the pencil skirt is. When I lift my foot to pull myself up into the cab, the skirt manages to hike itself up to my thighs *and* hamper my balance, and I'm falling backward. For a horrible, humiliating half second, I'm falling with my skirt up to my ass, I'm going to land in the mud, and it's going to be so fucking embarrassing, especially after I made such a show of not needing his help. And then he'll think I'm a *clumsy* awkward sausage on top of it all...

I brace myself for the fall and the ensuing humiliation, but neither comes. The moment I actually totter backward, Caleb catches me with a quick arm around my waist and a big hand on my—oh holy fuck.

His hand is on my ass. My almost bare ass, and because the skirt has worked its way up so high, the ends of his fingers are touching the exposed lower curve of my bottom. The arm banded around my waist is pure strength, and behind me he feels as solid and unmoving as a wall. A firm, warm wall made of swells and grooves of muscle and man.

I can feel every callus on his hand as he lets me find my balance, and then I feel the infinitely long second where it seems deliberately still, as if he's forcing himself not to squeeze my flesh, and that just makes my nipples hard all over again.

"Oh," I breathe out. "Oh—"

I can't remember being this turned on *ever*, and my body arches against his in unconscious feminine instinct. I want him to grind into me. I want him to bend me over the seat and fuck me until I see stars.

"Easy there," he finally rumbles, and with my back to his chest, I can feel the words moving through him and into me. And then like it's nothing, he lifts me up into the truck, handing me up into the seat, making sure I'm settled before his hands leave my body.

My heart is beating so hard I think it might leave my chest.

I have a brief flash of the time Brian and I went horseback riding on a date. I held out a hand to him, hoping he'd help me dismount, and he laughed at me. *Laughed.*

I'd flushed bright red. I didn't expect him to twirl me off the horse like a cartoon prince or anything, but surely it wasn't too much to ask for help? Surely even big girls deserve a steadying arm?

But Caleb—Caleb easily caught all two-hundred-odd pounds of me without so much as a grunt of complaint and then placed me as carefully in the seat as he would a stack of china teacups.

I turn to him to give him my thanks—thanks laden with possibly too much emotion from this dumb Brian baggage I have—but the words die in my throat when I see Caleb's face. His sensuous mouth looks tense and grim, and there are new lines around his eyes, as if he's experiencing some kind of strain. His hands are restless at his sides again, and he won't meet my gaze.

Immediately I panic that it was the effort of getting me in the truck, and I have to swallow back a dumb apology. But for what? For having a body? For being silly enough to try to climb into a truck in a pencil skirt?

No. *New Ireland.*

Instead, I just give him a "Thank you!" and he nods curtly, shutting the door after making sure my feet are safely inside, and then he walks around to the driver's door.

Greta hops in first, settling herself in a heap between us, and Caleb grates out a "Buckle in, please," not looking at me the entire time.

Clumsy awkward sausage. I knew it.

But I don't need his approval, even if he is only the second man in my life to touch my ass. Even if he is some kind of wholesome, all-American sex god. I lift my chin and stare out the windshield, which is smeared slightly with mud, and try to adjust my feet around all the stuff he has in the passenger-side floorboard.

Caleb starts the truck and then sees me trying to move my feet. A faint blush appears above the line of his beard, on his model-like cheekbones. "Uh, sorry about all this stuff," he mumbles, reaching over to move a brown paper bag that's full of...mason jars?

I peer inside. "Starting a pickle collection?"

The flush grows deeper. "It's a gift. From a friend."

A friend...like a lady friend? Maybe out in these parts, jars of pickles are some kind of flirtatious overture? Or maybe they're way past flirtation, and this lady friend likes to send him home after a long, sweaty night with plenty of sustenance. Because nights with him *would* be long and sweaty, I can tell just from looking at him.

"Is this an old laptop?" I ask, trying to shift a second brown paper bag with an old Dell inside, along with more mason jars of pickles and jams. The bag's got a logo printed on the side from a chain grocery store that's been closed for at least a decade—at least in the city. Maybe out here there's still a franchise open.

"The laptop is something my roommate repaired, and I'm returning it to a friend," Caleb says. "She's terrible with tech stuff."

Aha, so there is a *she*.

I don't know why this rankles so much, but it does. I frown as I finish moving the bag, which reveals a scuffed center console, and I give out an involuntary yelp.

Caleb startles at my noise and flings his arm across me, as if to stop me from going through the windshield—even though we aren't moving yet. "What is it?" he asks, alarmed.

"Th-There's bullets!" I manage to point to the center console, which has *bullets* just rolling around in there with a pack of gum and a small flashlight. I don't think I've ever even *seen* bullets in real life, not even once. Who even needs bullets in their truck? Serial rapists? Serial killers? What if my first instinct was right, and Caleb is actually going to kill me here in the middle of nowhere?

My squeamishness seems to confuse him. "Yes," he says slowly, "those are bullets." He says it in a voice like *what else would they be?*

"But why are they in your car?" I ask a little wildly.

Caleb tilts his head, his confusion growing into distinct amusement. "For the rifle mounted under your seat."

I nearly jump out of the seat. "There's a gun underneath me right now?"

"Relax," he says, barely keeping the laughter out of his voice. "It's not loaded."

"But...why? Do you use it"—I drop my voice into what I hope is my best serial-killer-soothing voice—"on people?"

He laughs, the rich sound filling the cab as he puts the truck into drive. "It's my varmint rifle, peach."

Peach?

Is he calling me *peach*?

"Varmint rifle?" I probe, deciding to leave peach where it is until I decide how I feel about it.

"For coyotes and foxes," he says a bit more seriously, his eyes casting around the surrounding fields as the truck works its way over the bridge and up to the distant county road. "They come after the chickens. Sometimes the coyotes will even give the cows trouble. Or they hassle Greta." He scowls as he says it, and I get the feeling he'd never forgive an animal for coming after his Greta-dog.

"Oh," I say. "But can't you just chase them off?"

Another laugh, and he's so handsome when he laughs that I have to look away. "No. They'll just keep coming back. And I'm not going to lose any of my animals because those pests are hungry."

The proprietary bent in his tone is so natural, so easy, and I can't decide why that turns me on. Is it the certainty? The strength?

Is it the sound of a male determined to protect what's his?

"There's a .410 shotgun under your seat too," he says all casual-like. "But that's for snakes."

"Snakes?" I ask, going pale because he's said the one word that can scare me more than *gun*. Oh God, if I'd known there would be snakes out here, I would have been way more terrified to be stranded!

"Okay, maybe the guns are okay," I grudgingly admit, because I don't like the idea of sitting on lethal weapons, but I like snakes even less.

Caleb chuckles, turning the truck onto a gravel road, and everything leaves my mind save for the way his hands look on the steering wheel. Big and rough and capable.

The turn points us right at the encroaching line of the storm, and I see lightning flickering in the distance. Caleb gives a sigh.

"Fucking storm," he says under his breath. Then, "Here's our pit stop. It'll just take a minute."

We're pulling into a long driveway—although "driveway" feels like an almost luxurious term, given that it's a dirt track with weeds growing up the middle and plenty of long grass along the sides. A low-slung white bungalow comes into view, all the windows covered with old-fashioned aluminum awnings. Several wooden outbuildings surround the house, gray and tired looking, and a gleaming twenty-year-old Cadillac nestles close to the house. A windmill spins in brisk, dizzy circles, and a couple of acres away, I see the slow nodding head of an oil drill.

"Is this your friend's house?" I ask, wondering if this is pickle lady.

"Yep," Caleb answers, throwing the truck into park and opening the door. Greta hops over his lap and is off like a shot, racing around the house like she's being chased. "Mrs. Parry sometimes has ducks wandering up from her pond," he says by way of explanation for Greta's bolt for freedom, but I stop at *Mrs. Parry.*

Mrs. Parry?

Surely that can't be the name of a lover—

The screen door of the house goes *whirr-BANG* as it opens and then slams shut behind an old woman in buttercup-yellow polyester pants and a white top with matching yellow flowers. Caleb gets out of the car and walks over to hug the woman—presumably Mrs. Parry—and gives her a kiss on the cheek. He's so much taller than her shrunken frame that he has to bend down considerably to do it.

"Now, what's this?" she asks, pulling away from him and eyeing me with some amusement as I climb carefully out of the truck and join them. "Caleb, have you found yourself a sweetheart?"

"Well, I—"

To my surprise, Caleb is stammering a little.

Mrs. Parry is already turning toward me and extending her hand. I take it and sense her approval of my firm grip. She makes no secret of how she appraises me, looking from my muddy flats all the way up to my lavender lipstick and windblown hair. She may be wearing a matching polyester set, but her eyes are still sharp, and I get the feeling not much gets past her.

I open my mouth to explain I'm just here to take pictures, but she interrupts me.

"She's a good, sturdy one," the woman says with a nod. "You and Ben did well."

Sturdy? I want to give a huff at that, but then my brain catches on the name *Ben.* Who's Ben? Why would she mention a Ben when she's sizing me up for suitability as Caleb's woman?

Also why am I even wondering this? Why am I even letting her talk about this when I am absolutely not Caleb's woman, or this mysterious Ben's?

"I'm Ireland Mills," I say as our hands finally part. "I came out to take some pictures of Caleb's farm for a client."

"Oh," Mrs. Parry says, and there's a real look of disappointment on her face. Real enough that I forgive her for calling me sturdy. "Well, then. I guess you'll still need some food, Caleb."

"No, ma'am," Caleb insists. "This morning, Mrs. Harthcock sent home more food than I know what to do with, and I—"

"Nonsense." Mrs. Parry is already bustling back toward the house. "You and Ben are growing boys still."

"—don't even like pickles," Caleb finishes his sentence in mumbled defeat as we watch Mrs. Parry disappear back inside. "You should see our pantry," he says, looking over at me. "It's *filled* with mason jars."

"'Our' pantry?" I ask. "Is this the Ben she was talking about?"

"Yes. My roommate." He looks like he wants to say more but doesn't know what he should say. He looks...uncomfortable.

A thought clicks into place.

Oh.

I guess I'm too used to how things are back home in Kansas City, because I should have picked up on the clues earlier. *Roommate* might very well be what a hunky farmer calls his boyfriend out in the Kansas countryside.

I feel a retroactive rush of embarrassment at how much I've been privately lusting after him. And embarrassment on his behalf that Mrs. Parry thought I was his girlfriend.

"And the pickles and the computer," I ask, looking for something to move me past this awkward realization. "That's from another lady like Mrs. Parry?"

He seems relieved at the change of subject. So am I.

"That's right. Mrs. Harthcock and Mrs. Parry got left all sorts of land when their husbands died. Some of it they sold, but the rest they rent out—to me."

"So you farm their land?"

Caleb does this very attractive squint thing where he looks out over the Parry fields. It's so unstudied and honest, and despite the *roommate* situation, something about it makes my toes curl in my flats, makes my belly clench low. There's so much strength in it, so little fear of hard work and dirt, and I've never seen anything like it. It's potent as hell.

"It's a touch more complicated than that, but that's the gist of it, yeah. I rent the land from them and farm it, since their kids aren't interested in the business."

"Is that what you're here for right now?" I ask, nodding toward the house where we can see Mrs. Parry moving behind the windows. "Farm business?"

More squinting—this time at the storm. "I like to check on them before the big storms roll in. There's a siren down in Holm," he says, naming the nearest town about four miles off. "And another at the intersection of the county road and Highway 50. But they can be hard to hear if the wind really gets up, so I like to make sure they have their weather radios and flashlights and fresh batteries. Mrs. Parry has a basement, but Mrs. Harthcock only has a cellar, and she has trouble lifting the door sometimes, so I come by and open it for her. Just in case the storm gets serious."

I stare at him for a moment, absorbing the fact that Caleb is not only handsome as hell, polite, and endearingly direct, but that he also takes time out of his day to go check on nearby widows. It's like he came out of some Perfect Man machine.

His roommate is a very lucky man.

Caleb notices me staring at him, and he gives me an easy smile, although his hands are back to that restless flexing again. And that's the moment Mrs. Parry emerges with a bag of jars, gives me a fond hug as if we've known each other for years, and lets Caleb kiss her on the cheek.

"I know the drill, son," she says as he's opening his mouth to say something. "I've got the weather radio on full volume and an arsenal of flashlights at the ready. Now you go tend to your work and let me tend to mine."

Caleb gives her a final peck on the cheek, along with a sheepish *you got me* smile that makes my pulse race, and then heads back for the truck. I'm about to follow when Mrs. Parry catches my wrist.

I stop and turn.

"You would be good for them, you know," she says softly. I'm about to gently deflect this, to find some way to hint to her that Caleb isn't interested in a sweetheart because he already has one named Ben, when she says, "It's more complicated than you think. Just keep an open mind."

"Mrs. Parry, with all due respect, my mind is plenty open, and I completely understand what's going on with Caleb."

The smile she gives me is a little sad and a lot pitying. "You don't yet. But you will. And I hope that plenty-open mind will stay that way when you do."

CHAPTER FOUR

CALEB

Ireland seems pensive when she finally climbs into the truck. Greta nestles her head in Ireland's lap without so much as a friendly lick first, and I find myself jealous of a damn dog. I want my head in Ireland's lap.

I want to give friendly licks.

Lots of them.

Until she screams my name.

I'm both irritated and grateful Mrs. Parry mentioned Ben. Irritated because I wanted to ease Ireland into the idea, because I wanted to seduce her to it slowly. Bracket her with me on one side and Ben on the other and palm her ass again while he kisses the lavender lipstick right off her mouth.

God. That ass.

The moment I caught her tumbling out of my cab with that madness-provoking skirt riding up her thighs...the moment I realized I had my hand on one of her softest, lushest curves—and so close to her most secret place—I nearly lost it. My dick, already thickening from the mere sight of her, went fully erect in less than a second. It was everything I could do to keep myself from pulling her tighter against me and grinding that hot column of flesh into her round cheeks. Everything I could do to keep from sliding my hand from her bottom to the luscious lace-covered lips between her legs.

Especially after that choked-off *oh* she made.

Especially after she arched against me.

Had it been some other woman, I might have. Because I wouldn't have cared what happened next. But I *did* care what happened next because I want more than a cheap grope with Ireland. I want to make her mine—make her *ours*.

Besides, Ben and I don't start things apart. Or finish them apart, for that matter. So yes, I was irritated when Ben's name came up, but I was grateful too, precisely because we don't do things separately. I needed that reminder, and it was as good a time as any for Ireland to learn there is a man named Ben who I live with.

I do wish I knew what Mrs. Parry said to Ireland before she climbed into the truck, though. She's very quiet now, and I don't know her well enough to interpret her silence.

I'm going to do everything I can to change that. Starting now.

"Your car," I say, giving a final wave to Mrs. Parry as we circle through the short gravel-speckled grass to go back down her driveway. "I can probably get it free now with my truck, but my concern is that it will get stuck in a different part of the road and you'll be in the same mess. It might be easier if we plan on coming back tomorrow or even the day after."

I steal a glance over at her, not missing the way her knee jogs slightly in agitation.

"I thought that might be the case," she says. God, her voice is irresistible. I can't wait for Ben to hear it, to hear how smoky and breathless it is. "I noticed there was a hotel off the interstate—I could take a cab there—unless there's a place in Holm I could stay."

She sounds doubtful about the last thing, and she should, because Holm consists of four hundred people, a bar, a volunteer library, and more churches than you'd think a town of its size could sustain. But no hotel. There used to be rooms for rent over the bar, but Ben stopped that when he bought the place, because the effort of keeping up the rooms wasn't worth the one or two customers a month.

"There's not a place in Holm," I say, turning onto the road to head back to my farm. "And I'll take you back to the hotel if you'd like, but you're more than welcome to stay at the farm. I could talk to your boss and explain about the car and the storm if you're worried about the extra time away from the office?" I know Drew would understand—he's one of the most laid-back guys I've ever met. The kind of guy who offers to help you move a couch and doesn't even notice if you don't offer free pizza in exchange.

"I can handle my own boss," Ireland says dryly, and I get the feeling my offer might have been overstepping a little.

Well, tough. She better get used to being pampered and taken care of, because I want to make it my life's work.

And that's after *only an hour together.* Christ, I have it bad.

The road is straight and easy, despite the mud, and I risk another look over at her. She has this look on her face—a twist of her lips that looks self-knowing and rueful, a slightly determined furrow of concentration on her forehead—and it's the look of an impulsive person who's trained themselves not to be impulsive. It's the look of someone spontaneous and brave who's forced themselves into a box of stiff reserve.

I should know. I've spent the last five years unboxing Ben after his last deployment.

"I promise I'll keep you safe from the storm. And that you're safe in every way in my house."

She lets out a long breath, and it's hard to read her tense posture. Is she tense because she wants to say yes? Because she doesn't know how to say *no*?

"It's not that," she replies. "I just don't want to intrude on you and Ben is all."

I'm back to irritated with Mrs. Parry.

"It's no intrusion, I promise. We've got a guest bedroom—shame not to use it when it's called for." It would be a shame to have her sleeping in the guest room instead of mine, but I keep that thought to myself.

Come out of that box, I want to coax her. *Be brave for me, little peach.*

"You know, it *would* make the assignment easier," she rationalizes aloud, her knee still bouncing. "Drew really wants to put together something magical for this client, and the more pictures I can gather, the better."

I nod. Drew mentioned the client on the phone to me—the Kansas Tourism Board—and how he hoped it would be a stepping stone to even bigger accounts.

"And it will be more convenient this way, certainly..." She smooths that tight, tempting skirt over her soft thighs, and I can't help but track the movement with my eyes, wishing it were my own hands moving over her body. "Okay. I'll stay with you, as long as it's really no imposition?"

I can still feel the warm heft of her peach-shaped bottom in my hand.

"No imposition," I murmur, shifting in my seat to relieve the pressure on my cock. "None at all."

⚛

My folks died when I was in college—my dad of a heart attack and my mom just a couple of years later from cancer—so the farmhouse has been officially mine for thirteen years...but hardly anything has changed since I took over the place.

Some of the equipment is newer, sure, and I have Greta-dog instead of my old collie Connor, but the house is still the same white, gabled affair—two stories of modest turn-of-the-century architecture, with a nice porch, big glinting windows, and a windmill right outside. I keep the land around it real trim and nice, and the same with the outbuildings and barns. All of it is freshly painted, and the grass is cut into a low green carpet nearly as far as the eye can see.

But it's humble for sure. It's practical. And I have to wonder what Ireland is thinking as we rattle down the gravel driveway to the house. Girl like her, with the slinky clothes and hair like silk, she's probably used to something more hip. Exposed brick and city views and all that. Here, the only view is of fields and the pond shining like a mirage behind the house—and the top of the water tower down in Holm.

I want her to like it anyway. I want her to like *me* anyway. And I think I get my first wish as she steps out of the truck and stares around her.

"Wow," she whispers, the wind tossing her hair. It also plasters her blouse against her body, showing me every place she curves and dips and rounds.

My hands are itching to touch her again, to shape over her body the way the wind is right now.

"You like it?" I ask, trying not to sound too eager.

She looks into the dark clouds crawling over the brown-green hills and then at the wind-whipped oaks and cottonwoods around the house. Tall, branching sunflowers bob and nod from the sides of the driveway and around the front porch. "It's beautiful out here," she says softly.

"It is," I agree with no small amount of pride. "Let's get you settled inside, and then I'll give you a tour before the rain starts for real. Maybe you can start finding places to take pictures. Forecast says it's supposed to be nice and sunny tomorrow after the storm blows through."

Ireland hums in agreement, and the sound goes straight to my balls. It's the kind of hum an aroused woman would make, and even though I know she's just stirred up by the pretty scenery and maybe the pictures she'll be able to take, my body doesn't care. My body wants to crush her back against the truck, shove up her skirt, and show her exactly what a country boy is good for.

I behave, though, and grab her bag from inside the cab and lead her into the house. She pauses at the porch to finger the petals of a sunflower, and I make a mental note to give her entire bouquets of them every chance I get—buckets and bushels of them if necessary.

Our footsteps echo across the old hardwoods once we come through the front door, and I point out the living room, the kitchen, and the old-fashioned parlor near the front.

"Is Ben here?" she asks, sounding a little nervous.

I wish I could tell her not to be nervous because Ben's going to be head over heels in an instant for her, but that would require too much explanation. And besides, I'm not aiming to yank her into our life without her having the chance to learn about us. What Ben and I share is...unusual. There was never a moment we didn't know we'd have to be real clear with any woman about what we wanted so she could choose that unusual thing for herself.

Some women chose yes. Some women didn't.

And after Mackenna left us when Ben got home from the war, we almost stopped looking altogether. It seemed easier to spend the nights alone than risk that kind of pain again.

But Ireland...something about Ireland makes me want to try again. *Well, not just something*, I admit to myself as I watch Ireland climb up the stairs and then follow behind her. Her skirt hugs the rounded curves of her ass and hips and pulls around thighs that I know would be so very plush around my waist and hips. Heavy and warm and soft over my shoulders as I settled in to taste her...

And her hair hangs like some kind of dark magic down her back, the sway and swish of it as she climbs mimicking the sway and swish of her hips and highlighting the contours of her waist—which dips in more than enough for my arms to slide around to toy with her breasts.

It's not just something *about her. It's* everything *about her.*

She's got that body that makes me feel like a caveman, a body that offers lush handfuls even for my big hands, a body that promises a warm welcome on cold winter nights. That hair and that playful mouth with its quirky lipstick. Her light-blue eyes and sultry voice.

But even more than that, there's something simmering under the surface of her that I want to touch, even if it burns me. She reminds me of one of the wild kittens we've got in spades out here—she'll play once she decides she likes you, but until then, all you'll get is quivering, wary stillness. But once you can coax her into playing, she'll play with claws and teeth and still you'll be grinning the whole time. She reminds me of Ben that way, although Ben's more lion than kitten.

Ireland turns at the top of the stairs, waiting for me, and I touch the back of her elbow to guide her to the guest bedroom, wishing I could touch more. The small of her back. The sensitive skin between her shoulder blades. Maybe even wrap my hand in her hair and pull until she gasps ever so faintly.

Ireland steps into the room, and there's still enough light even with the clouds rolling in that the dust is visible in the air. But the creaky metal bed has a fresh set of sheets and clean quilt laid over the top—it's not unheard of for Ben to bring home one of the town drunks to sleep it off here at the farm rather than in the sheriff's drunk tank—so we keep the room and the nearby bathroom pretty clean.

All the same, the room is fairly minimal—white walls, the quilt-covered bed, and an old dresser—with only the window and a framed cross-stitch pattern on the wall for decoration. There aren't even any curtains.

I fidget a little in the doorway, watching the storm-tinted daylight gleam along the silk of Ireland's shirt, and I have the same discomfort I felt outside the house. What if this isn't good enough for her? Nice enough or new enough or—

"I love it," she says simply, spinning to face me. There's that smile on her face again, lips twisting up in some kind of private joke, like she's only just caught herself from doing something she'll regret.

I'd do anything to know what.

I set her bag on the bed. "Do you have something you'd rather change into?" I ask, hoping that's not rude as hell to ask, but surely she doesn't want to tramp around the farm in that tight skirt—as much as I wouldn't mind the sight. Or the excuse to help her over fences or up into the hayloft...

"I do have some jeans," she muses aloud. "No other shoes, though. I just didn't think..." She drifts away to the window, looking out to the grass and sunflowers and, farther off, to the fields waist-high with golden wheat. "I guess I didn't think about how it would be different," she finishes in a soft voice, almost as if she's talking to herself more than me.

It seems like she feels good about the different, not bad, and I give a quiet exhale of relief. Of course, I want her to like it here. I want her to like everything about here.

I want her to stay here.

Slow down. You've only known her for half an afternoon, and Ben hasn't even met her yet.

And if Ben doesn't feel the same as I do...then I'll have to give up this craving for her, this clenching urge to bring her close. He and I are a package deal and have been since the day I helped him pick up a pile of spilled crayons in kindergarten.

"Ben's sister sometimes comes to stay with her wife and kids," I say, "and we have some boots for her here. If you'd like to try them out, they might be better than the shoes you've got on."

Ireland gives me a smile—a real one now, not one of her secretive and slightly unhappy ones. "I'd like that," she replies.

"Then I'll let you change," I say, and then I leave her in the room, closing the solid wood door and resisting the urge to linger like a pervert in the doorway. I don't need to hear the sounds of fabric rustling over skin to know it will make me hard. I don't need to hear her small sighs and steps to know I'll want to hear those sounds every morning for the rest of my life.

So I go downstairs, put out a bowl of food for Greta along with a bowl of leftover chicken for the barn cats, and then I finally text Ben.

You still coming home this afternoon?

Thursdays are one of the days someone else closes the bar down, and Ben and I have a standing...well, not date, really. It's not like that.

I mean, it's not *not* like that either.

Yes.

It's a terse reply, but it doesn't bother me—Ben's been short with words and even shorter with smiles since his first stint in the Korengal Valley. One of the reasons Mackenna left us all those years ago.

> *There's someone here from*
> *Drew's company to take pictures.*
> *Ireland Mills. She's staying with*
> *us because of the storm.*

No reply from Ben, which isn't surprising. He would consider that text a conveyance of information that doesn't require a reply, not a lead-up to something bigger.

Which it is.

> *I like her, Ben.*

That's all I have to say, because when it comes down to it, I'm pretty simple with my words too.

Three dots appear and then disappear and then reappear again. I must have surprised him.

Finally, he answers.

Be there in an hour.

And that's as much as I'll get out of him until he arrives, I'm sure.

I put my phone in my back pocket, and then footsteps down the stairs make me turn.

And swallow.

Ireland has toes painted a bright, cute kind of blue, and a toe ring winks off her right foot. I wasn't expecting these adorable wild-child feet to come out of those fancy office shoes of hers. And then—holy hell—she's in jeans.

Lots of girls Ireland's size don't wear jeans, or at least they don't wear tight jeans. But Ireland's got on jeans that hug every delicious line of her body, tight enough that I can see the tempting shape of her groin. And then she finishes coming down the stairs, and my brain sort of goes blank, white and blinded, like after a bright flash of lightning.

She's not wearing her shirt anymore.

Instead, she's in this painfully thin camisole thing—maybe what she was wearing underneath her silk shirt to begin with. I can see the lace whorls of her bra through it. I can see the slight shadows where her nipples are.

I can barely breathe. Between the tight jeans and the hardly-even-there camisole, I can visually trace every three-dimensional curve of her. The places where she's full and soft. The places that would give under my touch, under my body if I covered her frame with mine and slowly entered her.

When I was thirteen, we had to look at old paintings in art class, and lots of them had naked women. But not like the naked women you'd see in the dirty magazines a guy might steal from his old man. The women in these paintings were so *womanly*, with soft rolls of flesh around their bellies and dimpled asses and thighs. With the coy *vees* between their legs so plump and inviting. Some of the kids giggled when we looked at the pictures. But me, I couldn't breathe right, couldn't stop staring. After I raced home and did my chores for the day, I locked myself in my room and clumsily shoved my hand down my pants until I climaxed in a juvenile mess thinking of those plump pussies with their shyly pouting lips. Those navels buried deep in bellies you knew would be so soft, so giving, and those thighs and upper arms you could grab and grab and grab...

Ever since then, I knew. The way other boys had *types*—freckled or blond or dark-haired—I had a type too. Stretch marks are my freckles, and dimples and rolls are my hair color. I never worried so much about the why; it seems to me like men never have to defend liking blondes, after all. It's just my type. It's just what I like.

And fuck me, Ireland is *it*. Like every Rubens painting brought to life, with that plump shape between her legs, with her camisole revealing the places where her jeans can't contain her.

"You okay?" she asks as she finishes descending the stairs, her eyebrows furrowed a little. "You look upset."

Not upset, I want to growl. *Fucking horny.*

But I manage not to. I tilt my head toward the kitchen, where a back door leads to a screened-in porch and the spare pair of boots. After I find her some clean socks of mine—which bunch around the ankles they're so big on her little feet—and we get her into the boots, we head outside. I was so distracted by Ireland's body that I didn't notice she brought down her camera with her, but it comes out now as we walk around, with her pointing it at various things and then fiddling with the settings and muttering to herself and pointing it at the same things again. It slows down the tour, but I don't mind. I like watching her. I like how she looks in boots, silhouetted by distant hills and dark clouds, and I like how Greta plops down into the grass at her feet whenever she stops to mess with her camera. I like how the wind kisses the hair off her shoulders. I like everything about this moment, and if I had a fancy camera of my own, I'd take a picture too.

Finally we get to the old barn. Since I use the new, metal building farther out back for my big equipment, this one is mainly empty save for the tractor I use to mow and a single cow named Clementine. There's also a makeshift office in the corner—just a desk and a lamp, really—that I use to work on administrative stuff when the weather's nice. Or when Ben's in one of his moods and needs space.

Ireland stops by Clementine's stall. "This is your only cow?"

"This isn't a dairy farm, peach. We do wheat and some alfalfa, and that's about it."

"But," she says, peering into the stall where Clem is currently flicking flies off her back with her tail and staring at the wall, "I thought farms were supposed to have lots of animals."

"Here, we've just got Greta-dog, Clem, and too many stray cats," I say. *Way too many.* But I've never had the heart to do anything about them. Ben brings some up to the county vet when he has time to get them fixed, but it never seems to matter.

"Then why the one cow? For milk or something?"

"I get my milk from the SuperSaver." I laugh. "No, Clem was my Four-H bucket calf."

Ireland blinks at me as if I've just spoken in ancient Greek. "Four what?"

"Four-H—it's like—" God, how to explain Four-H to someone who doesn't know about it? Growing up, it had been just as much a part of life as church or the annual Holm parade. "It's a youth program all over the country, and I know they got lots of things you can do, but most kids out here did their plant and animal programs. When I was a boy, I had to raise a bucket calf, which is Clem here. Fed her from a bottle and everything," I say fondly, joining Ireland at the stall door. "She's plenty old now—older than most cows live to be, so she probably won't be here with us for much longer."

Clem huffs at that, which makes Ireland smile.

The wind is strong enough to make the wood of the barn creak around us, and outside the open door, I can see the first streaks of scattered silver rain. Won't be long before the storm's really here, and I send a quick prayer up to heaven that it won't tear up the fields or damage any of the equipment. Sometimes it feels like I can never get the weather going for me the right way—I need the sunshine but not the excessive heat that bakes the ground up drier than cornbread, and I need the rain but not the kind that comes with wind intent on flattening my barn.

Camera raised, Ireland snaps a picture of the scowling clouds framed by the door, and as she walks toward the opening, still snapping away, she becomes framed by it. Her curvy rear in those jeans, the dramatic inward dip of her waist, those bare arms...

I drift toward her without really knowing what I'm doing, my mind full of her and my body full of something hot and restless. She's just outside the doorway now, taking a picture and then frowning at the camera screen, and the indecisive rain has left a few plump droplets along her collarbone.

I'm transfixed by those raindrops on her skin.

You should ask. You should ask. Ask, ask, ask.

But I don't ask, and there's no excuse for it, and I deserve whatever hell she heaps on my head afterward. I know I do.

I reach out and touch a raindrop on her collarbone.

A breath stabs into her, and her startled blue gaze meets mine as her body shivers under my touch. I know how she feels—my own breath is stabbing at me, and I can feel every part of me trembling to touch her. Every part of me except for the one part that's rock hard and throbbing rather than trembling.

"Caleb?" She whispers the question and lets out a small puff of breath when I raise my rain-wet finger to my mouth.

"Yes, peach?" I swipe another raindrop off her collarbone, and another, enjoying the way the water then rolls down her chest and underneath her camisole.

Her nipples pucker into tight buds, and I think I forget my own name.

"I thought..." she says, all dazed and woozy sounding, "I thought that you—"

But she doesn't finish her sentence because I kiss her.

I kiss her hard and fierce, giving in to the hunger swelling up inside me, and I do what I've been longing to do all day and slide my arms around her waist and pull her body flush to mine.

I groan into her mouth the moment our forms meet. She's just as luscious and warm as I knew she would be, and my hard cock nestles right against her belly. Her full tits press hard against my chest, and I yank her even closer to feel more of them. More of her. Swallowing her kisses and moans all the while, demanding entrance to her mouth and then exploring inside the same way I want to tongue her cunt later—with flickers and licks and long, massaging strokes. And she opens to me so beautifully, arching her back into my hold and sliding her arms around my neck, kissing me back just as thoroughly as I kiss her.

My fingers twine through her hair, and I walk her back so she's pressed against the outside of the barn, raising my other arm to protect her bare shoulders from the rough wood. And then I really kiss her, pressing her hard against the wall, making her feel how tall and strong I am, making her feel how hard I ache for her. I slip a thigh between her legs, and she shudders at the contact against her pussy, rocks against me, and gasps into my mouth.

I drop my mouth from hers to the point of her chin and then up her jawline to her ear.

"What was it, peach?" I ask her as I nibble on her earlobe.

"What...what was what?" she asks hazily, still rocking against my thigh.

"You said before that you thought something about me, but you didn't say what."

"Oh," she breathes with a little laugh. "It seems silly now. Forget about it."

I've got my face in her neck now, and shit, she smells so good. Like flowers and all sorts of expensive womanly things. The kind of smell that makes you think of stores that have pianos and chandeliers inside them. "Tell me, Ireland," I say, nipping at her neck and then licking it until she shivers. "Say it."

I don't want her to censor herself around me. I don't want to be a reason for that twisting, self-mocking smile, and I don't want to be a reason for her to bite back what she really wants to say. Ever, and that means starting now.

She sighs happily at my attentions to her neck and then admits, "I thought you and Ben were a couple."

I stop.

Freeze, really.

And pull away.

She lets out a wrecked exhale as I do, as if it pains her to be separated from my body. Which, same. My own body is pulsing and aching and screaming to be back against hers. My mouth is lonely, and my thigh is cold without the hot weight of her cunt on it.

But still I pull back and run a hand through my hair. "Shit," I mumble.

She blinks at me. "I didn't mean to offend you," she says. "I just thought *roommate* might be some kind of euphemism, you know? And really, if you *are* offended, then I'm sorry because that's really narrow-minded of you—"

"I'm not offended," I interrupt. "Hell, Ben's sister is gay. Of course I'm not offended. I just..."

You just what, Caleb? Were about to ignore years of loyalty to Ben so you could dry hump next to a barn like a teenager?

Ireland is looking at me carefully now, and that kind of scrutiny plus her kiss-swollen lips and mussed hair is enough to make my torso clench again. Fuck, I want to kiss her senseless. I want to press myself back against her, but I can't.

Ben and I start things *together*. That means I need to wait for him.

"So you and Ben," she says. "Just roommates?" There's a hint of vulnerability in her voice as she asks, and I know what she really means.

She means: am I taken? Am I fucking around with her when I have no right to?

The problem is that I don't know what the right word is for Ben and me. We're not gay in the way Ben's sister is, and we're definitely not straight. But even *bisexual* feels incomplete to me, like it's one note on a piano, and what Ben and I share is a complicated but quiet melody.

A melody that needs a third person.

Shit, I'm no good at metaphors either.

"We're not just roommates," I tell Ireland honestly. "But it's not like... There's more to it than that." I run my hand over my hair again, feeling frustrated that I'm not better with words.

I'm a simple man. I like big girls, Kansas sunrises, and my dog, Greta. I like sharing those things with my best friend.

And as such a simple guy, I'm no good at explaining anything more complicated than a missing ball bearing.

"Oh," Ireland says, clearly still confused. She bites her lip, and my eyes fix on that spot like it holds the answer to every question I've ever wanted to know. "So this kiss...is it a secret from Ben? Because I don't like being a secret."

A small flame of hurt shines in her eyes, and I realize she's been someone's secret before. I wish I could find whoever it is and wring their neck, but I set that aside for now. I touch her chin and lift her face to mine so I can look her in the eyes. "It's not a secret, I promise. What I feel for you isn't a secret either; Ben already knows. But he and I—well, maybe it's just easier to explain when he gets here."

"Try me now," she says stubbornly, but at that moment a huge gust of wind catches the barn door on the other side, slamming it back against the wall with an ominous crack. More raindrops slice through the air, and I drop a kiss on her forehead.

"Gotta batten down the barn," I say. "And bring some stuff inside from the office. I promise, Ben will be here soon and we'll talk through everything, but until then, you should go inside the house and get you and your camera out of the rain."

I think she wants to argue more, but the racing wind makes it near impossible to argue, and she looks like she knows it. And I can tell from the way her hand tightens around her camera that she has very little interest in discovering how waterproof it is. With a frustrated shake of her head, she heads back to the house, Greta following at her heels without so much as a goodbye tail wag for me.

And even through the rain, I can still see the hypnotic denim-covered sway of Ireland's peach-shaped ass. God, what it would be like to peel those wet jeans off her.

Ben can't get here soon enough.

CHAPTER FIVE

IRELAND

I should be pissed, but when I get inside the storm-dark house, I only feel confused. Aroused. Achy in a way I never felt with Brian...or anyone else, for that matter. I stand there for a moment, unsure of what to do, simply watching the rain coming down in front of the porch. And then I turn back to the barn. I see Caleb outside, the mouthwateringly huge muscles in his shoulders and back straining as he struggles to close the barn door against the wind.

Jesus, everything about him. Those broad shoulders and sculpted arms, those flat abs and that thick erection I can still feel against my belly. It stretched all the way to his hip, a massive monster, and it wanted me.

I wanted it.

And then there's the way he touched and looked at me—all lust and grabbing and possessive. I've never been touched like that, like someone couldn't get enough of my body, and the parts of my body that Brian always avoided—hell, the parts I avoid touching myself—Caleb put his hands all over. He cupped my hips and slid his hands over the places where my waist turned into the soft convexity of my belly. He ran his hands over my ass *and* my thighs. His palm flexed against the parts of my back where my bra dug into my skin. And the whole time, I felt nothing from him but hot, throbbing desire.

This is bonkers, right? This whole thing. And yet it doesn't feel crazy at all. It feels necessary. Natural. The kiss and this hot longing I have in the aftermath. I try to remind myself that I started the day wanting to be professional, that technically this is a work trip, that Caleb is my boss's friend.

That it's unseemly to need to fuck under these conditions.

But watching Caleb in his wet T-shirt as he wrestles against the wind... Well, I'm willing to set aside professional seemliness just this once. After all, isn't it like a known fact that men fuck on business trips all the time? Why not me? If I'm single and Caleb and Ben are...well, whatever version of single exists for them?

Outside, the barn door is finally closed, and I watch Caleb go around the side to where I'm guessing the smaller door is, the one close to his rustic office setup. He said he had things to gather. He said Ben would be here soon.

I don't want to wait. Not for explanations and not for fixing the coiling need at the apex of my thighs.

It's more complicated than you think, Mrs. Parry said.

Well, it is certainly shaping up to be that.

I push open the door, and Greta looks up from her bed near the wood-burning stove, glances at the rain-soaked world outside, and lays her head back down, as if to say *thanks, but no thanks*. With a smile, I head out into the rain, cutting a breathless and wet jog across the short grass to the barn, having to circle around the long way to find the small door. It's propped open, and the growing roar of the rain is enough to mask my footsteps as I come inside.

And I thank God for that the minute my eyes adjust to the dim light inside the barn, because Caleb is standing slightly angled away from me with his jeans hanging open around his hips, the muscles in his arms bunching as he strokes and pumps at his straining cock.

Sweet merciful Jesus, the man is *big*. Long enough that the swollen head moves out of his giant hand as he fucks his fist back to the root and thick enough to make me swallow in a combination of lust and *oh shit*, because taking that part of him inside me would be a feat in itself.

The taut flex of his hips and the top of his ass where it peeks above his slackened belt is just the garnish on this masculine feast in front of me, and if I thought I was wet and aroused before, it's nothing like *now*. Now, when my nipples actually hurt they're so hard and I can feel the emptiness in my core like a living, keening thing.

I creep around the corner into an empty stall so I can stay hidden in case he turns—which is wrong. It's so wrong. In real life I'd never watch someone without their consent. But I *felt* him as we kissed. I felt his hands and his erection and his insatiable hunger for my body. And he didn't make it sound like he regretted our kiss, only that he wanted to wait for Ben...so maybe he wouldn't mind that I'm watching?

Maybe he'd even like it?

Except then again, maybe he wouldn't? Because he *did* lie to me, and he's not in here waiting for Ben by shuffling stuff around his office—he's in here jerking off his beautiful dick without me.

And okay, maybe it's a little bananas that I'm hurt by that, given that we just met and it's not *exactly* like I want him to go *Clan of the Cave Bear* on me and fuck me right in the wet grass...but also it's not exactly like I don't want it either? Sex with my ex-boyfriend was lights-out, missionary, and always came with this weird philanthropic vibe, like he was doing me a favor by fucking me. But with Caleb, it was like I made him wild, like I made him hungry for more of me, and seeing him do something as brutally primal as beat his cock the minute I'm not around him is rather exhilarating.

So maybe he wouldn't mind me watching or maybe he would, but the thing is that I've never had this feeling before—this *power*—knowing that I've driven a virile man past all politeness and civilized pretending simply just by being me, and there's no way in hell I can walk away from it now.

Plus there'd be no walking away from it anyway, because it's possibly the sexiest thing I've ever seen in my entire life.

Which changes in a matter of seconds with what happens next.

Heavy footsteps echo through the barn, and I nearly leap out of my skin when I realize someone walked *right past me* and I didn't even notice. The storm was loud and I was watching the delicious spectacle that was Caleb, and...yeah. Maybe I wasn't as alert as a voyeuring girl should be.

Luckily, the man walking up to Caleb doesn't seem to notice I'm here—I'm tucked far enough back into the empty stall that I'm probably hidden from view—and who would think to look in a shadowy stall for a peeping Tonya anyway? I almost wish he had seen me, though, so it would've given Caleb enough time to cover up his, um, activities. Because I have no idea who this man is, but there's no way he's not going to see exactly what Caleb is doing, and God, Caleb will be so embarrassed—

"'Bout time," Caleb says gruffly. His hand slows on his erection but doesn't stop, and he angles his body ever so slightly to greet this newcomer. Who steps into the lamplight coming from the desk, and holy fuck. Holy fuck. Holy fuck.

I'm glad the storm echoes and reverberates around the barn because the breath I draw seeing this man is not quiet. It's jagged and rough and out of my control. I can't help it, though, because this man is the perfect complement to Caleb's open, wholesome good looks.

Eyebrows slash over eyes so dark, they look nearly vampire-black in the shadowed barn, and a rough cover of stubble can't hide how *pretty* his face is—high cheekbones and a perfect jaw and a nose as straight and strong as any model's. Furthermore, the stubble only serves to highlight his painfully perfect mouth, which curls up slightly at the corners as if it was formed to do so. But nothing about his face looks happy, and if you mistook that curled-up mouth for a smile, those glittering onyx eyes would chill you right out of the notion that this man smiled. Ever.

Longish hair, dark and thick and tousled, frames that magnetic face, and it's paired with a body as tall and firm as Caleb's, though this man has a leaner bent to him—less bulk and more grace.

I breathe out again as it occurs to me in a clit-throbbing surge of insight that he must be—

"Ben," Caleb groans, his hand starting to speed up again. I watch, fascinated, as Ben leans against the desk and crosses his arms, his gaze on the other man's stroking hand.

"She must have you twisted up something good if you're out here like this," Ben says silkily.

"Yeah," Caleb says, dropping his head down. I can only just hear them talking over the din of the rain drumming on the barn, and I can't hear the sound of Caleb's hand on his flesh at all, which is very disappointing, as I think I'd like that sound very much.

I creep a little bit closer to the stall opening, hoping the two men are distracted enough that they won't see me peering out. Ben leans in a little closer, as if to give Caleb an order, and his voice carries over the rain, as if the words themselves are made of silk and can thread themselves through the raindrops.

"Show me how much you want her, Caleb. Show me how much you want to give her."

"Fuck," Caleb whispers. "I want her so much. I want to give her...so... much..."

His lips part as his hand pumps his cock faster, and his other hand drops to cup himself, and my cheeks burn with needy heat when I realize he's talking about come. He wants to give me lots and lots, and it's so caveman and so fucking hot. And even hotter is the way Ben stirs up Caleb more with his dark words, the way Ben ignores his own erection now straining at the front of his jeans.

"That's it," Ben coaxes. "Show me. I haven't seen you this worked up in ages. Is this all for her? Do you want to fuck her? Do you want to push into her pussy and fuck her until you come?"

"Yes," moans Caleb. "God."

"Did you make her wet, Caleb? Did you show off this big, strong body of yours to make her want you?"

Yes! I want to shout from my hiding place. *Yes, I'm wet. Yes, I want him!*

Caleb's response is another low moan, utterly helpless, and a wave of lust rocks me back.

It does the same for Ben, I think. His eyes flutter closed and his hand drops to his cock, still caged behind his fly. He doesn't stroke himself or even palm himself properly, simply pressing against his need as if he can make it go quiet.

Unfortunately, nothing is going quiet on my end. The raw sight of Caleb panting as he pumps into his hand and the somehow-just-as-erotic sight of cold, sharp Ben on the edge of succumbing himself is enough to make me desperate.

I slowly work from my half crouch to a kneeling position and unbutton my jeans, grateful again for the storm, which hides the metallic purr as I tug down my zipper. I slide down the front of my panties and shudder the moment my finger grazes my clit. I don't think that's ever happened to me before. Normally it takes a fair amount of porn or several pages of a smutty book to get myself going, but now I think I could climax with just a few circles of my finger.

"Come all over your hand," Ben urges. "All over this floor. Like you're coming all over her cunt and thighs to mark your territory."

My fingers delve lower, sliding between the lips at the apex of my thighs and finding them impossibly slick. Almost embarrassingly wet. But I don't care because it's all part of this heady feedback loop: Ben voyeuring on Caleb as I voyeur on them both, all of us unable to keep our hands away from the places where we ache to fuck and be fucked. It feels as undeniable as the rain, as urgent as the wind. If I don't come, I might die right here in this barn, only mere feet away from two men who look born to screw.

"Yeah," Caleb mutters. His head falls back, his face tilted toward the ceiling with closed eyes and an expression of ecstatic agony, and then with a soft grunt, his cock releases a fountain of thick, white semen. Jolt after jolt of it, landing all over the dirty floor, and it feels like it comes forever, like his orgasm must have been pent up for years and years, because there's so *much*, and the noises he makes are the noises of a man who's been denied for far too long. And I'm so close myself, so very close; I'm close enough that I bury my teeth in my lower lip in preparation to stifle my gasp, that I brace myself against the contractions I know are imminent.

Out in the circle of lamplight, Ben watches Caleb slowly go still, and they both let out a long breath.

"She must be something," Ben says, the heel of his palm still hard against his fly. He's just as affected by the unfiltered and brutish sight of Caleb coming as I am, but he seems to have more control. Me, I'm on the edge of my own orgasm, my eyes still riveted on the sight of Caleb's unflagging erection. But Ben is still all cool words and careful, catlike posture. Only his palm pressed to his covered cock gives him away.

"She is," Caleb rumbles, still catching his breath. "I can't wait for you to meet her."

"Oh, I don't think I'll have to wait long," Ben replies coolly. "She's right here in the barn with us. Aren't you, Ireland?"

CHAPTER SIX

BEN

I saw her the moment I walked in.

It's a good hiding place, I'll give her that, and with the storm trapping the barn under a dark bowl of clouds and rain, I'm not surprised Caleb didn't notice her in the gloom. Although it's also not hard to get past Caleb. He assumes everyone is as good and honest as he is. That everyone will play by the rules, wear the right uniforms, charge from the front. He made a great football player... Thank fuck he was never a soldier.

But me—I was an excellent soldier. Staying alive in the Korengal meant expecting no one to play by football rules. It meant knowing exits and potential cover. It meant knowing where people were hiding and why they were hiding. Five years hasn't been enough to break me of it—I don't know how many years it will take—and mostly I don't mind the ways the army's changed me. It makes it easy to keep my bar free of brawls and assholes, and right now, it's netted me a gorgeous woman currently staring at me with a bitten lip and wind-mussed hair.

She hesitantly steps out of the stall, a flush high on her cheeks—one I know will be matched on Caleb's face. Thirty-three years old, and he still blushes like he did in grade school when a teacher would call on him and he didn't know the answer.

He tucks himself away, zipping up with an embarrassed rush of breath. "Ireland," he says but stops after only her name. Which I understand, because really what can you say when a woman you like has just seen you beat off? In front of his best friend, no less? I'm not sure how much Caleb has told her about how we operate, but this is a much more dramatic introduction to our dynamic than usual.

However, dramatic or not, I was willing to take the risk. When I walked in and sensed her presence, glancing over to see her completely enraptured by Caleb's unintentional display of lust, I sensed she might be into whatever else I threw her way. And sure enough, I can see the evidence on her body plain as day as she comes closer—nipples like little bullets under her camisole, jeans unbuttoned, a certain breathlessness over and beyond the shock of getting caught.

And immediately, I *know*. I just do. Even without Caleb already wanting her, even without seeing the real and throbbing evidence of that want, I know this Ireland could be *her*. The one.

The one to break the spell of one-night stands and empty nights. The one to see us as more than just a fun joyride or a novelty.

The one to stay.

It's not just her looks, which are gorgeous, or her body, which is perfect, lush and soft and jiggly in all the places we like. But there's something about her gaze, her bitten lip, that suggests an adventuresomeness under the surface. A wildness that's been pinned down and glossed over but that's ready to break free. I'm fascinated. Hooked. I want to crack that glossy surface and tumble down into wild delights together.

Ireland stops a few paces away and tugs on her hair. "Um, hey. I was just..."

She's about to lie. I can see it in her eyes, which are all tensed up around the corners and refusing to meet mine. But I'm not going to let her lie. The stakes are too real, and it's been so long since I've felt anything other than tired and lonely, and I've learned the hard way that being a three takes much more honesty than being a two. Even when it comes to the little things.

So I step forward, grab her hand, and gently lick at her fingertips.

"*Oh*," she mumbles, her eyelashes fluttering closed. "Oh fuck."

Responsive too. I smile to myself as I give the pad of her finger a little scrape with my teeth and watch her shudder. I can already imagine having her and Caleb in bed with me, both of them following my orders...

She realizes too late why I'm licking her fingers and yanks her hand back. Her cheeks go redder than ever.

I run my tongue over my lower lip, tasting the lingering sweetness of her in my mouth. "You were 'just' nothing, Ireland. You were touching yourself. You had those pretty fingers in that sweet little cunt, didn't you? Watching Caleb and me?"

She swallows, blinking fast, but her stare doesn't leave mine, which I like.

"I—yes," she admits in a rush. "I was doing...that. What you said." And then she lets out a little snort of shocked laughter, as if she can't believe she just uttered such a thing out loud.

I'll have her more than simply talking about dirty things before I'm through with her, but I take this as a sign she's ready for something different. Ready for us.

"You were going to lie about it," I murmur. I reach up, wind one of her damp tresses around my finger, and give it a tug. Nothing too hard, not yet, but enough for her to know that when I'm here, I'm in charge. The other side of Caleb's sunny, happy coin. The daddy to our fucked-up little family.

She opens her mouth, and I tug on her hair again. "No lies to us, Ireland. Not now, not ever. Got it?"

"Got it," she whispers.

"Good." My hand still in her hair, I walk her back until her ass hits the edge of Caleb's desk. "Did you come?"

"Wh-What?"

"When you were playing with your pussy. Did you come? Did seeing Caleb jerk that cock make you clench around your fingers, wishing one of us were inside you instead?"

Another swallow. I'm beginning to grow addicted to the sight of them—how they move through her beautiful neck, how nervousness flits across her face right before she decides to be bold. "I didn't come," she says. She bites her lip for bravery and then adds, "But I did wish what you said. That one of you was inside me."

"Or both?"

She lets out a breath. "Or both."

Caleb steps up to her, his own face still flushed but his dick growing hard against his jeans again. "Can we touch you? For real touch you?"

"Oh God, please touch me," she half laughs, half begs. Then another small laugh of shock at her own boldness. "I can't believe I just said that."

I've known her for less than five minutes, and I can believe it. I can see the restless bird inside her fluttering to be free. I've always been good at seeing inside people. Letting them see inside me, however, not so much, but I try not to worry about that right now. I focus on the goddess in front of me with the red flush across her chest and the thighs unconsciously rubbing together.

I tug at Ireland's already-opened jeans just enough to slide my hand inside, pleased to feel the damp tickle of her intimate curls against my fingers. Caleb likes bare pussies, just like in the old paintings that had aroused him so much as a boy, but I like the secret of a woman's hair down there. A private thing, only for lovers to know the feel of. And hers feels amazing, soft and not wiry, gloriously silky. I run my fingertips over her mound, my other hand braced beside her on the desk and my feet crowding hers so she's effectively trapped between me, the desk, and the hulk of Caleb at her side. He runs his nose along the edge of her jaw, teasing her into letting out little huffs of anticipation, cajoling her into opening up to us.

We've done this so many times that the choreography is automatic, effortless, but the difference is that this time Caleb and I aren't just willing participants in some woman's search for a good story, and we aren't merely looking for the nearest consenting body to take the edge off our loneliness.

No, this time we are both shaking with the wanting of this woman. This time, the need to make her *ours* is exactly that; this isn't about fucking and then waking up alone again.

This is important. This is real. I survived four tours relying on my instincts, my ability to just *know* things, and I believe my instincts now.

Ireland belongs to us.

The moment my middle finger grazes her clit, she lets out a low moan and her head drops against my chest, something I like the feeling of immensely. Caleb is usually the one women go to for affection, the one they inherently trust, and it never bothers me. But for some reason, I want Ireland to be different. I want her to see past the parts of me that are cold or intimidating and trust me anyway. Trust I'll take care of her, keep her safe. That there's always gentleness behind the little cruelties I invariably want to give in bed.

I brush my lips against the crown of her head, smelling rain and something expensive, maybe the kind of shampoo you can only buy at salons, or perhaps some other, more mysterious product only those initiated into certain levels of beauty care know about. Either way, the combination of expensive and natural makes me want to kiss her skin until she's a wet, shivering wreck, but I settle for keeping my nose in her hair as my fingers go lower.

Wet.

She's so wet. The pleasing plumpness of her mound and thighs have kept all that wet heat trapped right inside her seam, and the moment I part her lips, there's slickness everywhere. The kind of slick that means a man could slide on in and have her coming in under a minute.

The kind of slick I like.

"Shit," she mumbles against my chest. Caleb kisses her neck and then raises his face to offer me a smile. A real Caleb smile, with a dimple deep enough to show even under his beard and with crinkles around his bright-green eyes.

My heart squeezes hard. The loneliness has been hard on both of us, but maybe on Caleb most of all. I can use loneliness like an armor, but Caleb's different—for him, loneliness will only ever be a cold dagger between his ribs, a slow poison swimming in his veins. We've known since college that whatever's between us only works with a third, but the years since Mackenna's departure have proved it time and again.

We need Ireland. Caleb needs her, and I need Caleb.

I just hope she needs us too.

It takes almost nothing to send her over the edge. I can't even imagine how strung tight she must have been from watching Caleb earlier, because it only takes sliding a finger inside her tight box to make her tense against me and then only a few rolls of my palm against her clit to send her fluttering around my touch. She cries out against my chest, and her hands come up to search for us. One hand fists in my shirt and the other hand fists in Caleb's, and my heart clenches again at the perfect symmetry of it. Her holding on to both of us, both of us surrounding her and keeping her upright as she rides out her ecstasy with my hand down her jeans.

My cock *aches* at it, with how sexy she is like this, with how perfect her cunt is against my hand. With how much I've missed being a three, and I mean really being a three—not picking up a woman for a night and then waking up with Caleb in a hotel room she's already abandoned before dawn.

I need to fuck. And soon.

Ireland slowly comes down from her climax, her body relaxing and her hands unfisting from our shirts. Her face stays against my chest, and I can feel the instant she goes from happily sated to awkwardly embarrassed.

I pull my hand from her jeans and tilt her head up to me. Her eyes are a darker blue after orgasm—something closer to an ocean than a sky—and I can see uncountable thoughts and questions swimming in there.

"Open your mouth," I say in a low voice, and she opens for me. I slide my wet fingers into her mouth, and she closes around them, sucking without me having to tell her to.

Oh yes, she and I are going to get along very well.

"Do you taste yourself?" I ask softly. "Do you taste how much you needed someone to fuck you?"

Her eyes dart over to Caleb, and whatever she seems to see there reassures her.

"Answer me with a nod," I say. "And no lies, remember? Can you taste how badly you needed to be fucked?"

Eyes huge on mine, my fingers in her mouth, she nods, and I remove them, satisfied. "That's right," I say. "And you still need to be fucked, don't you? You need to be between Caleb and me so badly. You need to feel two big cocks hard and leaking for you and you alone."

She looks like her breath is caught in her throat, like all those thoughts swimming in her eyes are just trapped, trapped, trapped, waiting to break free, so I coax her by leaning down and brushing my lips against hers for the very first time. She tastes like mint and lipstick, and her mouth is as soft as her cunt. I lick inside and then pull back to breathe against her lips.

"Be brave, Ireland. Say yes."

"Say yes?" she murmurs.

"Say yes to taking what you want. To taking us."

A little smile crooks her mouth. "You wouldn't be taking me?"

I nip at her jaw and then at that irresistible little smile. "Dirty girl. You know you'll be ours once you say it. So say it. Say yes."

CHAPTER SEVEN

IRELAND

It feels like Ben is asking me about something bigger than a roll in the hay.

I blink up at him and then over to Caleb, my heart racing along with my mind, trying to sift through Ben's words.

Be brave, Ireland.

You know you'll be ours.

Ours. He must mean that within the context of tonight. That if I go to bed with them, they'll be at my sexual service—not...not what my heart keeps tripping over itself imagining.

That there's more. That there could be so much more.

That these men not only want to fuck me but love me.

You're being silly, I scold myself. *And you're overly romanticizing sex. They must do this all the time, and you're just the latest one.*

It makes sense though now, what Mrs. Parry said. *Complicated.* Feeling the two of them touching me and kissing me, feeling their awareness of each other—it was completely different than kissing Caleb against the barn or watching Ben goad Caleb into coming all over his fist. Once the three of us touched, something new sizzled into existence. Something bright and searing. Something that took more than two people.

Yes, that's complicated. Different.

But however electric this thing between us is, however magical, I'm also realistic about what it actually means. I barely even know Caleb and Ben, so how could it mean anything more than just fucking? Besides, I'm very used to the idea that girls who look like me don't get swept into torrid love affairs with hunky country boys. That stuff happens to pretty girls. Skinny girls.

No, this will be sex, plain and simple, no matter what intense words Ben lobs my way.

I still want it.

Why not? Being invited to a threesome with the two handsomest men I've ever laid eyes on? Hell yes, I want that.

When I was a girl, I wanted to climb mountains and sail boats and go places no one else had ever been. I wanted adventures! I wanted fun! And right now, adventure and fun personified are staring me in the face, albeit in a way I never could have imagined as a girl.

Be brave, Ireland.

"Yes," I blurt out, taking Ben's advice and being brave. Being the woman that girl wanted to grow up to be before people started telling her she wasn't the right size for adventures and didn't have the right kind of body for fun. Being who I was before I started being the one to tell myself no—*no, I can't do that; no, people will think you're desperate or trying too hard or too eager to please.*

I've spent too long caging myself in, and it feels good to beam up at the men hulking over me with hungry eyes and big hands and emphatically repeat, "Yes."

It's easy to keep feeling brave as we dart across the grass, the rain coming down in cool silver streaks around us, the wind gusting past in huge buffets that nearly knock us off our feet.

Caleb grabs my hand, his fingers so warm and strong around my own, and then he's pulling me impatiently to the back door as Ben follows behind us. When I look back at Ben through the rain, the wind whips his T-shirt around the tight muscles of his stomach and chest, lifting the hem high enough to reveal glimpses of taut, olive-colored abs and a line of dark hair that disappears into his jeans.

Unf.

We stumble inside in a rain-wet and eager mess, and then I'm pulled up the stairs by Caleb while Ben stalks behind us, his eyes glittering with dark promises I hope to God he keeps.

Caleb leads me into the first room off the upstairs landing, and I know immediately it's his. There's something so basic about it, so *honest*, with the antique lamp on a wooden end table by the big, sturdy bed and a framed aerial picture of the farm on the opposite wall. A Carhartt jacket hangs off the doorknob of the small closet, and a paperback mystery sits facedown on the top of his dresser, the corners curling up slightly, like it got wet at some point. Like he took it with him one day out in the fields and got caught in the rain, or maybe he left it in the truck with the windows down.

For some reason, this little display of carelessness seals it for me. I've definitely got it bad for Caleb Carpenter. He spins me around so I'm trapped in his arms with my back to his chest, and I see Ben kick the bedroom door shut and prowl toward us.

I think it's only a matter of moments before I have it just as bad for Ben too.

It's deep evening now, and with the rain lashing outside, the room is almost completely dark—save for a nightlight glowing dimly in the corner, which is a rather endearing addition to a grown man's room. The light gives a faint burnish to Ben's cheekbones and a deep gleam to his eyes as he walks toward us, stopping a mere inch away from me. I could arch my back and my breasts would press against his chest, and the realization goes through me like a bullet. Suddenly it's all I want to do, to feel my nipples raking against his hard body. To feel one man solid and warm behind me as I rub myself against another. God, even just the thought of it makes me shiver. Talk about being spoiled.

But it's like Ben knows what I'm going to do before I do it; with deliberate slowness and care, he wraps his hands around my wrists and raises them to my chest, and it's less about restraining me than it is keeping me exactly where I am. Keeping me from rubbing against him like a cat.

"You want us to fuck you," Ben says, and he says it like a statement, not a question.

I answer him anyway. "Yes."

Lightning flashes outside, sending his beautiful face into sharp relief and showing me the primal hunger stamped onto his every feature. "Have you ever fucked two men at the same time?" he asks in a low voice, and God, those words in that voice go straight to my core.

Dirty, delicious words.

Dirty, delicious man.

"No," I whisper.

Caleb makes a noise behind me, his restless hands squeezing at me.

"What won't you do, Ireland?"

My brain struggles with a reply—partly because Caleb's hands are busy kneading my ass and hips and I can feel my body responding with fierce, wet need—but partly because I'm not sure I understand. "What won't I do?"

Ben may strike me as a hard man, but when he speaks, his words are patient, if cool. "You say you want to fuck, but fucking is an entire menu of things, sweetheart. It's always better to know your own menu before you start ordering."

I think about this. "Like hard limits?"

"Like hard limits. But also soft limits or preferences. You can do as little or as much as you like with us, and we'll be happy however we get to have you."

No one has ever talked to me about sex like this before. I've had boys ask if it's okay to move forward, if it's okay to do more, but *forward* and *more* always meant some vague notion of everything, like if you're agreeing to sex, then of course you'd also do oral and everything else in between. Like the only real boundary is between everything else and intercourse, and after intercourse, even that boundary goes away.

It's the first time I've thought about sex the way Ben describes it, as an array of things I can pick or not pick, and the freedom it allows me is almost giddying.

But then I genuinely can't think of much. Until Brian, I'd never gotten past some fumbling attempts at oral, and with him, our bed play was painfully tame. I almost *wish* we'd found some boundaries, because that would have meant some degree of exploration, of trying new things. Of being brave.

I look up at Ben, dangerous and sexy as hell in the darkness, and I feel Caleb breathing hard behind me, his thick cock brushing against my ass every time he exhales, and I seize on the impulse, on the adventure of the moment.

"I want to try everything," I say boldly. "All of it. Any of it."

Ben's hands tighten ever so slightly around my wrists. "All is a big word, Ireland. A very big one."

It *is* a big word. That's why it excites me so much. "You'll stop something if I ask you to stop?"

Caleb growls behind me, and I think I've maybe insulted his gentlemanly honor. But I have to know, and in order to know, I have to ask. "Yes, peach," Caleb says. "We'll stop."

I stare at Ben as he inclines his head in a polite nod. "Of course," he replies. "The very moment you ask. Or before the moment you ask, if I'm not certain you're into it."

"Then all of it is fair game," I say decisively. "There's so much I haven't done—so much I want to try. How will I ever know I don't like something if I don't try it?"

Ben's lips twitch. "How indeed."

He steps forward right as Caleb steps back, and he pushes on my wrists as Caleb pulls on my belt loops, and I'm walked backward toward the bed. And then suddenly both men are in front of me and I'm being pushed onto my back on the quilted mattress, and then Ben is crawling over me with predatory grace as Caleb settles next to my side. Ben's hair is long enough to hang around his bladed jaw and equally sharp cheekbones as he does, sending dancing shadows across his sinfully curved lips before he leans down and kisses me.

Hard.

I gasp up into his mouth, not prepared for the onslaught of his kiss after the rather gentle one he gave me in the barn. But I can tell by the way he settles over me, by the way Caleb groans at my side, that this is how Ben likes to kiss, with cruel pressure and deep, possessive strokes of his tongue, giving me no quarter. I can barely breathe, but I don't want to breathe, not if it means turning away from this kiss, a kiss that says *this mouth is mine now.*

You are mine now.

Ben breaks off the kiss to turn my face to Caleb, who kisses me just as deeply but more gently. More sweetly, though the subtle scratch of his short beard keeps it from feeling tame. It's like a reward for enduring Ben's punishing mouth, but if Ben's the punishment, then sign me up for a lifetime of being punished. I'm practically writhing underneath them in need, my body aching to be filled after Ben's claiming touch and then aching even more at Caleb's worshipping mouth.

Ben wedges his thigh between my legs as he lowers himself to his forearms to kiss me even harder, a look of dark pleasure moving across his face as my hips lift of their own accord to chase the friction. "Poor peach," Ben murmurs. "Isn't she a poor girl, Caleb, reduced to fucking my thigh because she's so hard up for it?"

"It's too bad," agrees Caleb. His hand drifts down to my chest, fingers circling one erect nipple, and even through the fabric of my shirt and my bra, it's excruciatingly good. "Wonder if we can help her with that."

Ben leans down for another kiss, and this one has *biting.* He nips at my lips and sucks my tongue and bites along my jaw. He sinks his white teeth hard into my lower lip, and I arch up into him with a cry, and then he turns my head for Caleb to soothe it better, which Caleb does with attentive licks and strokes and sucks.

On and on it goes—a kiss of darkness and near-pain from Ben and then a rewarding kiss of earnest passion from Caleb—one man leaving me wrung out and shaking and then the other man putting me back together again. Until I think I can't stand it anymore, until I think I might perish with the emptiness low inside me. Until I'm begging them shamelessly, with my pelvis rocking up against Ben's thigh and my hands clutching blindly at arms and shoulders and my voice quietly pleading against the rain, "More, more, more."

Ben lifts himself, and with some kind of wordless communication, he and Caleb both shift to peel my clothes off my skin. Ben is efficient, clinical even, but Caleb can't stop his hands from wandering over each new naked inch, and I'm grateful for the darkness. I catch his hand before he can move it from my sternum to my belly, a flush now burning my cheeks at even the idea of him touching me there. His caresses have been so worshipful, so eager, but will they change when he touches that part of me? Without the semi-smoothing barrier of a shirt or jeans, without anything between his fingers and my skin? My breasts and my ass and even my hips... They're the parts of me that are easiest to like for a man, I'm sure. The parts that could almost be like a Kardashian's body—sleek and flat-tummied, a two-dimensional hourglass.

But I'm not sleek. Not in my arms or thighs and definitely not in my belly, which is not two dimensional in the least. And it's stupid, given that Caleb has already pressed against me, given that nothing about my clothes earlier hid my body, but something about my naked belly feels more real and intimate than anything else we're doing.

I don't know if I'm ready to share it with these men. I don't know if I'll ever be ready to share it with any lover, come to that, but especially these two? As fit and tight and hard as their bodies are, how could they still want me if they know how soft and loose I am?

I guide Caleb's hand back to my breast, which is still covered by my bra, hoping to distract him from my belly, and he palms it with the awed happiness of a teenage boy, but I should have known Ben wouldn't miss it. I should have known Ben would see, even in the dark, the things I try to hide. He seems like the kind of man who's very good at seeing what people hide.

He also seems like the kind of man who's good at hiding himself.

Ben finishes tugging off my jeans and panties and then climbs back over me with glittering eyes. "All," he drawls. "*Any*. Those were your words, peach."

"Yes," I say with a dry throat, because I think I know what's about to happen. And it does.

Ben puts his hand over Caleb's and slowly pushes it down from my breast. Down to my belly.

I suck in a breath.

"You can say stop," Ben says in a voice that almost sounds indifferent, but in the haze of the nightlight, I can see the rapid pound of his pulse in his neck. He's aroused. He's edgy.

He likes this, I realize, and I realize also that it's not just the obvious—making out and now having me nearly undressed—but also him moving Caleb's hand. Him nudging me toward something that feels awfully like a boundary. Something scary.

He likes the thrill.

And...I like thrills too. Or I used to, and now I'm relearning how, and this is my first adventure. I can be brave.

I swallow and wet my lips. "I'm not saying stop."

"Good. Because Caleb wants to touch you here. Don't you, Caleb?"

"I do," Caleb groans, his hand flexing over my stomach, running along the curve of it until he reaches my navel. He even caresses the part where my stomach meets my hips and there's this crease I don't think a single other human has ever touched on purpose.

He touches it. Traces it. Follows it across my stomach while he bends down to kiss me.

"Caleb, I think you should take off your clothes now," Ben says in that bossy way of his, which isn't bossy at all. More like matter-of-fact. More like commanding. "Show off that big, strong body of yours and all the parts of you that want to feel her."

Caleb gives me a final kiss and then grins down at me, an irrepressible grin that I can't help but return.

"What about you?" I ask Ben, turning to look up at him. "Any parts of you that want to feel me?"

There's a flash of something like surprise, maybe even pride, across his face, and his mouth curls up at the corners. "There are some indeed," he murmurs, lifting himself off me. And while Caleb undresses, Ben pops open the button of his fly and works his jeans open enough to free the head of his erection, which even in the dim light looks florid-dark and swollen. The sight of him in his black T-shirt and jeans, with just the tip of his cock exposed, is the lewdest thing I think I've ever seen.

I'm panting for it.

Caleb is disrobing now too, fully, tugging off his T-shirt to expose a body unfairly masculine and perfect. His shoulders and chest and back are layered with swathes of swelling muscle, and when he unbuckles his belt and kicks off his jeans and boxer briefs, I see hard thighs that invite salacious squeezing and a tight, firm ass that does the same. Narrow hips, a lightly furred belly, and a heavy erection that bobs as he climbs back onto the bed. He wastes no time in helping me remove my bra, and then he and I are both completely naked. And then there's Ben, who somehow seems filthier than the both of us, more obscene, fully clothed with his rigid cock pushing through the fly of his jeans.

"Now," Caleb breathes, giving me another earnest, bearded kiss, "are you ready for all of it?"

CHAPTER EIGHT

CALEB

Ireland arches into my kiss, smiling into my mouth. "Yes," she says happily. Excitedly. "All of it."

I touch her again because I want to. I have to. I don't think I'll ever be able to stop. Her breath hitches when I run my fingertips over her belly, and I glance up at her face. She has her eyes closed now, as if she's steeling herself for something. For my touch.

"Now that just won't do," Ben says silkily from above both of us. "Open your eyes, Ireland. Watch Caleb touch you."

She blinks up at him and then over to me, her breath still stilted and her face uncertain. But she nods. "Okay." She swallows. "Okay. Touch me."

So I do. I touch the pale skin where the underside of her breast meets her chest. I trace down the slopes that lead to the sides of her waist. I stroke up to the middle and circle her navel, sunk like a deep well into her body, and then I move down to her lower belly with its gentle swell. And then—fuck—that plump pussy, the first time I've touched it. My cock jerks up as my fingers press into the giving flesh, and I groan, dropping my head onto her shoulder. She's even better than those paintings, better than anything a teenage Caleb could have imagined. I roll my head down and start kissing a trail down her belly, nudging Ben aside so I can settle between her legs and kiss at her stomach more easily.

She gasps at every kiss, trying to shy away, but I don't let her. I don't let her roll to the side or try to cover herself. I kiss her belly button and the crease of the place where her thighs meet her hips. And soon I have my mouth where I want it: kissing along her secret silk curls to her pussy. Pressing my lips to the coy little seam hiding underneath.

It's everything I can do to tease her like this, to keep my mouth soft and easy and almost chaste as I kiss the top of her mound and then at the sensitive skin on the outside of her cunt, where her thighs join to her body.

Because all I want to do is taste what's mine.

I want to part her pussy and revel in all the sweet heat there, all the slick wetness that Ben and I have made, and I want to feel the slick, tight channel my cock is about to fuck. I want to feel the new place I'll call home.

And even though I already knew, her pretty little gasps and stirs as I finally kiss her clit make it clear: this is for real. Which means one night won't be enough by far.

The thought sends a surge of possessive lust bolting through me. I seal my mouth over her swollen bud in a savage suck that makes her cry out and has Ben giving a low hum of approval. Using my thumbs, I spread her open like the world's best butterfly, pinning her lips apart so I can explore her. Her delicate inner folds and the tight hole tucked up inside them, all of it glistening in the dim light. Even like this, I can tell she'll be the prettiest shade of pink inside here, the kind of pink a man dreams about when he's got nothing but cold sheets next to him and a shameful fist.

I tongue and lick at her, like a boy with a county fair ice cream cone, trying to lick it fast before it melts in the sun. And Ireland is indeed melting, all of her shyness from earlier completely vanishing as her hands wind through my hair. Her thighs are warm and restless, pressing against me when she rubs my back with her feet, splaying open when she braces against the bed and tries to push her pussy against my face.

"He's good at that, isn't he?" comes Ben's voice. It's low and coaxing and just the tiniest bit cruel—it's sin incarnate. I grind my cock into the bed at the sound of it.

Ben's always been able to do that to me. Stir me up more, make me crazy, just with his words. And knowing that soon he'll be talking like this while I'm pumping away between Ireland's legs, well...it makes it hard for a man to be patient. I roll my hips against the quilt as Ben keeps talking over Ireland's whimpers.

"He likes that cunt of yours, I can tell," Ben remarks. "I can see the muscles in his ass flexing, and you know why? Because he's fucking the bed, he's that turned on. That turned on just from tasting you."

"*Oh,*" Ireland breathes out. Her thighs are tensing and her belly too, and she's getting close. So close.

Ben notices, of course. "You're going to come, aren't you? Because it's just so good to have his mouth there making you feel good? Can you feel his beard when he kisses you? You'll be feeling it tomorrow too, you know. You'll be Caleb's beard-burned little slut. Walking around in your pretty skirts with your pussy still swollen and marked up by him."

"Oh God," Ireland chokes out, falling total prey to Ben's words and writhing against my busy mouth. "Oh my God."

"You like that?" Ben probes, leaning down to run his nose along her pert chin and the apple of her cheek. "You want to be Caleb's little slut?"

"I—both of yours," she gasps.

"My slut too?"

"*Yes*," she moans.

"Then be a good slut and come for Caleb. His cock is full of come to give you, but it needs you wet and tight, doesn't it?"

Aw, shit. I'm practically boring a hole into this mattress I'm so fucking worked up now, and between Ben's words and Ireland's sweet pussy trembling against the flat of my tongue, I'm not sure if I'll even make it to fucking her.

"Answer me, Ireland," Ben says sternly.

I look up over the rise of Ireland's curls to see that she's cresting now, her entire body a tensed stretch of quivering curves.

"Doesn't it?" Ben demands again, reaching out and collaring her throat with a hand to turn her face to his. And that's all it takes—the combination of his filthy words and his hand at her throat and my devouring her pussy like I'll never get to taste a woman ever again—and she's right there, tipping over the edge.

"Yes," she says in a cry, and then she releases against my lips, coming with a final small slick of sweetness and a helpless arch of her back. I'm too far gone to stop eating her, though, lost to the taste of her and the feel of her on my lips, and it's Ben who pulls me away from her pussy by the nape of my neck.

"Look at what you've done," Ben says to our girl as I reluctantly rise to my knees. He runs a hand along Ireland's thigh, and she shudders under his touch, her body still visibly trembling with the aftershocks. "Look at poor Caleb. Look at how much he needs you."

The three of us look down at my cock, which is enormous right now, standing out from my hips in a hard, angry jut. I feel an uncommon surge of pride about how big I am, and it only surges more when Ireland's eyes widen ever so slightly as she takes in my size.

"Big," she gets out in a throaty voice. "So big."

"It's for you, baby," I say, giving myself a rough, helpless stroke from root to tip. "All for you."

Ben presses a condom in my hand, and I find my hands are shaking as I tear it open. Maybe I came earlier in the barn, but that feels like another life, another world. The tough, familiar fuck of my fist can't compare to even the promise of Ireland's body, so slick and soft and tight. It's like I've never come before, never in my whole life, that's how fucking keyed up I am as I finally get the condom pinched and rolling over my engorged shaft. That's how full my sack feels as I finally move between Ireland's legs, like I've got a lifetime of semen saved up just for her.

Even in the dark, I see that smile of hers that hurts my heart—the rueful one that means she's holding something back. That she's telling herself not to do or say something, and it makes me urgent to help her let go. To turn that troubled smile into a real one, into a smile that only knows pleasure and happiness.

Ben catches it too and slants me a look. He doesn't have to say anything, but we both know I'm better at this than he is. I've been practicing with him for years, after all.

"Tell us, peach," I say. I sit back on my heels between her legs, and Ben does the same at her side, the head of his cock still wedged out from his jeans but his body completely still.

She blinks in bemusement, her eyes still glazed with lust and post-climax bliss. "Tell you what?"

"You wanted to say or do something, but then you stopped. What was it?" I keep my voice warm, keep my hands to myself, even though in this position I can see the opened petals of her pussy waiting for me and my fingers are flexing with the urge to trace her secrets.

Her cheeks darken. "Oh. It's...it's nothing. Just me being silly."

"Nothing's silly to us," I assure her.

"I—" She bites her lip, and it's so fucking adorable and sexy I want to die. "I was just thinking about how I wanted to grab you and yank you down to me. Like pull you on top of me and just make you fuck me across the bed." She gives a little laugh. "And then I realized that would probably look too eager. Maybe even desperate."

I growl and lunge forward, sealing off her words with a hot kiss. "I'm the desperate one," I grate out against her mouth. "I'm the one who's too eager. I'm about to come inside this condom without even going inside you."

"Grab him," Ben says. "Use him. He likes being used, don't you, Caleb?"

I grunt in response, too busy kissing her to search for words, and she huffs out a little laugh against my lips. "So it's not too embarrassing if I want you that badly?"

Her voice is shy, and I pull up a little to search her face. "How could you even think such a thing?" I ask. "The only one about to be embarrassed is me because I'm not going to last longer than two thrusts inside you."

Her eyes shine up at me, and finally I get the smile I was hoping for—brave, bold, free. "Let's find out," she says, her hands trailing down my stomach to my hips. She grabs at my ass, and I'm done for. Done waiting, done holding on, done with everything that isn't fucking her until the bed falls apart. I dig my fingers into her hip to hold her steady, and then I wedge inside with one heavy, forceful shove.

And fuck *me*, she is even tighter and hotter than I ever could have dreamed. The squeeze at my head only grows more excruciating the deeper I push, until all of me is being clenched by her hot, silky grip.

She arches at the invasion, but I don't let up until I've got her seated on the full length of my dick and I can feel the intimate kiss of her pussy against my root. I keep my left hand at her hip, the right planted by her head, and I lean forward to give her another quick kiss and check in. "Doing okay?" I ask. I can hear how tightly strung my words are, and it's because my entire body feels like a rope that's about to snap. I have to fuck, I have to thrust, but I keep myself rigid and still until I know she's good. Until I know she wants to keep going.

She gives me a breathless nod. "More," she chokes out. "More now."

It's the only thing my body seems to remember how to do. I give an experimental pump, which makes her cry out, and then I can't wait any longer. I need more of those cries, more of her tits bouncing with every movement, more of her body giving and yielding under mine. I drive into her with a flurry of raw and hungry strokes, craving more and more and more, needing to fuck and fuck and fuck.

"Oh God," she manages, her hands flying up to brace herself against the headboard. "Oh *fuck*. Yes, yes, yes."

Ben is nearing his breaking point. His hand comes up to grip the headboard hard, and his chest is heaving under his T-shirt as he watches me plow into my peach. As he watches her moan and writhe under me.

"Ben." She whispers his name, looking up at him, and he looks down at her with an expression that might look buttoned up tight but I know is anything but. His buttons are unbuttoning, and his control is getting loose and hot, and I haven't seen it happen in so long, and even then I've never seen him quite like this. Never this close to wild, never so primitive that I think he might break the furniture.

With a low curse, he grabs his cock and feeds the tip of it into her mouth. "Just the head," he grinds out. "Suck on the head."

Ireland eagerly complies, craning her neck to accommodate him, and I ease up on the pace so she can suck his dick more easily. All the kissing and all the rain has exposed the natural berry-pink color of her lips, but I wonder as I fuck her if she's got any more of that pretty purple lipstick with her. I wouldn't mind seeing it on Ben's cock...or my own.

Wouldn't mind it at all, in fact.

Ben keeps his fist wrapped around his length, only allowing Ireland access to his tip, and he mutters instructions to her. "Suck harder. Swirl your tongue and lick the slit—yes, just like that. You're such a good girl."

With a groan, I speed up again, hardly able to stand it. How fucking sexy the two of them look like this, how fucking beautiful Ireland is, how fucking good she feels around me. How much I want this to last forever and ever. How much I want to keep her.

Ireland moans around Ben's crown as I screw her harder, and I bend down to suck at one of her pert nipples and then the other, noticing how she moans even more as my beard scratches along the sweet curves of her tits.

"I love that you love my beard, baby doll," I say. "Is it the pain? Is it being marked by me?"

Ben slides himself from her mouth, waiting for her to answer.

"I don't know," she pants out. "Both? Both. Just...more. More now."

More seems to be Ireland's new favorite word, and I vow again I'm going to marry this woman as I bite at her breasts and she whimpers *more*. As Ben feeds her his cock and *more* is what she exhales when he finally lets her come up for air. And *more* is the final word she cries out before she comes again, contracting down so hard around my cock that I have to fight to keep myself inside her as she rides it out on me.

Sated, she eventually stills underneath me.

"One more," I say, giving her favorite word back to her. "Give us one more."

"I can't," she pleads, but I can still feel her body responding to my own deep inside her.

"You can," Ben growls. I move my hand from her hip to her clit, giving her grinding circles that bulldoze past her *I can't*s. She's moaning again, loudly, even around the cock Ben keeps pushing in her mouth, and then he says, "Suck it, sweetheart. Hard as you can."

The hand on his cock clenches as tight as the hand on the headboard, and I see the minute he hits the point of no return, the moment he finally releases. His entire body tenses, and he gives a low grunt, still aiming himself down Ireland's throat and giving her every single bit of it, visibly pulsing in his hand, and Ireland works hard to swallow it as fast as he gives it to her. And I think she and I are both so helpless in the face of his rigid pleasure, with his locked jaw and fluttering eyes and massive, throbbing cock finally getting what it needs. She swallows his last gifts to her and then comes again uttering his name, and then mine, and then God's.

I'm like a freight train, barreling into her deep and fast, a near roar ripping from my throat as I finally fill that condom all the way the fuck up, still pumping the whole time through. I can feel it in my thighs and deep in my balls and all the way up my stomach, and still I throb into the condom as the last of her orgasm pulls every single drop out of me and closer to her.

And then it's finished. We gradually catch our breaths, unraveling into an obliterated kind of quiet, where there's only the storm outside and our still-rough breathing.

Ireland reaches up for me with one hand, the other resting limply on Ben's thigh. And then our amazing girl laughs. Laughs and laughs like she's just gotten off the best roller coaster of her life and she can't wait to get on again.

And I think Ben and I might be able to help her with that.

CHAPTER NINE

IRELAND

We fuck again. And this time, Ben flips me over onto all fours and slides his huge cock into me from behind while Caleb fists a hand in my hair and guides me all around his cock. Unlike Ben, Caleb wants my mouth everywhere—every crease and groove and needy inch—and also unlike Ben, Caleb has almost zero control over his own reactions as I suckle at him. He groans my name like a prayer, his hand trembles in my hair, and even his thighs shake as I tend to his cock.

Behind me, Ben is a force of nature. Like the storm outside but potentially more destructive. He fucks me like he wants to split me in half, like if he fucks me hard enough, he can break me open and eat my heart. And I'll be damned if it isn't tearing me apart with how much I like it.

I've never had sex like this before, sex like my lover's life depends on it, and that's how both men fuck in their different ways. Caleb with the mindless need of a caveman; Ben with the cold grace of a predator. Between the two of them, I'm going to set a world record for number of orgasms in one night.

Between the two of them, I feel like the sexiest woman in the world.

Again, Ben comes with stillness and a quiet, nearly regretful grunt, and Caleb comes loud with hips bucking and hands grabbing. I smile when I think about those hands earlier today. About how they seemed so restless by his sides, flexing and twitching. He clearly likes having someone to claim and grab, and tonight that someone is me, and I couldn't be happier. After we get cleaned up and tumble back into bed, he spoons me from behind and palms a breast with one hand and my cunt with another, not to start another round of sex but with a firm kind of possessiveness, as if to say *these are mine*.

I love it. I try not to think about how much I love it, and I definitely try not to think about how tomorrow is going to bring the harsh blear of reality over all of this. The tawdriness of taking two men to bed—even though I feel nothing but sheer contentment and a smug kind of feminine pride right now.

I wonder how the men will feel tomorrow. Politely indifferent? Trying to get me out the door as fast as possible before I get any wild romantic notions in my head?

Or, worst of all, embarrassed? For sleeping with me?

Ugh.

I push away the worry and the fear and try to settle into Caleb's possessive embrace. He's already asleep as Ben settles next to me—not on his side but on his back so that he faces up to the ceiling, and there's something kind of intimate about it, looking at him while he isn't looking at me.

In the faint gold light of the nightlight, aided by the occasional flash of lightning, I can study the sculpted perfection of his profile. The proud, nearly aquiline nose. The careful part of his lips. The stillness of his forehead and chin—the stillness of his everything, actually, which makes me wonder how much practice he's had at keeping himself motionless. Inert.

But his eyes—those aren't motionless at all. They gleam as they move from the window to the ceiling to me and Caleb and then back again, betraying a restlessness, a cloud of hidden thoughts.

It both fascinates and depresses me, that cloud. That fog of mystery that clings around him and covers him up. I want to burn away his gloom and see him smile.

"Thank you," he finally says. The lash of the rain almost swallows up his words, but I hear them anyway.

I don't know if I like them.

"You don't have to thank me," I say. "This wasn't me doing you a favor. And I hope," I add, in a mix of courage and insecurity, "that it wasn't you doing *me* a favor."

He turns his head and gives me a sharp look. "It wasn't."

"Then why even bring *thank you* into it?"

He lets out a long breath, and when he turns his head to look at the ceiling again, his expression is unreadable. "Because tonight is the first night in five years I've even been able to pretend I could fall asleep during a storm."

It's a strange thing to say—even stranger given I haven't seen him react to the thunder at all—but before I can ask anything more, he says, "Go to sleep, Ireland."

I want to argue, want to fight off the wave of drowsiness pulling at me and ask him more about it, but it turns out Ben must know me better than I know myself, because I open my mouth to tell him he can't boss me around, and before I know it, I'm asleep.

It's still storming and dark when I wake up, and it's disorienting, like I've slid into another world where rain and darkness are the defaults and I'll never see sunlight again.

Even more disorienting is the hard warmth enveloping me, the breath ruffling my hair, the huge hand cupping my pussy—but it's disorienting in the best kind of way, like waking up to find a dream is real after all.

Although the dream isn't perfect—when my eyes adjust to the dark and my mind unfogs, I realize the other side of the bed is empty save for a three-legged dog tucked into a circle.

Ben is gone.

"He always leaves," Caleb says sleepily from behind me. "Don't worry about it."

"Oh," I murmur, not knowing what else to say. What else do I have a right to say, really? I don't know Ben, and I barely know Caleb any better. I'm just a stranger in a strange bed listening to the rain.

So it shouldn't sting as much as it does that Ben isn't next to me.

This is all going to be over in the morning anyway. What does it matter?

But it does matter, it does bother me, and even though I want to be all sophisticated and casual about the fact that I just had the best sex of my life with the hottest men I've ever seen, I can't be.

This is just an inaugural adventure, I try to soothe myself. *There will be lots more. You're the new Ireland, remember? There will be so many other hot men in your future.*

The problem, I realize as I drift back into sleep, is that I don't want there to be any other men. I want *these* ones. I want Caleb and Ben.

After just one night.

God, I'm screwed.

It's the silence that wakes me for the final time, or maybe it's Greta's high-pitched whine as she paces on Caleb's side of the bed and tries to get his attention.

Maybe it's the strange light oozing in through the window. It's lighter than it was when I woke up earlier but darker than daylight should be and pitched in a color that makes me uneasy. I sit up, realizing what the silence is—no distant hum of the air conditioning or the refrigerator, no background hiss of plugged-in appliances. The power is out.

"Caleb?" I nudge Caleb's massive bulk, which is now prone and sprawled, although he's still kept an arm wrapped around my waist even in his sleep. "Caleb, wake up."

He opens his eyes right as the sirens start.

"Shit," he mutters, sitting up and wiping at his face. "Shit. We gotta get downstairs."

Greta whines in agreement, but I look again through the window and see nothing of alarm, really. A sky coffered with dark clouds, with a distant clear band on the horizon. "Do we have to?" I stretch. "It doesn't look so bad, and at home, I usually just ignore the sirens."

Caleb looks at me as if I'm some kind of lunatic. "We don't ignore them out here. We're going downstairs."

With a sigh, I roll out of bed, making a face at my jeans still damp and crumpled on the floor. I go to my room across the hall and pull on a pair of shorts and a tank top, and when I come back out, both Caleb and Ben are pacing the small landing at the top of the stairs. They're both still shirtless, with jeans clinging to narrow, fit hips, and I mentally curse the sirens. I want to take them back to bed.

"Downstairs," Ben says shortly, and when I don't move fast enough for him, he takes my hand and leads me down the steps. Caleb scoops Greta into his arms and follows, and our little parade climbs down a set of rickety stairs to a stone-walled basement by the light of a small flashlight Ben holds in his other hand.

Caleb sits down on a threadbare rug with Greta in his lap, holding her while she trembles, and Ben hauls out a dusty storage container and produces some candles and a lighter. Soon we're in a circle of flickering light, and in my sleepy state, I can almost imagine it's still nighttime. That morning hasn't come, and with it all the consequences of my adventure last night and all the decisions that now have to be made.

Except morning has come, and the soreness between my legs reminds me very much of the consequences and decisions. I fucked two men, came more times than I would have thought humanly possible, and now I have to figure out how to extricate myself with the most dignity possible.

Well, after the storm is over, I suppose. Then the dignity and such. For now, I'm content to watch the candlelight on Caleb's big hands as he tenderly pets his terrified dog. To listen to Ben move around the basement gathering up various items—a weather radio and batteries and a bottle of water and bowl for Greta—and to the wind shaking the house above us. Even in the basement, I can hear the distant wail of the sirens.

"I wish I had my phone," I murmur. I left it upstairs in the rush to get dressed and to the basement. "I could check the weather."

"Signal's bad enough around the house," Caleb says with an apologetic smile. "It's even worse down here."

I sigh and lean back. It's both boring and weirdly energizing to be without my phone at a time when I'd normally be using the hell out of it, and it makes me hyperaware of everything. The way the candlelight moves across Ben's bare chest and beautiful features as he sits on the floor next to Caleb. The way Caleb's eyelashes fan across his cheekbones as he closes his eyes and croons to Greta.

The way neither of them are touching me.

Oh God.

What if this is it? What if this is the beginning of the inevitably awkward end? What if it actually began ending the minute Ben left Caleb and me in bed? That's a very telling thing to do, right? One of those actions that speaks louder than words—so much louder it's practically a shout?

I don't want you again. That's what it shouts.

I adjust my position on the hard floor, again feeling the ache and lingering sting in my pussy from being so well-used last night. At least I don't feel ashamed. I worried about that last night, before I fell asleep, that there'd be some kind of *good girls don't have threesomes* panic, but I don't feel anything even approaching shame. If anything, I'm a little proud I had such a good adventure with such handsome men, that I was brave, that I did something impulsive and electrifying without stopping or censoring myself. Every part of it was good, and even knowing it's time for me to let go of the night and move on, I still only feel good things about it.

I only feel ashamed I want more.

I stare down at my knees as the wind picks up and roars around the house with a renewed fury that raises goosebumps on my arms. Caleb hugs Greta harder, mumbles something about hoping Clementine is okay in the barn. Ben is the picture of stillness, sitting with crossed legs and a straight back, his eyes on the weather radio as it drones on and on about tornado sightings near Holm and which counties need to take cover.

There's something about Ben's stillness that betrays *something*, however, even if I can't put my finger on it. It's not the stillness of a person at peace but the stillness of a person who's trained themselves not to flinch, and it makes me wonder what else Ben has trained himself to do.

And why.

A huge clatter comes from upstairs, followed by a glass-shattering crash, and Caleb jolts, as if to get up, but Ben clamps a hand on his shoulder. "Stay the fuck here," Ben bites out.

Caleb looks up the stairs, torn, and I remember he told me on our tour around the place that this is his family's house, that it's over a hundred years old. No wonder he feels protective.

But Ben is right—whatever is happening above us is too dangerous to investigate, and I watch his hand on Caleb's shoulder for longer than I should, something about it making me hot and squirmy all over again.

The weather radio keeps droning, but the wind and crashing get louder and louder, drowning out the robotic voice coming through the small, old speakers, and there's a moment when I think the house is going to come right off the foundations and just blow away. It rattles and creaks and groans mightily, and I realize I've grabbed on to Caleb's thigh only after he takes my hand and rubs a soothing thumb over the back of it.

The house seems besieged for hours, but when the weather radio announces the time, it's only been a handful of minutes, and from there on out, the wind slowly abates, retreating with erratic and fitful gusts, until all is silent once more. The next time the weather radio lists the counties that need to take cover, our county isn't on the list.

Ben clicks it off.

"Ready?" he asks us, as if we're about to go into battle and not upstairs. Neither Caleb nor I answer, although I notice Caleb gives Greta an extra pat before shifting her off his lap, and I think it's more to comfort him than to reassure her.

After blowing out the candles, we mount the creaking stairs up to the ground floor, with Ben's bobbing flashlight to guide us, and then he swings the door open to reveal a house that's still intact.

"Oh, thank fuck," Caleb breathes as we walk around to see everything is where it should be. The screen door came loose in the wind, apparently, and banged against the side of the house hard enough to shatter the glass in the lower half of it, but the rest of the windows are intact, and when we walk around the outside, the siding and the roof seem to be fine. Even Clementine is okay when we check on her, although she's agitated. The worst thing we can find is a tree on the edge of the property that's been blown over and some sunflower petals scattered across the lawn.

Caleb visibly brightens the more we walk, and he's nearly smiling when we get back to the house. Even Greta is wagging her tail, and for a moment, I think it's all over—the storm, the fear, the worry—all of it.

Then Ben's phone rings.

CHAPTER TEN

BEN

I don't like storms. Never have, actually, but after I got back from my last deployment, I realized I *really* don't like them. Not the unpredictable rolls of thunder that remind me of mortars echoing through lonely, scree-covered valleys. Not the strobes of lightning that remind me of muzzle flashes at a distance. But weirdly, it is the wind that gets me the most. My therapist says it's because the wind is as unpredictable as the thunder, but I know it's more than that.

The thing is, wind can sound like anything it wants—a screaming man, the whirr of helicopter blades, trucks rolling over the dirt. Any sound, every sound. One minute I'm in my own bed, and the next I'm back there. Kabul. Marjah and Musa Qala in the Helmand Province. The godforsaken Korengal. All I wanted was to come home. And then I came home and it was like it didn't matter.

But last night, I came the closest I have in years to falling asleep during a storm, to falling asleep in the same bed as someone else. Maybe it was the very thorough fuck session, but maybe it was also Ireland herself. Watching me with parted lips and openly curious eyes while a contented and happy Caleb snored behind her.

It's been so long since anyone has looked at me like that, like they genuinely wanted to know what was howling inside me, like they wouldn't be scared of it if I let it out. Like they wouldn't be upset if they cracked me open and actually found *nothing* inside, howling or not.

If they found there is no *Ben* inside me any longer, that I've somehow become a shell, a puppet pretending to be Ben Weber, going through the motions as if he never decided ROTC would be a handy way to pay for college. As if he just decided to stay near Holm and work at a bar and fuck women and his best friend at the same time.

Caleb's the only person I'll ever trust with the mess I've become, precisely because he doesn't demand to see those messy truths if I'm not willing to show them. But Ireland... Her gaze last night both demanded and conceded, and it evoked something fiercely needy in me, something that wanted to tie her to Caleb's bed and have her look at me that way forever. It was so unnerving that I had to leave after she fell asleep, although I would have left anyway. I'm too vulnerable in the nighttime.

I prefer to be vulnerable in private.

What is it about Ireland that makes me think I could change that? Even today, I find myself drawn to her clear blue gaze and her voice, which has the slightly husky sound of a woman who's just woken up. I want to fuck her right here in the branch-strewn yard right after a fucking tornado, that's how sexy her voice is.

In fact, I'm listening to her talk when my phone rings, jarring and loud compared to the low, sultry music of Ireland's words. With a muttered curse, I step away and answer it. It's Debbie, one of my two employees at the tavern.

"Ben," she says, and there's a peculiar and specific tremble in her voice that I've heard a hundred times before but never from her.

Never here at home.

Shock.

She's in shock.

I close my eyes, for a minute both smelling and tasting gunpowder. Feeling grit and dirt under my eyelids and on my lips.

"What is it?" I manage.

"The tavern," she shakes out. "Ben, the whole town, it's just—"

I understand immediately, even though I don't want to. I thought we'd been spared the worst of the storm; I thought we'd been lucky.

Turns out the worst of it didn't hit the farm because it was too busy tearing apart the town. The place I grew up, the place I earn my living. The place I call home.

"Are you safe?" I ask first because it's the most important thing. "Is everyone safe?"

"I don't know," she says. "I only just got here from my place. There's a police car, but I—I don't know. I don't know."

Shock will do that. Make the simplest sentences break off into fragments, make even the easy thoughts impossible to hold on to. I know exactly how Debbie feels right now because I've felt it so many times before. Although never *here*, never where I thought I was safe, with the wide green fields and leafy trees and sleepy creeks.

I squeeze my hand into a fist so tight I feel the nails dig into my palm.

"I'll be right there," I tell her.

Caleb didn't need to hear anything from me when I hung up the phone. Somehow he had shirts for us. Somehow he herded me toward his truck, and Ireland and Greta ended up between us on the big bench seat. Somehow we made it the two miles to Holm without saying a single word to each other.

And then we roll to the edge of our small town, and I'm beyond words anyway. I'm too busy remembering the sound of boots scrabbling over dusty ground, the heavy spray of gunfire in the heat. The scene we come upon is a scene I thought I'd never have to see again, a scene I saw far the fuck too often: the mounded rubble of a town gashed right off the map.

Holm is gone.

Well, maybe not *gone* entirely, but close to it—close enough that it's unrecognizable as the place I've called home for thirty-four years, and close enough that I almost wish it *were* entirely gone, because now it's become something tragic and alien and chaotic beyond belief.

The big trees shading Main Street are snapped and whittled to sharp, stark masts of stripped lumber, and the green lampposts that used to light the street— the ones the American Legion and Auxiliary Club decorate for Christmas each year—are knocked over like Lincoln Logs. Trash and debris litter every available surface—shreds of fluffy, pink insulation from the mowed-over homes a block away, glass and lumber snapped into toothpicks, paper and jagged slabs of sheetrock, and drifts of shingles and bricks piled as high as banks of snow.

"Fuck," Caleb says, stunned. "*Fuck.*"

I don't say anything but climb out of the truck and walk toward the bar. I hear Ireland and Greta follow me, but I don't turn back to look at them. I don't trust myself; I don't trust that Ireland won't give me one of those clear, demanding looks, and I'll crack into a thousand pieces right here in the middle of all this ruin. I can't crack, not yet. Not before I make sure everyone is safe and I know what all needs to be done.

Holm is small—less than four hundred people, and even that number has probably shrunk some since the last census—and our Main Street is only four blocks long. My bar is at the end of it, in an old brick building that's been around since the town's founding. It used to be the general store before they opened a Walmart off the interstate exchange, and the old salt who opened the bar in the 1980s called it General's to honor the building's past. I kept the name when I bought the place, and it's a strange relief to see it in faded paint still on the side of the building.

But everything else about the bar is wrong.

The windows are blown out. The door is gone. The brick structure survived, but the bricks themselves are blasted and chipped all to shit. And the inside looks like a ruin of glass, furniture, and ceiling tiles.

I crunch my way inside, squinting up into the shadows to make sure the ceiling isn't about to fall on my head, and call out, "Hello?" There's nothing but the sound of dripping water and voices from outside.

I step back out onto the street, looking for any sign of police or paramedics, wondering if the bar has been searched for people—and the other buildings on Main Street and houses too. It's been about thirty minutes since we left the basement on the farm. Surely that's enough time for first responders to arrive?

Caleb joins me after a minute, trailed by a shell-shocked Ireland and a nervous Greta. "Just talked to Harley from the gas station," he says. "They've been through all the buildings on this side."

"They find anyone?"

Caleb looks down the street in that *My Antonia* way of his, all stoic and solemn while the prairie wind tugs gently at his shirt and hair. "Three bodies. They've laid them out in the park, near the water tower. Called a funeral home over in Emporia already." Caleb names who they found, two of whom were Sunday school teachers of mine and one of whom we went to high school with, and I stagger—actually stagger—against the now-bruised wall of my bar. I lean my head back against the brick, close my eyes, and try to breathe, try to remain present, try all the tricks my therapist has given me, but it's no good. I feel jagged and angry and emptier than ever. I feel like the building I'm leaning against, like something that's been broken and tossed away and left to crumble in its own desperate mess.

And that's when Ireland steps past me to walk inside the bar. I open my eyes to see her curvy frame disappear into the gloom, and for a single, shining second, I recognize everything is going to be okay. That there might be a future with this sexy woman and her penetrating gaze and her secret bravery.

I take in a deep breath.

And then the ceiling falls in on top of her.

CHAPTER ELEVEN

IRELAND

"I'm fine!" I shout. "I'm fine! I'm fine!"

Okay, maybe *fine* is a little bit of a lie, given there's God only knows how many pounds of wood and metal pipe making a very unsteady tent above my head, but I'm not dead and I don't think I'm injured, at least not seriously so. Something hit my shoulder fairly hard on the way down, and I think I'll have an almighty scrape on my leg, but nothing's broken and nothing's bleeding in any alarming kind of way. Mostly I'm just covered in sheetrock dust.

"Jesus Christ," I hear Caleb swear viciously, and I see something in front of me shift, letting a little bit more light into the unsteady tent of mine. "You're really okay?"

"Help me," Ben's voice comes through. "Move that there—not that beam; it'll send everything else crashing down. Yes, there, that one. One, two, *three*—"

Ben's voice is knowledgeable, authoritative. Despite everything—the pain and the ruin around us and the very real danger I'm in of this stuff falling on me—I shiver a little at the reminder of how commanding he can be. How he commanded Caleb and me last night.

And in less than ten minutes, they've got the remains of the ceiling moved enough for me to wriggle free. There's an awkward moment where I don't quite fit and they have to shift more pieces around, and I have the sudden, familiar rush of longing for a different body—which is patently ridiculous, as *this* body was nearly just crushed by a building and I should only feel gratitude for being alive, so I shove that longing where it belongs and work my way free of the debris pile.

The minute I have my torso mostly out, I'm abruptly yanked into two sets of strong arms and crushed between two chests.

"I thought you were dead," Ben says roughly. I can barely breathe for how tightly I'm held between them, and I feel lips—his and Caleb's—all over my hair, and I feel their hearts drumming against my body in a frantic tattoo.

This is not how you treat someone you never see again.

Maybe they want to keep me.

But within seconds, Ben tramples the fledgling hope inside me. He pulls away from me so fast I almost stumble forward. And when I see his face, it's not even the cold expression I've grown used to from him. It's something wild and furious.

"You should go," he harshes out. "Go home."

Stupid me, I think *home* means the farm, and I say, "I'm not going home until you two are."

He shakes his head, almost violently, sending his too-long hair flicking into his face. "Go to *your* home, Ireland," he says, his eyes turbulent with something I don't understand. "You can't be here anymore!"

Oh.

Oh.

My heart sinks, even as I cling to any reason I can stay. "I still have work to do here," I protest faintly. "Pictures to take."

Ben makes a dangerous noise. "Look around you, sweetheart. You think this is the kind of picture your boss wants?"

I glance around the storm-wrecked bar and outside the door to Main Street, which looks just as broken, just as bad.

Caleb lets go of me, although I can feel the reluctance in him, and that gives me the courage to try one last time.

"I could stay...?" I offer. "And help?"

There's that cold curl to Ben's mouth now, something almost like a sneer, and I wonder how can this be the man who just crushed me against his chest, the man who just frantically kissed my hair as if to reassure himself I was alive? How?

How can he just *change*? Close off like this?

"Just get out of here, Ireland," Ben says, and his entire body is tensed with something that's either panic or fury. "Don't make this awkward."

And those are the words.

Those are the words that slap me across the face—more than *go home*, more than *it's time for you to leave.*

Don't make this awkward.

Don't be *that* fat girl. Don't be the girl so desperate for affection that she abandons all pretense of dignity and begs for it. Don't be eager, and don't be clingy.

Don't draw attention to yourself.

Don't ask for more than what people want to give you, because they won't want to give you much.

I know these *don'ts*. They've been my rulebook since high school, my guiding principles, and every decision I've made since turning down that photography scholarship has been because of the *don'ts*. How could I have fooled myself into thinking last night was something special? I know better—*I know better*—and I still let myself hope the adventure could last.

"Ireland," Caleb says, something pained in his voice. But I'm already turning away, I'm already leaving. Crunching over the bricks and glass outside to...to where, exactly?

To the farm, I decide. I'll walk to the farm. It's only a couple of miles, and there are only two turns. I can find my way, get my things. Then I'll walk to my car and leave for home.

They want me to go? Fine. I know the *don'ts* inside and out. I have them tattooed on the beating flesh of my heart. I know them even better than they do.

I won't make anything awkward.

I'll go.

&

"Ireland, wait!" Caleb calls, jogging up next to me. I'm already to the edge of town, past the place where he'd parked his truck. I'm guessing he stayed behind to talk to Ben, and I'm also guessing that whatever that conversation consisted of would piss me off, so I'm not going to ask about it. Instead, I turn and say, "Yes?" like he's a complete stranger to me.

Hurt flickers through those green eyes, and for a moment, I feel bad. Then I remember Ben's cruel words, and I regret nothing.

"Please, Ireland, I—" He squints down at the ground and scratches at his head, as if he's so lost for words he can't even remember how to speak them aloud. "I'm—I'm sorry, I guess. I mean, I don't *guess* that I'm sorry, I know I am, but sorry isn't all I want to say. I just don't know how to say the rest."

Just go. Just keep walking.

But it's like I unbottled part of myself last night, and I can't remember how to bottle it again. "*Sorry* isn't an even exchange for being treated like that," I say, hoping my voice flays him open. Hoping each word is a penknife under his fingernails. And he does flinch and opens his mouth to say something, but I stop him. "If you and Ben don't want to fuck me again, that's fine, but I don't deserve to be shooed away like a dog."

Caleb slumps his broad shoulders at this. "You're right. Of course not."

I start walking again, and he follows me.

I sigh and stop again. "Is this your way of offering me a ride to the farm?" I ask. And even as I ask it, there's a part of me that hopes he'll say no, that he's coming after me to tell me to stay, to tell me that Ben didn't mean it.

To tell me they both want me to stay.

But he doesn't tell me that.

"Yes," he replies. "I'm not letting you walk all the way back to the farm. Or to your car. And I've already talked to them on the phone, but I'd like to check on Mrs. Parry and Mrs. Harthcock, so I'm headed that direction anyway."

Ah, how gentlemanly, I think bitterly. A real gentleman should always give last night's trollop a ride back to her car, especially if it's on his way to do other things.

Caleb trots off to fetch his truck, and within a few minutes, I'm inside the cab as the ancient air conditioning roars hot air in our faces and as I try to wipe as much of the sheetrock dust off my face as I can. My hair is a lost cause—I look like I took a shower with grit instead of water—but I still pick out the bigger pieces of gypsum and flick them out the window. I'm examining the scrape on my thigh as we pull onto the gravel driveway of the farm.

Caleb parks the truck and then looks over at me for a minute.

"Get on the porch," he says gruffly. "I'll get something for that scrape."

"I don't need—"

He cuts me a glance that brooks no argument. "On the porch, Ireland. Before I haul you there myself." And then he slides out of the truck and slams the door behind him, stalking toward the house.

Sitting on the hot vinyl seat for a moment longer, I consider my options... and then decide it would be stupid to refuse a bandage just because my feelings are hurt. I'll get the scrape taken care of, and then I'll get my things, and then I'll go. Back to my empty apartment and my stable, safe job and my fridge full of whatever new diet shake my sister wants me to try.

And maybe I'm going to take a break from adventures.

Turns out they hurt a lot when they end.

I finally get out of the truck and sit on one of the old chairs clustered into a corner of the porch. Caleb emerges from the house with a first aid kit in hand. He drops to his knees in front of me, and he's so tall that even when he kneels, he's eye-level with me in the chair.

He clicks open the kit, reaches for my leg, and then hesitates. "May I?" he asks.

"Sure," I say. Grumpily.

The scrape starts near the outside of my knee and angles inward to the sensitive skin of my inner thigh. Caleb gently parts my legs in order to reach it, and my entire body lights up like a Christmas tree.

I suck in a breath.

So does he.

There's no denying the charge between us, despite what just happened, despite the fact that I'm going to leave. Despite the fact that he and Ben *want* me to leave.

No, feeling the warm brush of his torso and arms as he settles between my legs still affects me. Still makes my belly tighten low around the lingering soreness he left inside me last night.

And I can tell he feels it too. His hands shake the slightest bit as he grabs the antiseptic spray and a gauze pad, and when he looks back up at me before he sprays the scrape, I can see his pulse hammering in his neck.

"This may sting," he whispers.

"It can't hurt more than anything else that's happened today," I tell him, initially meaning the ceiling collapse but then realizing he may think I mean Ben's ugly words instead.

Well. Maybe I do.

His eyes look sad, and there's no trace of that amazing dimple under his beard. With an acknowledging nod, he bends low over my leg and sprays the scrape.

"Ouch!" I hiss, but my hiss turns into a moan as he leans close to my thigh and blows over the parts that sting. "Oh. *Oh.* Caleb."

He shudders at the sound of his name on my lips, blowing a little harder and then kissing all around the scrape, careful not to touch it, not to hurt me more. And then his mouth is moving up and up and up, right to the hem of my shorts, with licks and nibbles that have me squirming.

"Let me taste you," he begs. "Please. Let me taste you again."

And all of my hurt irritation vanishes in a puff of pure lust at the thought of Caleb's mouth on my pussy, at the promise of even more beard-burn, and suddenly I'm wriggling out of my shorts, half standing, half hopping, reaching over to the porch railing for balance.

I manage to kick them off, but before I can sit back down, I'm pushed against the railing and my panties are yanked to the side, and then Caleb's hot mouth is on me, sowing sweet fire everywhere he touches.

"God, you're already so wet," he mumbles against me, giving my pussy another openmouthed kiss, followed by a long lick with the flat of his tongue. "Always so wet for us."

Us.

Ben's absence is like a hole in the air, sucking all the oxygen away from us, and I hate that I want him here even after he kicked me to the curb. I hate that I miss his touch on me so much it hurts.

I hate it.

Even as I can't deny it.

"Fuck, you taste good," Caleb murmurs. His strong fingers dig into the soft rounds of my ass, keeping my pussy angled the way he likes, and the feeling of those almost-bruising fingertips along with the chafe of his beard drives me perilously close to orgasm. His tongue seems to be everywhere, until he gently takes my clit between his teeth and suckles at it.

My head falls back as I give a long moan. "God, Caleb, oh my God."

But I don't keep my head back, because he's too delicious right now, and I never want to forget how he looks like this. On his knees in front of me, those big shoulders tucked in, his dark head below the curve of my still-clothed stomach, tilting and working...

It's so much to feel, so much to see, even as awful questions filter through my mind.

Are you doing this out of pity?

Why doesn't Ben want me?

How am I supposed to walk away from this?

But even the questions disappear into smoky nothing as my impending orgasm winds closer and closer and closer, and I arch against the railing, trying to push myself harder against Caleb's wicked tongue.

He responds with a hungry, eager groan, sucking and licking like his life depends on it, and then I'm done for. I pant out his name right as my climax bursts, and then I don't know what else I'm saying. Curses, blessings, maybe even Ben's name leaves my mouth, but it doesn't matter, because it feels so fucking good. Waves and waves starting in my clit and radiating out through my stomach and thighs and all the way to the tips of my fingers. It feels like it goes on for hours as I ride it out against his mouth, with one hand braced on the railing and the other hand in his hair, clutching him tight.

And then, gradually, as all good things do, it subsides. It goes away, leaving only weak knees and a full-body flush in its wake.

Caleb seems reluctant to stop eating me, but he does, tilting his head up with half-lidded eyes and wet lips. He looks intoxicated—intoxicated from *me*, my body—which is a heady feeling. Heady as fuck. And when I look all the way down his body, I know for certain pity had nothing to do with what just happened.

He's hard.

Hard enough to seriously tent his jeans.

For a moment, we linger like this, my hand still twined in his hair and him on his knees with his face canted up toward mine, like a sinner before God. His eyes blaze earnestly across my face, and my stomach twists as I recognize what he's doing.

He's committing me to memory.

I let go of his hair.

"Ireland," he says as I bend over to grab my shorts. "Please."

I don't know what to make of him, this honest, passionate man who can make honest, passionate love to me and still say goodbye afterward. I don't know what to make of Ben either, and the thought that I'll never have the opportunity to figure them out is sharp enough to make me pull my shorts on with haste. I need to leave. Before I do something truly awkward, like cry.

Caleb stands, licking his lips like he's licking the last of my taste off them, and renewed lust hits me low below the belly button. I ignore it and fasten my shorts.

"I'll just go get my things," I announce, pointlessly, and he follows me into the house and up the stairs like a puppy. A big farmer puppy with big farmer muscles and pleading green eyes.

Ugh. Why do the two of them have to be so unfairly handsome? What chance do I stand against that?

I go into the guest room and pull together my things to pack, and from behind me, Caleb says, "Ben was in the army."

"Okay," I say, keeping my back to him as I fold up my clothes and stuff them into my bag. "Thanks for telling me."

"No, I—" Caleb makes that frustrated noise that tells me he's frustrated with himself, with the way he can't explain things the way he wants. "Ben was in Afghanistan. Four tours."

That slows me down. I put my camera on the bed next to my bag and turn to face him. "Okay," I say again, but curiously this time. I'm listening. Thinking of the way Ben kept so still this morning to avoid flinching at the *booms* of the thunder. Why he has trouble sleeping.

"I think it was bad. I mean, I know it was bad. He was in so many of the places you'd see on the news, and he knew so many people who died or were seriously injured, and I think he saw a lot of fucked-up things. He was always so sensitive..."

I make a noise at that, thinking of his cold eyes, his sneering smiles. "Ben? Sensitive?"

Caleb sighs. "Yeah. He used to get bullied a lot, as a kid, before he filled out in high school."

"God. Why?"

Caleb shrugs. "Because kids are awful? Because his sister was older than him and already out? Because he could never hide how he felt about anything?"

I ask the obvious question. "Were you two in love as kids?"

He rubs the back of his neck. "No...and yes. We've always been close. He lived with his grandma growing up, and after she had to move to a home, my parents unofficially took him in. His sister had already gone off to college at that point, but she wasn't ready to be responsible for another person, I guess."

"So you lived together? Is that when you found out you wanted each other?"

"It was complicated, you know? It didn't—I don't think either of us knew until the first time we had a third person. Someone between us."

"When was that?" I sit on the bed now, reluctantly enthralled. "High school?"

"A cheerleader named Serena." A faint smile blooms on Caleb's face. "She had a crush on both of us, and we both liked her. For a while, I thought we were going to fight for her, but then we all got drunk at a field party and the three of us ended up together in the back of my truck. We did that a few more times, until she started dating a basketball player instead."

"And you never..." I wave with my hand to indicate what I mean. "Never just the two of you?"

"We did," Caleb admits softly. His ears go red, but he meets my eyes so I'll know he's being completely honest. "Just the two of us. The summer after graduation."

"And?"

"It was still *fun*," he replies, with an almost shy smile, as if even the word *fun* is impossibly dirty, "but there was something about being a three that fit us better than being a two."

I think about that for a moment. Think about how electric it felt last night to be between the two of them, because it *was* electric and somehow also comforting—like nothing I've ever felt before in bed. As if between the three of us we could handle anything, we could explore everywhere, our shared strength and energy creating a web of safety and affection all around us.

I look out the window at the barn, where the three of us fooled around last night, wondering if maybe I fit better in a three than a two myself. Or is it just Caleb and Ben? Even if I left here and found another set of boys to play with, would it be the same?

I sigh. *How could it be the same? When it's them I want so much, not the number?*

"So we went to college and dated around for a while," Caleb continues. "And it was at the end of freshman year that my dad took me aside to have a chat. Turns out our little college flings had made their way through the town gossips back to him."

I grimace, and Caleb just laughs.

"Don't worry, he didn't kill me. Instead, he told me about Mrs. Parry's sister."

"What about her?" I ask, a little confused.

"She lived with two men on the other side of Holm for fifty years."

"Oh," I respond in a surprised voice. "That's unusual."

"The more unusual part is that I guess the town got used to it. She and her two men were part of everything—church, Rotary club, town picnics. And my dad told me if Ben and I wanted to live that way, the town would accept us. And he said if we wanted to be a couple, just the two of us, then he'd make sure the town accepted us that way too."

"And did they?" I ask. "Accept you?"

"Yeah," Caleb says with a smile. "They did. Mackenna lived with us for four years after college, and we never had to hide it. Not here in Holm, at least. People stared a bit in the beginning, when the three of us would hold hands or share a blanket during the town parade, but they got used to it fast. Maybe even bored with it. And after she left, when it was just the two of us together, it was the same way."

"Huh." It goes against everything I've ever thought about small towns, being a city girl myself, but maybe there's something about a tightly knit community that can absorb differences in surprising ways. "When did Mackenna leave? *Why* did she leave?"

Caleb's smile drops and drops fast. He looks out the window and rubs the back of his neck again. "She left nearly five years ago. Honest, it doesn't keep me up at night, but for Ben—well, Ben's the reason she left."

"Why? Was he a jerk to her too?" I ask a little bitterly.

"No," Caleb says simply. "He just...*wasn't*. Wasn't anything. When we met her in college, Ben was still that sensitive boy, but after each tour, it was like less and less of him came back. When he came back home the final time, he was sealed off so tight he could barely breathe. Mackenna always was an impatient kind of person, and it only took a few months of trying to bring him back before she gave up. She moved to the city, and that was that."

Even though he was a dick earlier, my heart still twists a little for Ben, the sensitive boy who went to war and came back a shell. "Has Ben...you know. Seen anyone? About what happened to him?"

"He's been going to a therapist weekly for five years now," Caleb says, a touch of pride in his voice. "He sees a psychiatrist too—meds for his panic attacks and sleeping problems—and he's in a community support group with other veterans. He's been working on himself for years, Ireland, so he hasn't just been lying around broken waiting for someone to fix him."

"I never said he was," I shoot back, ruffled. "Just that today he seemed awfully sealed off. And a lot like an asshole."

I watch as a certain kind of defeat scrawls itself across Caleb's face. "I know. I think—I think seeing the town gutted like that brought back some hard memories. And I think when that ceiling fell on you—well, fuck, Ireland, even I thought you were dead for a moment, and it hurt like nothing I've ever felt before."

I want to cling to the *maybes* his words raise in my mind—I want to cling to them too much, I can already feel it. Just like I can feel the tears burning at my eyelids when I ask, "If that's true, then how can *you* say goodbye?"

He rubs at his beard, his jaw tight and his eyes shining. "Because we start things together, and we finish them together. I'm sorry, Ireland, I really am, but that's the way it has to be."

Fifteen minutes later, I'm in my Prius, bumping toward the interstate. In my rearview, I still see Caleb's truck and him standing outside it. He refuses to leave until he sees me safely on my way. I know that's what he's doing, and it's the final straw.

I finally let the tears flow now. Now, when it won't be *awkward*. Now, when I can save my pride.

Everywhere there are signs of the storm and the destruction it scattered around the countryside. Branches down, big green road signs crumpled as if by a giant fist. Leaves and twigs everywhere, along with a scattering of things that are far, far from their homes. An Easy Bake oven lodged in a tree. A mattress blown against a fence.

And yet nothing the storm has left even comes close to matching how messy and broken I feel right now.

I think I fell in love. I think I fell in love in a single night. I think I fell in love with two people instead of one, and all of it is ridiculous, so fucking ridiculous, but that doesn't stop it from being true.

Doesn't stop it one bit.

Soon, Caleb's truck is out of sight, and I'm turning onto the paved county road that will take me back to the highway. Across the junction is a grassy field, but through the plot of knee-high grass waving in the sunny breeze is a meandering swath of flattened stalks, bent and speckled with flung mud. It's a near perfect depiction of the path of the tornado, and there's something singularly striking about it.

Possibly the lonely destruction matches my mood.

I reach automatically for my camera in the bag on the passenger seat, shoving my hand through my clothes in search of its reassuring shape, its familiar heft. But even as I riffle through the bag, a vision suddenly comes to me of my camera on the bed in the farmhouse's guest room. I put it there while Caleb was telling me about Ben and him, and I got so caught up in the story that I completely forgot to shove it into the bag before I left.

Which means it's still at the farmhouse.

Fuck.

I pointlessly and stupidly smack the steering wheel with my palm, which only hurts my hand and makes me feel childish. And childish is not something I can afford to feel right now—not when I'm already the awkward sausage who couldn't take a hint and had to be told to leave.

Humiliation and anger burn at me as I yank on the wheel of the car to make a vicious U-turn back to the farm. The humiliation is for obvious reasons, I suppose, but even I don't entirely understand the anger. I'm not an angry person normally; in fact, I'm always the first to say sorry, the first to make peace. I usually do everything I can to avoid conflict, to keep people liking me.

You're done with that now. No more apologizing just because you're scared of people walking away.

I straighten in my seat as I drive back to the farmhouse, and I allow the anger to wash away the humiliation. I allow myself, for the first time in my life, to hang on to my anger, to feed it and embrace it. Even with Brian and my sister, I never gave myself permission to be angry. Escaping those relationships were acts of desperate survival and retreat, not blazing righteousness. But it's like the storm—and what happened in Caleb's bed as it raged around us—has finally unlocked some new store of pride I've never had before.

I'm furious that these men made me feel any doubt or embarrassment about the night we spent together. I'm furious that the way Ben treated me made me feel like a stereotype. I'm furious that the whole thing made me feel ugly and unlovable.

And mostly, I'm furious that I live in a world that has the power to make me feel ugly and unlovable because of my body.

I'm very aware that Ben is still scowling and prowling his way around his wrecked business, that Caleb is off playing Farmer Do-Gooder, and that the farmhouse will be empty. All the same, I find myself rehearsing triumphant speeches and searing retorts all the way back to the Carpenter farm. For the first time in my life, I feel emboldened to defend my body. I feel proud of it, and I almost *want* someone to be at the house so I can tell them exactly how I feel. So I can hear my words scorching the air as I stand in my own skin and assert my right to be treated with dignity and to be loved. My right to live as everyone else lives.

In fucking peace.

Since the storm broke up this morning, the sun has been baking down on the prairie, and even the gloppy mud of the road has hardened enough for the Prius to wobble over it without issue. It wobbles back to the farm, and as I pull into the driveway, I see with a surge of excitement, dismay—and yes, lust—that it seems like I'll be getting my wish.

Ben is here.

CHAPTER TWELVE

BEN

I know it the moment it happens. Telling Ireland to go is the biggest mistake of my life.

I know it like I know the Kansas sun on my back or the weight of body armor on my shoulders. I know it like I know the green of Caleb's eyes.

I know it so much it hurts.

But even as I watched her wheel around to leave—gorgeous even covered in dust—I still couldn't make myself go after her. She almost *died* because of me, and how many people were hurt and killed right in front of me in rubble-strewn hellholes just like this one? It's sheer luck she's alive, and the knives of terror that stabbed through me while we were digging her out drove so deep I couldn't think straight.

Then the soldier in me took over, because that's what happens when I panic now. The sensitive boy who would have cowered behind Caleb at the first sign of trouble—he had no one to cower behind in Afghanistan. And so he learned to survive on his own.

I don't even really know what all I said to Ireland to make her leave—only that I followed her flinches to the words that would hurt the most, the ones that would drive her away. Words that would condemn me to hell, but even as I held her in my arms frantically kissing her hair, my brain wouldn't stop shouting *get her to safety, keep her safe, keep her safe, get her out—*

It was the only thing that penetrated the lingering terror and the relief she was okay—relief so deep that I knew I was already falling in love with her.

Keep her safe.

Keep her from harm.

Get her out.

"What the fuck?" Caleb demands. He's scrubbing at his face like he does when he's frustrated. When he's furious. "Why the *fuck* would you say something like that?"

My mind is still looping through its carousel of nightmares—the ceiling coming down over Ireland, blood-spattered dust in Helmand, yanking on debris not knowing if I'll find a corpse underneath—and I can't force out the right words. "She needed to leave," I say instead, my voice harsh and shaking. "She needed to go."

"No, asshole, she didn't," Caleb spits out. "I thought you liked her. I thought you understood that *I* liked her. That I wanted more than just a night with her."

I can't reply because I *do* like her. I *do* understand. I also want more with her, lots and lots and lots more, but my head is still crowded with flashes of her trapped under the wreckage and old memories from the war, and my heart is still squeezing with panic and the desperate need to get her to someplace safe, someplace *away*.

"Goddammit, Ben, answer me," Caleb grates out. "Just fucking answer me. You don't get to be a shell, not right fucking now. You don't get to go cold and empty after what you just did."

A shell. Cold and empty.

I hear the words like a faraway train, knowing what they are, yet they're so distant I can't reach them.

"She had to go someplace away from here," is all I can manage, and Caleb's jaw sets. He's so fucking handsome like this, streaked with dust, his beard setting off the perfect planes of his face. He's so handsome...but he's looking at me now with an expression of pure disgust.

"We've always done things together, Ben, and I won't stop now. But I also don't know if she'll ever forgive you for this, and I don't know if I ever will either."

And with that, my best friend, lover, and essential part of any relationship I've ever had, walks out the door.

It takes me almost an hour.

I'm behind the bar, sitting with my head between my knees the way I used to sit after getting roughed up by bullies in school, and I'm trying to do all the breathing exercises they teach you in therapy. I'm trying to put all the bad memories back where they belong and pull myself back to the present.

It's hard.

It's harder than it's been in years. It takes all the things I've learned plus the sedate presence of Greta-dog curled up next to me to claw my way up and out.

At some point, I slowly surface again. I can think Real-Ben thoughts and not Shell-Ben thoughts. I realize with dawning horror what I've done. I've hurt Ireland. In my mindless need to stop the terror, I've hurt her, and it gouges a fresh hole in my scarred heart.

I stumble out of the bar, my heart hammering against my ribs and anxiety crawling up the back of my neck, and there's no sign of Ireland or Caleb anywhere. Even Caleb's truck is gone.

He took her back to the farmhouse. Maybe they're still there?

God, let them still be there.

I bolt down the sidewalk, Greta at my heels, both of us dodging debris and the haggard townspeople milling around the ruined Main Street. It's a testament to how awful the day is that no one seems to notice or care that the town barkeep and his dog are sprinting back home, not that I'd care if anyone did notice.

My mind is full of Ireland and her blue eyes brimming with wounded hurt. Of Caleb and his disappointment.

I have to get to the farm. *Now.* Because I can't bear to lose Ireland, and if I do lose Ireland, I may also lose Caleb, and I also can't bear that. I won't survive losing either of them.

I'd rather go back to war.

The two miles home are hot and punishing, but if there's one thing I carried over from the army, it's the habit of going on hot and punishing runs, so I make decent time, even though I arrive a sweaty mess and Greta arrives soaked after taking her detours through farm ponds and stock tanks along the way.

It doesn't matter what time I make, though. No one's here.

I walk through the house in a numb kind of daze, set out cool water for Greta, and then wander upstairs. I don't bother calling any names—the emptiness in the house is palpable, almost like a living thing itself.

I go to the guestroom where Ireland would have stayed and stand at the foot of the bed, my hands dangling uselessly at my sides. I just stare in a kind of blank hurt at it. I know I don't deserve this moment of pain, so close to self-pity, because every part of this is my fault, but I'm also not strong enough to push the hurt away. I indulge in it and let it take me because I deserve to hurt. I deserve this shame and loneliness.

Sweat from my run here burns my eyes, and I wipe roughly at my face with an equally sweaty arm, which only makes it worse. With a sharp growl of frustration, I yank the unused guest towel that Ireland left folded neatly on the still-neatly made bed—neatly made because she slept with *us* last night—to dry my face.

That's when it catches my eye. Her camera, sleek and expensive, still nestled atop the faded quilt.

She wouldn't have left that on purpose.

Maybe she'll come back for it.

My heart lifts at the thought and then crashes back down, because even if she comes back for it, even if I get to see her pretty heart-shaped face and luscious body again, it doesn't mean I have a right to ask for more.

Like asking her to listen. Asking her to stay.

Making up for my earlier cruelty with as much pleasure as I can possibly visit on her body.

But still I find myself taking the camera in my hand, thinking about how her hands must have cradled it in exactly the same way.

It makes me feel closer to her.

I stopped questioning myself and my feelings when it comes to sex and love a long time ago—the way Caleb and I love each other necessitates a certain amount of adaptability and spontaneity—but I still can't help wondering about my feelings. To be so gone for someone after only a night? It's never happened to me before—not with Mackenna and not even with Caleb. Both of those relationships gradually evolved over time. But falling for Ireland was like an explosion—jagged and fiery and quick as hell.

By the time I heard the *click*, it'd already gone *boom*.

I go out on the porch, as if that will somehow bring her back to me. I'm clutching her camera like a child clutches a toy when I see the distinctive glint of sunlight on metal coming from the north.

My chest tightens; something inside it flips over and flips over hard.

Ireland.

The length of another breath brings a little Prius into view, bright blue and flecked with mud, and I know for sure it's her. I know that somehow I'm being given another chance, and I decide I'm taking it no matter fucking what. I'll beg her to listen, and I'll never stop begging if that's what it takes. I fucked up, but I'll spend the rest of my life making it up to her, if only she'll let me.

Oh God, please. Please let me, sweetheart.

"I'm just here for my camera," she announces briskly as she climbs out of her car. She's still in her distractingly sexy shorts and clingy tank top from earlier, and there's still sheetrock dust in her hair, but she has a bandage on her leg now and a heat in her eyes that means she's either furious or aroused. Or both.

Hot blood kicks to my groin, and I feel myself thicken against my zipper. Fuck, I want her. Even furious with me, I want her. I want her to scratch at me as she holds my face to her pussy. I want her to bite my neck and shoulder and chest as her heels dig into my back to drive me deeper inside her.

I hand over her camera without any additional urging from her. I'm not interested in holding it hostage or using something important to her as leverage. I'm only interested in *her*—her happiness and her safety and her pleasure.

She doesn't meet my eyes as she takes the camera, and she turns back down the porch stairs after she takes it without another word.

"Ireland," I say in a strangled voice. "I was wrong. I was cruel. I'm sorry for it, and it won't ever happen again."

My words halt her progress, and she slowly pivots back to face me. The hurt and anger in her expression would be enough to drive back armies.

"You're goddamned right it's never happening again," she hisses. "Because I'm never coming back here. Ever. *Ever.*"

Her words tear at me, tear at the part of me that wants her to feel safe. I should let her leave, and at this point, saying anything else aside from my apology is dangerously close to manipulation or coaxing, and I don't want that. I want her here because she wants to be here, not because she's guilted into it or convinces herself to stay against her better instincts.

That's what Caleb would do—clearly, that's what he *did*—given he's no longer here and Ireland is in possession of her car again. Ever the country gentleman, he escorted her to her car and honored her wishes the whole time.

I'm not Caleb.

I step down the stairs. "I don't want you to leave," I say in a low voice. She lifts her chin at me defiantly, refusing to step back as I approach.

"Then you shouldn't have *told* me to leave," she seethes.

"I shouldn't have," I agree.

"You treated me like shit for no reason," she continues, color rising in her cheeks, her eyes bright. "You made me feel stupid and awkward and embarrassed—and I don't deserve to feel any of those things!"

"Of course not," I murmur soothingly, because she's still letting me get closer and I don't want to spook her.

"I've spent so much of my life feeling like that, and I'm not going to feel like that anymore!" she says, blinking fast. Each blink feels like a blister rupturing open for me, knowing I'm the source of those tears. Shame and anger at myself stab deep, but I don't let it stop me from getting closer to her, close enough to reach out and stroke her cheek.

Her eyes flutter closed...and then snap back open. "Stop! You can't handsome your way out of this! You were an asshole!"

"I was."

"And you made me feel like I was the asshole!"

"I did."

A tear escapes one of her sweet blue eyes, and I catch it with my thumb. She bows her head slightly, as if defeated by the strength of her own emotions. "I'm so angry," she says to the ground. "I'm so furious with you. And I'm even more furious that I'm crying right now when all I want to do is yell at you."

"You can yell at me as much as you'd like," I tell her, sliding my hand to the nape of her neck while my thumb strokes along her cheek. "As long as you stay here to do it."

Another tear spills out. "I *want* to. Don't you see why it makes it extra awful? I want to stay here with you and Caleb so badly."

I don't miss how the present tense slips out in her words. A ray of hope shoots through me. "Stay, Ireland. Stay and let me make it up to you, make me suffer every minute you're due after what I did, just please"—I bend my face down and brush my lips against hers—"don't go."

She shivers at the touch of my mouth on hers. Parts her lips just enough to invite the gentle stroke of my tongue. And then we are kissing in truth, with her gathered in my arms and our slow kisses turning hot and sultry. Before long, my cock is burning against her belly and she's subtly rocking her hips against me.

When we part for air, her tears are gone, although her eyes are still vulnerable and glinting with turbulent feeling. "How?" she whispers. "How can you kiss me like this when just a couple hours ago...?"

I need to tell her about this part of me, but I don't want it to sound like an excuse, like I'm justifying my awful actions because I've had awful things happen to me in the past. I press my forehead to hers and accept there's no easy way to talk about the busted parts of one's mind, the broken and the healing parts. "Did Caleb tell you I was in the army?"

"Yes," she answers softly. "Afghanistan. PTSD?"

"And a sprinkling of garden-variety depression and anxiety. It's—well, it's a work in progress. *I'm* a work in progress. I was already on the edge after seeing the town like that, but when I thought you might have died, when I saw you were in danger..." My fist is clenched in the material of her tank top at the small of her back, and I force myself to uncurl my fingers. "We went through so many villages that looked exactly like that. Just heaps of stones and bricks. And you never knew what would happen when you were walking through. Would you be shot at? Step on an IED? Find the bodies of a dead family left out in the sun? It's like being turned up to maximum volume for hours...days. And then the volume knob breaks clean off and you can't turn it down anymore."

I stare at her, letting her see something I've only ever let Caleb see. Me, as I am, part shell and part sensitive boy who got beat to shit after school every day. "I'm so sorry, Ireland. I didn't want to hurt you. I wanted you *safe*...and I was so desperate to get you away from anything unsafe that I hurt you to do it. It's unforgivable, and I know that... I just also want you to know *why*. It's not because I don't want you or care for you. Just the fucking opposite."

Her eyes are huge and liquid, like deep-blue waters of emotion, and her lower lip trembles the slightest bit as she asks, "How can I trust you won't be awful to me again?"

All over again, I'm stabbed with shame and regret and self-directed fury. I know it's not helpful—I've spent the last five years listening to therapists and other veterans *tell* me it's not helpful—but the shame comes all the same.

And yet with it comes the faintest note of something else. Hope? Optimism? Certainty?

Yes, I think, *it's because I'm certain about Ireland.* I've never had a reason to believe in things like fate or destiny—the war was very effective at proving there's nothing but chaos in this world—but Ireland makes me doubt all that now.

"Because you're mine."

Her eyes flick over my face, searching me. "You mean that?"

My hold tightens on her. "Yes, baby. You're mine and Caleb's, and you'll remain ours until you don't want to be any longer."

"Yours." She tries out the word, as if the entire concept is foreign to her. As if no one's ever tried to possess her before.

Then they were all fucking fools.

"Ours," I confirm roughly, yanking her close once again. "As long as you want us."

She nibbles on her lower lip, and I can't help it. I bend down and bite that lip for her. "Do you still want us, Ireland?" I murmur against her mouth. "Will you stay and let me make it up to you?"

CHAPTER THIRTEEN

IRELAND

A couple of years ago, I was watching a movie with a handful of girlfriends as we traded gossip and passed around popcorn and bottles of wine. And we got to the part of the movie where the hero makes his grand gesture, chasing after the heroine and declaring his love for her. Declaring that she was *his*.

The room gave a collective groan at this, popcorn flying at the screen, and someone pronounced how utterly backward and chauvinistic that was and how she'd never be caught dead with a man who looked at her and said *mine*. A man who looked at her like she was a prize in the machine simply waiting to be claimed.

I stayed silent.

Because I wasn't going to argue that on a structural level men should act proprietary with women, and I never would. But on a personal level, well...

It was hard to look at my friend, who was slender and sleek and would no doubt have men wanting her everywhere she went and not think *easy for you to say*. Her body was the kind of body that people wanted to claim, wanted to stake some kind of sexual ownership of, and mine was not—never had been, and as years of pointless diet torture had taught me, never would be.

So it was hard not to *wish* I had the luxury of scoffing at male desire. It was hard to watch those movies and know that, according to them, people like me didn't have heroes chasing after them. People like me are the best friends, the comic relief, maybe even the villain.

And in real life? In real life, the kind of male attention I received was dangerous and demeaning. Aggressive frat boys who told me I should feel "lucky" to have them fuck me and then got belligerent and nasty when I refused them. Mean men at bars who grabbed and groped and assumed I'd be grateful for the assault since clearly nobody else would ever want to touch my body.

Girls like me, we didn't get chased, we didn't get claimed, we didn't get the happily ever after. Not in movies. Not in real life.

And was it such a crime to want those things? I burned to have them, ached to be the heroine standing in the rain or at the airport or whatever while the hero pleaded and begged and humbled himself for the privilege and honor to be with me. While he ached and burned for my attention and my body.

And now here I am, listening to Ben plead and beg. Listening to him lay his claim.

Mine. Ours.

The corollary to Ben's words darts around my mind, and it swallows up every other wound and worry: *Theirs.*

I've never belonged to another person before, not in the way that Ben is implying. Even Brian always made sure to tell people we were friends with benefits—or worse. At one memorably shameful work event, he told his boss I was his cousin in town for the week.

So, no, I've never had someone stand in front of me, eyes blazing with possessive lust, and practically vibrate with the need to claim me. Declare I'm *theirs.*

I've never been the heroine. Until now...and God help me, I like it. I like having this man on his proverbial knees while he also looks like he wants nothing more than to pin me against my own car and fuck me until the only word I remember is his name.

"Please, Ireland," Ben says, his voice hoarse and his eyes swirling with a mixture of desperation and lust that my body can't help but answer. "Please."

I suck in a breath, my anger blowing away into nothing. "You have to promise to treat me with dignity," I say, sliding my hands up his chest. "You can't hurt me again."

"Never again," he vows, and then his lips are tracing back over mine with hungry, greedy kisses. "God, Ireland, never fucking again."

He wraps my hand in one of his big ones and tugs me inside the house with the kind of uncompromising urgency that brooks no argument. Not that I'd argue anyway. There's something about having a six-foot-plus, square-jawed, dark-eyed soldier yank you up to his bed that makes a girl eager.

But he surprises me—he takes me to Caleb's bed instead, sitting back against the headboard with his long, muscular legs sprawled.

"Shorts off, panties off," he says. It's not a question.

"What about you?" I ask in a breathy voice.

Ben holds up a hand at my question, as if to say *in a minute*, even though I can see his thick erection stretching all the way to his hip and would hazard a guess *it* doesn't want to wait for any period of time. "Sit after you get bare for me. We're going to give Caleb a treat when he gets home."

God, yes.

I swallow with a combination of nervousness and arousal, but I've already gone to work on my buttons and zipper. As soon as I'm as Ben wants, naked from the waist down and settling between his legs, he finally answers my question. "Don't worry, baby. I'll get what I need very soon."

He arranges me with all the bossy precision of a field commander used to having his orders followed. I'm leaned back against his broad chest and my legs are arranged to drape over his in a way that exposes my pussy to the open air. I almost have a moment of self-consciousness when I feel how wide Ben's legs have to part to accommodate my ass, but it's erased the moment I hear his moan as his erection makes contact with my body. His control fractures the tiniest bit, and he pushes his swollen cock against the place where the small of my back curves into my naked bottom.

"Fuck yes," he grates in my ear. "I love your body. Caleb does too—should we get that pussy of yours ready for him?"

"Yes," I whisper, already wet from Caleb's earlier attention and now from the kiss of cool air along my intimate places. But then Ben strokes a hand down over my breast, over the slopes of my stomach, and down to my feminine place, and I instantly grow even wetter.

"Oh baby," he rumbles. "You need us right now, don't you? Need your boys to take care of that pretty little cunt?"

My head drops back onto his shoulder as his finger delves inside. "Yes," I moan. "I need it." And even just the thought of Ben and Caleb sliding their throbbing columns of unyielding flesh inside me is enough to make me clamp down on Ben's finger. He gives an answering growl.

"Careful, baby," he murmurs. "I'm not letting you come until Caleb gets here. It's going to be a long dance at the edge if you keep up like this."

But what choice do I have? With a handsome, tortured soldier holding me close with one arm while his other reaches between my legs to play with me as if I'm his new toy? What girl wouldn't already be on the edge?

"God, I love how you open up like a flower," he groans, his finger tracing my swelling, slick folds. He buries his nose in my neck and breathes me in. "You're perfect. Fucking perfect."

I'm nearly beyond speech with wanting his fingers to do more. "Ben..." is all I can manage, and then I'm just whimpering and squirming as he teases the pad of one finger around my budding clitoris.

Behind me, I can feel the heat of his erection even through his jeans, like a rod of scorching need. I want it *inside* me—anywhere, everywhere. And just the thought of having him *everywhere* launches me that much closer to orgasm.

"Ben," I beg. "Don't make me wait any longer."

"You'll wait as long as I say you will," he replies in that dark, authoritative voice that never fails to make me quiver in delight. "Even if it's *hours.*"

Hours?

And to prove his point, he trails his touch away from my clit...down, down, down.

"Oh!" I gasp as he presses against a place no one's ever touched before. His finger is slick with where it's been, and it easily penetrates the tight ring of muscle there. I writhe against the new pressure and the illicit thrill of it, and Ben ducks his mouth to my ear. "You want me to fuck you here? Caleb too?" His finger probes deeper, and I make a helpless noise of assent. "What about both of us at the same time, hmm? Working both your tight holes while you're pinned helpless between us?"

"Yes," I whimper, and he rewards me with the heel of his palm against my clit as he carefully fingers my ass. I'm so needful that his entire hand is now wet with me, and playing with my ass clearly gets Ben beyond needful too, because he grinds out several curse words as his other hand flies to his pants to free his cock so it can rub along my bare skin.

And that's how Caleb finds us just a few moments later—me shamelessly rocking against his best friend's hand, my dirtiest secrets penetrated and exposed for viewing, and Ben's erection grinding livid and hot against my skin.

Caleb stands in the doorway of his room, looking staggered. He runs a shaking hand over his mouth, his green eyes flickering back and forth between Ben and me, between the wet and ready place between my legs and the slow grind of Ben's hips against my ass.

"Peach," Caleb breathes, as if he can hardly believe I'm here, and my heart seizes. If I can forgive Ben for pushing me away, I can forgive Caleb for letting me go. In fact, I feel like I can forgive them for *anything*, so long as they finally fuck me. So long as I get to live out Ben's filthy suggestion and experience what it's like to be completely filled. What it's like to have both of them inside me at the same time.

"Caleb," I say, reaching for him, and he's suddenly unfrozen, racing to the bed as he tears off his clothes.

"I wouldn't let her come until you got here," Ben says with a trace of smugness. "She's so fucking wet for you."

Caleb finally kicks off his jeans and boxers and puts a knee up on the bed. My mouth goes dry at the sight of him—all that heavy muscle coiled tight with the need to fuck, those hands twitching at his sides like it's taking everything he has not to grab me and pull me right onto his turgid length. The length that now bobs proudly from his hips, the end of it shiny and tight and beginning to glisten for me at the tip, even though he's only just now joined us.

And when he crawls into the opening made by my legs hooked over Ben's, I can't resist the urge to touch him. To run my fingers over those bulging muscles and the light-brown hair that dusts over his chest and abs. He groans at my touch and then leans forward to nuzzle my breasts, turning his head to bite at the tender undersides through the fabric. It's raw and animalistic and even more so while another man is playing with my asshole as he does it.

Caleb lifts his head to look at Ben. "You said her pussy is ready for me?"

"See for yourself," Ben says and moves his hand to the side—but keeps his middle finger firmly inside my other entrance.

Caleb sucks in a breath. "Holy fuck," he mutters and then glances over to my face, where he no doubt can guess from my flushed cheeks and hooded eyes how much I like what Ben's doing. "Holy fuck," he repeats, this time to himself, as if he can't believe his luck.

I crane my own head now to look up at Ben. His jaw is working tight and his eyebrows are pulled together in strain, like it's taking everything he has not to be fucking me right now. "Are you going to fuck me there?" I ask shyly. "Now?"

He looks down at me, eyes glinting. "Do you want me to fuck you there? Now?"

"Yes," I say with a blush. "But...I haven't done it before."

"Ben is very good at it," Caleb says and then flushes deeply. I decide I want very much to hear more about this and how Caleb knows—and maybe have some demonstrations—but then Ben is sliding out from behind me and stalking to his room, his erection jutting up in a deliciously thick arc from his parted jeans. He returns without his shirt and with a handful of supplies.

"Lie down, Ireland," he commands. I notice his hands are trembling as he hooks his thumbs in the waistband of his jeans and pulls them off, and the evidence of his desire inflames me. Reassures me, even though I'm a little nervous about what comes next.

I move to the middle of the bed as Caleb easily rolls a condom over himself and joins me. He rolls me to my side so we face each other, and he runs the back of his fingers over my face.

"I'm so glad you're here," he says, and there's no mistaking the tenderness in his voice, the depth in his eyes.

Unexpectedly, emotion knots in my throat. "Really?" I whisper. "We only had one night together. If I'd left, it wouldn't have been that big of a deal."

Caleb's already shaking his head. "It would've been. I know it hasn't been long, but can't you feel it?"

"It?" I echo, and he takes my hand and splays it over his chest. Underneath my palm, his heart beats warm and steady and fast.

"Yes," he says solemnly. "It."

My lips part, but I'm not sure what to say. Because I do feel *it*, and if the boys feel it too...

Well, it makes me feel something I've never really felt before. Optimistic and confident and happy and...

Loved.

As if to shore up Caleb's sweet words, Ben kisses my shoulder from behind me and then brushes his lips over the shell of my ear.

"I feel the same way, Ireland. You're ours."

Theirs.

"Yes," I say almost dizzily. "I feel it. I'm yours."

What else can be said after that? Caleb reaches down between my legs to test my readiness and groans at what he finds. With a big callused hand, he pulls my knee up to his hip, and then I feel the broad head of his penis probing slick and latex-covered at my seam.

"Shit," he mumbles as he works the tip of his dick inside me. "Shit, Ireland, you feel so good."

I squirm on the end of his cock, trying to feed more into my body, and he gives a breathless laugh. "I got you, peach, hold on. Trust me to give you what you need."

"Want it *now*," I growl, and he laughs some more.

"Ben, how long did you tease her for?"

"Not very long," is the amused answer. "But you remember how responsive she is."

Caleb's eyes light back on my face, and his laughing mouth pulls into a wicked smile. "I do remember." And with a thrust of his muscled ass, he plows all the way home.

My fingernails dig into his shoulders as my sex stretches and ripples around him, and he gives me three deep and grinding strokes in return, the pressure of his thickness inside me and the gorgeous friction against my clit sending me over the edge. The tension inside my body shatters into a mosaic of delicious sensation—seizing waves low in my belly, flutters of pure pleasure radiating from my clit, tingles of electricity shooting down to the pads of my fingers and the bottoms of my toes.

"Fuck," Caleb groans, his head dropping back. "She's coming already. I can feel it. *Fuck.*"

Ben bites me on the shoulder with a pleased rumble. "Good. Come hard for Caleb, baby. Get all nice and tight for us."

His dirty words spur me on, and my head is tossing on the bed as I ride out my climax on his glorious organ. Caleb is gritting his teeth in order to keep from following me, and then we both let out agonized gasps as Ben's slick finger finds my pleated entrance once again and pushes inside.

"Oh God," I pant, my orgasm surging hard again from the extra stimulation. "Oh God, oh God."

"You better hurry," Caleb grinds out. "I'm not going to last much longer."

"Then how are you going to last when it's my cock pushing inside her?" Ben asks.

Caleb shivers at his words, biting off a curse as he no doubt imagines how it will feel, how tight I'll get with another huge shaft wedged inside me.

My orgasm finally subsides, leaving me limp and quivering, and Ben adds a second finger. "Push against my touch," he advises as I tense up. "It'll open you more to me. Good girl, that's it. Do you feel dirty with my fingers in your ass? Do you feel sexy?"

I give it a couple of breaths, adjusting slowly to the foreign feeling. It does feel dirty, it does feel sexy, especially when I see Caleb gazing at me with an expression bordering on awestruck as he slowly glides his girth in and out of me in time to Ben's pumping fingers. Especially when I look up at Ben and see a man who's about to tear the bed apart with his teeth if he isn't inside my body right this minute.

"I'm ready," I murmur up to him, turning as much as I can to look at the irresistible man kneeling behind me. "I'm ready for you."

"Are you sure?" he asks, and I can see the toll it takes on him to proceed with care. To delay. His shoulders are shaking, the muscles of his belly are clenched so tightly that every band and slab is etched in high relief and glistening with sweat. His cock is dark and distended. A large vein traces up the side, and the slit at his crown is wet and shining with pre-come. "I'll be careful with you, Ireland, I swear to God."

"I know," I say, giving him a sated smile. I'm still dizzy with all the hormones from my last climax. "And I'm sure."

He drops another kiss on my shoulder and then reaches for a condom, tearing the packet open with his teeth and sheathing himself in a quick, practiced movement. There's the click of a bottle cap, and then Caleb and I are treated to the sight of Ben spreading lube down the length of his rigid erection. Through the glisten of the latex and lubricant, I can still see all the veins and the plump crown in perfect detail, and my body craves it, longs for it, even though I have one hot erection already lodged inside my body.

"Same as before," Ben says, tossing the closed lube bottle to the side of the bed. "It's just like my fingers."

"He's lying," Caleb says, his dimple peeking out from under his beard.

"Okay, I'm lying a little," Ben amends. "It's just like my fingers...if my fingers were much, much bigger."

He lies down so the muscled length of his body stretches out behind mine. I feel another flash of bashful unease—there's something about having his firm chest and abs and thighs pressed against the soft gradients and creases of my back and bottom that brings up my worst feelings about my body. Between Caleb at my front and Ben at my back, there's no angle I can twist myself to try to make my waist look smaller, no hiding the crease between my stomach and my hip, no attempting to make my FUPA look smoother. There's no hiding the dimples in my bottom and thighs. I'm completely exposed, naked and squeezed between two men who could be on the cover of a magazine.

But my chagrin vanishes the moment Ben presses fully against me and lets out a groan that goes up to the rafters.

"*Fuck,*" he curses, unable to stop himself from stroking his cock along the seam of my backside. "I'm never letting you leave this bed."

I look back to Caleb, who seems to have the same idea, judging by his bitten lower lip and his roaming, grasping hands.

What girl would ever *want* to leave this bed? Between these two?

"I'm never going anywhere else ever again," I say with a half laugh that turns into a half gasp as I feel the broad tip of him press against my opening. "Oh, Ben."

"Gonna fuck you so good," he husks. "So good, baby."

The hoarse urgency in his voice is an aphrodisiac all its own—not that I need one with the two of them around. I'm so wet that whenever Caleb gives me a thrust, it's like a hot knife moving through butter, and I can feel the beginning of another climax twining into a tight knot right behind my clitoris.

The pressure as Ben begins to work his way into the small aperture is intense—intense enough that I bury my face in Caleb's strong chest as I try to catch my breath.

"Shh," Caleb soothes, stroking my hair and my arm. "This is the hardest part. You just have to breathe."

I breathe as he instructs, trying to push against Ben's invasion, but he's so big, so wide, and there's a pinching feeling that borders on pain as he finally works his way past my rings of muscle.

"*Tight,*" Ben grunts, shoving in another inch. "Fucking tight."

I press my face harder against Caleb, telling myself *breathe breathe*

breathe, and Caleb runs a gentling palm over my thigh and hip, his other arm underneath me and holding me close to him.

Ben curls a hand around my hip and uses another to anchor my shoulder, and then he gives me a final shove that rips the breath right from my body and sends him as deep as he can go.

"Are you okay?" he asks in a strained voice. I can feel him trembling and sweating with the effort to hold his body still, and when I pull my head back and see Caleb, I see the same strain stamped all over him too.

"A moment," I choke out, my entire body tense and aching with the invasion of not one but two massive erections. "Need a moment."

Now firmly in place, Ben readjusts so he's pressed all against me again, and he nuzzles my neck, my hair, my shoulder. Like an animal gentling its mate. And he praises me, telling me how sweet I am, how beautiful I am, how good I make him feel. He promises to make me feel good too. He promises I can use his body and Caleb's to sate my lusts any time I want.

He says I'm the sexiest woman in the world, and Caleb murmurs his agreement, kissing my mouth as Ben kisses the nape of my neck.

As they both throb inside me.

A minute passes, and then another, and between the kissing and the praising, the discomfort has melted away. Instead, I feel gloriously, happily *full*. Complete, even. Like this is the way I'm meant to have sex, like I was formed at birth to mold between these two men.

"Okay," I say, still a bit shaky but also aroused beyond all belief and ready for the climax that's waiting just a few thrusts away. "More, please." I think of what I said last night and smile. "*All of it.*"

"We're gonna give you all of it," says Caleb with a filthy gleam in his eye. "You better hold on tight, little peach."

Together they begin fucking me with careful, rolling thrusts, both of them completely attuned to me, watching and listening with an attentiveness that can only be called reverent. When I flinch, they pause and adjust the angles of their hips until I sigh again. When I gasp, they kiss and lick my mouth and neck until I'm squirming down onto them. And when I dig my fingernails into Caleb's shoulder and moan, they reward me with deep, railing thrusts that leave me seeing stars and panting their names.

My hovering orgasm only needs a few minutes of this to finally explode into release. With an unladylike moan, I detonate around the two cocks buried inside me. Hard, clenching contractions take me, make everything below my navel feel like a giant squeezing fist of pure pleasure, and I'm dimly aware my orgasm is driving the men wild.

Ben and Caleb link hands over my hip to hold me steady as I writhe through the delight, and together they surge into me as deep as they can.

"Gonna come...so hard," pants Caleb, and behind me, I hear Ben grunt in agreement. Then Caleb lets out an almighty yell, his head thrown back and the cords in his neck straining, and heat scalds my sheath through the condom after he pumps waves of his orgasm into the latex.

It triggers more pleasure of my own, and stars dance at the edge of my vision as a delicate pain lights up nerve endings everywhere on my body. Ben's sunk his teeth into my neck and, with a bitten-off noise, erupts otherwise silently against the tight, dirty glove of my channel, filling his own condom with spurt after spurt of hot seed.

Both of them keep thrusting through their ejaculations, and I keep undulating between them as my own climax ebbs gradually into satisfied exhaustion. In a tangle of arms, I'm cradled between them, and we're sweaty and the condoms need to be taken care of, and I have no doubt I'm going to be sore, but at this moment, all I can think is what I told them earlier.

I'm never going anywhere else again.

Yes, they were sex words, but I realize they're also true in every other sense as well. I want to stay.

I'm *going* to stay.

CHAPTER FOURTEEN

CALEB

The sun blazes nosy and chiding through the window, reminding us there's so much to do and fix outside these walls, but we ignore it, spending the afternoon as if it's the dead of night—doing all manner of wicked and depraved things normally saved for hours of darkness.

After we clean up, Ben and I spend a long time between Ireland's legs, jostling for space and the chance to lick at her sweet honey. And after she comes twice more, we once again cradle her between us and take her at the same time. This time, I'm the one fucking her tight, rear hole, and the grip of her is insane. And with the pressure from Ben's cock inside her pussy and the added stimulation of feeling him stroke against me through her thin walls, it's a miracle I last long enough to make sure she comes first. Somehow I manage it, lips thin and eyes shut, waiting until the last of her shudders die down before I open my eyes and let myself just *look* at her writhing between us. Those sweet slopes and tucks of her body. The way her curves yield softly to my form as I move against her. The way her body spills out of my hands as I fondle and squeeze at her.

She's straight out of my wet dreams, out of every fantasy I've ever had—dark hair soft as silk and flowing like water over Ben's arm. Blue eyes to rival the storm-cleansed sky outside. Perfectly formed lips that beg for my own.

And a body like those paintings in art class—with soft rolls and a round bottom and a plump little pussy that all but begs to be fucked and fucked thoroughly.

That's all it takes, looking at her, and I come with a bellow and a bowing body, pumping my condom full of hot, slick seed. Ben watches me roar and tense through it, and then he takes Ireland's mouth in a searing kiss as he follows me over the edge with a single quiet noise.

We've always used condoms with every woman we've been with, always, always, and a jolt of fresh blood hits my spent cock as I think about what it would be like to skip the condoms next time. To claim this beautiful woman from the inside out, to feel the slippery heat of Ben doing the same.

My cock gives another pulse, trying valiantly to rise to the occasion, and Ireland gives me a happy, if slightly rueful, smile.

"I need a break, cowboy," she says, wincing a bit as we tug free of her body. "Another few minutes, at least."

"We have all the time in the world," Ben says. His brows draw together as he gazes down at her. "I hope."

For a moment she doesn't answer, simply searching Ben's face and then mine as if trying to read our thoughts. Apparently satisfied by what she sees, she gives us a lazy nod, like a queen.

"All the time in the world."

࿎

When late afternoon begins to crest into evening, we drive back to Holm. Ben needs to start making calls and contacting insurance companies about the tavern, and after making sure Mrs. Parry and Mrs. Harthcock are safe and settled, I'm anxious to get back to town to help in whatever way I can.

To our surprise, Ireland is just as eager to go. She changes into fresh clothes and slings her camera around her shoulder.

"What?" she asks, catching Ben and me looking at her.

"You don't have to come," I tell her gently. "It's not your town, and anyway, I don't know how much there will be to do—"

"There will be plenty to do, for one thing, and for another, while this may not be my home, it *is* yours. I'm not a totally heartless city girl; I want to help, and I can help, and I'm coming along too. So long as it won't be hard on Ben."

Ben crosses over to her and yanks her close. "I swear it won't be," he murmurs, training those intense, dark eyes on Ireland's mouth. And then he gives her a kiss like he's just come home from the war all over again.

Holm is flooded with people when we get there—police cars and pickup trucks crowd the debris-choked streets—but Ireland is right. Even with so many people here, there's plenty to do. While Ben focuses on the tavern, Ireland and I spend the next five or six hours working to help shift rubble and sort through wreckage. We work deep into the humid dark, Greta sticking close and providing moral support by licking everyone's hands and doing enough tail-wagging for an entire pack of dogs. And Ireland frequently pauses in order to snap pictures of the town at work righting itself.

I don't know much about photography beyond taking pictures of used farm equipment to sell it on the internet, but even I can see her pictures are striking. An older woman crying in front of the flattened house where her sister died. Dirt-streaked faces gazing out at the sunset. Ben, head bowed in misery as he stands in the doorway of the tavern.

The pictures give me chills, and as we're sitting around the kitchen table, each with a well-earned glass of bourbon as the night presses in through the windows, I ask her, "Why didn't you become a photographer for real? Why go work for Drew?" I like Drew quite a lot, but that doesn't mean Ireland isn't wasted writing tweets for microbreweries or creating brand strategy for a sandwich chain. Pictures like these could be in newspapers, on the covers of magazines; she could be anywhere, with her pick of people wanting her pictures.

Ireland takes a long drink of bourbon and reaches out to idly finger a sunflower sitting in an old jelly jar on the table. I saw the bloom as we walked in, still fresh and healthy and sheltered from the storm by the porch stairs— knowing Ireland's fascination with them, I made sure to come out and pick it for her while she got cleaned up. I'm glad I did, because watching her face soften as she studies the flower makes my chest puff out with pride. "I, uh, I turned down a photography scholarship in college," she says eventually, eyes still on the flower. "And decided to stay local. Major in something more practical."

It sounds plausible enough—hell, I did the same, choosing a college only two hours away so I could be close to the farm while I got my degree in Ag Econ— but there's something about the way she doesn't look at us as she answers that makes me think there's more to the story than she's willing to share right now.

She's saved from me pressing further by Ben's stifled yawn, and we abandon our bourbon for a shower and sleep. Ben surprises me by climbing into bed with us, folding Ireland into his big arms, and reaching out with one foot to touch mine like we used to do when we were boys sharing a bed. But when I stir in the middle of the night, I find Ireland in my arms instead, my foot encountering nothing but cool sheets under her tucked-up legs.

He still doesn't trust himself to sleep with us the whole night through.

"...haven't talked to them yet at all. I wanted to ask you first, of course."

Ireland's voice filters through my groggy brain, and I roll over to see her perched on the edge of the bed, her legs curled up beside her, a phone to her ear. Like this, the mouthwatering angles of her hips and ass are perfectly delineated by the morning sunshine pouring in through the window. I move closer to her and start shamelessly squeezing her curves and stroking her stomach. She ineffectively bats at me as she keeps talking.

"I'm so glad you like them, and we're going back today, so I'll take more. I think this is a much stronger pitch in the long run, but I'll need to come back a few more times. I want to capture all the rebuilding efforts and stuff like that."

I hear Drew's voice on the other end, but I ignore it, busy exploring Ireland's body and teasing fingers over her hip to the soft vee of her pussy.

She gives a delicious shiver, and her voice when she answers her boss is a little strained. "Yes, let's make sure to add this to the meeting tomorrow. I want everybody's feedback."

They exchange a few more words before she hangs up, and I curl my hand possessively over my new favorite toy.

"You're going back to Kansas City," I say. I knew she'd have to, but I can't fight the irrational urge to truss her up to my bed and keep her here at the farm forever.

She sighs and parts her legs enough for me to pet her cunt properly. "I'll leave tonight, since my meeting is first thing tomorrow. I'm going to see if we can pitch a different angle to the Tourism Board. Rather than 'farmers at work' for *Real Kansas*, I want to show Holm. The citizens working together after the storm, grieving together and helping each other."

I think of her pictures last night, of the goose bumps they gave me, and make an approving noise. "I like that idea."

"So does Drew, so it's really down to convincing the client. At any rate," Ireland says, her eyes shyly glancing away, "Drew thinks I should sell some of the pictures too. He's reaching out to his friends at some local and national papers now."

"That's wonderful!" I slide my arms around her and tug her even closer so I can reward this good news with more caresses and strokes where she's growing wet and needy. "Your pictures should be in every paper, in every magazine."

"You're just saying that because you want to have sex with me again," she mutters, but she blushes.

"No, I'm saying that *and* I want to have sex with you again. Now, I'm going to holler for Ben, and when he gets in here, I suggest you be ready."

Watching Ireland leave is painful, even with as tired as Ben and I are from working in town all day. We each kiss her senseless before she climbs into the car, crowding her against the car door and taking turns with her lush mouth until we're all breathless and she can barely stand.

"Come back to us," I plead against her lips.

"You're ours," Ben says simply, and then he leans down and bites at her neck. She shudders against us.

"Yours." She smiles. "I'm yours."

She calls us every night, and for once, the internet connection at the farmhouse is strong enough for the three of us to use video chat for its best purpose—so she can see Ben and me stroke off for her while she leisurely fingerfucks herself. From her calls, we also learn the Tourism Board is thrilled about the new pitch and that the *Kansas City Star* has been running her pictures with the promise to buy more.

She awkwardly, adorably, asks if she can come visit this weekend.

"How about you move in," Ben says.

She laughs, but I know he's not joking. The time away from her has done nothing to dull our certainty that she's our girl, the missing piece to our hearts, and every moment she's away from us is painful. After she offhandedly mentions being able to work remotely, it makes it impossible not to dream and hope of a time when she can stay here always. But Ben and I agree not to push her too fast. We've had years and years to adjust to the way we like our love and our sex, but Ireland's only had a week.

We can be patient. Maybe.

When she returns on Friday afternoon in her gravel-dusted Prius and with a fresh coat of lavender lipstick on that irresistible mouth, Ben and I are waiting.

She parks in the driveway and climbs out of the car, looking a bit shy, like she's not sure what it will be like to be with us in person again. She's wearing another pencil skirt, this time with heels and a clingy cardigan thing that shows off all my favorite parts of her breasts and stomach and waist. The pencil skirt hugs her tightly enough that I can easily perceive the inverted triangle of her crotch, and even though I was already hard with anticipation simply knowing she was on the way, seeing her in the flesh is like a kick of heat right to my dick. My balls tighten and my shaft swells even more, needing to be buried inside her at the first opportunity.

Ben is the first to move, prowling toward her like a wolf and then seizing her in a lewd kiss that has her nipples poking through her sweater.

"Inside," he growls, all beast to Ireland's beauty. "Fucking *now*."

We go inside, and we fuck Ireland in her pencil skirt, and then in nothing but her heels, and then again in nothing but her lipstick.

"Move in," Ben says again as we all lie in bed that night, naked and sweaty and spent.

Ireland laughs again, burrowing into us and falling asleep in a record amount of time.

This time, Ben almost manages to stay the entire night with us before creeping back to his own bed where he feels safe.

CHAPTER FIFTEEN

IRELAND

"No way," I say firmly. "Uh-uh. Nothing doing."

It's my fourth weekend with the boys—*my* boys—and the miserable August heat has driven us to the big farm pond at the back of the property. I thought we were heading back here simply to sit beside the water and let the breeze cool us off, but that notion evaporated the minute we reached the small wooden dock and both Caleb and Ben stripped completely naked. I barely had a chance to ogle their big, muscled bodies with those delightfully taut asses and heavy, semihard cocks, before they launched themselves into the water.

Completely naked.

"Come on, peach!" Caleb says with his customary grin. "It feels amazing!"

I shake my head vigorously. It's hot as hell out here, and while I normally love swimming, I love swimming in a *swimsuit*. One that has been carefully selected to support and flatter. The idea of stripping naked in all this bright sunlight, every wobbly inch of me exposed, and then jumping into the water with all those wobbly inches at maximum wobble is enough to make me wince.

It's strange, because a month ago, I would have avowed the new Ireland was confident and fierce and no longer cared about wobbles at all. And you would think having two hunky farm boys jumping my bones every few hours would have cured me of any insecurity at all!

I'm annoyed with myself about it. It feels like I'm going backward...and with no good reason. These boys adore me. I adore them. They've never done anything to make me feel anything *but* the sexiest woman alive.

But, if I'm honest, when Ben and I fought and I left, there was this tiny part of me that said, *Oh. Of course. What did I expect would happen? Plus-sized girls don't date cute, fit guys. Men like them won't want to keep you around.*

I know it was his war trauma talking, and Ben never made that moment about my body—but I did. I definitely did. And there's this weird little place in my mind that won't let go of it, like a dog with a bone. Just chewing over this insecurity until it's gross and splintery and rank. Until it whispers things like *how long do you really think this can last? How long until they* really *look at your body and decide not to want you anymore?*

"I don't like swimming with fish," I lie, sitting on the dock instead. I stretch out my legs and smooth my skirt primly down my thighs. The fabric sticks to my skin because I'm so sweaty, and I try not to think about how cold the swimming hole looks right now. How refreshing. "I prefer to swim in clean water. Without living things in it."

"The fish are very nice fish," Caleb promises. "They haven't eaten a person in years."

"Funny," I reply. "Very funny. I'm still not coming in."

"I think you are," Ben says from next to the dock. The water flows gracefully over his strong shoulders as he effortlessly treads in place, the tantalizing lines of his firm body disappearing into the green depths and hiding the most interesting parts from view.

I try to catch a glimpse anyway.

I bet even the cool water swallowing up his body is doing nothing to diminish that perfect penis of his.

Caleb is the first to haul himself up the dock ladder, but Ben follows right after, and then I don't have to crane my neck anymore to see their beautiful cocks because they're right in front of me.

"No," I say, having a feeling where this is going. "I'm not going in."

"You're all flushed, peach," Caleb coaxes. Even as he says the words, a drop of sweat drips down from my hairline. "A nice dip would make you feel better."

Ben just stares down at me with that penetrating way of his, like he can see all the things I don't want him to see.

I look away, pretending to fuss with the hem of my skirt and also pretending my dress isn't sweat-soaked and clinging to my back because I'm dying in the sun. "I'm not actually that hot," I fib. "The breeze off the water is enough to cool me down."

Ben drops to his knees and moves over me so he's straddling my legs. He plants his hands on either side of my hips and leans forward, his lips grazing my jaw. "If you don't get into the water, I'm pulling you in."

I narrow my eyes. "You wouldn't."

He shrugs without answering, leaning in to kiss my neck, heedless of the sweat there.

"You monster," I accuse. "What if I can't swim?"

At this he pulls back and searches my face. "But you can swim, can't you? This isn't about swimming at all. There's something else holding you back."

He's so close and so beautiful and his expression is unnervingly kind. I can't keep looking at him; the gross little voice in my head won't let me.

"Ireland," Ben warns. "Talk or be thrown in."

"I'm not doing either—"

With a movement so quick I barely see it, he's on his feet and has one of my hands while Caleb has the other. I'm yanked up, and before I can catch my balance, I'm in the water, my toes touching soft, cool mud before I kick back up to the surface, spluttering.

They stand naked above me, looking very proud of themselves. "There," Caleb says, laughter in his voice. "That wasn't so bad, was it? Aren't you cooler now?"

"This dress is dry-clean only, you dicks," I grouse. But I can't lie... The water does feel good.

"Now that it's all wet, you should take it off," Caleb suggests. His cock seems to agree, thickening as he peers down at me in the water. "Your underthings too. You know, in case they're also dry-clean only."

I think for a moment. I can't help but be squeamish about the idea of stripping in the bright, unforgiving light of the summer sun, but if I get in the water right away, maybe it won't feel so exposing...

I swim toward the ladder and pull myself up, and before I can reach for my zipper, Caleb and Ben are helping me unzip and peel off the wet dress. I shoo them away out of instinct, and with schoolboy laughing and whooping, they jump back into the water.

Too late I realize my mistake. Right next to me, they wouldn't have been able to properly see my body, but now that they're back in the water, I'm totally exposed again. It's like being on a fucking runway, and their view up at me is far from the ideal angle.

Just finish undressing quickly and get down the ladder, I coach myself, turning away before I unhook my bra. Then I discover facing away from them means they'll see more of the cellulite on my ass and on the backs of my thighs— but being in profile means they'll see my belly. Facing them means they'll see my breasts under the cruel duress of gravity.

Fuck.

But when I drop the bra and turn, I don't see two pairs of judgmental eyes cataloging my every stretch mark and dimple. Instead, both men have swum to the edge of the dock and are watching me with hot gazes full of hunger. One of Caleb's hands is moving lazily under the water, and I flush when I realize what he's doing.

"Now your panties," Ben grates out. He's breathing hard as he watches me.

"Those too."

Their hungry stares fill me with power, and my insecurity melts away as if it were never there. I shimmy out of my panties and even give a little hip swivel as I do.

"Fuck me," Caleb groans. "Get in here, peach. Now."

I do. I run and jump in, wobbles forgotten, and later that afternoon, when the three of us fuck under the shade of a big cottonwood tree, I can't even remember what it feels like to be embarrassed at all.

The nightlight in Caleb's room is for Ben.

I have this epiphany as I'm gently turned into Caleb's arms and Ben slides out of the bed to go to his room.

The nightlight is so Ben can find his way in the dark.

Away from us.

My heart squeezes as I press my face into Caleb's warm chest and let the steady swell of his breathing lull me back to sleep.

I wake alone in the morning, which is normal for us. Ben never sleeps the whole night in here, and Caleb gets up around dawn to tend to the farm. I stretch and sigh at the darkened nightlight. I want Ben to stay the night with us. His bed is only a twin—something I think was an intentional choice, meaning no one could ever sleep in his bed with him—so it has to be Caleb's bed. I wish there was a way to tell him I'd be happy to sleep with lights on, the television on, anything he needed, without it becoming awkward, but I can't think of the right words. The words to reassure him that I don't think he's broken or damaged, that I simply want to share everything with him. Sleep included.

I'm going to talk to him about it, I decide as I shower and get dressed. *Today.* If it's nightmares, then we'll work through it. If it's space, then I'll sleep on the floor. I'll do anything it takes, but it makes me miserable to feel him slipping away every night when the answer could be within our reach.

However, talking to him may come sooner than I planned. I get downstairs to find both men waiting for me in the kitchen, which is *not* normal.

"I made breakfast," Ben says, pulling out a chair for me and presenting me with a mug of coffee and then a plate of irresistible farm food. Fried mushrooms, eggs, and bacon, with a thick slab of toast, butter melting on top.

"Thanks!" I take the plate, and I'm about to demolish the toast when I notice them looking at me.

I've never liked being watched while I'm eating. It makes me immediately and terribly self-conscious, as if I'm doing something wrong by it. As if I should have refused the food or asked for raw kale and sunflower seeds instead.

But there's nothing about Caleb or Ben that looks anything other than their normal handsome and slightly-obsessed-with-me selves right now. Caleb has his usual bearded grin as he sits next to me, and Ben his usual hungry gaze as he sits on the other side.

Relax, Ireland. They aren't Brian and your sister. They're not judging you.

It's still hard to take that first bite, but Ben's look of masculine pride as I moan around his meal is worth it. They love to take care of me—I'm in danger of being downright spoiled. They wash my hair in the shower, they launder my clothes, and they pack my bags. They plug my phone and laptop into chargers if I forget to at night, and they put jars and vases full of fresh sunflowers in every room simply because they know sunflowers make me smile. They give me the second-best spot on the couch—Greta-dog gets the first-best—and then, of course, there are the hours and hours of mind-blowing sex.

So it's not unusual for them to pamper me with a delicious meal, but it is unusual for them not to be working right now. For them to be here watching me eat instead of out in the fields or in town, or even working on restoring the tavern now that some of the insurance money has trickled in.

I glance between them, wondering if I should stop eating.

"Move in with us," Caleb blurts out, and Ben groans.

"We were going to wait until after she ate," he says irritably. "Remember?"

I swallow and look at them both. They are deadly earnest, sitting on the literal edges of their seats with green and brown eyes trained on me.

"You aren't serious," I say weakly.

"We've never been more serious about anything," Ben says after giving Caleb a *let-me-handle-this* look. "We're in love with you."

My mouth drops open.

Caleb laughs. "Peach, it can't be that much of a surprise. We can't keep our hands off you, we call you constantly when you're away, and we never let you out of our sight when you're here. Of course we're in love with you."

"I just—I—" I'm stammering and also trying to keep my chin from quivering. "No one's ever said that to me before."

Both boys blink at me with such sweet surprise that I have to rub at my nose to fight off the sudden about-to-cry sting there. And then before I can do or say anything else, I'm being yanked into a fierce embrace between the two of them, and even on their knees around me they're still tall enough that I feel completely surrounded.

I bury my face into Caleb's neck, rubbing against his soft beard.

"We've been in love since the moment we met you," he says softly.

Ben is moving my hair aside to kiss the nape of my neck with firm, warm lips.

"We've known you were ours since day one," Caleb continues. "Please say yes, Ireland. Please say you love us back. Move in with us."

My heart's so full it feels like it will burst.

How can this be real? How can this be true?

And how is it that I've never wanted anything as much as to be with these two men for the rest of forever?

"I love you back," I mumble against Caleb's skin. "I think I've been in love with the both of you since the first day too."

I'm rewarded for this admission, squeezed and kissed and loved on. Petted and stroked until I feel all spoiled again.

"You haven't answered us about moving in," Ben says. "Why? Is it work? Family?"

I can work remotely, and I would probably pay money to not see my sister, so it's not either of those things. But I'm not really sure what it *is* either. Some kind of lingering insecurity, maybe? This stubborn doubt that I don't really belong with them because of my body?

I hate these gross thoughts. I banish them to the back of my mind and try to focus on what I know instead—Caleb and Ben love me and I love them, and there's no practical reason keeping me from moving in other than that it's fast and this relationship is still so new. Well, that and one person in our bed can't seem to stay there for the whole night.

Maybe this is my chance to be brave...and to nudge Ben into bravery along with me.

"I'll say yes," I decide, "if Ben can sleep the whole night with us."

Behind me, Ben's body goes still and stonelike. "Pardon?" he asks, as if he didn't hear correctly.

"I think you heard me," I reply gently. "If we can find a way for you to sleep through the night with us, I'll move in."

CHAPTER SIXTEEN

BEN

Ireland is looking at me over her shoulder, her blue eyes clear and serious, and Caleb's looking at me the same way. All concern and desire. It makes my chest tighten, and I stand up to get some space while I think.

"I didn't think anyone cared much one way or the other," I say, going over to the counter and bracing my hands against it. I take a few deep breaths, trying to organize my thoughts, which are currently in a defensive swirl. "It's not like we fuck any less because I sleep alone."

"It's not about fucking," Ireland says, and I hear her stand up and walk over to me. She slides her hands around my waist and leans her head against my back, molding her curves to me.

It feels so good. Good enough that I realize how tense my body is, as if I'm fortifying myself against some kind of danger.

I inhale, forcing myself to remember that I'm *here*, not in Marjah listening to the sporadic crackle of bullets and the distant thuds of mortar shells. I'm here at the farm with the two people I love. Two people I'm trying to love better than I have been.

"I have trouble sleeping," I admit, and even that admission is harder than it should be. I don't know why, when Ireland's arguably seen the worst of my baggage already, but I can't stand that I'm not able to do something as normal as sleep with the people I love—or hell, sleep properly at all. It makes me feel juvenile and antisocial and abnormal, and I hate it.

But Ireland deserves the truth, and I made promises to her that I plan on keeping.

I take a deep breath and keep going. "It's hard to get to sleep, and I have nightmares when I do. Bad nightmares that leave me sweaty and thrashing and kicking. The TV and lights help sometimes but not always. I *want* to sleep with you two—God, I want to so much—but I'm terrified of hurting you while I'm dreaming—and on top of that, it's not fair to make your sleep worse just so I can share a bed with you. You deserve rest."

"And you don't?" Ireland murmurs.

I make an impatient noise. "Not if it makes it *harder* for you to sleep!"

"I can handle myself," she says stubbornly.

"Me too," says a deep voice next to me. I look up into the soft-green eyes of my best friend and lover.

"It's not that easy," I say. "*I* don't even like being around myself at night. I would never ask someone else to be."

"But you're not asking. We are." Ireland squeezes me tighter and then slips under my arm so she can peer up into my face. "Please, Ben? Can we try it?"

What man on earth could resist these hopeful big blue eyes? This soft, pouting mouth? I'm nothing but weakness when it comes to her, and I think she knows it because her pleading expression starts looking more and more triumphant the longer we stare at each other.

Finally I heave a giant breath. "Okay," I agree, and I know I sound reluctant as fuck—because I am. "We'll try tonight. And then you'll move in with us."

The firmness in my words leaves no room for argument, and it sounds more like a military command than a boyfriend asking someone he loves to share his life. But I don't care. I don't care at all because she gives me a sweet smile and an even sweeter "Yes, Ben."

And then breakfast is left to cool on the table as we yank each other upstairs to fuck in the bed we'll all share tonight.

The thought of tonight haunts me as I toil over the new floors in the tavern this afternoon. As I work, my mind fills with worrisome scenarios ranging from good-old-fashioned insomnia to the humiliating release of tears I sometimes wake to find on my face.

It's not a big deal. It's not a big deal, I repeat to myself as I work on fitting and gluing the floorboards down. People sleep with their lovers all the time, and surely I'm not the only person in the history of human relationships to have trouble sleeping. *Ireland and Caleb love me,* I remind myself and feel the tight anxiety in my chest loosen a little.

I want to make them happy. I want to be closer to them.

I can do this.

I've survived years of bullying in school, and I've survived war zones that have since become legendary for how hellish they were. Fists and bullets and fire—I've lived through it all.

I can survive the night snuggled against someone I love.

The tavern door opens, letting in a welcome rectangle of warm sunlight and fresh air, and I look up to see Ireland in the doorway wearing the short skirt Caleb and I beg her to wear all the time and a blouse thing tied around her waist, showing off a tempting tease of pale skin. With her blue lipstick and colorful clothes, she's like kissable, lickable city-girl candy, and I want to wrap my fist in all that dark, silky hair and press my mouth against all her sugar. My cock is pulsing to life just looking at her.

I wipe the sweat from my brow with my forearm and get to my feet, taking off my work gloves so I can grab at her and kiss her. She giggles as I do, fussing about her lipstick and halfheartedly trying to keep her distance from my sweaty, sawdusted body, but she eventually gives in, letting me crowd her against the wall until she's moaning into my mouth and arching her soft breasts into my hands.

The door opens again and Caleb walks in. "Oh fuck, you guys," he says in a husky voice. "Fuck yeah."

"No, no, no," Ireland protests as Caleb joins us and starts in on her neck. "We just fucked this morning. Twice!"

"Doesn't matter," I mumble, brushing my thumbs across her hard, needy nipples. My cock is raging to be inside her, and with her short, flirty skirt, it's all too easy to push my hand between her legs to find out if she's wet enough to fuck.

She is.

She moans again as I slide my thumb under her panties and start rolling it against her stiff little clit.

Caleb's already grinding his erection against her hip, taking up where I left off on teasing her nipples, and I whisper in her ear, "We could do it a third time... and a fourth time...and a fifth time...right here against this wall. You coming so hard on our cocks that you can't even hold yourself up..."

Her eyes are fluttering almost all the way closed, and for a minute, I think she's going to agree, but then her phone buzzes in her skirt pocket and she jolts.

"You guys," she admonishes, pushing us back with a flat palm to each of our chests. "I'm supposed to meet a reporter from the *Star* at any minute, and I can't do that with lipstick all over my face and a used condom in my pocket."

"Well, obviously we'd throw the condom away after—"

Her hand moves from my chest to my mouth. "Your talking privileges are suspended for the time being." Her half smile fades a little. "It's important to me, Ben. My pictures of Holm and all the rebuilding that's been happening here could be the start of something exciting, and I don't want to fuck it up. Now where can I fix my lipstick?"

Caleb points her to the bathroom—which has running water and a mirror, even if it's still trashed from the storm—and then turns back to me with a thoughtful expression. "You think we should go with her to meet this reporter? Like emotional support?"

I'm already walking toward the bag I've got sitting on a makeshift table made out of sawhorses and plywood. I rummage for a clean shirt and wipe the sweat and blue lipstick off my face. I'm thinking of her anxious, hopeful expression just now, and also about the way she's been all over this town taking pictures of both the tragic and the hopeful.

I wonder again why she isn't already doing something she obviously loves so much.

"Yeah. I think we should."

The reporter and her accompanying photographer are friendly and engaging. The reporter interviews Ireland for a good forty-five minutes as we stroll around the recovering but still visibly scarred Main Street while the photographer drifts away and back again to take pictures of various buildings and piles of construction materials. Caleb and I more or less hang back, and I'm sure we look like country boy versions of bodyguards as we trail behind our girl and cast looming six-foot-plus shadows along the street. The photographer seems a little nervous around us, but the reporter is just curious, peeking back over her shoulder and then back at Ireland, as if trying to guess if we're related or something. It's strangely irritating, but I force myself to remember that two is not the usual number of boyfriends to have. And also that Ireland wants to impress this person, so it won't do her any good if I spend the rest of the afternoon scowling.

Ireland herself is adorably oblivious to our presence as we go, so used to us following her around like overgrown—and overprotective—puppies that she only spares us a glance every now and then. But each glance is elated and grateful and makes me fall in love with her all over again.

"Well," the reporter says, hitting *stop* on her phone's recording app and giving Ireland a warm smile, "I think that's probably all I need. We'll just get some photos of you and then head on out."

Ireland freezes, and I can see the moment the panic hits her like a lightning bolt. She swallows, and there seems to be effort in keeping her voice light when she says, "Photos of me?"

"Of course!" the reporter chirps. "I think it will really drive home the point of the piece, which is all about the girl behind the camera, you know? The face behind the pictures that everyone's been talking about."

It's astonishing how fast the well-kissed, confident, animated woman taking them around the town vanishes. In her place is a woman who looks terrified, tugging unconsciously at her hemline and rounding her shoulders ever so slightly, as if she's trying to hunch into herself.

As if she's trying to hide.

I don't understand it, but every protective instinct in me roars to life, and they must be in Caleb too because he's already taking a step forward, as if to put himself between Ireland and danger. Danger in this case being a chirpy, five-foot-four reporter.

I step forward too and put my hand against Ireland's back.

"Do you want your...friends...in the picture?" the reporter asks, looking at us with avid interest.

"Boyfriends," I correct automatically and then realize I've made a mistake. Ireland stiffens against my hand at the same time as the reporter's eyes gleam with unmistakable delight. I can practically see her brain whirring with ways to work this juicy tidbit into the story.

Shit.

"Boyfriends?" she repeats and gives us the *oh cool, uh-huh, uh-huh, I'm pretending to think this is totally normal* nod and smile. "And you met after the storm?"

I can feel the deep breath Ireland takes. "Actually, no," she answers, and she answers with a lifted chin and the confident, cheerful smile I've come to know and love. "We met before the tornado." And she gives a charming and PG-rated account of how we all came to know each other and how the storm brought us together.

The reporter can't hide her excitement. "This is such a cute story," she gushes. "Can I make it part of the feature? I mean, with a picture of the three of you..."

I'm about to say no on Ireland's behalf. It's clear there's something about being in a picture that makes her uncomfortable, and I won't have anything making her unhappy, but she beats me to an answer.

"Yes," she says, and while I can sense her bravery, I can also sense her pride. "You can put it in the article, with a picture of the three of us."

And when Caleb and I arrange ourselves around her, our arms crossing behind her back to wrap around her waist, it feels like the most natural thing in the world. Not just the holding of her between us, which isn't new, but doing it publicly.

I give her a kiss on the head between flashes of the camera.

"I love you," I tell her.

"I'm real proud for the world to know I'm your boyfriend," Caleb adds quietly.

Ireland flushes a happy flush, and her smile for the camera goes brighter.

"Okay, I think we've got it," the reporter says cheerfully after the photographer gives her a nod. "I'm going to work fast—we're hoping to get this up by late evening!"

It's enough to send another nervous look flitting across Ireland's face, but the reporter and photographer are quick with their goodbyes, and there's no chance for Ireland to change her mind about anything. When they leave, she turns back to us, chewing on her blue lower lip. "Do you think I did okay? Did I talk enough about the rebuilding and the storm? And the picture—"

"You did great, peach," Caleb says, wrapping his big hands around her shoulders and dropping a kiss onto her hair. "You did perfect."

She sighs like she doesn't believe him but isn't willing to argue and turns back to the tavern. We follow, stepping onto the sidewalk right as Mrs. Parry's nephew walks past with a bucket of paint in each hand, headed for the little volunteer library next to the tavern. I give him a nod, although something about the way the older man eyes Ireland has me pressing my hand more firmly against her back, those protective instincts still rearing strong.

Ireland, probably still chewing over the interview in her mind, doesn't notice Lyle Parry or my reaction to him. I shoot a glance at Caleb, who also takes note of the smirking way Lyle is staring at Ireland, and Caleb understands immediately. He hangs back, ostensibly to talk to Lyle, but really to step between Lyle and Ireland while I shepherd her back inside the tavern.

Caleb and Lyle greet each other and make some small talk as we all move down the sidewalk, and it's with some relief when I get to the door of the tavern and push it open. Ireland is walking inside as Lyle lowers his voice and mutters to Caleb, "She must be something else in bed, huh?"

"Excuse me?" Caleb asks coldly.

"You know what I'm talking about," Lyle says in a winky-nudgy kind of tone, which is still loud enough to carry easily through the threshold of the open tavern door. I try to shut it, but I'm not quick enough. Lyle's stupid voice still reaches us. "The chunky ones are always better in the sack. More grateful, you see? Makes them try harder."

Next to me, Ireland goes completely still, and I'm torn between the need to comfort her and shield her from every shitty thing in this world and my rage. I want to go out there and beat the teeth out of Lyle Parry's head. I want to wring him like a towel and hang him up to dry.

But one look at Ireland's face reminds me what my priorities are.

I gather her into my arms and hold her to my chest. "Fuck him," I murmur.

Caleb outside growls, "You'll talk about Ireland with some fucking respect, Lyle, or face the consequences." And then Caleb storms inside amid Lyle's shocked sputters, slamming the tavern door shut behind him.

"God, Ireland, I'm so fucking sorry he said that," Caleb says with misery painted all over his expression. He comes to stand next to us, putting his hand on Ireland's shoulder, but she shakes her head and takes a step away from us.

"It's fine," she says in a falsely bright voice. "I've been one of the 'chunky ones' for a long time. I'm used to it."

Everything about her is armored right now—her forced smile and her tense stance—and when I reach for her again, she moves out of range.

"Ireland," I say, and my voice is lower and sharper than I want it to be, but seeing her upset like this has me on edge. "He's a fucking idiot. You're beautiful and perfect."

If my words were arrows, they'd be bouncing hopelessly off her armor now and dropping uselessly to the floor.

"Of course I am," she says with more of that false, hard brightness. "I know that. Well, I think I'm going to head back to the farmhouse now—I should probably get some work done before dinner, and I thought I could make dinner tonight since you guys usually make it, so I should also head out to the store..."

She's babbling, talking fast and lively, as if worried that if she doesn't, we'll try to comfort her again. She gets her things, and I grab my things too, deciding to call it a day at the tavern. I don't want to be apart from her even in the best of situations, but especially not when some shitbag has said something awful about her.

We all head outside together, Ireland still chattering until the moment we get into separate cars and drive home. And once we're in the kitchen—Caleb and I taking over dinner preparation by unspoken agreement—with her working at the table, Caleb tries to bring it up once again.

"I don't like that he said those things," he says while stabbing his fingers through his hair. "I hate even more that they've upset you. Tell me how to fix it, peach. Tell me how to make you feel better."

She looks up from her laptop, and when she does, her eyes are hard and her mouth is set in a mulish line. "You can make me feel better by not talking about it."

Caleb opens his mouth, and she holds up a hand. "I mean it, Carpenter." Her voice is truly serious, absent any fake cheeriness or falsely casual confidence now. "I don't want to talk about this."

A limit is a limit is a limit. An entire adult lifetime of polyamory has taught us that. Caleb gives me a helpless look, and I give him a small nod, telling him I understand his frustration, his need to protect our woman from any and all pain, but also that we can't do that if she doesn't want us to. And hell, maybe it would be impossible anyway, because I'm not sure *how* to comfort her. How can she not see how fucking beautiful she is? How devastatingly sexy that body is? How much we want to love and cherish it and her?

We make dinner, and then we make love, shower, and make love again. As I watch her pretend her way through a normal evening, I see the waves of hurt and anger flicker through her like electric currents. I see her swing between the unfocused and unconscious real confidence I've grown used to from her and the almost-harsh forced confidence she had in the tavern after we heard Lyle. I see her move from happy and sexy to insecure and worried and then back to happy and sexy again.

And I realize something about myself as I watch her. Something not even years of therapy could teach me—something that seems painfully obvious now that I see it.

People aren't just one thing.

People aren't just confident and then that's it, there's nothing that can dent that confidence. People aren't just brave and then free from fear their entire lives. We exist in tangles of virtue and weakness simultaneously—we are the best and worst of ourselves all at the same time.

A soldier who faced bullets and bombs but is now afraid of the dark.

A scared, sensitive boy who made himself so tough he's forgotten how to be vulnerable.

A man who is fierce possession and cold reserve all at once.

And maybe all that is okay—maybe words like *best* and *worst* or *virtue* and *weakness* are misleading. Maybe they incorrectly assign value to things that aren't good or bad in and of themselves; they're simply *human*.

And it's with this epiphany that I climb into bed with the people I love. I wrap my arms around Ireland, one of my hands finding Caleb's and lacing with his fingers, and I close my eyes against the darkness. For the first time, I don't fight the fear. I don't struggle with it. I allow it just to *be*, bobbing on the surface of my mind along with all the other things I'm thinking and feeling. Like that I love Ireland and Caleb, that I want this to be for the rest of our lives, that I want them inside every wall or gate I've ever erected. That Greta-dog is almost out of dog treats, and that once I get the next insurance check, I should be able to order stuff for the new tavern kitchen.

That actually it's okay to be afraid, okay to be anxious, and it would be okay no matter what, but it's especially okay with the woman I love nestled against my chest and the man I love snoring gently beside her.

Somehow, by some magic, as I trace the oval glow and shadow of the nightlight on the ceiling, I manage to fall asleep.

And I sleep the whole night through.

CHAPTER SEVENTEEN

IRELAND

He did it.

I wake up wrapped in the world's warmest, best-smelling blanket, and when I open my eyes to see Ben's face all open and young-looking as he sleeps, a spike of joy goes right through my chest.

He did it.

He did it for me—for all of us—and suddenly, with a crest of dizzying happiness, I can see the future ahead for the three of us. Me moving in, us sharing sex and sleep every night. Maybe someday we could share even more... weddings and babies and all the things everyone else gets to have. Why not us? It may look different, it may take figuring out, but to share forever and more with these men would be worth it. So fucking worth it.

I slide out of bed and take a quick shower as they doze on. Dawn is breaking and they'll be up soon, and I want to have a big breakfast waiting when they are. I'm already smiling to myself as I imagine giving them the news. I'll tell them I'm going to move in, and then they'll grin—even my broody soldier will be smiling—and then they'll start thanking me with their mouths and their fingers and their cocks...

With a full-body shiver of anticipation, I grab my phone to go downstairs and the screen goes bright. Notification after notification are stacked—some from social media, some from email—but what strikes me first is a text from my boss, looking like it came in right after my three-hour fuckfest with Ben and Caleb began last night.

> *Great interview! We've already had two*
> *potential clients contact Typeset wanting*
> *your photography as part of a campaign!!!!*

So the interview did go live last night...and presumably the picture along with it. But before I can properly process my panic, I see a text from a contact I should have deleted a long time ago: Brian.

Still look like a cow. Guess you're a slut now too.

I nearly drop the phone.

Oh God, oh God, oh God.

I look over at Ben and Caleb—both of them still stretched and sprawled like teenage boys across the bed—and for one painfully acute moment, I want to wake them up. I want them to pull me back into bed, where it's warm and cozy and where I'm loved without reserve. I know if I tell them what Brian said, they'll be furious. They'll scowl and make angry bear noises and threaten to kill him. And then they'll fuck me with all that pent-up anger—not directed at me but *for* me—anger stemming from the need to protect me. And I'll feel better.

Except maybe I won't. Not until I figure out exactly what's going on, at least.

And maybe, a cold, slimy voice whispers, *they wouldn't do that at all. Maybe after what Lyle said yesterday, they'll start to realize you're not worth protecting. You're not worth the effort. Why would you be? It's not like there are men lining up to take their place.*

"Shut up," I whisper back to the voice. "Shut up, shut up, shut up."

But it doesn't shut up as I creep down the stairs in the near-dawn darkness. The voice keeps going. And the longer it talks, the more sense it starts to make. Especially as I open up my laptop at the kitchen table and see an email from the reporter in my inbox, with the subject line *Here it is!!!*

I open the email and click the link.

I immediately wish I hadn't.

The picture of me with Caleb and Ben is at the very top, and right away I can see it's not a flattering picture. The skirt I bought in a fit of bravery after breaking up with Brian—the same skirt Caleb and Ben beg me to wear all the time—does nothing to hide thighs that are too wide and too pale and too dimpled. My cropped blouse that felt so cute when Caleb kept trying to yank it off me so he could nuzzle my breasts looks embarrassingly small now. The little strip of belly that seemed spunky and adorable looks sad and not a little oblivious on the screen. Even the long wavy hair and colorful lipstick—a look I'm normally so proud of, a look I've shown off on Instagram more times than I can count—seem pathetically desperate. When I went into town that day, I felt bold and sexy and fun, but looking at the picture now, it's like every single element that makes Ireland Mills interesting or pretty or *anything* has been flattened into an image that screams *trying too hard.*

Not for the first time, I wish I weren't so goddamned short. I wish I were five foot nine or ten, like the famous plus-size models on the covers of magazines, and not five foot two. I wish my curves were spread out instead of all squished together, I wish I carried my weight differently.

The cold, slimy voice chants wishes along with me—wishes that pass through my mind in less than a minute but get darker and darker as they go. I wish my breasts were smaller. I wish my belly were too. I wish I looked thin...I wish I *were* thin. I wish I were born that way.

I wish I wasn't born at all.

A pulse of jagged, ruthless satisfaction follows the thought; it's like pressing down on a bruise.

It's starkly comforting to acknowledge the truth at last.

I wish I wasn't born at all, not into this body. I hate this body.

I run my hands through my hair, tugging at it. How can this be me thinking these thoughts? Me, who just a month ago was a newly confident woman with tons of body-positive bloggers in her Instagram feed and a wardrobe full of clothes she actually wanted to wear? I thought I was over feeling bad about my body, that I'd solved my insecurity, and all it takes is one picture to make me wish I'd never been born? How weak am I?

Desperate for any new input to shake me away from my thoughts, I look back at the picture. The boys look amazing, of course, even though they'd both been working outside and sweating that day. They look like models for some kind of country boy calendar, T-shirts clinging to tight stomachs and belted jeans showing off narrow hips and distinct bulges behind their zippers. They look like the epitome of alpha males, like they should have a willowy, all-American blonde between them, not a dumpy brunette who looks like an art school dropout.

Although I'm not *even* an art school dropout. I'm something much worse: a girl who was too chicken even to go in the first place.

The caption for the picture is journalistically spare:

Mills, 24, and her two boyfriends,
Caleb Carpenter, 33, and Ben Weber, 33, both of Holm, Kansas.
They met the weekend of the tornado.

The article itself is fantastic—I can recognize that in a distant part of my brain. The reporter paints a picture of me as smart and vibrant and creative, all of my quotes sound insightful and intelligent, and all the photographs of mine they feature are strikingly composed and emotional.

But I of all people know it doesn't matter how smart I am, or how talented. When you're fat, all of those qualities are erased. All that exists to represent you as a three-dimensional and nuanced human is your fatness, and your fatness is translated in a kind of visual shorthand for all sorts of moral failings. Laziness. Gluttony. Uncleanliness. An unholy lack of self-control and self-discipline.

The very sight of you is almost like an affront; your existence is almost offensive.

I could have invented CRISPR or fed thousands in the streets of Calcutta and it wouldn't have mattered so long as my picture was at the top of the article. It's why I've hidden behind the camera for so long—because to be in front of the lens is to acknowledge that I exist in this body. To be smiling is to not participate in the expectation that I should be ashamed.

I should close the tab. I should, I should, but the rational part of me is gone, cowering and crying somewhere, and all that's left is the part of me that can't resist pressing on the bruise some more.

Which is why I scroll down to the comments section.

It's a mistake.

Even the awful part of me that whispers about how much I hate my own body sees that it's a mistake, because it turns out that even the worst cruelty I can muster toward myself is nothing compared to what strangers can say on the internet.

Why are *they* with *her*? one anonymous commenter says. *Two hot guys with an overweight girl just doesn't add up.*

Another anonymous commenter adds below, *I bet there's not even room in the bed for all of them.*

Why is the Star *glorifying this unnatural sex cult?* SoonerInTheKitchen replies. *This is clearly a relationship built on sin.*

xfitwarrior says, *Shame on this paper for promoting disease and glorifying overweight ppl when being overweight is the number one cause of death in America and costs billions of dollars to taxpayers every year. Obesity IS UNHEALTHY. Obesity KILLS. Shame on you!*

A reply to that comment by ketogoddess87 says, *You don't know where she is in her journey! She might have already lost a hundred pounds and be on the way to getting healthier! You can't judge someone's health by just one picture!*

QueenSizeGirlsDoItBetter replies to that comment, saying, *Wherever she is on her journey, she shouldn't be wearing clothes like that. I'm a plus sized girl myself, and even I know that nobody wants to see allllll that body hanging out everywhere!*

I guess there's no accounting for taste, KSUBetcha says. *'Caleb' and 'Ben' here prove that. Chubby chasing much?*

CalebAndBenLovePiggies replies to that comment with *oink oink.*

My fingers are trembling as I scroll down, but I can't stop myself, can't look away. It's some kind of sick impulse, forcing me to read every nasty comment, every judgmental observation about my size, every reply that seems well-intentioned but is actually still incredibly hurtful.

I can't breathe. I can't think. At some point, my brain begins sending out panic hormones, flooding my veins with the need to run, to fight, to scream.

Danger, my nervous system blares at me. *Danger.*

It doesn't matter that it's "just" the internet, that I can't see the faces or hear the voices of the people who've written these things, because it's still real. Real people still said these things in a place where I, a real person, could see them. Where I could see myself talked about with—at best—condescension, and—at worst—hostile disgust.

This is what you get, the awful voice whispers. *For thinking you could have more. Wanting to be a famous photographer. Dating two men way out of your league.*

The voice is right. I was stupid and foolish to ever believe otherwise.

And I'm not really sure what to do with that epiphany, or with the nauseous, panicked urges roiling through me, until I see the last comment and feel like my heart is going to explode from beating so fast.

An anonymous commenter has posted a link to Ben's tavern on Yelp, and when I follow the link, I see the page has been spammed with one-star reviews. They're predictably pointless and crude—mostly rehashing the same kinds of awful things said in the comments section of the article—but they hurt me in an entirely new place. It's one thing to be insulted and dehumanized, to have my potential photography career burned down before my eyes. Those things stab at places that have been stabbed at before.

But to have Ben and Caleb insulted and dehumanized—and to have Ben's livelihood threatened—all for the sin of loving me, well...

There's no scar tissue there. It's a fresh, new, terrifying pain.

I was reluctant to allow that photo for a few reasons. Because I wasn't mentally ready for it. Because I've spent the last ten or so years defining myself as the person *behind* the camera except for carefully angled and curated social media pictures. Because I was nervous about publicly declaring myself in a poly relationship.

Never, ever, not once, had it occurred to me the picture would hurt Ben and Caleb. I never once considered the cost they would pay to love me and my body.

God. What have I done?

I'm about to close out of everything—a survival mechanism, really, not out of some admirable display of willpower—when my phone chimes again, an innocent little *pling* of a text message. Except it's from Brian again. And it's actually a voice message this time.

I know, on an instinctual level, that I shouldn't play it. I know that nothing good can come of it, that there's nothing helpful or insightful that he can say to me. But I'm too broken down not to crave that last strike, one last wound, and my hand is moving over the phone before I can stop myself. I hit play.

"You know"—Brian's voice comes over the speaker, loud and brittle and mean—"if you wanted more than one dick, I could have paid a friend to fuck you. I would've had to pay him a *lot*, though."

He's drunk. I can tell by the wobble of his voice, a wobble I heard frequently enough, although never at—I check the clock above the stove—six thirty in the morning.

"I kept wondering," he rambles on, "how the fuck dare *you* break up with *me*? Me, when I was being so fucking nice to you in the first place? And now I know why—it's because you're a whore. And I don't know what you did to make those men pretend to like you, but I know for a fact they're just pretending." A hiccup. "And I'm going to prove it. I found your boyfriend's little tavern, and I posted it on that bullshit article, and I'm going to tell everyone what a fucking pervert he is—him and his fucking farmer friend. We'll see if they're willing to be nice to you after you've ruined their lives."

The message ends, and with it, the last, tiny thread of self-control I'd been clinging to. I shouldn't be surprised at his hateful words, that he's the one who outed Ben's tavern on the article. And yet, I am. I'm exhausted by it, by the relentlessness of having a body that's such an easy target, by the cultural certainty that anyone who loves me or my body is some kind of deviant freak. That anyone who cares for me deserves to be punished, and I do too, for not staying where we're supposed to—in the neatly cruel categories the rest of the world decides.

I press my face into my hands, tears running out of my eyes like water dribbles from a tap—steadily and without effort. It barely even feels like I'm crying. It barely feels like anything, as if my body has put the act of crying on autopilot as my mind races through the implications of this.

I've been stupid.

I've been selfish.

I thought people like Lyle Parry were the exception. I thought the little cocoon of sex and domesticity we spun here at the farm could last forever. But

I forgot the rules, forgot the lessons that all those cheesy romantic movies had taught me.

There is no forever for girls like me. There is no happily ever after for a curvy girl, and if I try to force it, I'll only end up hurting Ben and Caleb more. I'll only end up wrecking their lives. The town will scorn them, just like Lyle did. Ben's tavern business will wither under the scorch of online mockery, and gentle, sweet Caleb will be torn up from the inside out with every cruel comment that comes our way.

No, this was doomed to fail from the start, and I'm so ashamed it took this long for me to figure it out. I feel greedy and grasping and worse—I feel naïve.

So fucking naïve.

With a swallowed sob, I slam the laptop shut.

I know what I have to do. It's awful and scary and I already hate myself for it, but I'll hate myself more if I stay, knowing what it will cost Ben and Caleb to love me.

I stand up, wipe the tears from my face, and turn to go upstairs.

And find both men standing in the doorway to the kitchen, watching me with clenched fists and heaving chests.

"Was that him?" Ben asks quietly. "Your ex?"

I don't even know what to say or what to do, because the humiliation of them hearing Brian's message blocks every neuron in my brain and every nerve ending in my body. I am living humiliation. I am shame and anger embodied.

I am shaking.

"I'll kill him," my normally sweet Caleb vows, his jaw tight under his beard, and something in my chest snaps in half. Gentle Caleb all murderous and Ben looking like a cold, clinical soldier instead of the complicated, sensitive man I know him actually to be—it's too much. This is breaking them in every possible way. It's breaking me too, and it has to stop.

"No one talks to you like that," Caleb seethes, every cord in his neck and forearms standing out. "Fucking no one. We're going to take care of it, peach, trust me."

Ben's gaze is astute, piercing, when it locks on my face. "Don't believe a word of it," he orders. "Not a single word of it. He's bitter, and bitter people will do anything to make someone else feel as shitty as they do."

"And he's an asshole," Caleb adds.

"And he's an asshole," Ben concedes, his eyes still pinned on me. "He can't hurt us, and we won't let him hurt you. Got it?"

But can't they see that I'm already hurting? That they will be hurting too? All because we forgot the rules?

"I'm going," I say. "I'm going back to Kansas City."

Caleb's eyes flare green with panic. "No, peach. Don't say that."

"I can't do this!" The words are ripped out of me, right from the gut. I'm crying again. "I can't do this with you two."

They flinch at that, and I use their momentary surprise to push past them and go upstairs, throwing all my stuff into my bag once I get there. The toothbrush knocking cutely against theirs on the bathroom counter. The salon shampoo and conditioner perched on the shower ledge. All the lacy, sexy things I bought to please them...and all the lacy, sexy things they bought for me. All the clothes and half-read paperbacks and charging cords and other evidence that I'd been slowly moving in all this time.

It all gets packed up, and when I get downstairs, Caleb and Ben are sitting on the sofa by the front door—Caleb with his head in his hands and Ben in the deliberate pose of a hawk visually tracking prey.

I need to walk to the door now. I need to go. And yet I can't make my feet move. Can't force myself to admit this is the end.

"Don't do this," Ben says. The sharp cuts of his cheekbones are flooded with color, and in his utter and perfect stillness, the corners of his sensual mouth have gone white. "Don't let him win."

"It's not just him," I say. "It's everyone. Everything."

"But it's not everyone," Caleb whispers, looking up at me. "Because the three of us know the truth. That we're in love and nothing will change that."

Sweet Caleb. "It's easy to say that now," I tell them. "But it won't be for long."

"Ireland," Ben says, and that's all he needs to say. He packs every feeling, every question, and every plea into those three syllables. I promise myself I'll hold on to the sound of him saying my name forever.

"It was beautiful, loving you," I say to them both. "I wish it could have lasted."

"No." They say it at the same time, and I take a breath.

"I'm the one saying *no* now," I tell them. "This is my limit. I finally found it." I try bravely to crack a smile. "Goodbye. And please don't follow me, I have to do this. For all of us."

I finally make myself take those steps across the room, past two wonderful men who deserve better. And then I walk out the door and out of their lives.

CHAPTER EIGHTEEN

IRELAND

Two Weeks Later

"Ireland, there's someone here to see you."

I look up from my desk to see Drew standing next to it, looking mildly uncomfortable. My heart seizes at the same time as my stomach clenches. "Is it Caleb?" I whisper, hoping for it to be and also dreading it at the same time. It's been two weeks since I left the farm, two weeks of nonstop calls and texts and voicemails from my boys. Caleb's resorted to trying to get a message to me through Drew.

And Ben...he's mailed me letters. In his heart-wrenchingly precise print, he begs me to come home, tells me he loves me over and over again, will sleep the whole night through with me every night for the rest of our lives...

I've broken their hearts by leaving, but what could I have done? What could I have said? *I have objective proof that I'll ruin your lives if I let you love me? The world will never accept that you love me and my body....and I don't know that I can accept it either?*

They would have tried to talk me out of these conclusions, they would have fought for me to stay, and I wouldn't have been able to bear it. I would have caved and stayed and then hated myself for my weakness as the months dragged on and their lives became worse and worse.

No, this was for their own good, and my own good as well. I needed a harsh dose of reality.

That doesn't make it any easier, though. Drew has found me crying in the break room more than once, and I've fallen asleep at night only by drinking way too many vodka lemonades and sleeping on the couch.

It's too hard to sleep alone in a bed now that I know what it feels like to sleep tangled and warm with two other people.

But I did the right thing. Of that, I'm certain.

So I push away my disappointment when Drew shakes his head. "No, it's a woman. But Caleb did call again this morning. Are you sure you can't—?"

"I'm sure," I interrupt, the lie stinging my lips as it comes out. "As sure as sure can be."

☘

Typeset is a very typical kind of marketing office—it's almost insufferably trendy, with exposed brick and an open workroom with rows of shared desks. Only the meeting rooms provide any modicum of privacy, and even then the privacy is fairly notional, given the walls and doors are made of glass.

This is where I meet my visitor, a young woman standing by the window looking out over the skyline. She's wearing jeans and a tight T-shirt, so she's not the typical Typeset client or the kind of young professional who haunts this part of the city. She turns to face me, and I realize two things at once.

First, she's got the kind of body I long to have. Small breasts, model height, the majority of her weight around her hips and in her thighs. Pear-shaped, but the sexiest fucking pear in the world. Even though she probably weighs as much as me or more, she looks like she belongs in a catalog or on a runway, whereas I look like an extra bar wench on a medieval film set.

The second thing I realize is that she's also staggeringly beautiful. No makeup. Simple clothes. She's flawlessly skinned and glowing, gorgeous without all the things I use as a mask—the lipsticks and the bright colors. She's effortless and easy and perfect. Damn her.

"Hello," she says, picking a chair and sitting down, as if this is her meeting room and not mine. "You Ireland?"

"Um, yes," I say. "I'm sorry, have we—?"

She waves a hand. "No, but why would we have? I'm Mackenna."

"Okay..." I say hesitantly, feeling like I should be able to infer more from her name than I am.

"Caleb and Ben's ex-girlfriend," she supplies.

"Oh," I say, surprised, and then, "*Oh*," as I realize I have no idea why she's here, but it can't be good. "Look," I say, trying to head off any ex drama at the pass, "we're actually not together anymore—"

Another hand wave. She's got the Deathly Hallows symbol tattooed on her wrist and an old-fashioned *Mom* tattoo splashing across her upper arm. She has gold-brown skin, coffee-colored eyes that gleam in the hot sunlight coming in through the window, and glossy, thick hair that looks so good I want to bite my knuckle in jealousy.

Impatient. That's what Caleb had said about her, and as I look at her now, I can see it. In the way she shakes her silky hair out of her eyes and sucks the front of her teeth, in the tapping of her foot and the quick smooths over her clothes.

"Caleb said you'd left them when I called," she explains. "You don't have to walk me through the timeline."

"Caleb said—wait, what? When you *called?*" Jealousy more bitter and distinct than body envy scratches at the inside of my chest. "Do you call Caleb a lot?"

Mackenna rolls her eyes. "It's not like that, princess. I saw your article in the paper. I was already meaning to call after the storm—to check in and all that. See if my favorite tree was still there by the creek. *Anyway,*" she says loudly, as if bored by her own story, "after I saw the picture of you three, I really wanted to call and tell them, well, you know." She stares at me as if the end of her explanation is obvious.

I feel silly. Abashed. Significantly less pretty and interesting than she is.

And still wildly jealous. "I actually don't know," I say. "Sorry."

"You *know,* all that mushy, happy-for-you ex stuff." She's gesturing again, as if acting out a one-woman play. "When I broke up with them, I did genuinely want them to be happy. I just knew I was never going to be the woman to do it, and I definitely knew it when I met my two fiancés here in the city a year later. But even though I'm not in love with Caleb and Ben anymore, I still care about them, and I still want them to find a happy ending." She pauses. "Not in the splooging sense, I mean. Like in the emotional sense. But I guess also in the splooging sense."

I have no idea what to say to this, so I don't say anything at all.

"*Anyway,*" she says, again in that bored, impatient-with-herself voice, "I called to say 'I saw your new girl in the paper, I'm glad you're happy, yadda yadda,' and then instead of telling me how happy he is and how Robot Ben has become a human again because of you, he proceeds to wail about how you left them without a fucking word, and now you refuse to talk to them."

My brain snags on a word. "Caleb *wailed?*"

Hand wave. "Sniffled, wailed, whatever. Caleb doesn't *cry,* Ireland. Sniffles from him might as well be sackcloth and ashes."

Ugh. The thought of happy, dimpled Caleb sniffling is enough to tear at my heart. I try not to think about it.

I made the right decision. That's all there is to it.

Mackenna leans forward. "So I have to ask...*why?*"

"Why what?"

"Why, when you three had been happy for a month, did you just pack up and leave?"

I look at her, gorgeous and confident in her body, and immediately feel stupid. "Why do you care?" I deflect.

"Because I feel protective of them," she answers bluntly. "Because I know under those big muscley chests beat two adorable hearts that want to spend the rest of their lives worshipping the woman they love. Because I saw how happy you looked in that picture, and why would anyone abandon people who could make them smile like that?"

Overwhelmed, I press my face into my hands. It's like every feeling at once—every agonizing, earth-ripping emotion I've been burying over the last four days—is scrabbling to the surface.

"I thought it would be better that way," I say into my palms. "For them."

"*But why?*"

How can I even begin to explain it? The terror and shame of reading those comments? Of knowing that nothing, *nothing*—not my career, not Ben's, not even the simple fact that we loved each other—was enough to stand against my size in the eyes of the world?

"Because I'm fat," I say bitterly. As bitterly and meanly as I can, pouring every drop of pain and fury and shame into the word that I can. "I'm fat."

"So?"

Mackenna says it blandly. Almost uninterestedly.

I look up from my hands, shocked. Actually shocked.

No one has ever said *so?* about my body before.

Not once.

People have protested when I've said the word—*no, you're not fat! Don't say that about yourself!*—or they've substituted euphemisms that amount to the same thing—*you're not fat, you're curvy! Voluptuous! Plus-sized! There's more to love!*

And sometimes in Brian's or my sister's case, it was an excuse to be cruel, to point out if I just wanted it *more*, if I just tried *harder*, I could be thin like them. It was an excuse to tell me I was unhealthy, that I clearly didn't love myself enough, to hint that my fatness actually meant I was a bad person. A weak or greedy person. A worse person.

But never, ever, *ever* has anyone just said "so?" Like instead of me declaring I was fat, I told her I love baseball or that I've never been to Idaho.

I blink.

"So what?" Mackenna repeats. "You're fat. So am I. By the way, nice to meet you. Now what does having a fat body have to do with dumping Caleb and Ben?"

I feel like some kind of rug has been yanked out from under my feet. "I—"

I don't actually have words to follow that. I don't have words at all. The only thing in my mind is a vague protest that she doesn't really get it because she's such a cute kind of fat girl, but maybe I'm wrong about that too. Maybe she gets it just as much as I do, because while I see her as having this magically-easier-than-mine body, the rest of the world may not. The rest of the world may see just another body that doesn't fit.

Mackenna squints at me, tilting her head. The light catches again in her glossy, trendy hair, and a new kind of jealousy thrums through me. A softer kind of jealousy than being worried about her relationship with Caleb and Ben. I'm envious of her confidence. Of her utter and complete okayness with who she is. It makes her so fucking cool, so fucking magnetic.

She comes to a conclusion, apparently, bestowing a giant grin on me. "It's that word, isn't it? Fat?"

"Well, I don't—"

"Do you think fat means *bad*?"

"I mean, I—"

Hand wave. "It's just a word, princess. A word like *tall* or *short* or *Nebraskan*. It's an adjective that doesn't have to mean anything negative. The world thinks that fat is the worst thing a woman can be, but the more we use the word like a neutral description, the more we say *fuck you* to that idea."

"But," I say, "it's one thing to say it about yourself, you know, to use it as a hashtag and make it your choice. But other people don't use it like that."

"Aha," Mackenna says triumphantly and stabs a finger up into the air. "I knew it was about that article!"

I flush.

"Let me guess... You read the comments?"

"Yes," I mumble. "I know. It was stupid to."

She gives me a rueful kind of smile. "It's okay to forget to expect the worst sometimes."

I let out a long breath, staring past her and out the window. "I felt so idiotic after I did. Because I've spent this year trying to be someone more like you. Confident and happy in my body, like all the body-positive people I see online. And I thought I'd done it! I thought I was over ever feeling bad about my body again—but all it took was one freaking picture."

"And a hell of a comments section," Mackenna adds.

Sigh. "And that."

"Look, princess, body positivity doesn't mean you flip a switch and walk around feeling great for the rest of your life. It's not even really about feelings at all. Body positivity is about what you *do*. It's about daring to live your life as

270

you are—not fifty pounds from now, not six dress sizes from now. And there are going to be days when every bad feeling comes back for you again. When you feel all the messy, hopeless things you thought you were past feeling. Those are the days you *do it anyway*."

"Do what?" I ask, my voice bleak. "What is there to do?"

Mackenna practically erupts. "Everything! There is everything to do! You post pictures of yourself, or you dress the way you want, or you push back against a flight attendant who's treating you like trash. You unapologetically pursue your photography career, and you date the people you love, even if other people don't like it. Not because it makes you feel good but because it helps change the world. Do you see? Even just living your life is a radical act. *That* is body positivity. *That* is what matters, not an emotion that can change at the drop of a hat."

I understand what she's saying, although I don't know if I like it. It feels *hard*. It feels unfair.

It feels unfair because it is unfair, I remind myself. *It shouldn't be this way. It should change.*

Maybe I can be someone who changes it. Who fights against the unfair parts, because what's the other option? To live like I did before? To be and die alone?

I press my fingertips against my eyelids, careful not to mess up my makeup but also wanting to keep the tears inside. "But what about Caleb and Ben? Those trolls and my ex were coming after the tavern online, and I couldn't—" I break off, really about to cry now. "I couldn't bear the thought of Caleb and Ben paying any price to love me."

"And?" Mackenna says.

She says it so matter-of-factly, as if there's definitely something else I need to say, that I don't even question it.

I answer her, as surprised by the words as she isn't. "And what if this was the first time they noticed I was fat? What if they hadn't really noticed before, but then after they learned how everyone else sees me, they would realize they didn't really love me after all?"

And then I clap a hand over my mouth. Where the hell did that fear come from?

Mackenna nods as if she were expecting this. "Well, you're a dumbass if you think they hadn't already memorized your body from head to toe long before this article. They know what your body looks like, Ireland, and they worship it. I promise. Also, look at me!" She gestures to herself. "Do you think I would have dated them—*lived* with them—for years if they were capable of that kind of behavior?"

Her eyebrows are arched in challenge, her mouth pursed in a knowing smirk. She looks like the kind of woman who wouldn't stand for any hint of dickish behavior.

"No, I guess you wouldn't have," I say. A new thought occurs to me. A new fear. "Do—do they only date girls like us? Like a fetish or something?"

The thought makes me deeply unhappy. What if all the wonderful, sexy, ecstatic moments we shared were because they had an unhealthy fascination with my body—not because we were simply Ireland and Caleb and Ben?

"Okay, A of all, I don't like the way you said the word *fetish*," Mackenna responds, doing this thing where she aims her pointer and middle fingers at me and waggles them. "It's very kink-shamey, in general, and I don't stand for that. B of all, I don't understand this need to pathologize people who find fat folks attractive. You wouldn't be asking me if they only dated brunettes or Catholics, so why do we have to label normal desire as something twisted just because that desire isn't for a thin body? And C of all, no." She drops her fingers. "They don't only date girls like us. I went to college with them, and I can tell you they've dated all kinds of girls—even dated a boy once."

I let out a long breath.

"D of all," she says, "I feel like you're asking all the wrong questions."

I'm chewing over all the things she's said to me, so it's in an absentminded voice that I ask, "What are the right questions, then?"

"Will your boss give you the afternoon off, and how fast can you get back to Holm?"

My chin quivers with the force of unshed tears. *God, if only it were that easy.* "You don't understand. I'll make their lives harder."

Mackenna rolls her eyes again. "You won't. But also, that's not your choice to make. What if you did make their lives harder...and they still choose to be with you anyway? What if Ben would rather have zillions of one-star reviews and have you in his arms? What if Caleb wants you in his life no matter the cost? Give them a chance to choose you, because, spoiler alert: they will."

I press my fingertips back into my eyelids again, but it's too late, the tears are everywhere.

Mackenna's voice softens. "You're thinking right now that you don't deserve it. That you don't deserve to be chosen. And I'm not telling you to believe it or to feel like it." I hear her stand up and walk over to me, putting a sisterly hand on my shoulder.

"I'm only telling you to act like it," she says. "Fake it 'til you make it, gorgeous. Act like you deserve to be loved, and I promise, everything else will work itself out."

And then she leaves.

I try to hiccup a goodbye or a thank-you, but I know it only comes out as incomprehensible syllables. All my choices are flickering through my mind like the world's most depressing movie, fueling more and more tears.

Leaving the farm.

Dating a man who made me feel awful about myself. Letting my sister make me feel the same.

And possibly the most life-altering choice I made before I met Caleb and Ben: turning down the photography scholarship.

I've lied to so many people about why—I've said it was because I wanted to stay close to home, because I wanted a marketable major—but the real reason is because I went to visit the campus that spring, and everywhere on the grounds and in the halls were girls who *looked* like artists. They were slender and bohemian. They had long, coltish legs coming out of adorable, spaghetti-strapped rompers and hipbones that jutted above distressed jeans. I was the only fat girl in sight, and suddenly everything about me felt fraudulent. I didn't look like I belonged there, and what if that meant I actually didn't?

I wouldn't have fit in—and I felt that on a literal level as well as a social level—and so I tearfully turned down the scholarship and hid myself someplace safe. Someplace invisible. Someplace where I hoped my body wouldn't matter.

I robbed myself of my own future because I was terrified of what people would think of me in the present.

It's only now, after talking to Mackenna, that I realize I'm about to do the same thing. I'm giving up everything I ever wanted from love because I'm scared. Because I think I don't deserve it.

But you don't have to believe you deserve it. You only have to act like it.

I know I'll have to try to find Mackenna online somewhere to give her a proper thank-you. Because her words...her words have freed me from somewhere I didn't even know I was trapped. They've electrified someplace deep inside, and what I feel burning at my fingertips now is not a *feeling* or even a *belief*. It's something much, much more powerful.

It's a decision.

I push away from the table with tears still wetting my face and go find Drew.

"I need to take the afternoon off," I say, swiping at my eyes and in general trying to look like a professional person. "And maybe the day after that too."

"Of course," he says, his ginger eyebrows drawing together. "Is everything okay?"

"Not yet," I say honestly. "But I think it might be."

Sympathy floods his face. "Do you want me to help? I can call Caleb—"

"No." I'm shaking my head. "Thank you, but I think I need to do this myself."

He nods. "Okay. Take all the time you need—you've got plenty stored up."

I give him a teary smile and then go back to my desk to grab my purse and my keys. I'm practically vibrating with all the new parts of me Mackenna has helped unlock, thrumming with the near-violent need to find my men and tell them—what? That I believed the worst of them? The worst of myself?

Yes. I need to be honest about why I left. But I'll also tell them so much more.

I'll tell them how desperately I love them and how my days at the farm were pure magic and my nights in their bed were pure heaven. I'll tell them I don't want any future without them, and if they're willing to jump into this with me, then I'll jump in too. Feet first, eyes wide open, just like I should have done at the pond.

So long as I'm with them, I'll jump anywhere.

I'm practically running down the stairs of the building to get to my car, wondering if I should call first or just show up at the farm, and it's when I get to the first-floor doors that I hear a sound so achingly familiar that the tears nearly start up again.

The happy, chipper yap of a dog followed by the *rattle-bang* of an old truck.

I push open the door to see Caleb's truck wedged awkwardly between two electric cars plugged into charging ports, Greta-dog sticking her head out the window and barking wildly at the silver streetcar gliding by. Caleb and Ben climb out of the truck, looking like Kansas versions of Adonis, with their broad shoulders and narrow hips, and when they catch sight of me frozen in the doorway, they freeze too. They both have big bouquets of buttery yellow sunflowers in their hands.

None of us move for a long minute—a minute when I quietly panic that I've ruined everything and I've ruined it so thoroughly that they've driven two hours just to tell me they never want to see me again.

Hi, is what I should say.

Sorry, is what I should say.

"I love you," is what comes out. So softly that I'm not even sure they hear it.

And then they're loping toward me with big, half-jogging strides, and I'm suddenly crushed into two sets of strong arms and pressed between two hard, warm chests, the sunflowers crushing in there with me. My chin is taken between Ben's firm fingers, and my face is turned toward Caleb. I'm kissed—passionately, tenderly—with a scratch of soft beard, until my knees weaken and

I can barely stand. When I start whimpering against Caleb's lips, Ben turns my face back to his and rewards me with a long, thorough kiss of his own.

"Fuck, I missed you," Caleb groans into my ear, hugging me tighter as Ben continues to conquer my mouth with his. "Missed you so damn much."

We break apart with a gasp, and I'm shocked to see Ben's eyes are just as red-rimmed as mine probably are. I reach up and touch the corner of his eye, where even now a tear is beading. The touch of it is scalding—burning me with regret.

"I'm so sorry," I whisper to them both. "I'm so, so sorry."

"No, *we're* sorry," Caleb says, pressing his face into my neck. "We started this whole mess. We should have never told that reporter we were dating if you didn't want us to. If you don't want to be openly dating two men at once, we get it. We'll have you however you want."

"That's not—" I take a breath and pull back enough so I can see both their faces. "That's not why I left. I'm ready for the world to know I love two men. I was a little surprised by it coming up during the interview, but when I chose to pose for that photo, I chose to be ready. I'm proud to be with you."

I receive two dazzling grins in response to that.

"No, it was more like...I was worried you wouldn't be proud to be with me. That even if you were, it would mean subjecting yourself to all kinds of things..." I trail off because Ben's expression has grown stormy and Caleb's thick eyebrows have pulled together in confusion. "The comments people were leaving on that article, the things my ex said...and Ben, your Yelp page..."

"What's Yelp?" Ben asks, his storminess giving way temporarily to puzzlement. "Is that on Twitter?"

"It's a thing on the internet for reviewing restaurants and stuff? Super popular?"

He shrugs, his face getting dark and thunderous again. "I don't care what happens on a Yelp. Do you think the people in Holm are having drinks at the tavern because of reviews on an internet site?"

Having grown to know the people of Holm over the last month, I have to admit it's unlikely. I shake my head.

"Even if loving you meant selling everything I own and going to work at the meat-packing plant in Emporia, I'd do it. I don't give a shit about what people say or do, as long as I have you. As long as *we* have you."

Caleb's nodding in agreement, pressing his face to the back of my hand, as if he can't bear not to touch me for even a moment.

"Ireland," Ben continues, his voice growing raspier, more pained. "It kills me that you'd ever think we wouldn't be anything other than ecstatic to be with you. I don't know what it's like to be fat"—he uses the word in the same mild, casual tone Mackenna did—"and I can't pretend to know all the ways society makes your life harder because of it, and that means I'll be learning as we go sometimes. But I do know how I feel. I don't love you in *spite* of your body. I love you with it, as you are, and I'll never be anything but fucking proud to be yours."

Caleb assents to this last with a nuzzle of his face against my hand and a murmured, "Me too."

My heart lifts. I knew Mackenna was right about everything, of course, but having it confirmed nearly makes me break into tears again.

"You mean all that?" I whisper to them.

They nod solemnly at me.

"We mean it, peach," Caleb says. "And we'll beat the hell out of anyone who says different."

"And we possibly have," Ben says.

I look up at their faces, mischievous and possessive all at once. "Oh, you didn't."

"We just paid your ex a little visit is all," Ben answers mildly. "He won't be bothering us again anytime soon. And he says he's sorry, by the way."

"I feel like I should scold you," I tell them, shaking my head, "but I have to admit, I'm not sorry."

"Good!" Caleb grins. "Neither are we."

Greta barks and prances around our feet, as if trying to signal that she's also not sorry.

I take in the happy dog and these two perfect, amazing men, who are currently trying to kiss me around their hug-crumpled sunflowers.

"Let's go home," I say, kissing them back. "Let's go home together."

And we do.

EPILOGUE

CALEB

Christmas Eve

"Greta! No! Bad Greta!"

My dog has grabbed the end of Ireland's long scarf with her teeth and is trying to tug it free of its owner, growling a little at the red fabric when it doesn't do as the dog likes.

Laughing, I come over and pry Greta's teeth off the scarf and then banish her to the kitchen to her bed by the wood-burner. Normally we don't get much snow in December here, but as an early Christmas surprise, the skies darkened and rumbled and dumped a good eighteen inches onto our hilly stretch of the plains. Enough snow to cover the long grass on the hills that crest around the farm—more than enough to sled on.

And sled we did, Greta-dog bounding through the drifts around us as we took turns on my childhood Flexible Flyer, and we went down the hill so fast that even Ben giggled.

Ben. *Giggled.*

And now we're back home, red-faced and snow-crusted, and I know exactly what I want to do with the rest of my Christmas Eve. I unwind the rest of the scarf from Ireland's neck as she pulls off her hat. Clouds of silky dark hair glisten with specks of powdery snow, and as she tosses her hat onto the table, I can see several big snowflakes still caught in her eyelashes.

Beautiful.

Ben catches on to what I want to do right away and joins me in undressing our woman. He tugs off her gloves, slowly, finger by finger, and then kisses her red, cold-nipped fingertips until she's shivering from something other than cold. We unzip her jeans and peel the denim from her legs, and I drop to my knees and press my face against the cold skin of her thighs while Ben takes off her sweater.

"Your beard tickles," she says, but her laughter changes into a soft gasp when I mouth the soft triangle between her legs, letting my warm breath blow over the silk that cups her pussy. Even after all these months, she still gets this hitched, surprised breath when I touch her there. It goes to a man's head, all that wonder. And the look on her face when I make her come? Makes me feel about eight feet tall.

I want to see that look now, even though we aren't anywhere near a bed, and I press my lips harder against her and kiss her through the fabric, licking and licking until she's soaked through and rocking her pussy against me.

"Put your hands in his hair," Ben grates out. "He likes that. He likes being your toy, don't you, Caleb?"

My nod has the added bonus of stroking my tongue against her clit, and she cries out, her hand threading through my hair and holding me fast to her cunt.

I obey the unspoken command, sucking her pouting little bud until her thighs are quivering against my face, and then I hook a finger around the wet fabric and allow myself a taste straight from the source. I slick my tongue between her folds as I coax one of her legs over my shoulder, and she leans back against Ben for balance as I fuck her cunt with my mouth.

"That's it," Ben coaxes darkly. "Open up your pussy for Caleb. Let him inside."

She slides her leg farther across my shoulder, and the plump outer petals of her sex unfurl even more, allowing me to lick deep, right at the very heart of her. I fumble with my fly as I taste her, unable to stop myself from pulling out my erection and giving it a few rough strokes.

Fuck, she tastes good. Sweet, with the tiniest hint of sour and salt. Her pussy is so tight, even around my tongue, and it makes me shudder with anticipation to think of how it's going to feel on my cock. Wet and hot and squeezing me, like her body is demanding my come.

I'll give it to her. Now that we've all been tested and she's on birth control, we can finally fuck raw, and the feeling is like nothing else in this world. My cock gives a hard flex just knowing what it's about to get.

Ireland writhes against my mouth, and I realize Ben has his cock freed too so her silk-covered ass can rub against him. He's got his big hand wrapped around her throat now, and whatever he's murmuring in her ear has her getting more and more worked up. I can taste her need, and I can feel it in the fierce tug of her fingers through my hair.

"Enough," Ben finally growls. "Up to bed. I need to fuck."

Stumbling upstairs, Ben and me shedding clothes as we go, we kiss and grope and grab until we're all in our bed. I drag Ireland against me so her tits are crushed into my chest, and I lick at the seam of her mouth until she parts it and lets me in. I can never get enough of kissing her, of feeling her lips so soft and yielding against mine, and her tongue like hot silk with her perpetual cinnamon taste from her favorite gum.

I reach down to mold my hand over her cunt, and my fingers brush against Ben's fingers as he plays with the little star of her ass, probing it open a little more roughly and urgently than normal.

He knows what we're going to do tonight, and it's got him all worked up. I can't blame him. I could almost come against Ireland's soft belly right now just thinking about it. But I hold it together long enough for Ben to order Ireland to take my cock and feed it inside her.

There's a moment—always that first moment—when the plump head won't fit. When my erection is too big and her pussy is too small, and the pressure is so insane that I think I might erupt right then and there, before the entire tip is even inside.

I live for that moment.

Holding my cock in both hands, she stirs the swollen head against her opening before she tries again, rocking and circling until finally, finally, I start to sink into her tiny channel.

The hot squeeze of her is like the grip of heaven itself, and I push in, needing to fuck, needing to thrust. With a sucked-in breath, her hands fly to my shoulders, and she holds on as I work the edge off my need by giving her a few rough strokes.

"Hold still," Ben says in a voice that demands obedience. "She's gonna take me too."

Ireland moans her assent, arching as much as she can while pierced with my length so she can make her little entrance more available to Ben.

The usually stoic Ben isn't immune to the sight. A muscle in his tight jaw jumps as he looks down at us, her intimate place speared by my flesh and her ass presented to him the way he likes. With a harsh swallow, he grabs the lube and slicks himself up until his cock is a glistening column of need, and then he swirls some against Ireland's tight hole for good measure.

"Ready, sweetheart?" he rasps.

"Please," she breathes. "Yes, please."

It's slow work. Each inch makes her squirm and pant, her fingertips digging into my shoulders so deeply that I know I'll bruise, but I'll happily wear the bruises as badges of honor. Every single one is worth the look on her face now, with her eyes hooded and her lips parted and a flush that dusts the apples of her cheeks and the top of her chest.

Each inch is also work for me, because the extra pressure is almost too much for me to handle without coming—especially coupled as it is with the erotic squirm of Ireland on our cocks and the rough, reassuring rasp of Ben's legs against my own. The firm brush of his sack on mine.

Soon, he's fully seated, and you'd never guess the three of us have ever been cold, because now everything is heat and sweat and damp. With long, rolling movements, we fuck Ireland in tandem, keeping her filled and stretched, rubbing each other through the thin, shared wall of her body in a touch more intimate than almost anything else in this world.

It doesn't take long. It never does like this. Ireland says it's like being split in half, but being split in half by an electric rainbow made of orgasms. I don't know about all that, but I do know having her sweet body pressed against me, her clit grinding on its favorite place above my cock, and Ben's erection fucking against my own is more than any man can handle. The moment Ireland comes apart in our arms, we follow, grunting with a few final fast strokes and then erupting inside her. My balls draw up tight as my shaft swells, and then I release wave after hot wave of my seed inside her, spending so hard that my vision grays out around the edges. I let out a satisfied roar as all the sizzling, aching pressure finally relieves itself, and Ben gives his usual bitten-off grunt—the most he ever loses control in bed. I savor the feeling of his cock throbbing so close to mine as much as I savor the lingering flutters of Ireland's pleasure, and I allow both to pull the very last drops of my climax out of my cock.

"God, you're such a beauty," I say, kissing Ireland everywhere, petting her and praising her for taking both of us like such a good girl. Ben echoes my praises, kissing her neck and stroking her hair until she's practically purring. We both slip free from her body in a wet rush, and Ben goes to get things to clean us up.

He and I exchange a look as we do.

It's time.

"What do you say we change into our pajamas and go have some warm apple cider by the tree?" I ask casually. Too casually maybe, because Ben rolls his eyes behind Ireland's back at my bad acting as he scoots back on the bed with a towel.

However, Christmas and everything Christmasy is Ireland's favorite thing, so she just nods happily. "Sounds amazing." And then she rolls over like a princess to let Ben attend to her while I clean off, get dressed, and go downstairs to get everything ready.

A few minutes later, we're around the tree with the fire going and steaming mugs of spiked cider for us all. Greta-dog nestles on the couch next to Ireland, who's cute as a fucking button in her flannel pajamas covered in snowmen, but Ben and I remain standing.

"I can make room," she says, preparing to move. "Or we can put Greta on the floor?"

Greta gives a huff, as if she knows she's about to be evicted.

"Don't move," Ben says in his soldier voice, and Ireland goes still, looking confused. We go over to the tree to get the two little boxes we've nestled in the branches. She blinks at them and then blinks at us.

They're not wrapped, tied only with small red bows, and her breathing speeds up as we pull off the ribbons together and open the boxes together.

As we kneel together.

"Ireland," I say, my mouth suddenly dry with nerves. "I know it's only been five months, and I know it's all moved fast. But I've never been surer of anything in my entire life—that I want to spend it with the two of you."

"We want you to be our wife," Ben continues for me. Tears glimmer in Ireland's eyes as he speaks. "We want to marry you and cherish you and spend forever with you. And I know there will be so much to figure out legally, and I know it will never be the easy road, but it's the only road I want. Marry us, baby. Please."

"Oh," she says, starting to cry in earnest now and putting the back of her hand to her mouth. "Oh God. Yes. Yes, of course."

My sternum cracks open and pure sunshine beams out. I'd hoped she'd say yes, of course—I wouldn't have asked if I thought it was unwelcome, but still—to hear your woman say yes to forever is still the best kind of feeling. My own eyes are wet as Ben and I slide our rings onto her finger, each ring one half of a diamond-studded Celtic knot so that when they're put on together, they make one whole design.

Ireland flexes her hand, enraptured by the glitter of our rings, and it's both unbearably arousing and unbelievably—almost spiritually—gratifying to witness.

Ben is ready to fuck her again, I can tell, but we're not quite finished. I reach into the pocket of my pajama pants and pull out another ring.

It's made of beaten metal that's been hammered and burnished to a dull gleam, as quiet and strong as the man it's going to belong to. I take Ben's hand, which is suddenly shaking, and I slide it onto his finger.

"I love you," I tell him, my best friend and lover and weary, mysterious soldier. "I want all three of us to be married, together, in a ceremony apart from anything we do legally. Maybe only two of us can be married on paper, but in our hearts, it will be all three. Tell me yes, Ben. Tell me yes."

The corner of Ben's mouth hooks up in a smile at my command. "I thought I was the one who gave the orders around here."

I kiss him. Hard. And then Ireland is joining in, and the three of us are kissing with more fierce possession than we ever have before, the firelight catching the new rings and sending beams of reflected light around the room.

"Well, then," I finally manage. "I'm ordering you to order us around for the rest of our lives."

"Yes," Ben says. "Yes, of course, and fuck you, I'm crying now."

He is.

Ireland kisses the tears off his cheeks, and somehow that turns into the three of us on the floor, kissing and grinding and eventually fucking while the fire crackles and more snow spits outside. I catch Ireland and Ben looking at their rings more than once as we make love, and if I felt eight feet tall before, there's no telling how I feel now.

Like the luckiest man alive, the luckiest man who's ever had the privilege of being alive. With my farm and my Clementine-cow and my Greta-dog and my truck.

With my broody ex-soldier.

With my curvy girl.

Lucky doesn't even begin to cover it.

ACKNOWLEDGMENTS

Firstly, I have to thank my amazing agent, Rebecca Friedman, who co-pilots with boundless energy and kindness.

A resounding *thank you* to my heroic editor, Scott Saunders, who cleans up tenses and straightens out straggly subplots with the patience of a saint—and to the rest of the Waterhouse team: Meredith Wild, Robyn Lee, Jennifer Becker, Yvonne Ellis, Haley Byrd, Kurt Vachon, Jonathan Mac, and Jesse Kench. And my eternal gratitude and awe go to Amber Maxwell for creating a gorgeous-as-heck cover for Ireland and all her curves!

An especially deep and humble thanks are owed to Julie Murphy, who spent long, late hours talking over plot points and characterization with me, as well as helping me catalog Channing Tatum's and Adam Driver's best physical attributes.

To Ashley Lindemann, Serena McDonald, Candi Kane, and Melissa Gaston for their tireless toil and love! To the Snatches and other authors who make working in this bananas industry possible—especially Tess and Natalie, who keep plenty of beer and sparkling water in their house for me, and any author who has tolerated my lust for dance parties on a retreat: thank you. I owe the Kiawah crew a special shout-out for plot help and, in particular, Ally C for helping me with the nitty-gritty details of Kansas farming.

Loving and margarita-soaked thanks to the Jarrett girls—Aunt Paula, Aunt Jan, and my own Grandma Sandra—the farm girls in my own family!

And finally, I have to thank you, the reader. Thank you for going on this journey with me and Ireland!

MISADVENTURES

IN

BLUE

To Josh, for all these years of couch time.
I love you.

CHAPTER ONE

JACE

A burglary sounds more exciting than it is.

Burglars are opportunists, generally, and the ones smart enough to do it more than once are smart enough to know how to do it right. Know what you want and take it while no one else is around.

Sticking a gun in a bank teller's face isn't going to get you anything but a prison sentence—but if we're talking the kind of theft that happens without anyone getting hurt? And for shit that isn't federally protected? Well, be clever and you might just get away with it.

Anyway, alarm calls for business structures at night usually turn out to be nothing. Bad wiring or teens goofing off or—most commonly—a night cleaning crew with an old alarm code. And the turns-out-to-be-nothing calls are frequent enough that I'm surprised when I get to the scene and actually find broken glass everywhere. A brief and welcome shot of adrenaline pulses through me as I call it in and draw my weapon to search the premises.

Empty.

With a disappointment that is as irrational as it is unwanted, I update dispatch and call my sergeant.

"Russo," she answers in her usual clipped way.

"Hey, Sarge, it's Sutton. I'm responding to that alarm at 10533 Mastin, and I think you should call Detective Day in. It looks like another one of her doctor's office robberies."

I can tell by the pause on the other end of the phone that my sergeant has no idea what I'm talking about.

"She sent an email about it last week," I add. "Asking to be alerted if there was another one, which I think this is."

I hear clicking and sighing and guess that Russo is double-checking her own inbox to find Detective Day's email.

"All right, kid," Russo says. "Found the email. Looks like calling her in is what we need to do."

That at least gives me some kind of satisfaction. Maybe there is no one to chase, nothing to *do*, but at least I can make sure the right person gets the right information.

But it isn't a lot of satisfaction.

Well, Jace, what did you expect when you took a job working for a suburban police department? Firefights? Car chases?

No. I knew exactly what I was doing when I applied at Hocker Grove Police Department. My sister just had her second baby, my folks were retiring, and I wanted to put down roots. I wanted to buy a house and maybe get my degree and settle down. I wanted something more than the stop-and-start life of active duty in the army like I had before.

I wanted to come back to the place where I grew up.

I walk out of the doctor's office and crunch across the broken glass back to my car for the crime-scene tape, taking in the typical Hocker Grove night as I do. I take in the empty parking lot, still puddled and damp from an earlier storm and lit by lonely light poles, and I take in the distant roar of the interstate and the rustling of wet tree leaves in the wind.

I smell the suburban air, a mix of wet grass and gasoline. The almost-country and the almost-city mixed together.

I smell home.

Although for being home sweet suburban home, Hocker Grove is plenty busy and plenty grim. As the second-most-populous city in the state of Kansas, with almost two hundred thousand people, every type of crime comes out to play. Domestic abuse, drug abuse, battery, assault, theft, and so many auto burglaries that they have their own unit in the investigation division.

As I know from my own childhood growing up in a shitty apartment tucked behind a Walmart, Hocker Grove isn't all happy middle-class families and prosperity. But even with all the work that needs to be done, the pace of life here after six years in the army and three hellish stints in Afghanistan feels, well... boring and uneventful.

Russo arrives right as I am pulling the tape from my car, and after her come Coulson, Romero, and Quinn. Together it doesn't take long to get the scene roped off and secure, and afterward, I slide into my car and start sketching out the beginnings of my report. I hate paperwork, but if there's one thing I learned from the army, it's that there's no point in putting off things you hate. *Especially* paperwork. It just bites you in the ass harder when the time comes.

"I heard they called in the Ice Queen," Quinn says, coming over to lean against my car and talking to me through my open window. Quinn's fresh out of field training, like me, but a couple of years younger, and sometimes that couple of years feels like decades.

But as my grandmother used to say, I'm an old soul, and I'm sure fighting in a literal war did nothing to make that soul any younger. So I take a deep breath and try to be patient with the fact that this guy wants to shoot the shit while all I want is to get my work done.

"Ice Queen?" I ask, not looking up from the report screen of the mounted tablet in the car.

"Yeah, man. Cat Day. You haven't heard about her?"

I could point out that in a department of nearly four hundred commissioned officers, there are a lot of people I haven't heard of, but I don't bother. Quinn doesn't need my help keeping a conversation going.

"So get this. Years and years ago, she was engaged to another cop, and he was killed in the line of duty. Killed *right in front of her*. And when the other officers arrived on the scene, they found her sitting on the steps outside the house where he was killed and she's covered in his blood from trying to do CPR, and the first thing she says is, 'Can I wash my hands?'"

He pauses for effect. I keep typing.

He keeps going, with more hand gestures now, to drive home his point. "Not 'Oh my God, my fiancé is fucking dead' or 'Someone wheel me to the psych ward because I just watched the man I love bleed out' or anything like that. Nope. 'Can I wash my hands?' She wasn't even *crying*. And they said she never did cry, like ever, not even at his funeral. How messed up is that?"

Honestly, I don't think it's messed up at all.

Everyone reacts to trauma differently. I once saved a civilian's life by shoving my fingers into an open wound in his thigh, and three hours later I was eating nachos in the DFAC and complaining about how the Chiefs couldn't get their shit together. The only way to keep living after these moments is to focus on the tiny realities that, when stitched together, make life normal. Washing your hands. Nachos. Talking about things that don't matter.

To stay normal you have to pretend to be normal.

It's compartmentalization—but you can't say that word to the therapists and counselors because then they start nodding and writing stuff down.

"Who's *they*?" I ask, looking up from my tablet.

Quinn's red-blond brows furrow together. "What do you mean?"

"You said *they* are saying this stuff about Detective Day. Who?"

He waves an impatient hand. "It's just like—stories, man. Gossip and stuff."

"Why does anyone care?"

"Because she's still, like, a frigid bitch," Quinn states as if it's obvious.

His words piss me off. "That's unprofessional to say," I tell him. "Not to mention shitty."

Quinn rolls his eyes and his body at the same time in a kind of *oh come ON* gesture. "You're no fun, Sutton."

"So I've heard," I say, getting back to the report.

"Ugh. Fine. But mark my words when you meet her. Frig—"

I give him an irritated glare, and he finally, thankfully, shuts up and leaves me alone.

Ice Queen.

I wonder what she's actually like. My mom was a firefighter, and I know being a woman and a first responder means walking along a wire with no safety net. Too passive and you get ignored for promotions and recognition. Too aggressive and you get labeled a bitch. Act like a man and you'll succeed—but then you'll be punished for not being enough like a woman.

This reflection, along with random thoughts about being home and being bored, filter through my mind as a civilian car rolls into the parking lot. A very nice civilian car.

I watch with interest as it coasts into a spot and stops and then with even more interest as a woman climbs out in a blouse and skirt—no uniform, although there is a badge clipped to the waist of her skirt.

Detective Catherine Day.

She's slender, upright, with posture and movements so graceful that there must be ballet shoes in her past...ski trips and horses too. Light-blond hair waves just past her shoulders, sleek and glamorous in that Old Hollywood kind of way, and the drape of her silk blouse and the fitted hug of her pencil skirt scream money and delicacy and restraint.

She is sophistication embodied.

And all of this refined dignity is coupled with a direct, determined stride and quick, efficient assessments of her surroundings. She exudes confidence. Independence. Power.

I don't know about the *ice* part, but the *queen*?

Yes. I can sense it from here.

In the thirty seconds it takes her to tuck her leather portfolio against her stomach and walk into the building, Catherine Day obliterates any thoughts of boredom or disappointment, and I feel a strange jolt of unhappiness when she walks out of my sight.

I close out my tablet with a few impatient stabs and get out of my car. Talking to her is the only thing I want to do.

CHAPTER TWO

CAT

I'll never concede that crime scenes and high heels don't mix.

I duck under the yellow tape to find the on-duty sergeant and notice a spray of broken glass on the ground. With a rueful glance down at my nude Manolo Blahniks, I pick my way carefully through the sparkling debris to the woman facing away from me, talking into the radio on her shoulder. I've never been more grateful for my years of ballet and yoga as I am when I make it to her with my balance and dignity intact.

Sergeant Russo gives me a friendly—if slightly disbelieving—once-over as I reach her, eyeing my silk blouse and tailored pencil skirt. A sleek leather portfolio is tucked under my elbow.

"Just rolled out of bed like that, huh?" she asks, letting go of her radio and gesturing for me to follow her through a doorway to the real crime scene.

I smile as we walk in, but I don't answer. Nicki Russo and I went through academy together, and while we're friends, her remarks about my clothes have always been more than a little pointed. *Detective Dry Clean Only* is her favorite nickname for me—which I suppose is nicer than the one they call me when I'm not around.

Officer Ice Queen.

They've been calling me that since Frazer's funeral twelve years ago. The funeral where I didn't cry, didn't mourn, didn't expose a single sliver of the raw, howling pain I actually felt.

"Tell me what we've got," I say, setting aside the sharp memories and taking in the scene. "Same as last time?"

Russo nods. "Even down to the timing. Doctor's office, hit after ten. The window around the door is broken—likely what triggered the alarm. We had a uniform here within seven minutes. He searched the office and the rest of the building. No one in sight."

I look around the half-lit waiting room. There's glass from the broken window out on the sidewalk and a spray of shards glinting on the carpet. The usual array of pointless, uninteresting magazines are still neatly arranged on the tables, and the corner houses a collection of wooden toys. Except for the glass, it could be any well-kept, undisturbed waiting room, all but—

"The television again," I murmur, finding what I was looking for. A bare TV mount on the wall, random wires and cords dangling from the ceiling above it.

"Yep," Russo agrees. "My guy saw it right away. He was the one who told me to call you, by the way. Actually read your email about it all."

"And you didn't read my email?" I ask absently, walking up to the wall and examining the mount.

"Do you know how many emails I get in a day?" asks Russo.

It's a rhetorical question, so I don't bother answering, but I do say, "That was attentive of your officer to remember it. I'd like to speak with him, if I may."

"Sure. And the office manager is here too. She might be able to give you a preliminary report of what's missing."

"Nothing else will be missing," I say, more to myself than Russo, still looking at the mount. It was poorly installed, and drywall dust litters the carpet below, as if dislodging the television from the mount sent a shower of the stuff everywhere. "They just want the TVs."

A string of similar robberies has plagued the city for the past two months. It's always doctors' offices, it's always TVs, and it's always at night.

I normally work in crimes against persons—homicide, stalking, assault— but my experience working a similar case for the Kansas Bureau of Investigation a few years back had my sergeant pulling me to work this one. I don't mind, since my usual caseload is a lot grimmer than stolen televisions, but it has been unexpectedly frustrating.

I have one of the highest case clearance rates in the department; I'm not used to failing. Yet I've been on this one for four solid weeks with nothing to show for it.

It's galling, and an unfamiliar itch of restlessness works its way down my spine. It's everything I can do to maintain my poise as I turn back to Russo.

"The scene techs are taking pictures?"

"Already done. They're working on trying to lift prints now, but good luck with a fucking waiting room, you know?"

I make an agreeing kind of noise as we head back toward the scheduling desks, where a wan young woman stands next to a copier. She looks stunned, a confused kind of afraid, and a frisson of impatience skates through me.

There are far worse things than a stolen television—particularly one stolen when no one was around—and I want to tell her that. I want to tell her she doesn't realize what horrors life can present. What fears. Even when Frazer died, I still managed to keep my pain and terror and guilt locked safely inside—

I stop the train of thought immediately. It's not helping the strange restless itch burrowing deeper and deeper into my chest. An itch that seems to be equal parts vexation over the case and some indefinable physical need.

I take a subtle breath, remind myself that this girl is probably in her early twenties and that I don't need to infect her with my jaded, thirty-seven-year-old weariness.

"I'm Detective Catherine Day," I say, extending my hand.

She looks at it for a moment, lost, and then seems to remember what's expected and shakes it. "Gia," she replies.

Russo grins at her. "Good Italian name."

"Uh, yeah. Pisani. Last name." She lets out a huffy little laugh, as if realizing how wooden she's being. "Sorry. This is just so weird."

I give her a small smile. "We'll need you to submit a complete list of everything missing or disturbed in the office, Gia, but whatever you can tell me now will be helpful for the initial report."

She shakes her head, looking lost. "It's only the television... It's bewildering. It's just *gone.*"

"But no one was hurt," Russo tells her. "And in the grand scheme of things, a TV is not the worst thing they could have taken. They could have taken medicine to sell off or all sorts of expensive medical equipment."

Gia chews her lip. "You're right, of course. Absolutely right. It's just this is my first real job out of college, and I have no idea what to do or if it's somehow my fault..."

I catch her uncertain gaze, touching her elbow as I do. "It's not your fault, and I'll guide you through as much of this as I can."

With Gia somewhat mollified, I manage to get a decent preliminary interview out of her, arrange for a follow-up later this week, and ask for a complete inventory of the equipment and other valuable items in the office. Then Russo and I head back outside to the parking lot to find the responding officer.

"*Bewildering,*" Russo echoes. "Can you imagine using the word 'bewildering' out loud?"

"The diploma over her desk was from Vassar," I say a bit distractedly, feeling a short buzz from my phone and looking down to check it. Even with the parking lot lights sending a diffused glow over the pavement, the screen is painfully bright after I tap the notification open. "Maybe she's simply well-spoken. Excuse me. I need to check this."

Russo stops and politely waits for me to check my latest email. I register a small click of satisfaction when I see it's something I've been waiting for.

"Boyfriend?" Russo asks, noticing my pleased expression.

"Crime Analysis," I reply. "Extracted data from the license plate readers in the area of the last burglary."

She rolls her eyes. "Day, you need a boyfriend. Or a girlfriend. You can't fuck extracted data, or at least so I've heard."

"I'm fine, Nicki."

She gives me a mock scowl at the use of her first name. "You seem fine, *Cat*. Really, really, superduper fine."

We're angling toward a clump of officers standing next to a patrol car. Even in the dark, they've all got the requisite patrol cop sunglasses propped on their heads, and every last one of them has a gas station coffee cup clutched in one hand—vital medicine for any officer on any shift, day or night.

"I *am* fine. I promise."

She softens, going from friendly ribbing to the earnest tomboy I met fifteen years ago at academy. "Frazer would want you to be happy, you know," she says quietly enough that the uniforms can't hear her as we approach. "He wouldn't want you to live like this...married to the job since you couldn't marry him."

My chest tightens uncomfortably.

It's been twelve years since he died, and there's been plenty of therapy and life between then and now—and still her words sting. I tuck my phone carefully inside my portfolio, swallow, and say, "I'm happy, Nicki. Truly."

It's a lie, but she doesn't press me on it, for which I'm grateful. "Okay," she says. "I just want to see you have a little fun is all. Live a little."

"I know. And thank you."

She gives my shoulder a little shove, a playful gesture literally no one else in the department would attempt with me, and then we're to the chattering cops and the conversation is over.

The restless itch, however, is back, tickling between my shoulder blades and tugging deep in my belly. Damn her, but Russo's words have gotten under my skin.

Am I lonely? Am I married to my job and starving myself of happiness?

Of course not. How ridiculous.

But if it's so ridiculous, why this itch? Why this feeling like I'm waiting for something, missing something? Or someone?

"Sutton," Russo calls out. "Someone here to talk to you."

One of the uniforms breaks away from the knot of gossiping cops and turns toward us. He's young—very young—no more than twenty-three or twenty-four, but he's without the swagger most cops have at that age. And it's obvious he doesn't need it.

Serious gray eyes stare out from under equally serious brows. A slightly Grecian nose leads to a sculpted mouth currently pressed into a solemn, no-nonsense line—which only serves to highlight the tempting peaks of his upper lip and the subtle fullness of the lower even more.

His high-and-tight haircut is relaxed just enough that I could run my fingers through the dark thickness at the top but still short enough to show off his uplifted cheekbones and strong jaw. And his body—his body is pure sex. Young, vigorous, twenty-something sex. Broad shoulders testing the seams of his uniform shirt arrow down into trim hips neatly circled by a duty belt. His uniform pants cling to hard, athletic thighs, and right below his belt, there's the bulge of a mouthwatering cock at rest. Oh God, oh God—

I blush, my eyes snapping back up to his face. There's no way he didn't see me giving him such an obvious once-over. Except he doesn't look proud or amused—the two reactions I'd expect from a hotshot-looking rookie.

He looks thoughtful. And maybe a little curious.

"Sutton, this is Cat Day. She's the lead detective on these robberies."

"I remember," he says. His voice is deep and rough—just like sex with him would be—and at hearing it, something behind my sternum pulls free with enough force to make my lips part on a silent gasp, and heat spills from my chest to my belly to somewhere lower down.

That itch from earlier is resolving itself into thudding, hot aches everywhere. Everywhere I thought my body had gone quiet over the years. The tips of my breasts, the neglected bundle of nerves between my legs. My lips and my fingertips and even the skin of my belly, all craving heat and friction. All craving *him*. His combination of strength and power and youth—that thrill of seeing a man so young and virile vibrate with such restrained intensity.

Now is when I should speak, when I should take control of the situation again, but I can't trust my voice not to betray the sudden, purring desire currently humming across the surface of my skin. Instead, I extend a hand for a quick, professional shake.

His hand is larger than mine, warm and dry and calloused, and the moment our skin touches, I know it was a mistake. Electricity sizzles through me, and with his eyes locked on mine as we touch, it's impossible not to imagine that gray gaze on me as he pumps between my legs. Staring down at me as I take his heavy cock into my mouth. Touching him, no matter how professionally, only drives me to further distraction.

"Nice to meet you." That *voice*. Even listening to him, no matter how bland the words are, feels like a prurient act—like I shouldn't be doing it in public. Surely everyone around us can see how my skin is catching fire? How my nipples are beading through my lace bra and silk blouse?

"Nice to meet you," I manage back, praying I sound composed. "I appreciate you making sure I was brought in tonight."

"I read your email," he explains and then says nothing else. A man of few words, I suppose, although there's no mistaking the intensity at which he operates. It's in his extreme focus, the predatory stillness of his form. In the tension around his mouth and the alert tilts of his head.

It's hard to mind either the silence or the intensity when his eyes are shimmering mercury in the hazy radiance of the parking lot lights. They're the kind of eyes that seem to say everything his mouth won't, and it's next to impossible to tear myself away when Russo breaks in and asks me a question.

"Hey, do you need Sutton much longer? He's an evenings boy, and his shift finished an hour ago."

Right.

Shifts. Robberies.

Police work.

Focus, Cat. Work the case.

"Only a few minutes more, Nicki," I tell her and then turn to Sutton. "Do you mind going over what you found with me?"

The shake of his head is deliberate, precise. No motion wasted, no emotion betrayed. "Whatever you need."

God. I could listen to that voice say *whatever you need* every night for the rest of my life. Low in my ear...against the nape of my neck...from between my legs.

I curl my fingers around my leather portfolio so hard that I know my knuckles are going white.

"Thank you," I say, and thankfully my voice is as calm and cool as ever. "Can you walk me through what you saw when you pulled up?"

Sutton nods but not before his eyes drop to where my hand clenches around the portfolio. I angle myself away from him ever so slightly so he can't see, and he looks back up. I can't read his gaze...and I'm not sure if I want to.

"I arrived about ninety minutes ago—dispatch sent it out as an alarm call," he starts and then proceeds to give me a clear and concise accounting of his arrival and subsequent search. I'm impressed with his eye for detail—most rookies don't know what to look for on calls like these—and I'm also impressed with the way he describes his search. Brief and without posturing or flourish. Even Frazer couldn't resist the occasional showboating back in his time.

"Thank you," I say when I've finished. "And you're back on duty tomorrow?"

"At three in the afternoon. I'll have my report to you by five."

"Don't make promises you can't keep," Russo advises in a half-supervisory, half-cynical tone, and then she turns to me. "You'll get it at some point in the next forty-eight."

I make a mental note of that. "Then you're free to go, Officer," I tell him, my eyes dropping one last reluctant time to the hewn, lean length of his body. My little ogle is snagged by the embroidered *J. Sutton* on his uniform shirt.

"Jace," he says softly.

I glance back up at him.

"J is for Jace," he explains. "Oh," I say and then notice Russo is narrowing her eyes at me. I clear my throat and offer my hand again. "Then thank you, Jace. This has been very helpful."

And I manage not to shiver when he shakes my hand a second time, his eyes falling to my mouth. I also manage not to make a disappointed whimper as his skin parts from mine and he turns to leave.

After he's several paces away, Russo crosses her arms and squints up at the fingernail-shaped moon. "He's only just graduated from field training a few months ago," she says conversationally. "Very young."

"He's very adept," I say in a neutral tone.

"Hmm." She makes the noise in a way that lets me know I'm not fooling her. "Okay, well, I think we're close to being able to release the scene if you're all good?"

"I've got everything I need," I say. "Thanks, Nicki."

She waves me off, reaching down to say something into her radio, and I walk away, trying very hard not to notice the stoic shadow of a certain police officer walking back to his patrol car.

I still notice.

I make a final round through the scene and then walk back to my car, portfolio cradled under my arm. I open it up to where I keep my car key in an inside pocket, and as I'm unlocking the passenger door to set my portfolio in the seat, a patrol car slides into the spot next to me.

The window rolls down, revealing the startlingly handsome profile of Sutton.

"I wanted to make sure you got into your car okay," he says quietly.

I glance around me and then raise an eyebrow. "There are at least seven cops in this lot. And lest you forget, I'm a cop too."

"You don't have your service weapon on you."

"Don't I?" And I'm not exactly sure why I do it, but I can't say my motivation is entirely professional defensiveness. I pull up the hem of my pencil skirt to show where my small Glock is strapped to my inner thigh, revealing my garters and stockings in the process.

I can hear Jace's audible inhale, and when I glance back up at him, his eyes burn with something like fury. But I'm guessing the strain around his mouth and the way he works his jaw to the side has nothing to do with anger.

"It's safer to carry your gun on your hip," he says tightly.

"I don't like to ruin the lines of my skirt," I say. Yes, I'm that vain, although at the first sign of danger, I would have had my weapon out and ready.

I realize I'm still showing off my lingerie when he lets out a low groan. My body responds to his response like he's just touched a match to gasoline, and Russo's voice echoes in my head: *have a little fun.*

Be happy.

It's reckless what I'm about to do. Stupid in ways I'm never stupid in, yet I'm going to do it anyway because I want to. Hell, maybe I *need* to. Maybe my body is so desperate for friction and release that it could have been any man who crossed my path tonight.

But I don't think that's true.

It's something about this too-young-for-me rookie, with his earnest seriousness and intense eyes. With that body that practically thrums with strength.

Every part of it is wrong for a thirty-seven-year-old woman, for a professional, maybe even for an officer of the law, yet I still lean down to his window and say, "Fifty-one thirty-seven Norwood Avenue. The door will be unlocked."

And without waiting for his response, I walk around to the driver's side of my car and leave.

JACE

An hour later I'm in the station, staring at my open locker as if it has answers.

It doesn't.

Fifty-one thirty-seven Norwood Avenue. The door will be unlocked.

My cock, which has been pushing against my zipper since she flashed me that impossibly sexy combination of gun and garter, is hot and throbbing at the idea of going to her house. It's swollen and proud at the pleasure of being picked. My cock wants to go.

Hell, all of me wants to go, if I'm being honest.

Being interviewed by her did nothing to diminish my slow but growing fascination—a fascination that felt more and more possessive as our conversation went on. The more her aqua eyes flicked over me in that endearingly unchaste way. The hauntingly sexy arch of her eyebrow as she listened. The inadvertent pout of her mouth as she took notes.

The flare of ownership I began to feel was so powerful, so urgent, that I could barely breathe. I didn't care that she was older, that we just met, that while technically permissible, fraternization within rank was still frowned upon.

She was mine.

My ice queen who would thaw only for me.

Except now as I'm changing out, hanging up my duty belt in my locker and lacing up my civvy boots, I'm plagued by questions.

Is this something she does often? Am I not the first young, unattached officer to be picked for this?

Am I imagining her attraction to me? My reaction to her?

And do any of these questions actually matter? It's a spontaneous lay with no promise of more. A single, near-strangerly fuck and then a parting of ways. For all I know, I'll be pushed out the door with a wet dick and one of those small, enigmatic smiles, never to see her again.

I nearly growl at the thought. I don't want a single fuck with Catherine Day. I don't know what I *do* want, but I know this thing stretching and flexing to life inside me won't be satisfied with only tonight.

I'm going to need more.

I'm going to need a lot more.

CHAPTER THREE

CAT

I'm shaking as I walk into my house.

Wild doubts and frenetic surges of panic tumble around inside my mind as I lock up my duty weapon and put my badge and my notes away.

What am I doing? Have I lost my mind?

And will he come?

What if he doesn't?

What if he does?

I pace around the house, turn on some modern cello music, and pour myself a large glass of white wine. It's been three years since I've screwed someone, and even that barely counted because it was the tentative and too-sweet fuck of a successful first date. The man treated me like a china doll—like I'd crack at the first sign of rough handling—and I didn't come. It was rather embarrassing for both of us afterward.

I found excuses to avoid dates after that.

So for three years it's just been me and a small collection of carefully curated toys, and the idea of letting a man back inside my body has me more excited—and more terrified—than I thought possible. What if I've forgotten how to be good at it? What if it's as disappointing as the last time I invited someone into bed? What if—oh, this is a big one—what if this young man doesn't like my definitely-a-woman-in-her-thirties body?

Worried, I drink more wine and wander back to the front door, debating on whether or not to leave it locked.

Maybe I should. Maybe I should call this entire impulsive, preposterous thing off. I'll leave a note on the door telling him as much and spare us both our pride.

But dammit, I don't want to.

Every time I conjure up an image of Jace Sutton—gray eyes and that young, vigorous body—my own body sizzles with unmet need. And as nervous as I am, I'm certain that if I don't do this, I'll regret it for the rest of my life.

No, I want this. I'm doing it. No matter how embarrassed I'll be in the morning.

I unlock the door.

I'm still dressed, though, and as I finish my wine and set the glass down on the counter, I wonder if I should change that—if I should strip down or don something a bit more overtly sexy. Hell, I'm still in my heels even, still Detective Dry Clean Only.

With a sigh, I decide to change, but as I walk out of my kitchen, I feel it. The distinctive prickle at the back of my neck telling me I'm not alone.

I look up into the window across the breakfast nook and see Jace in the reflection, standing at a careful distance behind me. I'm impressed with how silently he entered my house; I'm not easy to sneak up on.

Even in the reflection—and superimposed over my dark, private backyard—he looks painfully well-built, with the curves of his shoulders and arms pushing at his T-shirt and his jeans showing off his narrow, perfect hips. His chiseled features are still set in that stern, ultraserious expression that I found so compelling earlier, but now there's something else behind that solemnity. Something darker. More primal.

Neither of us says a word, as if we both know that speaking will somehow dilute whatever this is. This assignation. This mystifying attraction between us.

So instead, I give him a steady, almost regal nod, like a queen to her young knight, and he understands immediately, a slow ripple of dangerous lust coursing visibly though him.

He strides forward like a conqueror, and before I can turn to meet him, he has his hand flat between my shoulder blades and he's bending me over the table.

I bend, all the blood in my body pooling in my cunt.

"Jace," I say.

He says nothing in reply but yanks my pencil skirt up to my hips and lets the cool air of the room caress my panty-covered ass. Still silent, his hands find the tops of my stockings and then move to stroke along the lines of my garters. I can't help the moan that escapes me once his fingertips trace up the curve of my ass. Or the second moan when he slides a finger under the edge of my panties and explores the needy kiss of my pussy. He removes the finger and gives me a hard cup, letting me feel the unraveling threads of his control.

Letting me feel how rough he wants to be.

And the ensuing shove and grind of his denim-covered erection against my ass almost feels like an indictment, like he's accusing me of something. I roll my face into the wood surface of the table and shudder.

I like it all way too much.

Have I ever felt like this before? Like a present being unwrapped? Like being both the best and worst thing to happen to a man?

And how does someone so young know to fuck like this?

My panties are torn off—just torn right off my hips without so much as a by-your-leave—and Jace gives my high-heeled foot a vicious kick with his own. It spreads my legs apart, like he's searching me, frisking me, and the thought of that is so wrong and dirty that I whimper into the table.

A long finger makes an approving circle of my now-exposed cunt and then penetrates me in an unhurried but persistent slide. I arch, which earns me another finger and a pleased grunt from him. He gives me a few lazy pumps, paying special attention to the textured spot inside that sends frissons of electric sensation everywhere through my body, but just when I'm starting to get really wet, truly squirmy, he withdraws his hand.

When I look up at the window, I see him staring back at me with darkened, unknowable eyes. He has his fingers in his mouth, and he's sucking my taste right off them.

"Oh God," I whisper. "Oh God."

What have I gotten myself into with him?

A small, barely there quirk of his lips makes me think he can read my thoughts. And the next thing he does is just as carnal, just as vulgar. He unzips his jeans, pulls out his naked cock, and lets it drop right onto the top of my ass. A heavy, marking weight that tells me I wasn't wrong earlier about that superlative bulge in his uniform pants.

Without a word, he extracts a condom from his back pocket and tears it open with his teeth—a move I find animalistically, almost violently, sexual—and then rolls the sheath over his turgid length.

I'm grateful for the condom, really, I am. But at the same time, I almost regret it. I almost wish he'd just penetrate me without one—which is patently nonsensical, as I have no doubt a man like Jace Sutton is fucking his way through the greater Kansas City area. Most cops his age are, which is one of the reasons I've refused to date any of them after Frazer's death.

But Jace has bulldozed past all my usual, prudent precautions. Younger man. Fellow cop. And apparently he's even bulldozed past my common sense about casual sex and protection.

God, I'm fucked in the head.

I can feel the scorching heat of his tip even through the latex as he lazily maps the hollows and folds of my flesh, making everything wet and ready for his invasion.

Then he invades.

The spread of his wide crown into that long-untouched place makes my breath stutter and my fingers curl against the wood, and he's relentless with it, driving in and in and in, tunneling through my tight, squeezing flesh. He pulls back to the crown, and with a hard hand on my hip and a low grunt, he pierces me all the way in.

He stays just like that for a long moment, my body flush against his hips and his free hand smoothing over the strappy bits of garter belt on my bottom and the rucked-up fabric of my skirt. I can't imagine how wanton I look like this, how debauched, my skirt shoved up and my cunt stretched—and all of it without foreplay or an inaugural kiss. Without even a word.

I'm so turned on by it all that I think I'll scream if he doesn't start moving.

I'm shorter than him by a significant amount, even in the steep Manolo Blahniks, and he nudges my feet back together with him still inside in order to get me at the angle he wants. And then he starts to fuck.

Each pull out to the tip is a thrill of friction, and each shove back in is a sear of pressure and heat. He fucks me unapologetically, thoroughly, shoving and driving inward until I can swear the end of his cock is somewhere in my chest, his hands fisting in the expensive fabric of my skirt to bring me back against him harder, faster.

I look up at the window again just to see him—just to see that tall, sturdy body at work—and find him looking at the same thing. Watching us, still clothed, bucking and sweaty. Two cops seeking a desperate, dirty cure for an ancient ache.

His face like this is spellbinding—his dark brows are drawn together in focus and his full mouth is pressed into a solemn line, and he doesn't look like a predator who's caught his prey. He doesn't look like a victorious male who's managed to pin a mate. Not yet. I'm not sure what else he wants until his hand gives my ass a quick *crack* and then just as quickly finds my clit.

Then I know. He wants more from me. He wants me wild. He wants me to come.

I arch, I purr, I twist—his fingers are expert and sure, and they know exactly how to work my flesh, exactly how to circle and press and rub. He watches me carefully in the window, studying my face, and I realize he's learning what I like, gauging my reactions to what he does.

So he sees the frustrated pout when he touches me gently, the ecstatic gasp when he gets rough again and demands a response from my body.

I'm spanked and I let out laughs of surprised pleasure because who knew that could feel so good? So naughty and invigorating, the contrast of the sparkling pain only serving to highlight the pleasure I'm feeling around his thick erection and under his skillful fingers? And there's more, so much more.

My nipples are plucked and rolled through my blouse and bra. My hair is wound in his fist and pulled. My asshole is pressed and played with—with ownership, with male prerogative, as if he has no doubt that he has every right to it.

There's no china doll treatment from Jace Sutton. None at all, and I'm on fire with how much I love it.

My orgasm comes with three years of need roaring behind it—more, *twelve* years of need, twelve years since I've been properly fucked, and even then it still wasn't like this. It still wasn't as dirty or as hard or as fundamental. *This* is how I need to be fucked—how I've always needed to be fucked—and I never knew. I never knew until this one-night stand with a young man I have no right taking to bed.

Bed...kitchen table. Whatever.

With a sobbed moan, I feel the orgasm catch fire around the buried tip of his cock, starting in my belly and yanking at my clit and flickering across every single nerve ending I have. He sucks in a breath as the contractions grip his erection, as if my body is trying to milk the come right up his shaft and into my body, and then he lets loose.

Truly lets loose.

His cock swells bigger and harder than ever, and his hips hammer into the curves of my bottom as if he's trying to wedge his way inside me. I know he wants to come, I know he wants to pump his condom full, and knowing that is enough to set off a second, stronger orgasm inside me.

I let out a soft wail, writhing and kicking my feet as his relentless fucking pins me to the table, and it's too much, it's all too much. I can't handle how viciously my pussy clenches with pleasure. I can't handle the sensory overload of being screwed so ferociously through it all. I wail and I kick, and he grunts and keeps thrusting, and then he lays his upper body over mine, wraps his hand around my throat, and spears me harder than ever, going so deep that I can feel the hair below his navel tickling my ass and the zipper of his jeans biting the tender skin of my thighs.

In near silence he comes, with only a ragged groan on that first exquisite throb to let me know his control is also shaken, and the scalding heat of his seed is palpable even through the latex. His erection flexes and pulses inside me, doing the job it was made for, and I love the feeling of it so much that I tuck my cheek against my shoulder so he can't see the delirious grin on my face.

God, I'd forgotten. Forgotten everything, really, but mostly how good it felt to have someone releasing inside me, filling me with heat as their body jerked in pleasure.

He stays bent over me even after his cock goes still, and he brushes the hair away from my ear so he can ghost his lips over its shell. And for a minute, I think he's going to kiss me. Going to shatter the potent fantasy of this magical encounter with some banal *thank you* or *how was it for you?*

But I underestimate him.

"Don't you ever, *ever*, leave your fucking door unlocked," he whispers against my ear. "Ever fucking again."

Without waiting for a response, he pulls out and steps away, leaving my entire body wet and empty and cold. I hear the clang of the kitchen trash can lid as he throws the condom away, and the purr of his zipper, and then his footsteps to the front door. It opens.

I hear the pointed, deliberate sound of the lock turning and then the door closing behind him.

Jace is gone, having left me bruised and flushed and happy—and safer than how he found me.

And I stay bent over that table for much longer than necessary, smiling into the wood because that unsettled itch from earlier is finally, finally scratched.

CHAPTER FOUR

JACE

I'm edgy as hell as I walk into the station.

I barely slept, could hardly eat this morning, and even the usual grind of weights and cardio at the gym wasn't enough to sharpen my focus. All I could think about was *her*.

Catherine.

Cat.

She was catlike indeed last night, all purrs and sinuous, needy arches. I wonder if she bites. I wonder if she scratches.

I think I might die if I don't find out.

The problem is that I'm not sure I'll have the chance—and even I see the irony of that, because ever since I've come home to Hocker Grove, I haven't exactly been a "find out more" kind of guy.

I left the army, expecting to marry my high school sweetheart, and came home to find that she'd been sweethearting plenty of other guys while I was away. It hurt less than it should have, and I think we'd been nothing more than friends with benefits for a while. But it still made me wary of anything lasting longer than a couple of hours. Once bitten and all that.

Except I want more than a couple of hours with Cat. I want much, much more, and it was only respect for what I thought she needed from our encounter that made me leave. I wasn't going to force myself on her for longer if all she wanted was a nice little fuck to finish off the day.

Not that our fuck was *nice*. Or *little*.

My dick swells as I remember how rough my ice queen wanted it. How she moaned as I pulled her hair and spanked her ass. How fucking sexy and sluttish she looked with that prim skirt over her ass and her pricy garters framing her cunt.

I get to the locker room and lean against my locker, my mind crammed full of last night, my body aching with the memory of it.

What is it about her?

Is it that she's older? Elegant? Mysterious?

Was it the bewitching discovery that if you bent her over a table, all that good breeding disappeared?

I'm not sure. It's all of it combined, maybe. All of it plus seeing her at work last night, so fearless and intelligent and methodical. Knowing her slender, wanton body came paired with steel resolve and a sharp mind.

I'm still chewing over this as I get to roll call and take a chair. Russo goes over the normal beginning of shift stuff—traffic assignments for the afternoon, new slides from vice about a drug ring up north—and then swivels her chair toward me. "Investigations is asking for a uniform to help with the television robberies. I volunteered you."

I'm only half paying attention, my thoughts still fixated on a certain detective. "Pardon?"

"You did a good job last night," Russo says honestly, and it's one of the things I like best about her. She's fair, and while she doesn't effusively praise her squad the way some sergeants do, she consistently recognizes good work. "I was impressed, and Captain Kim in investigations was impressed. We both agree you'd be a good fit to help Day with some of the investigation grunt work."

Hearing her name out loud is like a shot of adrenaline. I sit up straighter, alert. "I'd be working with Detective Day?"

Russo tilts her head at me. "Yeah. That's what I said. That a problem?"

It's the furthest fucking thing in the world from a problem. "No, of course not. Do I need to change shifts?"

"You'll be working whatever they tell you to work," Russo says. "You're temporarily assigned to Day's sergeant and Day's squad. I imagine you'll be working some days, some overnights, that kind of thing. Will that work?"

I have no life outside of this job except for the gym and playing with my niece and nephew. And I'm to the point where I'd happily donate an organ if it meant I could see Day again.

I give Russo an affirmative nod.

"All right. Then get your rookie butt down to investigations and report to Day."

In the history of the HGPD, no one has hauled ass to the investigations station as quickly as I do now, and I test more than a few speed limits as I try to get there before Day clocks out. I park the car and practically jog into the building.

I search out the investigations sergeant for a quick check-in and to verify whom I need to report to for the evening portion of the shift, and then I'm free to find her.

I can admit it now, as I'm stalking through the maze of cubicles to find hers. I can admit how badly I want to fuck her again. How much I hated walking away last night, how my stomach twisted all night long at the thought that she might think badly of me, that she was displeased or unimpressed with what happened.

I want very much for her to be pleased. To be impressed.

I knew all of this earlier, of course, but it's only now as I'm eating up the space between us that I acknowledge the implication.

I want her to be mine.

At least one more time.

Cat's cubicle is tucked away in a far corner, and it's larger than most. A subtle indication of her position in the unit. A little digging this morning while Romero and I were at the station gym netted me the information that Cat is the lead persons detective and usually takes point on the city's homicides, when we have them—which is rarely—working assaults, batteries, and stalking the rest of the time.

She has the highest case clearance rate of any other detective in her unit and has for years. She did a stint with the KBI—HGPD loaned her out for that one—and frequently gets called in by other agencies to help with difficult cases. The "frigid bitch" Quinn was talking about is possibly the best cop in the department—and manages to be the best without fanfare or arrogance.

And she surrendered all that intelligence and discipline into my hands last night. The significance of that is potent. Intoxicating.

Russo made it sound as if Captain Kim had decided to put me on the burglary case, but I can't help but hope that Day asked for me. That she liked my performance—both at the scene and in her kitchen—enough to trust me with her presence again. I want her to trust me. I want it as directly and forcefully as I've wanted anything else that matters.

And now I'm thinking about wanting her in the noisy, fluorescent bullpen. *Get it under control, Sutton.*

I'm always professional and respectfully subordinate—a gift from the army days—but even walking up to her cubicle has my cock thick and my blood hot. My heart is in my throat like I'm a teenage boy about to ask a girl to his first dance, and I'm itching just to *see* her, just to be *close* to her.

Except when I get to her, she's not alone.

A man, probably just on the young side of forty, is standing in the cubicle opening with an elbow propped on the chest-high wall and one dress-shoed foot crossed behind the other. He's in a tailored blue suit, the kind that costs as much as I make in a month, and it showcases an impressively fit body. There's no wedding ring on his hand, and he's leaning in to talk to Cat in a familiar manner that makes me want to smash something.

When I get to the cubicle entry myself, I see Cat sitting in her chair, looking radiant in that tasteful way of hers and laughing at something he's said.

I hate him immediately.

Her eyes slide over to me and widen, and for a moment, I see desire flash in those sparkling depths—but as soon as I see it, it's gone, and she's the aloof queen once more.

"Sutton," she says calmly. "What brings you to this station?"

Ah, so she didn't know I was coming. Which means she didn't ask for me. Shit.

Pushing down my disappointment, I reply, "Russo's lending me out to you. It's gone through Kim and everything, so...I'm at your disposal. Starting now."

I feel a rush of male satisfaction as my subtext sends pink blooming along her cheekbones.

"How nice," she murmurs, her sea-colored eyes dropping down to her shoes. She takes a breath, and when she looks back up at me, she seems to have control of herself again. "Sutton, have you met our new assistant district attorney, Kenneth Goddard? He used to be one of the best defense lawyers in town before he moved away a few years ago, but now he's back and fighting for the side of good." She gives him a quick, teasing grin with her last statement, and I hate him even more.

Kenneth laughs. "Good is subjective. You know that."

She makes a face. "Maybe in criminal defense, but you were getting doctors and rich kids out of DUIs, Ken. Not exactly a hero's fare."

"But you admit I *was* good at it." He grins and then turns to me, extending a hand. He's good-looking, damn him, in a WASPy way. Medium height, dark-blond hair, and a fucking cleft in his chin. His fine-boned face and expensive haircut make me think he's known wealth long before defending assholes for lots of money.

"Nice to meet you, Officer Sutton," Kenneth says easily. It takes every ounce of self-control I have to shake his hand.

"Likewise," I lie.

Cat stands up, smoothing down her skirt as she does. It's another pencil skirt, dark gray this time, and I nearly need to excuse myself after thinking about how good it would look shoved up to her waist.

She seems to have the same thought, because her hands shake as she smooths the fabric again and she can't look me in the face.

"Kenneth is the ADA who will handle most of the medium-level persons crimes moving forward, so he was just in to talk to Kim."

"Well, and to catch up with you, Cat," Kenneth interjects.

He calls her Cat. I don't fucking like that. Not at all.

And I like it even less when he catches her hand and gives it a quick squeeze. Jealousy flares through me so hot and fast that I think I might erupt, because how dare he touch her in front of me?

Stop it, my conscience warns. *She's not yours.*

For her part, Cat seems as surprised by the hand squeeze as I'm not. Any idiot can tell that this Kenneth is interested in her, that he wants her. It's all over his body language, in the gaze that can't stop dropping to her tits and tracing the subtle curve her pussy makes against her tight skirt.

He wants her, and worse—I think there's some history here. When he lets go of her hand, it's with the satisfaction of someone reclaiming lost territory.

"I hope you don't mind if I give you a call?" he asks, touching her elbow. I nearly deck him.

Her eyes dart to me, her mouth pursed in a moue that I'm beginning to recognize as her thinking face. "I suppose that would be okay," she says hesitantly, and something inside me dies a little.

It's impossible not to notice how good they look together. Not to notice he's got the same elegant, well-bred features she does. The same expensive taste in clothes. They're the same age and have the same precision of speech and bearing.

Compared to him, I feel young and dumb. A blunt, inexperienced instrument. A big, strong body to ride and then forget about the next day.

I take a step back as he gives her a winning smile and then turns that smile on me. I don't think I'm imagining the glint of victory in his stare as he holds out a hand for me to shake again. Nor the trace of smugness in his voice when he says, "Officer Sutton."

I shake his hand, letting my nod be my only response.

"I'll talk to you later, Cat," he says, the words laden with meaning, and then he leaves.

And I'm not sure what I feel, except jealous and possessive and maybe the tiniest bit insecure. Especially looking at Cat, now leaning over her desk to get her portfolio, her pale-blond hair swinging in soft, coiffed waves, one delicate high heel kicked back for balance.

She looks like perfection. Like the kind of woman who should be with a hotshot lawyer, pampered and taken to restaurants I've never even heard of—

and wouldn't be able to pronounce their names even if I had. Kenneth is the right kind of man for her. Not me.

But I don't think I care.

I don't care because I may not be rich, but I've known rich men and I know how they think. I know exactly how Kenneth sees Cat. She's a shiny, beautiful thing to him, like a sleek sports car glinting in the lot, and once he acquires her, he'll want her off the streets. He'll want her sitting at home, safe and gathering dust, until he sees fit to take her out and show her off.

I don't care because even though I barely know her, I can see a life like that would make her miserable. She can't be fettered down to play house, leaving only to be gala arm candy. She needs to be handled according to her strength—used and adored in equal measure—and she needs someone who doesn't want to change a single fucking thing about her. Not her job or her drive or anything.

And I don't care because I felt her body against mine last night. I heard her fingernails against the wood and her soft, euphoric moans as she came over and over again. I saw her quiver as I spanked her and pulled her hair. I felt her get wetter and wetter as I kicked her legs apart and played with her asshole.

There's no way in hell Kenneth would be able to give her what she needs.

And I can.

Maybe it's as simple as that.

But as Cat straightens up, gives me one of those thoughtful half pouts, and says, "Okay, Sutton, what am I going to do with you?" I worry that it's not going to be simple at all.

CHAPTER FIVE

CAT

The sight of Jace standing in front of me stunned me so much that I don't know how I fumbled my way through the rest of the conversation with Kenneth. There I was, praying Kenneth couldn't tell how gingerly I was sitting on my office chair because I'd been reamed to heaven and back by a gorgeous man who'd been a baby while I was in high school, and then Jace just *appeared*, as if my tender cunt had summoned him into existence.

The difference between Jace and Kenneth was beyond startling. Next to the raw, potent presence of Jace in uniform, Kenneth looked like a photocopy of a Brooks Brothers ad. Where Jace was hard and lean from PT in the desert, Kenneth had the sort of self-conscious physique that came from paying a trainer a lot of money. And where Jace's almost-rugged features are pulled into a look of stern detachment, Kenneth was all genteel symmetry and practiced smiles.

I've never felt that Kenneth was *unattractive* before now, but with Jace next to him....Jace might as well have been the only man on earth as far as my body was concerned. The sheer power radiating from his wide shoulders and crossed arms and wide, booted stance was enough to make me embarrassingly, shamefully wet. I stood up before I left a damp spot on my skirt.

"Okay, Sutton, what am I going to do with you?" I glance down the bullpen, relieved to see that no one is watching the Ice Queen blush over a rookie, and then I glance toward the door as I think. I have a few follow-ups I need to do, and I could probably task some of those to Jace, but if I'm honest, I'm not ready for us to part ways just yet. It feels like some kind of bizarre gift from the universe that he's here at all. One of those coincidences that I'm in danger of making too much of, when I should just be grateful for the extra help. Especially when that help is as capable and competent as Jace Sutton.

The thought grounds me in the here and now. Back to reality and the case. With a deep breath, I turn to him and force myself to be nothing more than professional. At least in my words, if I can't be in my thoughts.

"I think it's best if we go through the evidence together, make sure you know everything I do," I say. "Kim's given me the meeting room across the hall as a base camp, so let's start there."

I gesture to the meeting room in question, but Jace doesn't look where I indicate. Instead, he gives me a slow, heated once-over that makes my belly clench.

"I'm happy to start wherever you are," he says after a minute, with just the barest hint of an eyebrow raise to underscore that he's not only talking about the case, and then he turns and walks to the meeting room with the confident stride of a man who's been to war.

It's that presence that seals the deal, I decide as I follow him out of the little hallway made by my cubicle and the meeting room. With his kissable lips and long eyelashes, he could easily be too handsome to be powerful, but there's something about those stormy gray eyes and the low voice and the authority he exudes simply by standing in place. It's what makes him look like a cop and not like an actor who plays a cop on TV.

He opens the door to the meeting room and flicks on the light, and I can't help it. I really can't. It's these fucking uniform pants and how they display the molded, muscled curve of his ass.

I look.

I *gawk*. Like a schoolgirl after the cute boy, I gawk.

And then I remember I'm thirteen years older than him and my gawking probably looks more like a leer.

Stop it, Cat. This can't happen.

There's a million reasons I can't fuck Jace Sutton again. In our department, officers and detectives share the same rank, and fraternization is allowed within rank, but it's still wildly unprofessional...even more so now that he's been assigned to my case.

And then there's the age difference. A twenty-four-year-old cop with a giant cock and flat abs? I have no doubt there's a bevy of badge bunnies with limber, nubile bodies waiting to crawl into his lap face first and that he probably went home so fast after fucking me because he had no desire to fuck me again. Why would he want to fuck an old lady when there's probably an infinite supply of eager twenty-somethings waiting to fall into his bed?

The thought is depressing.

But I'm not in the habit of allowing myself self-pity and never have been, even after Frazer's death. I enjoyed last night, and I refuse to regret it. Even if it's time to get back to real life now.

And I'm all ready for real life, for the contained control I normally enjoy, just as soon as I'm done looking at Sutton's ass. Which I am. I definitely am done looking—okay, maybe just one more peek—

Jace turns faster than I anticipate, and there can be no doubt he catches me looking. His usual brooding scowl gets scowlier.

Which is fair. There's no doubt it's improper to be caught ogling your young coworker's ass, even if you did fuck him the night before. But I can't pretend shame. I can't pretend there isn't a tiny part of me that feels entitled to look.

I tilt my head and allow him a little smile. *You caught me.*

He kicks the door shut, and in a heartbeat I'm pushed against the wall and trapped between his hands planted on either side of my head as my phone and portfolio tumble to the floor.

I'm caged in by two hundred pounds of angry male muscle, but I haven't been afraid of big, grumpy cops since I started academy—and anyway, my body associates all this intensity and closeness from Jace with something close to danger but much, much more fun.

"You're looking at me like you want to be bent over a table again," he says in a silky voice.

"Maybe."

He glances down at my nipples, erect and making themselves known against the thin fabric of my blouse.

"Is that for me?"

"Who else would it be for?"

"Kenneth."

I make a dismissive noise, and my cop narrows his eyes.

"He wants to fuck you," he growls. "I don't like it."

I lift an eyebrow. "I don't see how that's any of your business."

More scowling. "Still. He's an asshole."

It's so churlish, so very male, that I have to laugh a little, and his gaze snags on my smiling mouth and goes from angry to something different. Something greedy.

"He's not an asshole," I say. "He's very nice. Even if he were an asshole, however, it still wouldn't be any of your business."

"You've fucked him," the sulky rookie says. "Haven't you?"

There's no point in lying, not when Jace and I are as little to each other as Kenneth and I are. Or at least as little as Jace and I *should* be to each other. "Three years ago. One date. He ended up moving right after to be closer to his kids, and that was the end of it."

"Except he's back now," Jace points out. "And he wants to pick up where you left off."

"I'm reiterating again that this is none of your business."

Not that Jace is wrong. I think Kenneth would very much like to pick up where we left off. Have more china doll sex. And in the three years since he left, I've thought about it. Thought about how long the nights are getting, how my house seems to feel emptier and emptier and emptier. I never cared too much about becoming a spinster—I've even railed against the label as patriarchal bullshit—but though I don't feel desperate to marry or start a family, I do feel... lonely.

And wouldn't Kenneth be an easy solution? He already has two lovely daughters, so if we had children, it would be because we wanted them, not because we felt middle age bearing down on us. And we run in the same circles, share many of the same friends. It makes sense.

In contrast, Jace makes no sense. He's the opposite of the pro-Kenneth list. Too young to settle down, and I bet too wild too. Just like Frazer at that age, working hard, playing hard—drinks and girls and danger. There's no easy security in Jace, no clear path to a future.

So why am I uninterested in Kenneth?

And why am I so inexorably drawn to this young cop instead?

I look up into Jace's stern face. "Why do you care?"

It's the wrong thing to say. It betrays too much of my own conflicted desires, and Jace, like any good predator, smells my weakness.

"Do you want me to care?" he asks, his voice turning low and rough.

He's visibly shaking with restraint now, his hands balled into fists on either side of me, his pulse thrumming fast in his neck. Every long, diamond-cut inch of his body is desperate to press against mine; I don't have to look down to know he's hard. His jaw is tense, rigid, a small muscle jumping along it. He looks like he wants to fuck me right through the wall.

God, this is sexy. It's all so fucking sexy...

My composure is gone. My control is shot. There's only him, smelling like leather and the barest hint of tea tree oil. Rugged and clean. I lean forward and run my nose along the edge of his jaw to smell it better.

He freezes.

His jaw is clean-shaven, but that five o'clock shadow is beginning to make itself known—just a hint of raspiness over his warm, sculpted jaw. It tickles against my nose, and his scent is even stronger like this. If the Yankee Candle store sold a candle that smelled like Jace, women would stop going on dates altogether.

"Cat," he rumbles in warning.

This growling version of Jace is going to be the death of my panties. I rub my chest against his hard, body-armored one and smile into his neck.

He lets out a long breath. A "now I see" breath.

"Do you like me being jealous of him?" His hand drops from beside my head and slowly, deliberately palms my cunt through my skirt. "Do you like it when I'm possessive?"

My head drops back against the wall as my hips push against his touch. Pleasure curls, dark and smoky, through my belly and chest, and I know the answer before I admit it aloud. "Yes."

"I know you do." He says it matter-of-factly, in this almost-arrogant way that leaves no room for doubt.

I do like it. He did know.

It's that straightforward.

He reaches over with his free hand and locks the meeting room door, and for the first time, I appreciate how isolated it is. Near nothing else except my cubicle, with no internal windows or shared doors. And when Jace flicks off the light, leaving only the afternoon sunlight straining against the metal blinds of the exterior windows, I know we're essentially hidden here. As long as we stay silent, no one will know.

Ohhhh, this is such a bad idea. But it doesn't stop me from rocking my cunt against Jace's peremptory touch.

"Tell me," he says, leaning close and ghosting his mouth over my jaw. "Did he fuck you right? Did he make that little pussy of yours happy?"

My eyelids flutter at his dirty words, even as the sensible part of my mind rears up to scream *it's none of your business!* I shouldn't betray poor Kenneth's ego this way. I shouldn't. But then Jace presses hard enough to make me moan, and I think maybe I don't care and that I'll tell him anything to keep this jealous, ravenous side of him around.

"Did he?" he demands again, impatient with my silence, curling his fingers to catch my clit with more pressure.

"No," I relent in a whimper. "No, he didn't."

Jace nods to himself, as if confirming knowledge he already had. "He was too gentle, wasn't he? Tried to fuck you easy and sweet?"

His fingers are now at the hem of my skirt, dragging it up to my waist. I'm squirming to get his touch back where I need it, back where I'm wet and aching, back where only he can soothe me.

"Too bad he didn't know there isn't anything easy about you," Jace says, one hand pushing my panties aside and the other hand fisting in my hair. He makes me watch as he pushes his fingers inside me and fucks me with them. "Too bad he didn't know you're the furthest thing from *sweet*."

"Then what am I?" I dare him, as if any dare has teeth when you're fucking yourself on someone's hand.

But Jace responds immediately, his nostrils flaring and his eyes blazing bright. "You're *mine*," he seethes and yanks me in for a brutal kiss.

Our lips meet, hot and urgent, and then his tongue seeks out the seam of my mouth, demanding entry, demanding succor. I let him in. I let him taste my mouth for the first time as he finger-fucks me against the wall and fists my hair. He sweeps through my mouth the way he does everything—quietly, intensely, and with raw, male power. But I manage to break his silence and elicit a long groan from him when I kiss him back, when I stroke my tongue along his the way I would his cock, with flickers and swirls and promise.

I shouldn't do this. Fraternization is fine, but sex on duty definitely isn't—and we're not only on duty but also on police department property. In the same building as twenty other cops. I should push Jace away, straighten up my skirt, and act like Catherine Day again.

I'm tired of acting like Catherine Day. The thought adds to the restless itch that's been crawling through my blood since I saw Jace standing firm and sure next to my cubicle. I'm tired of being lonely, of being the best, of being the sort of woman that would fit a man like Kenneth.

And as foolish as it is, something about Jace drives back this lonely ache and makes me feel alive again—and I can't surrender that to the faceless pestle of propriety and professionalism. Not yet, anyway.

I reach up and grab his collar. "I want to get fucked again," I say against his mouth.

He doesn't flinch. Doesn't hesitate.

"Here?" he asks.

"Here."

His mouth comes back over mine, hard, as he adds another finger inside me. "I don't have a condom, Cat."

My high heels make it difficult to rise and press to get the friction I want, and Jace knows it, using my inability to move to tease me, to edge me along the brink until I think I might go mad.

."I don't care," I pant. "I'm using birth control. I'm clean. Fuck me bare."

He pulls back enough to catch my eyes, and the raw lust there is enough to make my knees buckle. "Cat."

"Are you clean, Jace? Say you are. Say you'll stick that beautiful cock inside me. Say you'll do it now."

"I'm clean."

I nearly faint in relief.

"If I do this, I'm going to come inside you," he warns. His fingers stroke inside my cunt to underscore his words. "Going to make that pussy mine. Got it?"

"Oh God, yes, please, please do that." I'm dangerously close to babbling now, my hands still twisting in his collar.

He gives me a nod. "And you have to be quiet," he says, his free hand unbuckling his duty belt. "Can you do that?"

"I'd like to promise that I can?" I offer, and for the first time in our acquaintance, I see his mouth hitch up in a smile. It kicks the breath right out of my lungs, he's so handsome.

He slides his fingers free and says, "Open." And then my mouth is filled with his fingers—which taste like me. It's so filthy, I can't stand it.

"Keep your legs spread for my cock," he rumbles, and I obey.

CHAPTER SIX

JACE

I'm about to fuck Catherine Day in the investigations station.

More than that, I'm about to fuck her surrounded by boxes of evidence for the case we should be working on, with my new supervisor down the hallway, in broad fucking daylight, and I don't care.

In my defense, I didn't stand a damn chance after she murmured those magic words.

I want to get fucked again.

Although it's possible I didn't ever stand a chance. Not after catching her staring at my ass in that obscene way of hers. Not after seeing her beautiful and polished, sitting in her cubicle. Maybe not even after last night.

One hit and I'm a goner. Cat Day: gateway drug. Except she's a gateway drug to more of her. She's got me craving and trembling for just one more taste. Just one more touch.

Running me extra ragged is the slow unraveling of her own self-control—all that equilibrium and poise vanishing under my lips, my fingers. Seeing my scent drive her wild, feeling my jealousy get her wet. Her plea for us to fuck bare.

There's a good reason I don't pack condoms in my badge wallet or uniform pockets, and it's because it's against policy to fuck on duty. And when I say *against policy*, I mean I'll be outside on my ass so fast I won't even have time to put on my sunglasses.

But I don't even care right now, because right now? With my fingers in Cat's mouth and her eyes burning aqua against mine?

It would be worth it.

It only takes one hand to unbuckle the duty belt and only a moment to pop off the keepers and drop it to the ground. I don't bother pulling the underbelt free—I unfasten it to expose my pants button, and then I'm able to unzip.

Cat makes a noise around my fingers—a sort of whine that communicates one thing: *hurry.*

My cock is so eager to be free that it nearly slaps up against my abs after I tug down the waistband of my boxers. And I can already feel the cool kiss of air along my tip, telling me I have pre-come beading there. After that, it's just some pragmatic rearranging of fabric to make sure my cock is unimpeded and her panties are shoved well free.

"Shh," I tell her and remove my fingers from her mouth. I need both hands to do this: a hand for grabbing one stocking-covered thigh to hike to my hip and the other to stir my head around her opening.

But she can't *shh*, at least not very well. The minute the hot, taut skin of my crown kisses along her pussy, she lets out a noise that has me ready to blow—and would also let anyone walking by know what we are doing.

A quick time-out then. I drop her leg, and amid a whine of protest at the lack of contact between us, I unclip her garters and pull down and remove her panties.

And then I put them in her mouth.

Not a lot—not enough to truly gag her or make her uncomfortable— but enough that she has to work to keep them in place. Enough that she'll be reminded to stay silent, because we can't get caught.

Not only do I not want to get fired, but if I manage to get one of the best detectives in the metro fired because I couldn't keep it in my pants? I'm never going to not hate myself.

So it's panties and silence for now.

Her eyes are wide and wondering on mine as I trace a finger around her perfect mouth. The lace spilling out of it only highlights the smoothness of her lips, the natural, lipstick-free pink of them.

"That's better," I say quietly. "Can't have you getting caught, can we? Can't have you trying to explain why you needed my cock so badly you couldn't wait."

She closes her eyes and nods, and I use the moment to bring her leg back to my hip again. With her opened up and her mouth full, I can now freely nudge at the entrance waiting for me without worrying about her pleasured noises bringing the entire investigations unit running in.

She's hot and slick, and shudders race up and down my spine as I find the little opening all tucked away in her wet folds and forge in. I've never felt this— *never*—not even as a dumbass teenager or when I thought I was going to marry Brittany. Never had my bare cock surrounded by a hot pussy, skin to skin, with nothing in between. It's impossible to describe, impossible even to process, and I make an unholy grunt as I finally reach home.

Cat makes a noise around her panties, and I look into her wide, surprised eyes. She looks down at where we're joined, past my rucked-up uniform shirt and her crumpled skirt to where only a glimpse of my thick shaft is visible before it disappears inside her.

She makes the noise again, and I realize she's saying *oh*.

Yeah. *Oh*.

"Shit, Cat," I whisper, feeling undone, vulnerable with the sheer experience of taking her like this. "How the fuck did I walk away from you last night?"

I emphasize my point with a thrust, testing the angle and the pressure of us like this. "How did I not stay and fuck and fuck and fuck until neither of us could walk?"

Her eyes flutter closed in that way I'm learning means she's aroused beyond belief, and I reward her with another slide—this one with a little grind against her clit at the end. Her supporting leg nearly buckles, and she grabs on to my shoulders for balance, her manicured fingernails digging in through my shirt as I start truly pounding into her.

Even in her sexy-as-fuck heels, the mismatch in our heights make the angle a little rough, a little desperate. I have to bend my knees and palm her ass to hitch her higher against me, and she finally wraps her other leg around my waist and locks her heels at the small of my back, now fully pinned against the wall by my cock and the force of our need.

It's grinding and wet and messy. She clings to me, carrying most of her weight with her clenched thighs and her arms braced on my shoulders, but I have to keep her pressed against the wall for balance. Which keeps the swollen bead of her clit tight against me, keeps it rubbed and squeezed and all the good stuff that makes her writhe and quake and pant around the lace in her mouth.

It's the lace I watch as I fuck her, focusing on the delicate clovers and whorls of the fabric. On the glimpses of full pink lips underneath, of pinker tongue and white teeth. At first, I do it to distract myself from the insane feeling of her pussy around my cock and that shapely ass cradled in my palms, but then it becomes its own torture. Her perfect mouth, tempting in its lush elegance, crammed full of my homemade gag. And she let me—she just *let me*—as if I had every right to gag her. Every right to do whatever I want.

I curl in, snag her earlobe with my teeth. "Get there, Cat," I grate out. "You feel too good, and you have to get there because I can't last."

She nods, and the movement brushes her panties across my polyester uniform shirt with a gentle rasp that drives me wild. I have to close my eyes and conjure up memories of crawling through frozen mud at boot camp and eating rubbery DFAC food to stave off the knot of orgasm that's currently pulling tight at the base of my cock. I can't come yet...I can't come yet...her first...*I can't come yet*—

Cat manages to find a new way to bear down onto me that gives her clit even more attention. We're toiling hard, the both of us, sweat misting damp across our skin and breathing fast, short, feverish breaths, and I see the moment our labor pays off. The moment she finally catches hold of her release, and with a whimper, she drops her head onto my shoulder and quivers around my cock. Big, rolling quivers that clench down at the tip of me buried somewhere deep inside her.

She's mumbling something around her panties as she rides out her orgasm, the same thing over and over again, and it takes me a few times hearing it to realize it's my name. It's my fucking name.

Jace jace jace oh god jace—

My orgasm slams into me so hard that I want to roar with the sheer ecstasy of it, the primal victory of pumping my come deep into a woman and giving her everything I have, every last fucking drop.

It's messy, so much messier than usual, and as I keep fucking her through the hot slick of my own seed, I remember that it's because there's no condom to keep our bodies separate, no barrier to contain the biological result of thrusting, pumping pleasure.

It's just my come and the wet evidence of her orgasm, mixing hot and perfect around us, and feeling it drives my climax on and on and on. I ejaculate with brutal, seemingly never-ending throbs, each pulse like a jolt of pure heaven sizzling straight through me, and for a moment, I feel more naked than my still-clothed situation should permit. Like Cat can see more than just my face or my bare cock but something inside me. Like she can see me in a way no one ever has before.

It freaks me the fuck out—but maybe not as much as it should.

Maybe I want her to see me because I want *her*. Period. Everything about her I want, and I want more of it, and I want more of it for a long time.

When I set her carefully on her feet and slide out, come drips out of her, and one slow drop lands on the toe of her red high heel.

"Jesus fucking Christ, I might need to come again," I say as I watch it happen.

Cat just gives a little croon in response, yanks out her makeshift gag, and then uses the panties to clean off the inside of her thighs.

I groan again. "Fuck, now I really need to."

She looks up with some amusement and then back down at my cock, which is already stiffening, ready for round two.

"*Young* man," she purrs.

I have no doubt she could keep up with me, though, given the way she's biting her lip and eyeing my erection right now. If we were at her place or mine—if we were anywhere else—we could go as many rounds as we needed to scratch the itch. As it is, I'm almost considering asking her for another—just one more, just real fast—because I'm not satisfied, not satisfied at all.

She's still all rumpled and flushed, and that pussy is still exposed and taunting me with its silky blond curls and swollen, florid petals, and I just need one more time, one more fuck. Then I can start thinking straight again.

Cat's cell phone rings from the floor where she dropped it earlier, and as she bends down to get it, I hear a voice from outside the door. Two voices.

Shit.

The look of alarm I shoot Cat is reflected right back at me, and she ignores the phone in favor of setting herself to rights as quickly as possible. She doesn't bother fastening her garter—simply yanks down her skirt, smooths her shirt, and digs in her portfolio for a small elastic hair tie. She pulls her mussed hair into a ponytail as I zip up and manage to get my duty belt on with some degree of quietude, although the keepers I have to shove into my pockets because I don't have enough time to fasten them on. I shove her panties in my pocket too, unlock the door, and flick on the light.

Within seconds of us getting seated at the table, there's a casual knock and then the door pops open.

"Hey," Sergeant Hougland says. The door opens more, and he's with—aw, fuck—he's with Captain Kim.

I see Cat swallow in the corner of my vision.

But both administrators seem unsuspecting and oblivious as they come in, and they don't seem to pick up on Cat's pink cheeks or the smell of sex in the room.

Not that I can relax any. I just had delicious, wet, unprotected sex in a police station. Sex that is still all over my skin and probably my clothes too, and now my new supervisors are strolling in for a chat. I hold myself as rigid and as detached as I can manage, hoping it's not obvious that I was a rutting, eager beast just a few minutes ago.

"Day, we're just swinging by on our way out to a meeting to see if you got that report I sent over from KCPD."

Cat nods, folding her hands over her crossed legs, looking every bit the untouchable ice queen she's rumored to be. Except between those crossed legs is a cunt that's currently leaving a wet spot on that dry-clean-only skirt.

I feel a jerk of primitive satisfaction at the thought.

"I did," she says crisply. "It was a report full of nothing, which I expected."

"No leads on their end?"

"No leads," she affirms. "Same as what KCKPD and the other Johnson County agencies said. The televisions aren't being sold in the area, if they're being sold at all. It's like they're being stolen and hoarded."

"That's not the usual way of things." Hougland sighs, as if personally put out that these criminals aren't following the template. "You think they're planning on selling them in one big shipment?"

"It would be foolish," Cat says and lifts a shoulder in a graceful shrug. "But I suppose we can't rule anything out. I'm pulling together a list of plates that have hit plate readers mounted on traffic lights near the burglarized offices. Any duplicate hits—especially in the hours before and after the burglary—I'm going to follow up on. I suppose a next step could be seeing if any of those car owners have made payments for a storage unit in the metro. We might find our televisions there."

Hougland and Kim are nodding. "When it's warrant time, loop me in," Hougland says. "I want to look it over before we submit it to a judge."

"Of course," Cat says coolly, and then Kim and Hougland ramble on a bit more about this and that before one of them glances at the clock on the wall and gives a theatrical sigh.

"It's time to head out. Great work, Catherine," Kim says, and they finally leave.

When the door closes, I look across the table at Cat and see a peculiar tightness around her mouth. If I had to guess, I'd say she looks pissed, but on Cat, it's hard to guess at any emotion because she's constantly wearing this forbidding, almost haughty shell.

"Hougland tick you off?" I hazard.

She looks back at me with some surprise and then gives a reluctant, sly grin. "That obvious, huh?"

"Nothing about you is obvious," I say, and I mean it. "But I'm determined to learn every single thing about you. Including how you feel and what you hide."

Her lips part, ever so slightly, and she shakes her head. "I keep thinking I know the box to put you in, and then you keep surprising me..."

I'm dying to know what box she wants to put me in, but she continues.

"Yes, Hougland has been frustrating to deal with. He just transferred into investigations last month, after I'd been put on the robberies. He's old and a man, and he has old-man ideas about what I'm capable of. He's been micromanaging the hell out of this case, and me, and I don't deserve that."

I love how unapologetically she talks about this. How fearlessly she calls out Hougland on his bullshit.

I don't know what she sees in my face just now, but she raises an eyebrow.

"I have pride too, you know," she says. "Cop pride is not exclusive to people with penises."

"That's not what I was thinking."

"What *were* you thinking?"

"That I'd like to have a few rounds in the ring with Hougland until he started treating you with respect."

This seems to please her—fine little lines bracket the corners of her full mouth and spread out from her eyes. "*Young* man," she says again, but this time she says it with fondness. With affection.

I don't realize how long our gazes are locked in this sort of baffled, lustful fascination with each other until she clears her throat and looks down.

"Jace, about today," she begins, and my stomach sinks. I know that tone of voice. I know it because I'm usually the one to use it. Usually the one to tell someone I just fucked that it's been a great time and now I'll get them an Uber.

I don't help her along with this because I don't want it. I know I almost got her fired just now by screwing her in her own police station. I know this is nuts, but dammit—I don't care.

"You know what I'm going to say," she says tactfully, gently. "I am...rather charmed by you, but I think you also charm me out of all reason. And it doesn't make sense anyway."

"What doesn't make sense?" I genuinely don't understand. I find her wildly sexy, wildly intelligent, and I want to fuck her every chance I get from now until...well, I don't know until when, but for a good long time. What else does there need to be?

Her eyelashes sweep down in a dark fan over her cheeks as she chooses her words carefully. "Me and another cop. I haven't dated another cop since Frazer, and I shouldn't start now."

"Why?" The word is out of my mouth before I can really process that she just brought up her dead fiancé and that I should proceed with diplomacy.

She's still looking down as she thinks. "What happened when he died—I can't live through that again. I barely survived it the first time." She meets my gaze again, and I'm nearly rocked back by the emotion simmering in her blue-green eyes. "I know what they say about me. That I'm incapable of grief or love or any feeling at all. The Ice Queen. The truth is I wanted to die with Frazer that night, and a part of me did. And what's left won't survive if it happens again."

"So no cops...because they might die? Hate to tell you this, Cat, but everyone dies. In every profession."

She presses her lips together. "It's not the same. And cops are reckless, risky, and rough. They get hard. Now that I'm older and know that, I don't know if it's what I want in my future."

"I didn't hear any complaints about my getting hard earlier."

She looks like she wants to roll her eyes. "And you're young, Jace. Inappropriately young."

"I don't mind," I tell her. "The difference in our ages doesn't bother me at all."

She looks away. "It will."

"Why?"

She still won't look at me. "Because you're young and sexy and you'll have equally young and sexy girls raining from the sky. You deserve better than wasting your time on me." She stands up to leave.

I stand up too, not willing to let this go. "Cat—"

She holds up a hand. "It's enough, Jace. It's enough to make it a bad idea. I'm thirteen years older, and you're the kind of man I've sworn to stay away from anyway. Maybe you can fuck the same person over and over again without feelings getting involved, but I look at you and I know that's not going to be possible for me." She takes a deep breath and meets my eyes. "I look at you and I think you might be capable of breaking my heart."

And with that bombshell, she crosses to the door without so much as a *goodbye* and leaves me alone in the meeting room. The room that still smells like us.

CHAPTER SEVEN

CAT

It's quite frigid between us after that.

Perhaps the frigidity is all on my side. Perhaps I'm the one making it cold, because more than once this week, I've caught him staring at me with a heated need that nearly made my skin catch fire.

He still wants me. And fuck all if I don't still want him.

But life isn't that easy, and after the close call of Kim and Hougland nearly walking in on us, I'm reminded of what matters most.

Working. The. Damn. Case.

So we work the case. Jace has officially switched to day shift now, so I actually do get him up to speed on everything. I assign him to some follow-ups and calls to witnesses to verify reports, and we manage to get through it without any unprofessional interaction. Or, you know, more police station intercourse.

I can't stop aching for him, though. Those intense gray eyes that get darker and stormier when they look at me. That frowning mouth that I now know can be kissed into softness. Those big, rough hands that handle my body the way I've always needed to be handled, even if I hadn't known it. More than once when we're working in the meeting room, I excuse myself to use the restroom and then rub myself to a quick, urgent orgasm in the stall just to take the edge off. It's the only time I've ever been grateful for the gender disparity in the police force—more privacy in the bathroom to indulge this unseemly need for a much-younger-than-me man.

It's a long week, with both of us unhappy and strained and physically uncomfortable. And the week gets even longer when I realize I have my low-light range recertification waiting for me at the end of it. It's the annual test I have to take to prove to my department I can operate a firearm in the dark. But I know I can operate a firearm in the dark and operate it well.

It was how I killed Frazer's murderer all those years ago.

And therein lies the problem. It's the one thing I do each year that brings it all back. The dark, shitty house in the worst part of town. The frantic babbles of the meth addict who'd just stabbed Frazer and left him to bleed out on the dirty floor. The kick of the gun in my hand as I fired and the killer fell. Trying to save the man I was supposed to marry...

My hands shake as I pull my vest over my shirt. I opted out of my usual uniform of silk and tailored skirts today, knowing I'd be striding and darting around the darkened range rooms. I'm wearing the blue, like a real cop. Something I rarely do since I transferred to investigations after Frazer's death, leaving the world of uniforms and midnight stabbings behind.

So here I am—polyester uniform shirt, utility pants, load-bearing vest. I'm even wearing boots instead of my customary heels. I have to force myself to breathe as I tighten the laces, I'm so agitated by what's about to come.

It's stupid to feel like this, I chastise myself. It's been twelve years, and anyway, it's never permissible to be afraid of the dark.

But the minute the lights go down, my mouth goes dry. I can make myself move through the cinderblock rooms, shining my flashlight onto faceless paper targets. I can make myself shoot perfectly, hearing only the dull *pop pops* through my earmuffs, but it doesn't matter. I still see that house, the terrified and blank face of the perp, spattered with Frazer's blood. I still smell old food and vomit and the coppery scent of my fiancé's life soaking into the old, stained carpet. I still remember Frazer's vacant stare.

I relive it every single time I'm forced to do this.

When I finish, I'm as empty as the magazine in my gun.

"Two hundred forty-six out of two fifty." The firearms sergeant grins at me as I'm taking off my vest. "That's a new personal best."

"Sure."

He laughs. "Don't act too excited now."

I try to give him a smile in return, but it feels all wrong on my face. Everything feels wrong.

Nothing will ever feel right again.

Making excuses, I stride quickly out of the training center and get to my unmarked car. I go back to my station and finish up for the day, staying a couple of hours late because I forget to look at the clock and can't seem to feel the time passing. Jace has gone home—the keys to his patrol car are hung back up, and I recognize every personal car left in the lot, meaning none of them are his.

Not seeing Jace makes everything worse—makes everything so bad that I just want to curl up and cry and cry and cry.

But I don't cry. I never do.

Somehow I make it out to my own car, with my portfolio and purse in the passenger seat and my phone in my hand. I've dialed Russo.

What the hell am I even doing? I don't know.

"Russo," Nicki answers in her familiar brusque way.

"Nicki, where do your evening people go to unwind?"

A pause. "Whyyyyyyy are you asking?"

"I'm looking for someone."

"Is it Jace Sutton?" my old friend asks in a too-casual voice.

Oh no. Like any cop, Nicki smells gossip, and I'm searching for a plausible reason—any plausible reason—why I'd need Jace after hours.

"I have a couple questions about his contacts today. He was out of the station his whole shift, and I didn't have a chance to catch him before he left." Even with as shaken up as I am, as empty and wrong-feeling, my voice is still perfectly steady, perfectly cool. I know I sound convincing.

"Okay," Russo says, and I can tell she's torn between her instincts and how well I sold that lie. "Well. The eves crew usually heads over to the Dirty Nickel after a shift or on their days off. He might be there, I guess."

Her guess is my hope. I don't have his cell number, and I don't feel comfortable digging through personnel records to get it when this isn't police business. Ditto with his address.

But showing up at his favorite dive is any better? Get a grip, Day.

"Thanks, Nicki."

"Anytime. And hey..." She stops for a moment, as if deciding how to proceed. "I saw in payroll that you had low-light range today. And I know that— well, what I mean is, if you ever need to talk, I'm here."

My throat feels as if someone's cinching a ribbon tight around it. "Thank you, Nicki. That's very kind."

"I mean it, okay?"

"Okay. Good night."

And Russo hangs up without saying goodbye, per usual. I drop the phone in my passenger seat and sigh.

I should go home.

I should go home and do what I've done every year after low-light range: pop open a bottle of wine, drink the entire thing, and then fall asleep curled around Frazer's college sweatshirt.

I should not go to a place called the Dirty Nickel to find a man thirteen years younger and...

And what? What is my plan? That Jace will take one look at me and know I need to be hugged? That I need a warm chest to finally, finally cry into?

No. If anything, we'll fuck, because that's the only connection we have, and then we'll both be miserable after because every time we have sex, we're courting major professional trouble.

I should not go to the Dirty Nickel.

I should not.

I start my car and tell myself to drive home.

The Dirty Nickel is in a rougher part of town, in a cluster of old strip malls and used car lots, tucked away at the end of a low-slung building that also contains a thrift store and a vape shop. It's a far cry from the martini bar I occasionally venture out to with my girlfriends from college.

I nearly almost go home to change into something less fancy...and then remember I'm not in my usual silk and tailored wool. I'm in the dark-blue polyester of my uniform, with utility boots and a ponytail.

All I'm missing are the sunglasses and I could be a cop for Halloween.

With a sigh at the uniform—and at everything, absolutely everything—I get out of the car and walk inside. It doesn't matter what I'm wearing. It doesn't matter because I shouldn't be here, shouldn't be doing this, but it's the only thing I can think to do. It's the only thing that feels right when everything else feels so wrong.

The inside of the bar is only marginally better than the outside. Pool tables hunker down under dim lights, a couple of televisions play a baseball game between two teams no one cares about, and an unseen jukebox issues forth music the other detectives and I call "construction worker rock."

At seven, the place is just picking up, and I catch a table in the far corner with a few faces I vaguely recognize. Young cops. It's awful, perhaps even a little elitist, but I don't bother to learn a rookie's name until *they* bother to stick around for five years. Or more.

So I'm not entirely certain who they are or what shift they work or how long they've worked for Hocker Grove, but they're definitely HGPD. Even if I didn't recognize their faces, I'd be able to tell they were cops immediately. Legs sprawled but eyes alert, everyone in those free T-shirts you get for working golf tournaments or charity 5Ks or holiday parades. The men with short, inexpensive haircuts and the women in low ponytails or messy buns.

Not every woman.

In a table of about twelve, five are women, and three of those five are definitely cops, but the other two are just as definitely not. They've got impeccable makeup and glossy hair, and they're young, so fucking young.

Badge bunnies.

I've never liked the term—it seems vaguely sexist to me to disparage young women for the type of men they like to take to bed—but right now, something about their shiny, giggling youthfulness sets my teeth on edge. Especially after I see that one of them is curled around the one cop I *do* recognize.

Jace.

He hasn't seen me yet. He's peering up at the baseball game with his fingers wrapped around a beer bottle, but the bunny sees me standing in the doorway. She watches me watching them with her salon-perfect ombre hair brushing against Jace's shoulder and her hand on his thigh. He's in street clothes, the same kind of free-event T-shirt the rest of the cops are wearing, and battered jeans and boots.

And he still looks magnificent. All rounded, muscled shoulders, long, firm thighs, and a stubbled jaw that looks like pure sex. A warrior at rest, with the requisite maiden waiting to comfort him.

I have to go.

That's the only thought that registers in my mind—the rest is an awful kind of static. A static that hisses *what did you expect? You pushed him away. How long did you think it would take him to find someone else to screw?*

Oh God. I've made a giant mistake in coming here.

I'm turning to leave when he sees me, and it's like all the air is sucked from the room. His eyes meet mine, and I can't read them, can't even try, because there seems to be every feeling inside that silver gaze. Anger and hurt and lust and longing, and they're all directed at me. Right at me.

The bunny looks up to Jace as if she's trying to read his stare like I am, except she takes the extra liberty of sliding her hand up his thigh to rest against the unyielding contours of his abs. I think she also managed to graze his cock on the way up, and Jesus Christ, who was I kidding with that whole *if I break it off earlier, I won't be heartbroken* bit?

Because I did break it off early, yet here I am, feeling like someone's using the jaws of life to cut through my ribs and expose my beating heart. On top of what I went through today at range, it's too much.

It's too fucking much.

I break our gaze and wheel around, opening the door into the summer evening and making my escape.

I have to go.

I have to go home to my wine and to Frazer's sweatshirt and the loneliness I chose for myself. At least that way I can be vulnerable in front of nothing more important than a sweatshirt. At least I'm not making a scene in a begrimed bar in front of a whole table of cops.

And I can leave Jace to the bunny and the inevitable outcome of the night. She can kiss that pouty, serious mouth as bad music blares through the bar, and she can have those big hands drag her back to the bar bathroom for impromptu sex. She can feel the ruthless thickness of his cock wedging inside her. The hard flex of his abs and hips against her ass. His teeth biting her neck as he releases inside her.

They can have each other, and I'll have myself and an old sweatshirt that doesn't even smell like the man it used to belong to, and it will be fine.

The summer air is still hot, still waving above the pavement and trying to pull sweat out of my body. It feels like a punishment, and one I deserve.

The door opens again, and the cop in me can't help but turn at the knowledge someone's behind me.

"Cat." Jace's voice is husky. "What the hell are you doing here?"

"Going home," I say. I turn away from him because I can't look at him. I can't look at the man I pushed away, because I can't lie to myself and pretend I don't regret it. Pretend I feel some kind of wise, selfless pleasure in seeing some girl almost two decades younger than me crawl all over him.

A hand grabs my arm, and I'm spun to face him.

"The fuck you're going home," he says roughly.

I'm brittle, I'm so damn brittle, and I can't keep my tone even as I say, "I'm leaving and you're free to go back inside to your *friends*." My voice hitches over the word, and again that awful feeling of having my ribs cut open returns, even though I deserve it, even though I did it to myself.

"I don't want to go back inside to my friends," he says, clearly missing my implication in the word. "I want to know why you're here."

I twist myself out of Jace's grip and start walking to my car. "I shouldn't have come," I say, more to myself than him.

"But you did," he says as he follows me. "Why, Cat? Why did you come here?"

I have my car unlocked before I get to it so I can make a quick escape, but Jace isn't going to make it that easy for me. Before I can open the door, his hands land on either side of me, caging me in. The hot metal has to be uncomfortable, but there's no pain in his voice as he leans down to my ear.

"Tell me."

The moment seems to intensify, crystallize, and become something sharper, more vivid.

Cicadas are chirruping madly everywhere, and a breeze is blowing an empty soda can across the lot. It's so humid that the air is a heavy blanket over my skin, and behind me I can feel the press of Jace's body. His biceps crowding my shoulders. His chest against my back. His massive erection against my rear.

And then there's that scent. That leather and tea tree oil scent, and I hope it's rubbing on my clothes. I hope I smell like him when I get home.

That, more than anything, defeats me. How can I stay strong when Frazer's sweatshirt smells like nothing and Jace is here and vibrant and alive and he smells like everything? How can I stay strong when I realize that maybe I want Jace more than I ever wanted Frazer...and how can I stay strong when I realize that *today*, of all days?

I hang my head forward in surrender.

"I came for you," I admit in a tired voice. "I came here to find you."

CHAPTER EIGHT

JACE

Hot, raw joy floods through my veins at her confession.

I open up the car door before she's even finished speaking. "Get in," I say shortly, and then I'm around the other side of the car in a heartbeat, climbing into her passenger seat after carefully setting her portfolio on the floor.

I'm already buckled by the time she manages to sit down. She doesn't start the car.

"Jace..."

"Ninety-three eleven Reeds Road," I say. "Unit ten. My place."

She bites her lip. "What about your friends inside?"

"My tab's paid," I reply. "And those assholes will be fine without me."

A little huff. "I'm not talking about assholes or your *tab*, Jace. I'm talking about the girl who was in your lap."

Oh. *Ohhhh.*

I look at her more carefully now, at the burnish of red along her cheekbones and the press of her lips. She's jealous. She's jealous, and that sends a whole stir of male pleasure swirling in my chest.

"I don't care about that girl because I'm leaving here with you. You're the one I'm taking home."

Her forehead makes contact with the steering wheel; for once, that perfect ballet posture is slumped. "This is a bad idea."

I touch her shoulder, the familiar fabric of the uniform made sweetly exotic over her slender, lithe muscles. And then I touch the pale silk of her thick ponytail because I can't resist it. "I'm not taking you back to my place to fuck you."

She lifts her head, eyes me warily. "You're not?"

"No." I'm still toying with her ponytail. I'm totally entranced by the sight of all that exquisite hair bundled into a rope that practically begs to be wrapped around my fist. "I'm taking you back to my place so I can take care of you. In a not-fucking way."

"I don't need taking care of," she says defensively, stiffening back up to her normal erect bearing. I can't play with her ponytail like this anymore, dammit, and I settle for curling a finger around her chin instead and making her look at me.

"You came here to find me and you found me, and now this is what's going to happen, okay? Start the car and drive, Cat. Drive us home."

I know she's wrestling with herself, nibbling more on that plush lower lip until she finally relents and starts the car. "Okay," she says. "But I don't have to stay."

"Of course not."

But of course she does.

I don't mean that in a nonconsensual way—she's free to leave whenever she wants—but in an emotional sense. I know she needs someone with her, and that someone should be me. I've seen this look in soldiers' eyes before. I've seen faces full of vacant restlessness. I don't know what happened to Cat today, but I know whatever did happen was Bad. Bad with a capital B.

And with a Bad thing, you can either shove that shit way down and hope nothing ruptures, or you can find someone you trust and find a way to bleed it out. Talking, drinking, fucking, music—anything is fair game.

I think Cat has been shoving her shit down for years, and I think she's finally rupturing. I want to be the one to help her bleed it out instead.

I don't even really know why—in no way should I feel like I deserve that place in her life or in her hurt and healing after just two screws—but I do. This week did nothing to slake my thirst for her. In fact, it just got worse and worse as the days rolled on without the chance to hold her slender wrists in my hand or the opportunity to run my thumb along the luscious lines of her mouth.

I jerked my dick raw thinking about her at night. I throbbed in mute agony as I sat across the meeting room table from her during the day. I wanted her so badly that I thought my bones might crack from it.

And don't get me started on what happens whenever I think of her words ending our little fling.

I look at you and I know that's not going to be possible for me.

I look at you and I think you might be capable of breaking my heart.

I think of those words—and let's be honest, I've probably thought of them every ten minutes since she said them—and this fierce, strange urgency comes over me, like I'm at the top of the roller coaster and ready for the plunge straight into danger. It makes my stomach twist up into my chest. And then something vital in my chest twists up into my throat. And then I just want to throw her over my shoulder and do something drastic. Abduct her like a Viking. Marry her. Hell, even cuddle her on the couch, which is something I haven't done in years and never thought I'd want to do again.

For now, though, I'm taking care of her. Whatever she needs is what I'll give, for as long as she'll let me.

"You're in uniform," I remark as Cat pulls out onto the street and angles the car toward my apartment. "I've never seen you in uniform."

"I had range today," she says, not taking her eyes from the road. "I'll wear the utility uniform for training and, you know, the dress uniform for the official department stuff." Her mouth gives a self-conscious twist. "I wear it so rarely that it almost feels like a costume now."

"When I first saw you standing there, I thought I was going to come in my pants."

My words are so surprising that she snorts out a very unladylike laugh, which makes me smile. I like seeing these cracks in her control, these glimpses of the warm, funny woman underneath her shell.

But I'm also not kidding. Cat in her silk shirts and high heels is a wet dream come to life, but Cat in uniform? I don't even have the words. It's like all that strength and resolve she normally hides under a veneer of cold dignity is even more on display, stripped down to the essential power and discipline she exudes.

The fitted lines of the shirt highlight her delicately squared shoulders and reveal the tight swells of muscle in her arms. The pants cling to her taut ass and legs. And her hair in that ponytail—without the gentle, Hollywood-starlet curtain of it softening her features, you can see exactly how ethereal she is. High cheekbones and big, fragile eyes. A comely jawline that ends in a pointed, adorable chin. Coupled with that booted, confident stance of hers and her svelte form, she could be one of those elves from the fantasy novels. Otherworldly and lethal. Deceptive beauty concealing deadly dominance.

God, what man doesn't want to tangle with that?

It only takes a few minutes to get to my house, which is one of the reasons I like the Dirty Nickel. It's a short ride home or only a medium walk, and while I'm not hung up on things being convenient in my life, I do like simple. Straightforward.

So what are you doing right now, then?

We park and get out, and then I lead her up the stairs to my door. It's only as I'm letting her in that I have a burst of sudden self-consciousness about how she will see my place. She of the flawlessly decorated bungalow. She of the kitchen piled with fresh fruit and flowers. She of the real-ass art hanging above her sofa.

What is she going to think when she sees my Craigslist

couch and inherited recliner? My collection of signed baseballs and the empty QuikTrip cup on my counter I forgot to throw away this morning? I keep the place pretty tidy, but for all that, it's undecorated and shabby, and it looks like it belongs to a twenty-four-year-old guy without a girlfriend.

My cheeks flame as we walk inside, and I'm waiting for her to say something, waiting for her to raise a sculpted eyebrow at the place, but instead she just turns to me and goes straight into my arms. Without asking, without hesitation, as if she belongs there. And whatever has been twisting from my chest into my throat now twists so hard that the back of my eyelids are burning.

"Are you ready to talk about it? About what made you come find me?" I whisper into her hair.

Her face is buried in my chest, and she just shakes her head, a *swish swish* of that tempting ponytail.

"Can I take care of you, then? Without talking?"

A bob of the ponytail. *Yes.*

I wrap my arms around her slim frame, just taking a moment to relish the feeling of her crushed to me, so elegant yet so strong. And then I walk her backward in slow, careful steps to my bathroom, where I flick on the light and pick her up to set her on the counter.

She watches me with wide, red-rimmed eyes. She hasn't cried yet, but I can feel the force of her tears pushing against her restraint, flooding her control.

"Do you trust me?" I ask.

"Yes," she murmurs.

"I'll stop when you say. Always."

She blinks up at me, suddenly looking very young and very, very lost. "I know."

I take in a deep, shivering breath as I reach for her.

The thing is that our first time, and our second, Cat initiated. Cat told me her address or purred that she wanted to get fucked again, and then I followed where she led. I knew exactly what she wanted out of me, which was a big cock and a dirty mouth.

But now? Now when she's sought me out, looking like the sun's been darkened to ash? It's different. This isn't just a quick, hungry screw. This isn't a primitive urge let out to play. This is me giving something to her, not us trying to take from each other in a frenzied embrace, and I want to get it right. I want to get it so right that she trusts me to give it to her again and again.

I want her to always find me when she needs something. I want to always fix anything that's hurting her.

And now my throat is so tight I can barely breathe.

I begin unbuttoning her uniform shirt, taking care to keep my fingers from grazing against the silky fabric of her expensive athletic shirt underneath. Once I get the top few buttons undone, I can access the hidden zipper behind the placket of dummy buttons and unfasten the shirt all the way. I pull it from her arms and then drape it over the towel bar.

Next come her boots, which I unlace and gently remove, as if I'm handling glass slippers and not steel-toed footwear. She flinches when I get to her socks—I imagine in Cat's head, someone seeing and interacting with something as shamefully human as her socks is very embarrassing—but I don't let her move away. I'm not afraid of her socks. And nothing about her wonderful body should make her shy. After pulling the socks free, I give her bare feet several kisses to prove it.

I nudge her off the counter and remove her belt and pants, which also go over the towel bar, and now she's only in her undershirt and panties.

"Do you trust me?" I ask again, and she knows what I'm asking. Does she trust me not to make this sexual? Does she trust that I'm not doing this for me but for her?

She nods.

And then I strip her completely bare.

It's the first time I've seen her naked, and even though I ignore my erection, my body's response to her unclothed form is like being struck by lightning. Heat everywhere. Light behind my eyelids. My life poised on a razor's edge.

She's porcelain, rare and precious.

Her breasts are little teardrops, still pert and high on her chest and tipped with pale-pink nipples. A narrow waist curves in and then gently flares into her hips, and an adorable navel studs her belly along with a couple tempting freckles. Below that belly is the sweet cup of her pussy, covered by neatly—almost primly—trimmed blond curls.

But she's also so *real*. There's a few thin white streaks along her hips and on the sides of her breasts—the kind of stretch marks that come from living, not from babies—and a small curve below her navel that softens her belly out of true flatness. Slightly too-large areolas and a little mole under one breast.

She's real. And perfect.

I pull her into me and kiss her hairline because I can't not kiss it.

"You're so fucking beautiful it hurts to look at you," I say roughly.

She only rubs her face against my still-clothed chest in answer.

I step back and quickly undress, doing my best to ignore the throbbing erection currently aimed at the ceiling. I turn on the shower and coax her inside once it's warm.

I start washing her. Methodically, scrupulously. Avoiding the stiff buds of her nipples and the plump weight of her ass and the silky curls between her legs. Instead, I focus on her arms and her legs and her feet. I spend a long time soaping up her back and shoulders and then kneading her tight muscles until she's limp and heavy-eyed. The familiar smell of my body wash rises all around the shower stall, mixed with something fragrant and female that is uniquely her. I wish we had her soap here, her scents, but at the same time, I can't deny the primitive pleasure in having her covered in my own. Marking her skin with my smell.

After her body, I wash her hair.

I mean for it to be comforting, soothing, and maybe it is at first. As I pull her hair free from her ponytail with solicitous care—making sure not to yank or tug—and as I begin working the shampoo into her hair, she makes low, happy noises in her throat and leans back against me. For a while, it seems like she's practically purring under my touch, and I make sure to massage her scalp as I work. To pamper her.

But after I rinse the conditioner from her hair, I notice that her shoulders are hitching in barely perceptible jerks, rising and falling in the suppressed, shuddering way of someone trying to hide their tears.

She's finally letting it out.

"Cat, baby," I say, turning her so that she can bury her face in my chest again, which is what she does. I wrap my arms around her and cradle her, my broad back shielding us from the spray as she sobs against me and I stroke her hair. She cries so hard that her entire body shakes, that she can barely breathe, and I wonder if she cries like this often.

I wonder if this is the first time she's ever let herself cry about anything.

I chafe her back and kiss her wet hair that smells like my shampoo, and I simply hold her and let her use me. Use me as a safe place for her, use my arms and my chest and my silence. My strength and my body are hers. And I'm beginning to think my heart is too.

After a good ten or fifteen minutes, her sobs begin to space apart, quiet down into muted sniffles and sucks of breath, and she tilts her head to look up at me with owlish eyes still glassed over with tears.

"Thank you," she whispers. I can barely hear it over the running water.

I give her temple a kiss in response, using every last shred of my control not to kiss her full on the mouth and stroke her tongue with my own. In fact, we've both been very maturely ignoring my hard-on as it dug into her back and stomach, knowing it was a lost cause. I'm a little proud of how well-behaved I've been, considering the naked, slick, emotional circumstances.

"You said you weren't going to fuck me," Cat says, reaching up to touch my face. I cradle her face in response, feeling the fragile flex and work of her jaw as she speaks. "What if I've changed my mind? And I want to be fucked?"

I peer down at her, water droplets dancing off my shoulders to make a heavy mist around us, and I study her expression through the haze. Study her aqua eyes, as open and vibrant as any tropical sea. Her mouth, which is currently in a shape of worried hope. Vulnerable excitement.

"We don't have to," I tell her. "I know I'm hard—that's just what happens when I'm around you—but that doesn't mean we have to do anything."

The elegant and refined Catherine Day gives me an eye roll worthy of any teenager. "Do I seem like the kind of woman who would give out pity sex just because a man had a sad, lonely boner?"

Hearing the word *boner* from her pretty lips is enough to make me laugh. "Okay, maybe not."

"I want to because I want to, Jace. Because I want you." Her eyebrows pull together a little, as if she's trying to puzzle something out. "I *need* you."

"Then you can have me," I rumble, sliding my palms down to the delicate bevel of her collarbone. And then down farther so I can feel her heartbeat under my fingertips and her nipples harden against my palms.

"Bare again," she begs as I start toying with them.

"Yes, ma'am," I murmur, and then I duck down and take her nipple into my mouth.

She gasps and arches, her hand coming to the back of my head to encourage me. I groan at the feeling of her fingers in my hair, tugging at the short locks, and I nearly growl at the sensation of her nipple stiffening even more between my lips.

I suck and suck with hot pulls, and then I catch it gently with my teeth until she gasps again. I move to the other side to torment her other one until they're both dark pink and jutting out from her breasts in inflamed need.

Then I drop to my knees.

Cat moans in anticipation as I brush my lips over her mound, and then she breathes out a long *ohhhhh* when my flickering tongue finds her clit. The shower has washed away most of her flavor, so I sling her leg over my shoulder and spread her open with my thumbs so I can taste the very heart of her.

I taste it, finally, with her pushed open and my face practically buried between her legs. I grunt as the sweet and salt of her blooms on my tongue, and my cock jolts with so much need that I have to jack it even as I service her just to keep my limbs from shaking.

"Oh God," she says once she catches sight of me handling my dick. "Oh

God, get up here, get up here—"

I stand, careful to make sure she has her balance as I do, and then I press her against the shower wall and kiss the hell out of her. I kiss her until she can taste herself on my tongue, and I kiss her until she's trying to grind her pussy against the thigh I put between her legs.

I break the kiss and look down, thinking I could watch her needy pussy rocking against my bare thigh all day long, but of course my dick doesn't think that.

"Ready?" I ask.

She whimpers out a *yes*, and then I lift her into my arms so that her legs go around my waist, notch the head of my cock at her opening, and impale her in one smooth and delicious glide.

She wraps her arms around my neck for more leverage, and I brace her against the shower wall again. It's so much like the time we fucked in the station, except it's completely different. For one thing, it's slippery and wet, so we have to be more creative, fucking more with arms and twists of hips rather than with the grunting, battering force I used in the meeting room.

And instead of wearing the uniforms and badges that define our lives, we're stripped bare, right down to the skin. Even our expressions are naked, and Cat's is showing me all the fear and hurt and longing she carries around inside her every day, and her eyes are shining down at me like I single-handedly saved Christmas. There's a new kind of intimacy between us. Something more than sex—more than friendship or respect, even—and it feels fragile and breakable and beautiful beyond all reason.

Oh God. She's twisting me up so badly, twisting my heart right up.

I catch her lips with mine. "Do you..." I start to ask and then stop because what I was about to say was *Do you feel what you're doing to me?* And then maybe I would have also said, *Do you know I'm falling in love with you?*

I'm terrified of scaring her off, so I don't finish what I started.

And maybe I don't need to. Maybe Cat can see it in my face anyway, because she presses her forehead to mine and murmurs, "Yes."

Just that one word to my half question.

Do you...?

Yes.

I'm not going to survive her, I think.

She comes apart into a slippery, shivering mess, her cunt pulsating all around my shaft and squeezing me on to my own orgasm—as fierce as it is tender, surging into her warmth with her blue eyes on mine and her hand in my hair.

For a minute, we simply pant together like that, the water still spattering our shoulders and feet and our shared essences beginning to seep out from where we're joined. It's a surprisingly cozy feeling—or maybe cozy isn't the right word.

Restful, maybe. Familiar in the sense that it feels *right*.

In that I want to feel it again and again and again.

I comb her hair once we leave the shower and then bundle her into a big T-shirt of mine, and we nestle into my bed together. I'm too sated and sleepy and filled with this big new feeling for her to care that my bed is a store-closing-sale mattress on a plain metal frame or that my comforter is an old threadbare thing from my sister's college days. And Cat doesn't seem to notice. She just tucks her hands under her cheek like a fairy-tale princess and closes her eyes.

Not good enough.

I wrap an arm around her waist and pull her snug against my chest, allowing her to wriggle a bit so that her backside is pressed against my ever-present erection and her back is to my chest. I tell my dick to settle down, tuck her head under my chin, and completely encase her in my arms.

For a long time, we lie like this in the darkness, breathing together, her feet idly rubbing around my calves, and I think she's asleep. Until she takes a deep breath and says, "Frazer died at night. In a dingy little house in the bad part of town. The electricity had been shut off at some point, so when I went in, there were no lights on..."

She pauses, tensing in my arms, and I wonder what she's remembering. What she's seeing in her mind as she shares her pain with me.

"It was dark and so hard to see, and everything happened so fast. And Frazer—" She stops abruptly, and I guess that's a part of the story I won't get. At least not yet.

Another breath. "I shot, but I wasn't fast enough. It was dark, and I didn't want to hit the man I was going to marry."

I squeeze her close, knowing there's nothing I can say that will fix it.

"It was so stupid of me, but after...everything...I went outside to wait for backup, and there was blood everywhere, just everywhere. And it was starting to dry on my hands in this awful, sticky way, and all I wanted was to wash them, just *fucking wash them*, because all that blood was supposed to be inside *him*, not on *me*, and he was dead and I'd watched him die and it was all over my hands..."

"Cat. Babe." I hold her tighter, wishing there was some way I could cage her in my arms and keep her safe and free from bad memories forever.

"I did all the mandatory counseling after it happened, all the therapy for PTSD, and I'm fine most of the time. Nearly all of the time, in fact. But there's something about squeezing the trigger in the dark that makes it all come back."

I let her words fall back down around us like rain and soak into the ground. Soak back into silence. Sometimes that's all that's needed.

But this is something she and I share. Maybe we don't share an age or the same kind of upbringing, but tragic violence in the course of duty...yes. I know it too.

My voice is tired with experience when I speak. "Knowing you killed someone is hard. Knowing you didn't kill them fast enough to save someone you care about is even harder."

She considers this. "Did you kill anyone in the war?"

"Yes."

"And watched someone you care about die?"

"Yes. Not a fiancé, but a friend. Yes."

"Oh, Jace."

I press my lips into her hair. "It's okay. I did all the counseling too. And it's still hard, but I'm going to be okay."

Cat sighs. Rubs her toes on my shins. "I'm going to be okay too." And then more silence.

This time I think she's really drifted off, and I'm about to follow her, when she whispers, "Jace?"

"Hmm."

"Were you going to fuck that girl if I hadn't shown up?"

I don't know what it says about me that I'm a little glad she's still jealous, even though I left that girl in the cold so I could bring Cat home instead. Even though it was Cat who got her hair washed and then had my tongue in her pussy.

But I want her to know the truth. I want her to know where this is going for me. "No, I wasn't going to fuck her, no matter what happened. She's a friend's sister, so I didn't want to shove her off of me in public and embarrass her, but I planned on letting her know it wasn't going to happen."

"Why not?" Cat asks, and she asks it almost like she's afraid to hear the answer.

"I think you know why not," I reply. There's a long pause, and I may not have a ton of experience with delicate talk like this, but I know I've gone as far as I can go tonight. "Good night, Cat," I add softly, and she nestles her nose into my bicep in response.

And this time we really do fall asleep.

CHAPTER NINE

CAT

I wake up still wrapped in Jace's arms, with an almighty erection wedged against my bottom and soft snores in my ear.

The sun is bright and new, telling me it's still fairly early, and the lack of any alarms chiming in the room reminds me that we both have the day off. I stretch my legs and arms and back as much as possible inside his giant bear hug, wonder if I could possibly doze back off, and then reluctantly concede that I'm awake for good now.

I pry myself free of his embrace and make to slide out of bed and investigate Jace's coffee or tea options—but I'm immediately seized and hauled back against his big, sleepy body.

"No," comes his half-awake growl. "Stay."

"It's morning, Jace."

"It's our day off." His voice is petulant, adolescent even, and I roll over to look at him, to coax him awake, but I'm simply crushed back into his chest. I can feel the snores vibrate through him when he falls back asleep seconds later.

"*Young* man," I whisper to myself, smiling a little. I manage to push away enough that I can stare at him—really stare at him—as he sleeps. At the adorable sprawl of his big body, the pout of his parted mouth, and the long eyelashes resting dreamily on his cheeks. All those handsome features, normally so severe, normally so stormy and scowly, are relaxed into a boyishly sweet expression in his sleep. He barely looks twenty-four like this, and you'd never guess he's a cop or a former soldier. You'd never guess he's known grief or fear or anger. That he's haunted by the memories of war.

He looks gentle and dear and young. So young.

I try to get out of bed again, this time more because I need a moment to process my feelings. About this young man, about how tenderly and thoroughly he made love to me last night. About how he wanted to take care of me beyond sex and outside it, before he even knew what was wrong.

Do you...?

Yes.

Even now, I'm not sure exactly what he was going to say, but it didn't matter. Whatever he wanted to know, the answer was yes.

This is skidding off the rails fast, Cat.

But I never do get a chance to process my feelings. I'm grabbed again, and this time Jace wakes up enough to put that massive erection to good use.

For two weeks, I am unbearably, abominably weak, and for two weeks, Jace and I fuck constantly.

And everywhere. We fuck everywhere.

At my place. At his place. Twice more in the station—after the brass went home this time. In his car, in my car, in the bathroom of an office building after interviewing a witness.

And every night as I fall asleep with his arms around me and his lips pressed to my neck, I think *you have to stop this—you have to end this pointless fling because it's going to hurt one or both of you.* It's unprofessional to have sex with a coworker, and it's a fireable offense to do it on duty, *and* it's just... unseemly, given his age.

Catherine Day doesn't do unseemly things! It isn't me, this torrid, sex-fueled affair, yet every time I convince myself to end it, something else happens and my resolve vanishes like it never existed in the first place. Jace will yank me into a searing, movie-worthy kiss or send me a heated gaze from the passenger seat of my car. Or he'll rumble *Cat, baby* in that husky growl of his, and nothing else will matter. Not our jobs or my reputation or seemliness. The only thing that matters is him and how close I can get my body to his in the next thirty seconds.

But despite the sex and the snuggling in bed and the occasional domestic moment of making coffee or dinner together, there's not another vulnerable moment like there was that night in the shower. I don't cry, he doesn't ask *do you...?*, and we don't talk about our pasts again. We have sex and talk about the case. Professional and age considerations aside, it should be perfect.

Why isn't it perfect?

Why do I keep thinking about that moment in the shower? Why do I keep wishing he'd finished his question?

Keep hoping he'll ask it again?

My confusion isn't helped any by Kenneth, who's been trying to corner me into dinner for a few weeks now. Would I say yes if I weren't screwing Jace? *Should* I still say yes? I mean, Jace and I haven't defined what we are to each other, and it's not like he's the loquacious type and full of effusive raptures about how much he adores me. For all I know, that night in the shower was a fluke and I really am just a convenient lay. For all I know, I'm just a fun way to pass the time until something better comes along.

But.

But.

Even though the entire thing is ridiculous, even though I'm worse than foolish for carrying on with a man so much younger than me, I can't bear to entertain even the thought of another person while I'm with Jace. Maybe I'm being too romantic or overly monogamous, or maybe it's some kind of transferred loyalty from Frazer, who was the last cop I dated before Jace—but whatever the reason, I won't start something with Kenneth. I don't even want to.

I call him back and agree to dinner, deciding I owe him this conversation face-to-face. I won't tell him about Jace—certainly not—but I'll tell him there's someone else right now. It will be a hard conversation to have, but Kenneth will understand. I doubt he spent his three years in St. Louis pining for me, and surely he didn't expect to come back and find me pining for him.

But now it's nearly time for that dinner—just a few hours away—and I still haven't told Jace that I'm going out with Kenneth.

He won't understand, I think.

But you know that he'd want to know about it anyway, I argue with myself, and then I sigh. I'm thirty-seven, and I'm obsessing over boy drama like I'm in junior high. What the hell has gotten into me?

With a sigh and a quick press of my fingertips against my forehead to help alleviate some of the pressure building there, I refocus on the files in front of me. I've been combing through them ever since our last two leads ran dry.

In a case as big as this, there's always another lead. Always another angle. I just have to find it.

I'm deep into the file on the last burglary—the one where I met Jace—and I'm clicking through the photos on my laptop when I hear a deep voice ask, "Drywall?"

Startled but happy, I turn to see Jace leaning against the edge of my cubicle, looking like a cop from a cop calendar with his crossed arms showing off biceps and forearms and his pretty mouth lifted into the tiny crook that passes for a smile for him.

"Drywall?" I ask back, trying to think through the temporary haze of electric lust and happiness that descends upon me every time I see him.

He tilts his head at my desk. "You were staring at your laptop, muttering 'drywall, drywall' at the screen."

"Oh." I turn back to my desk to make a quick note while gesturing for him to come in. "I hadn't realized I was talking out loud. How was the warehouse search?"

"Nothing there," Jace says and takes a seat in the spare chair next to me. He brings the chair close enough that our knees touch under my desk, and I want to melt. I want to run my fingers along the cut hardness of his thigh up to the heavy cock currently pushing at his zipper.

I don't. But the temptation is agonizing.

"Any chance they could have moved the televisions before you got there?" I ask, forcing myself to focus on the task at hand. I sent Jace to check out a couple locations that had been used to hide stuff like this before. A shot in the dark but worth looking into.

Jace shakes his head. "One warehouse is being renovated into lofts, and the place was crawling with a construction crew. No one I talked to had seen anything being moved in or out. The other was completely abandoned but had a few squatters staying inside. They swore up and down they hadn't seen any trouble."

"They would say that," I murmur, but I trust Jace's instincts—for now.

"And the drywall?" Jace asks.

I frown back at the screen. "I'm not sure yet. There's just something about all that drywall dust at the scene that keeps tugging at me. It will come."

"Mm," Jace says, and from the way he says it, I can guess the word *come* sent his mind in a very different direction than police work.

I'd roll my eyes, but that wouldn't be very fair of me since I've spent the last five minutes vaguely considering pulling him back into the meeting room for a quick round to help me last the rest of the day. The day that I'm—sigh—spending part of with Kenneth.

Tell Jace. Tell him now. He'll be pissed, but he'll be less pissed than if he finds out later.

I open my mouth to speak, but Jace gets there first. "I have my niece's birthday party this evening," he says quickly, almost as if he's blurting it out. "It's nothing super formal, just a barbecue and cake at my sister's house, but I thought you could come with me. And, um. You know." He looks down at his boots, suddenly bashful and boyish and so...un-Jace-like.

The first time I ever drove a car faster than one hundred miles per hour, I was in academy and terrified beyond all reason. Yet there was this moment as

I accelerated—adrenaline screaming through my veins, and my stomach back where I left it at the starting line—when my heart floated in my chest out of sheer, exhilarated joy.

I feel that now.

Jace's invitation to meet his family and the unusually shy way he asked— it makes me feel like I'm driving one hundred miles per hour, with my heart hammering fast and happy even as my body registers unheard of terror.

Because I know what happens when you drive fast.

You brake hard.

I can't meet his family tonight because I have to have dinner with Kenneth, and anyway, it would be ludicrous for me to meet his family. How would I even introduce myself? As the coworker he's been jeopardizing his job with because we can't seem to wrangle our hormones under control? As the cougar who caught his poor, innocent body in her claws?

Jesus.

No. I can't meet his family and his parents, who will only awkwardly be a decade or so older than myself.

And I shouldn't meet them because we aren't a *thing* anyway. We aren't going to be together for long, because these flings never last, and then when his family doesn't see me again, they'll know for sure that I was the predatory sex-harpy taking advantage of their handsome son.

All the euphoria, the heart-floating-in-my-chest, it just stops, like I really have mashed on the brakes with all my weight. And I suddenly very much want to cry.

I glance at his face, with its red of embarrassed hope burnishing his cheeks, and hate myself. "Jace, I'd love to go, but—"

"It's okay," he says, very fast. "It's okay. I didn't really think you'd want to go anyway, and I only thought it would be an easy way to get dinner and stuff, so—"

He's killing me. My cubicle has become the scene of a homicide.

"Stop," I say, grabbing his hand and hating myself even more for the white lie I'm about to tell. "It's just that I've made plans with a friend for dinner already. But I will see you tonight at my place after? Just let yourself in through the garage if you get there before me."

"Sure," he says, and there's so much in his voice, so much that isn't normally there for this quiet, primal cop, and I think my heart is breaking. And that's almost the scariest part of this.

I've gotten to the point where his unhappiness is more painful than my own.

☖

Kenneth and I meet at one of the understatedly elegant restaurants that suits us both so well, and it's as I'm walking in that my work phone rings.

"Day," I answer after I fish it out of my purse.

"Hey," comes the person on the other end. "This is Jessica in Dispatch. We just had a woman call in trying to speak to you. She says she works at one of the doctors' offices that's been robbed and needed to check something on the missing items report."

I see Kenneth at a far table, already with a bottle of wine on the table, and I give him a small wave before I turn away. "Did she leave a number?"

"She did. I'll email it, along with the call notes. She sounded pretty upset about something, but she only wanted to talk to you."

That isn't unusual. Speaking to the detective on a case is like speaking to the manager at a store—there's an imagined aura of authority cloaking the interaction. And I certainly wouldn't turn down the opportunity to talk to anyone directly. Our dispatchers are good, but there's a limit to what they'll be able to lift out of a conversation if they're not familiar with a case. And at this point, I need every lead I can get.

After confirming that she'll email the details, I hang up with Jessica and then make my way over to Kenneth, who stands to greet me.

"Cat," he says warmly, taking my elbows and kissing me on the cheek. It's shocking how unpleasant it feels, how very wrong to be kissed by someone who's not Jace, and I'm quiet as I take my seat, trying to process the tumult of troubled feelings currently jostling around in my chest.

You're a detective, Cat. You know how to read evidence.

Being irritated at Kenneth's touch combined with how miserable I felt today turning down Jace's invitation seems to point toward a very obvious conclusion. One I don't want to think about because what it means is too maudlin. Too destabilizing.

Far too real.

"I'm so glad you could meet me," Kenneth says as he pours me a glass of sauvignon blanc.

I take it gratefully, determined to fortify myself before the hard conversation starts. "Thank you for being patient while we were making plans. This case has been eating up lots of my evenings." *Well, the case and sex marathons with a man almost half your age.*

Kenneth waves the hand holding his own wineglass, in a *don't even worry about it, I totally understand* gesture, and I can't help but fixate on that hand. On the difference between his manicured fingers under the pale wine and how Jace's fingers looked wrapped around a beer bottle at that bar a few weeks ago. How casually masculine Jace was. How unselfconscious.

Kenneth pretends to be casual too, with his air of careless sophistication, but his mannerisms are too studied for that. The wine label faced outward so the rest of the diners can see that he spent eighty dollars on a single bottle. The angle of his shoulders so that his thin sweater over his button-down will pull just the right way over his arms and back to display his physique.

I think of that date three years ago and the terrible sex that followed— the kind of sex you'd expect from someone who focuses more on style than substance.

This is the person I thought made the most sense for me?

We make small talk for a while, mostly about work and his daughters, and then we hem and haw over whether we want to order the rabbit or the octopus, because that's the kind of restaurant this is. I wait until after we eat and after Kenneth has his third glass of wine to turn the conversation to our non-future.

"Kenneth," I start, searching for tact. "You're a good friend, and—"

"Oh, Cat," he says and reaches for my hand across the table. "I thought you'd never broach the subject. I don't want to dance around this because I think we are both too old and too tired for that, don't you?"

I hate the way my hand feels in his. How funny that Jace can bend me over a table and plug my ass with his thumb while I babble incoherent, orgasmic *thank yous*...and yet the peremptory way Kenneth takes my hand in a public building raises my hackles.

I gently remove it, giving him a small smile. "I agree."

"I like you," he continues, although he stares at his own hand with a furrowed brow, as if confused about what just happened. "I know our last foray into romance was interrupted by my move to St. Louis, but I'm here to stay now, Cat. And I want to make a new life here. Find a partner to share that with. Do you understand what I'm saying?"

I do understand. He's thinking exactly what I've thought before: the two of us make sense on paper. We're the logical and inevitable pairing of upbringing and profession. Two rich kids who caught a case of conscience and went into the field of justice instead of finance or medicine or literally anything else more lucrative? That's us. We'd be able to kvetch about judges and defense attorneys while we shopped for antiques and took winery tours.

But in the last few weeks, I've discovered I don't want that...if I ever did.

"I understand, Kenneth, and three years ago I might have wanted to be that partner," I say. "But that's not why I came here tonight."

A hard anger passes over his features so quickly that someone less perceptive might have missed it. But I catch it.

I catch it, and I'm suddenly beyond grateful that I'm not going to entwine my life with his. Not when his first response to rejection is anger. Not when all my cop senses are currently on high alert at the prospect of a man so much larger than me suffering from the side effects of a fragile ego.

Fortunately, that ego appears to value public perception over personal slights, because he doesn't seem inclined to make a scene. Instead, he takes a deep pull from his wineglass and leans back in his seat. "Is there someone else?"

"There is."

He looks off into the middle distance and then looks back to me after a long, pensive moment. "Why did you come to dinner tonight, Cat?"

"I came because I respect you and I thought this conversation deserved care and attention."

He sighs, rubbing his forehead, and then gives me a rueful kind of smile. "That's how you know we're old, by the way. Seven years younger and you would've just DMed me on Twitter. Seven years younger than that, and it would've been a passive-aggressive Snapchat story."

I laugh a little and so does he, and my tension slowly ratchets down. *He's taking it okay. It's going to be okay.*

"I am sorry," I say. "I truly enjoyed the time we spent together before you moved. But then I met"—I stumble, almost saying Jace's name and only barely catching myself in time—"someone, and I'd like to see where things go."

Kenneth shakes his head, seeming sad. "I should've reached out earlier. It's my loss, Cat. I hope he makes you happy."

I don't miss the bitter edge in his tone, and my cop senses prickle again. Outwardly, he seems like he's adjusting well, but there's something emanating from him that makes me uneasy. I never ignore these instincts, and I feel abruptly grateful that I drove here on my own and don't have to rely on him for a ride home.

"Thank you," I say. "He does make me happy."

There must have been too much truth in my tone, because there's more irritation in Kenneth's expression now. Luckily the waiter comes by with the check. Kenneth and I politely argue about who will take the bill—a pointless argument because the money isn't significant to either of us. We agree to split it, and then we pay and make to leave.

Kenneth catches my hand a last time after we stand up, and he kisses the back of it. "I hope we stay friends."

"Of course," I say, but I doubt it.

In fact, I'll probably make sure to put some distance between us...at least until his bitterness fades and I sense he's safe again.

I get in my car and text Jace.

I really need you tonight.

And I mean sex—always that—but I think I might also mean more. I need his chest to bury my face in and his hands petting my hair. I need to tell him everything about Kenneth and apologize for not telling him sooner.

I need him to know that I only want him.

And I think I need to know that he only wants me. I think I need to be spanked, mounted, and fucked. I think I need all Jace's intensity centered on marking my body as his. I think I need my choices anchored in this raw connection Jace and I can't seem to shake.

I'm pondering all this as I drive home, chewing over the dinner and my uncomfortably big feelings for Jace, and I'm so wrapped up in my own thoughts that I don't notice anything different when I park my car in the garage and walk inside my kitchen.

"Have a good time?" says a low voice from behind me.

CHAPTER TEN

JACE

I almost didn't believe it when I saw them through the window. The restaurant they were at is in this fancy mixed-use development thing—the same complex that houses the bakery that made my niece's cake. I volunteered to pick up her cake so my sister could focus on getting everything else ready, and then I saw Cat's car—with the license plate number I couldn't help but memorize the first time I saw it.

I thought I'd pop in and say hi because that's where I'm at right now. I'm at the point where two hours away from her is bone-cutting agony, and I needed a fix. I'd just pop in, fake a smile to whatever martini-drinking girlfriend she was with, and then lean in to kiss her cheek. I'd smell her hair and her skin as I whispered what I was going to do to her later tonight. Where I was going to fuck her. How hard she would come.

But there was no martini-swilling girlfriend.

Instead, she sat across the table from Kenneth—fucking *Kenneth*—who looked handsome as always in his "only the best from JoS. A. Bank" way. And they were talking. And smiling. And drinking wine.

And the *rightness* of them in there tore through me like a shotgun blast. Because of course Cat looked like a movie star with her expensive clothes and soft blond hair and those high heels that give her feet that glamorous, Barbie-style arch. And of course she looked like she belonged there with a man who knew what kind of wine to order, what kinds of arts events and charities to make small talk about.

Fuck.

And she lied to me about it.

Double fuck.

I should have left immediately. I should have stepped away and shelved this for a later discussion, but I didn't. I stayed and watched for another ten minutes, jealousy and hurt pounding through my veins. I stayed until my sister called and asked me what was taking so long with the cake.

It wasn't a surprise that I wasn't much in the mood for a party after that. I went, gave little Abigail her cake and her present and a big hug, and then decided to go home.

Which was when I got her text.

I really need you tonight.

I leaned my head back against the driver's seat and tried to talk myself out of it. I could cancel. I could tell her I wasn't feeling well, or that my sister needed help with the babies, or even that I saw her out with another man and didn't feel much like fucking tonight.

Which would be a lie. I want to fuck her now more than ever.

I want to feel her body pressed against mine. Feel her mouth moving over my own. I need to reassure myself with thrusts and moans and searching fingers that I'm not imagining what's between us. That she is still mine.

No. No fucking. Not until you've figured this out.

So I'm at her house because she asked and because it needs to be figured out. Even though the thought of *figuring it out* sends fear bolting through me like jagged sparks of lightning.

What if we *figure it out* and that is the end of us?

I pace through her sleekly renovated bungalow until I can make sense of my feelings. Until I can admit to myself that *falling in love* somehow turned into *being in love* without me realizing it, and now I have to deal with it. I have to admit to myself that us ending would destroy me.

She has to know.

But I won't be a dick. I'm here because she asked me to be. I'll tell her I know about Kenneth, and then I'll tell her how I feel. The choice is hers. I've been here before, after all, with Brittany and her reverse harem of jackasses who worked in cell phone stores or did car detailing or whatever it was that kept them here and available and not off fighting a war. I survived that with a woman I thought I might marry. I could definitely survive this.

Even if it doesn't feel like it.

Even if it feels like I already love Cat an infinite amount more than I ever loved Brittany.

Face it. You're in way deep. Deeper than you've ever been.

When Cat walks through the door, I don't mean to scare her, but that's what happens. I speak, and she spins in a sharp turn, her hand dropping to her hip as if she's reaching for her duty weapon.

Shit. I'm a dirtbag. I take a step back, my hands in the air like a suspect.

"Christ, Jace," she says, her hand falling away from her hip and her posture going from alert to its usual straight-backed poise. "You frightened me."

"I'm sorry," I say, and I mean it. "I didn't mean to...loom."

She sets her purse down on the counter and presses her fingertips against her forehead for a minute. "No, I—I should have remembered you might get here before me. I was just distracted."

By Kenneth? I want to ask, but I'm not going to. If I'm brutally honest with myself, we've never talked about being exclusive. We've never set any parameters around our relationship. Yes, fine, I'm still jealous as fuck, but I know I don't really have the right to be.

But I've underestimated Cat and her powers of observation. She gives me a once-over with those sea-blue eyes, with one delicate eyebrow arched and her lips pursed, and then she says, "You know I was with Kenneth."

God help any suspect who tries to lie to her.

"Yes," I say. "I know."

She looks at me almost like...like I don't know. Like she's disappointed. But disappointed in what? That I know? That I admitted it? Am I not being as calm as I think I am?

I take another step back, trying to reassure her that I'm not going to give her a hard time. That I'm not going to try to use my body to intimidate her. Her gorgeous, pressed-together lips grow more disapproving.

Does she want me to talk more? I don't trust myself to talk more. I don't trust myself not to blurt out *you're mine, you're fucking mine*, drop to my knees, shove up her skirt, and prove it with my mouth. Prove that her body already knows who it needs, and it's not Mr. Men's Wearhouse. It's me.

"I thought you'd be jealous," she murmurs, still studying me.

"I *am* fucking jealous," I say tightly and then snap my mouth closed so fast my teeth click. *Don't be a dick, don't be a dick, don't be a dick.*

She takes a step forward. Another and then another while I stay completely still, unsure of what she's thinking.

"Prove it," she says, folding her arms across her chest.

"Excuse me?"

"Prove you're jealous."

It's like I'm in some alternate dimension—one where my primal, Freudian id makes all the rules. "I'm not sure what you're asking."

She sighs, suddenly looking very much like an impatient schoolteacher, which is not helping the angry lust roiling in my belly in the least. "What do you want to do to me right now, Jace?"

"I don't—"

Another step forward. "You want to screw me in the heels I wore to dinner with him? You want to handcuff me to the bed so I can't leave until you say I can?" She presses a hand against my chest. "You want to see your come on my stomach? Or my tits?" Her hand drops down to my belt, and I catch her wrist before it can go somewhere farther down.

I can't tell if she's in earnest or she's goading me. "Stop it."

"Why are you asking me to stop?" she asks. "Is it because you actually don't want this? Or is it because you doubt I'm really asking you for it?"

"Of course I doubt it," I say through clenched teeth. "What I really want would terrify you."

She gives a beautiful, rich-girl scoff. "Try me."

I lift a hand and slide it though her silky hair, fisting it at the base of her neck and holding her head back just enough that she won't be able to move without disrupting her balance. And then I lean in so my lips brush the shell of her ear as I speak. "I do want to fuck you in these heels. And in handcuffs. I want to fuck your mouth, and then I want to bend you over my knee and redden your ass until you think of me every time you sit down. I want you to take me everywhere in your body—and I mean *everywhere*, Cat—until you feel as owned by me as I'm owned by you."

Confident my little speech has frightened some sense into her, I let go of her hair and pull back. But instead of seeing her face tight with fear, I meet eyes with pupils blown wide with lust and blushing cheeks and her tongue working at her lower lip in a kind of fervent anticipation.

"You feel like I own you?" she whispers, searching my face.

"Isn't it obvious?" I ask.

She just keeps blinking up at me, like she can't believe it. Like she can't believe I feel it, and I trace that doubtful mouth with my fingertip as I speak.

"And I may be young, but I know what I want, Cat. I want you. I want to make you mine."

Her hand goes back to my belt, toying with it, but her eyes stay glued to mine. "Then make me yours, Jace. Right now. I won't break, I'm not"—a small smile here, as if at some private joke—"I'm not a china doll."

I consider her, reading her body's signs. Her nipples poking through her blouse trying to get my attention. Her pulse thrumming at the base of her neck. The blush below her collarbone that disappears down into that sexy silk shirt. She likes it when I'm possessive. Jealous, even. I remember that from the first time we had sex at the station.

But this is something different. "You're asking me to claim you," I say, making sure we're on the same page. "While I'm angry and hurt and jealous. While I want to be rough."

"Yes," she moans, pressing her breasts against my chest as her hand wraps around my denim-clad erection.

And that's all I can take. All the permission I need. I scoop her up and sling her over my shoulder, just like the Viking I wanted to be a few weeks ago, and smack her ass hard as I walk toward her bedroom. I feel her stomach hitching where it presses against my shoulder, and for a moment I wonder if she's crying or trying to speak, but then I hear—

She's laughing.

She's happy.

It's a roller-coaster laugh, the kind of laugh that's pulled out of you by adrenaline and joy and terror all mixed together, and I take it as extra confirmation that she's on board. I still say over my shoulder, "Say stop when you need to stop, baby."

Her voice is full of smug cop pride when she answers, "Fine. But I won't need to."

I don't think she will either. She's tough, tougher than anyone gives her credit for, and I think under all that good breeding and money is a woman who wants to test her limits. Who wants the edgy, filthy, primitive challenges no one else has known to give her.

But I know. I know what she needs.

I drop her onto her bed without warning, without delicacy, without even flicking on a light, and then I fall on her like a predator in the dark. I nip at her jaw and throat until she whimpers, and then I eat her mouth with stark, brutal kisses until both of us are breathing hard and my dick is leaking all over the inside of my jeans.

Taking her wrists in one hand, I pin them above her head as I grind into her clothed pussy with merciless hips. "How much did this cost?" I say, working a hand between us to pluck at her silk blouse. "Two hundred? Three hundred?"

"Three hundred," she pants.

It'll be hell on my bank account to replace, but so fucking worth it. I let go of her wrists and move up so I'm straddling her hips, and then I take one side of the blouse in each hand. She's wearing it in her usual way, unbuttoned to expose just the right amount of décolletage, and the fashionable part of the placket gives me just the right handholds to grab and tear the blouse apart.

It's a well-made shirt, and it takes plenty of strength to rip the buttons from their moorings and send them scattering across the bed, but I manage, revealing a lacy bra and Cat's stomach, both ivory-pale in the moonlight streaming through her window.

She looks wrecked like this, wrecked already, with her shirt rumpled and torn around her breasts and her hair mussed and her lips swollen from my attentions. I run my fingers over the swells of her lace-covered tits and down to her quivering belly. "All this is mine," I tell her.

"Yes," she says.

I move off her. I find the zipper to her skirt and yank it down with impatience, peeling the fabric from her body and tossing it on her floor like I don't know it probably also cost an unthinkable amount of money. And before I straddle her again, I allow myself to appreciate the vision she makes like this, with her white garter belt highlighting the nip of her waist and her nude stockings giving off a faint sheen in the moonlight. With her heels still curving her feet into sexy, chic arches.

She looks expensive. Cultured.

And I'm the man who gets to bite and bind and dishevel it all. I'm the man who gets to make her mine.

I remove the remains of the blouse from her and then straddle her again to knot her crossed wrists in the fabric. There's plenty of it, and it's soft and thick enough that I can bind her tightly, and I do, relishing the jagged exhale she gives when she tests the knot and finds it unyielding.

"Now," I say, climbing off her. "Let's see what the queen keeps in her toy box, hmm?"

With as much sex as we've had in the last few weeks, we still haven't dipped into her toy collection, although I know it's in her end table, and I know she must have some things in there that are at least mildly shocking, because she blushes whenever I ask her about what she has.

Well, there's no time like the present to find out.

I leave her trussed up on the bed while I make my way to her nightstand and pull open the drawer. I growl when I see what's inside.

"Dirty girl," I say, holding up the cool metal of a jewel-ended butt plug for her to see. I toss it on the bed, along with the bottle of lube she has stashed inside the drawer. "So fucking dirty. I knew you were. Knew you were keeping all kinds of secret filth wrapped up in all that silk."

She makes a needy noise and drops her bound hands to her stomach, and I only realize why when I see her fingers sliding under her panties to get at her pussy. I'm back on the bed in an instant, pinning her arms above her head again.

"Bad," I tell her. "You're doing bad things when you should be trying to be very good for me right now."

"Just make me come first," she demands, trying to rock her hips against my erection. "Make me come, and then I'll be good."

"Nice try," I rasp, biting her breasts until she listens. "You are mine right now, which means your orgasms are mine too. And you're not going to come until I know you're very, very sorry."

"Sorry for what?" she asks breathlessly.

"For making me want you so much. Now *shhh*."

I go back to the drawer and riffle through all the interesting items in there. In addition to the jeweled plug, she has a vibrating one, along with a very realistic dildo—which I'm boorishly proud of being bigger than—and three different vibrators. I pick a vibrator and then join her on the mattress, where she's currently trying to rub her thighs together for friction.

I pinch her nipple. "Knock it off."

"Make me come."

I pinch again, giving it a tiny twist through the lace this time. She gasps and then moans.

"Jace, please," she begs. "Just once, and then you can do whatever you want."

I don't bother responding to her ridiculous demand. I'm already too wrapped up in how *I* want her to come. How I want to stake my claim all over her body until it's mine, mine, mine.

I take the vibrator, turn it on, and lie on my side next to her, propped up on one elbow so I can watch her reaction as I buzz it over her nipples and navel. As I run it along her inner thighs and ghost it over her folds until her pleas start falling out of her mouth faster than her breaths.

She'll do anything, she says, anything I want. She'll suck me, jerk me, take me anywhere in her body, she'll do any depraved thing I ask...as long as I let her come right now. So long as I ease her misery just a little.

"No," I say simply.

But I do find her clit with the vibrator and give her a little taste—just a little hope—before I click the vibrator off and deny her again.

She writhes on the bed, trying to free her wrists from the blouse I tied around them, which is when I flip her onto her belly and prop her up on her elbows and knees.

"I like the thought of you with these plugs in your drawer, dirty girl," I say. I unhook her garters and garter belt and fling them to the floor. Her panties are lace, real and delicate, and it takes nothing for me to rip them off. And finally, I get the view I've been wanting all day. A cunt so wet it glistens in the near darkness and the tight star of her asshole above it.

I press a thumb against that star now, testing its tight resistance. "I like the thought of you so desperate for it here that you do it to yourself. That you squirm in bed alone at night, just needing it. My filthy baby."

She's moaning now and trying to push back against my touch.

"Have you ever really been fucked here, Cat? With a cock?"

"N-No," she answers, still seeking out more pressure and friction from me. "Just toys. But I—I want it. Wanted it for so long."

"None of those rich boys knew what to do with you, did they? They didn't know how shameless you really are. How much you need to sin." I palm her cunt, feeling how wet my words have made her, and she shudders at the contact.

"Jace," she pleads.

"Baby, you know the only answer you're gonna get is *when I'm good and fucking ready*, so instead of asking, why don't you tell me how you feel? What's happening inside that amazing mind of yours?"

"I-I feel like my skin is too tight," she manages, still trying to buck against my hand. I use my other hand to toy with her clit a little to reward her for obeying. "My cunt feels hollow. My nipples hurt, they're so hard. I feel like I haven't come in a thousand years."

I frankly feel the same way, with her wrists tied and her pussy against my palm, and I have a dizzying moment when I realize that my anger and my jealousy have turned into something else, something different. Like desire—but darker, because it's the desire to see her fall apart for me like I'm falling apart for her. Like possession—but better because she's begging to be possessed.

If I had to call it anything, I'd say it was love. Rough and elemental, the only love I'm capable of giving.

Ah fuck. I can't spin this game out for much longer. Not when the urge to claim her and to love her is pounding through me so hard that my cock throbs in time with it.

I take the plug in my hand, admiring its weight and its cute little jewel at the end, before I trace the cool tip of it down the curve of her spine.

She shivers.

"Plug first," I say. "Then me. And when I'm inside your ass for the first time—that's when you can come."

She gasps when she feels the cool drizzle of lube on her and again when I add the extra coolness of the plug pressed against her rim.

"Okay?" I ask, meaning all of it. "Need to stop?"

"No, no," she says. "Just—I usually warm it up first."

I test it with my finger and find that the metal is already warming up against her skin, so I decide I can push her a little here. "I'll give you something very warm in a minute," I tell her and begin working her rosebud open.

She breathes out and relaxes against me, but it still takes some coaxing to get the plug inside, and then a long, quavering moan as the widest part of the bulb stretches her open. Once it's seated in her ass, the jewel winking sweetly between her cheeks, I reward her with the vibrator on her clit, letting her get almost to the brink before I pull back again.

"Jace!" she cries out, frustrated.

"I know, baby," I soothe. "I know." I run a gentling hand over her ass and up her back, petting her. "You're being so good for me right now. So good letting me have what I want."

"Oh God," she says, rolling her face into her forearms. "If I don't come, I'm going to die."

"Then you better be ready for heaven because we aren't done yet."

We play like this for a few more minutes—some buzzing on her clit, some toying with the plug until her entrance is kneaded into pliancy and ready for my cock. She's a moaning, wet mess with slick arousal now coating the outside of her pussy and her inner thighs, and when I see that, I feel like I've been kicked in the stomach.

How am I going to last long enough to make her feel claimed?

Fuck, I'll be lucky if I last another minute.

I climb off the bed and move in front of her so she can see me undress and also so the tempting shine of her wet cunt is out of view. She watches me peel off my shirt and kick off my boots. She watches me unzip and sees my cock push through my fly with wetness all over the blunt tip of it, all for her. Her eyes are huge in the darkness, and her tongue can't seem to stop darting out to lick her lower lip. As if she's desperate to taste me.

I'm light-headed at the thought, and also, Jesus Christ, light-headed that she's here with *me*—dumb, young *me*. She wants me, and I'm going to give her everything in return.

Once she truly knows she's mine, that is.

"Let me see you lube up," she whispers. "I want to see it."

I decide I don't have any objection to this, and I let her watch me as I coat my shaft and the big head with lots of slick lube. I give myself a few more strokes than necessary because it feels so fucking good to squeeze against the ache building deep in my groin.

"I'll go slow," I promise as I mount the bed behind her and remove the plug. "You tell me if you need me to stop."

"Just hurry," she says in that trembling, needy voice that kills me to resist. Resist I must, though, because ideas like *fast* and *rough* don't belong anywhere near *anal*—at least not for the first couple dozen times or so—and I'm determined only to be a caveman in the ways that are fun for us both.

I go slowly, knowing that I'm bigger than the plug, that there's no narrow base at the end to give her relief. I coax my plump crown past her rings, smoothing my hands along her bottom and back as I do, and then I give her a moment to adjust.

"I feel like you've gotten bigger," she says, a touch grumpily, as I slide forward another inch.

"No, baby, you're just small here. Let me in."

She takes a deep breath and forces herself to relent against my intrusion, but it's still a labor of love to get deeper. Still a few hot, urgent moments to get in all the way to the hilt. But then I am, and the sensation of her so tight and hot and smooth around me has all my muscles clenching and rigid against my impending orgasm.

Her first, her first, her first.

I reach for the vibrator and find her clit with it. "You can come now," I say. "Anytime you'd like."

"You don't have to sound so gracious about it," she mumbles, but I can already feel her tightening around me, see her hips trying to chase the delicious rumbles of the toy. I can see the muscles in her thighs trembling and hear the whine building in the back of her throat.

I turn up the vibrator's strength at the same moment I begin thrusting in short, grinding motions to maximize the indirect pressure against her G-spot. Her reaction is instantaneous.

"Oh God, *oh God oh God*," she whimpers, and the whimpering dies off into a series of sexy-as-fuck, animalistic grunts. "Coming *coming, oh God*, Jace!"

She dissolves. She's shaking, sweating, screaming, her entire body spasming around my cock as she kicks her stockinged feet against the bed and wails her pleasure into her forearm. Each squeeze of her climax clamps down hard on my erection, massaging it, yanking me closer to ejaculation, and I can barely wait for her tremors to subside before I'm flipping her over onto her back and pushing into her ass again.

"Fuck, it's tight," I hiss through my teeth. Her pussy is so wet against my skin as I curl my body over hers to fuck her harder, and I can feel her beaded nipples against my chest and her goose bumps against my own. I meet her gaze and take in her wrecked, dazed expression—hooded eyes and parted lips—and know that I made her that way. I fucked her so thoroughly that she looks like she can't even remember her own name. I gave her what she needed, every filthy minute of it.

"Look at me when I come inside you," I order her. She obeys, her eyes so soft and adoring up at me, even while I'm inside her ass, that I fall in love with her all over again. "Look at me while I take you in a place no one else has. While I claim you."

"Jace," she whispers, and I feel her start to come again. "I'm yours."

Those are the words that push me over the edge. The fist of pleasure that was clenching at the base of my spine finally unclenches, and my orgasm tears through me like a tornado. A hot wave of come spills out of my cock and then another and another, until I'm nothing but jerking, throbbing spurts of ecstasy. Slick and scorching jolts of unraveled man.

I empty my balls inside her and then manage to arrange us so I can collapse on my side, spooning her, with her tucked to my chest and my cock still buried inside her. I want the intimacy of it for another moment longer, just while we come down and catch our breaths. Then I'll untie her and we can clean up.

I stroke along her bare arm, reveling in the silky softness of her skin. A cloud of blond hair is in front of me, giving off some kind of expensive floral scent. Her ass is plump and pressed against my hips, and even as I'm softening, I can feel her body give rhythmic aftershocks.

I think *I'm* the one in heaven now.

"Okay?" I ask.

"Very okay." She sighs in contentment. "I feel very claimed."

"Good. You're mine now. Not his."

She stretches a little, and I slip out of her, wincing at the cool air of the room. This is my cue to untie her, but I have to mourn it a little because elegant Catherine Day looks so fucking good trussed up with her own shredded blouse.

"I was never his, you know," she says as I roll her to her back and start unknotting her shirt. "I agreed to dinner to tell him that nothing was going to happen between us."

I pause my work and search her face. She's telling the truth. "Really?" I ask anyway, needing to hear it.

"Really. I don't want him, Jace, and I think now maybe I never did, even three years ago. He was just there and he made sense, and...I was too lonely not to try."

I wonder if I make sense to her. If I'll ever make sense with my age and my background and my job. I wonder if I'm something she's trying out of loneliness and nothing else.

"Why didn't you tell me this earlier?"

A naughty, kitten-like smile. "I wanted to see what you'd do."

"Dirty girl. And how did he take it?" I ask, finally unlooping the silk and throwing it on the floor. I grab her hands and start massaging them.

She makes a noise of pleasure at my efforts. "Outwardly, fine. But inwardly...I think he was angry and jealous. Bitter, even. It makes me nervous."

Her words cut through me like a knife, and I swallow, forcing myself to focus on doing the best possible job anyone can do massaging a hand.

"And," I say, trying not to sound suddenly suffused with panic and self-loathing, "is that any different than how I acted tonight?"

"Oh, Jace, of course it is." She sits up, presses her hand against my jaw.

I meet her gaze, miserable. "How?"

"Because I asked."

"Oh."

"And you asked me back. It's that simple, Officer. Now let's take a shower."

CHAPTER ELEVEN

CAT

I wake up in a cloud of happiness so thick that even breathing feels like an act of joy, and in my drowsy state, I can't quite remember why—until I stretch, of course, and my well-abused internal muscles fuss and shout at me.

Oh yes.

Jace.

Last night.

After the anal and a shower, there was more sex—the gentler kind this time, although the orgasms that followed were no more gentle for it. And then we fell asleep snuggled together, spooning as I like to do, with my head pillowed on his big bicep and his legs tangled with mine.

A low male rumble comes from behind me, letting me know that Jace is awake, and I feel him stretch a little and then seek out the back of my neck with his mouth.

"Good morning, baby," he says in a sleepy voice. I shiver at the touch of his lips to my sensitive nape, and he notices—because he's a good cop and notices everything—and then kisses me there again while his hand seeks out a nipple to toy with. "Sleep well?"

"I'll say." I stretch again and roll over into his arms so I can look up into his face. In the fresh morning sunlight and having just woken up, his face is open and boyish, his silver eyes shimmering with molten sin. The place between my thighs tightens at the promise there.

"Shit, you're beautiful," he breathes, ducking his head to kiss my breasts and belly. "So fucking beautiful. I love you so much."

I love you so much.

Love.

A tidal wave of ice-cold water crashes over me, and I'm choking on my own panic. Drowning. Dying.

No. No. He couldn't have said those words. He couldn't have just...*said* them. Like they were no big deal. Like they were beyond self-evident.

Jace lifts his head. "Cat? You okay? You went tense all of a sudden."

"You said you loved me." My voice sounds strangled even to myself.

His handsome face looks so adorably confused, and my heart twists. "Of course I love you," he says, puzzled. "What did you think all that was last night?"

I pull my lower lip between my teeth, distressed.

His expression goes from puzzled to something else. Something wary. Watchful. "I said I was claiming you," he says slowly. "Making you mine. What did you think that meant?"

Excellent question. Even more excellent because didn't I realize last night that I wanted only *him*, that I was falling for him—and doesn't that mean I feel the same way? Doesn't that mean I'm in love with him?

Oh my fucking God, I'm in love with him.

I can't breathe. I can't think. The tidal wave is everywhere, and I'm all cold, flailing panic. I push him away and sit up, needing space, needing...a moment to just fucking think.

"Cat," Jace says, letting me move away but not letting me wriggle out of answering. "Tell me what you *think* this is between us. What we have."

"It's supposed to be just a sex thing," I say, pressing the heels of my hands into my eyes. "Just sex, just fun. That's it."

He takes my wrists and gently tugs my hands down so I have to meet his gaze. "This isn't *just* anything, baby. Not between us. This is real."

I search those gray eyes, so strong and young and sure. "That's what I'm afraid of," I whisper.

His jaw is tight. "Why?"

That he even has to ask reminds me of how new and naïve he is, and the unfairness of it all, the stupid, pointless *waste* of it all cracks me wide open. "Because this can't go anywhere, Jace! It never can! You're just starting, you have your entire life ahead of you, and you are going to find your wife and marry her and have lots of babies, and all of that is still going to be after several years of fucking anything that moves. I'm not going to be the reason you miss out on all that."

If I thought his face was tight before, it's nothing compared to now. I can see the muscles working along the sharp line of his jaw and around the sculpted corners of his mouth, like he's working very hard not to shout. "You don't want me to *miss out*," he repeats.

"Right," I say, even though as I say it, something twists inside me, hard. I know what I just said is true and I know it's necessary, but God, it feels uncommonly depressing to think about. Jace's life after me. Him falling in love and marrying and—

"Fucking other people," he says flatly.

And that.

"So you'd be okay with me sleeping with women who aren't you," he clarifies in a bitter, awful voice. "You'd sleep just fine saying goodbye and knowing I've found a new place for my cock."

I can't help it—I wince. Because I hate it. *I hate it.* I hate the thought of any other woman getting to see the dark line of hair arrowing down from his navel or the way his long eyelashes rest on his cheeks right after he comes. I loathe the thought of anyone else knowing the flex and clench of his ass as he fucks... or the hard lengths of his thighs straining as he gets ridden...or the rough, male authority of those hands that grab and hold and squeeze as he makes love.

Most of all, I hate the thought of someone else using his bicep as a pillow. Knowing the warm fan of his breath in their hair. Getting to wake up to sleepy gray eyes already blazing with possession.

And I can't meet those gray eyes now as I think about all this.

Hating it doesn't change anything, I remind myself. He's still too young. He's still a cop. This is all still so wrong.

Jace catches my chin with his fingers and forces me to look at him. "Is it really such a huge thing? Our ages? Because it's not to me, and if anyone says anything to you about it, I'll tell them as much." His gaze darkens. "Or more."

The noise that comes out of my mouth is a sour, scoffing noise that I'd ordinarily be appalled at making. "What are you going to do, Jace? Beat the shit out of every person who calls me a cougar?"

He starts to object at the word, but I go on. "Are you going to shake up every person who stares at us, wondering if I'm your older sister or an aunt—or worse, your mother? Walk around with a sandwich board telling people to fuck off?"

His eyes are narrowed now, and I feel the heat of that cop gaze scrutinizing me, and I hate it. I hate that he's examining me while I'm shredded with fear and messy with feelings I didn't ask for. Catherine Day isn't supposed to be shredded or messy—I'm always contained and cool. Icy, just like the rest of the department says I am. And not being icy when I most need to be is infuriating.

I toss my head away from Jace's fingers like an agitated filly. "And what are you going to say to yourself, Jace? In a year? In five? In twenty? When you've thrown away your life chasing something ridiculous instead of living it the way you should?"

I'm pinned to the bed before I can blink, two hundred pounds of pissed-off cop looming over me and pressing my body into the mattress. "You are *not* ridiculous," Jace growls. "And you're not allowed to say that shit about yourself.

Not while I'm around. Got it?"

Despite everything, the insane chemistry between us is setting my skin aflame. I can feel my nipples pebble between us, his cock go rigid and hot in the notch between my legs, both our hearts hammering hard against our chests as if they're trying to trade places. I want him to kiss me. I want him to eat my mouth like he's starving and then fuck me screaming into the bed.

Jace looks like he very much wants the same, his arms trembling where he holds himself above me and his eyes dropping to my mouth like he can't decide whether he wants to kiss me or shove his cock down my throat.

I moan, and his control breaks—for a single instant. He drops his mouth onto mine for a crashing, ragged kiss, but before I can even begin to kiss him back, he's gone. He's off the bed, staring at me, naked, his denied erection dark and bobbing between his legs. He ignores it and bites out, "We're not going to do that."

"Do what?"

"Fuck the fight away," he says shortly. "That's not going to help anything."

"Because it can't be helped, Jace."

He ducks his head, muscles popping in his jaw, but he doesn't argue my point.

Which leaves me feeling a little stung, although I'm not even sure why, given that I started this fight. And I'm not even sure *what* I feel anymore, actually, just that it's a million things at once. Like maybe a secret part of my mind was hoping he'd keep trying to convince me that we could overcome this.

"I can't help my age, Cat," he finally says.

"I know," I say. "But it's not just that."

"Oh," he says, his posture stiffening even more. "That's right. The badge."

I blink, and in that blink, I see my dead fiancé's sightless stare and an ocean of blood.

I sigh. "Yes."

"You're a cop too," he says. Accuses.

"Exactly." I get to my feet now as well, which maybe is a mistake because it only serves to highlight how much taller he is, but I don't care. "I already carry all the fear and the trauma for myself. I can't carry it for another person. I can't wait up every night wondering if this will be the night you don't come home. I can't be the one waiting on that phone call, Jace. I just...can't."

"Are you saying you don't worry now?" he asks, taking a step forward. "Are you saying because it's only been a few weeks, because we haven't put labels on anything, you wouldn't give a shit if I lived or died?"

My mouth drops open. *Of course not*, I want to sputter, but he keeps going.

"Because maybe you feel that way, but if you don't think I'm already in so deep that I wouldn't be in fucking agony if you were hurt, then think again."

I'm staring up at him—defensive and confused—and whatever he sees in my face is not the right answer because he reaches down for his clothes and starts yanking them on in jerky, vicious motions that make me suddenly desperate to take back everything I've just said.

"Jesus, Cat," he mutters, pulling his T-shirt over his head. "You can't freeze out everything, you know. And I'll be damned if I'll let you do it to me."

"Where are you going?" I ask as he shoves his feet in his boots. "You can stay. We can...talk."

He shoots me a dark look. "If I stay, we're not going to talk."

"I'm okay with that," I whisper.

He gives a cheerless laugh. "Of course you are. I'm good enough to fuck, but that's it, right?"

Irritation stabs through me, fast and sharp. "I never said that."

"You don't have to." He gets to the doorway, swiping his keys and wallet off the dresser and turning to face me. The morning sunlight pouring in from the living room outlines his hewn, perfect form in hazy gold. "Here's what I can't figure out," he says with a glare that raises the hairs along my arms. "How can you say you're afraid of having your heart broken if you can't even admit you have a heart at all?"

It's a fair question, and it lands with a punch. I stagger backward a step and sit heavily on my bed, unable to meet his eyes.

And he leaves without another word. He leaves me naked and alone and searching for an answer to a question I should have asked myself the moment we met.

It's the weekend, and since Jace is on my mini-task force of two, he has the weekend off as well. But he doesn't call that night or the next day. He doesn't text or stop by.

I don't reach out either.

Instead, I catch up on work email and a few other cases I've had to shelve while I've focused on the burglaries. I go grocery shopping. I do a yoga class. I call my parents, who've retired in France, and we catch up on the last couple of weeks. They beg me to come out and stay a month. They drop hints about how much fun their little farmhouse and pond would be for children.

I usually dodge the hints easily enough, but this time, my voice catches when I say I haven't been really dating anyone.

"Catherine?" Mom asks. "*Is* there someone?"

I don't know how to answer that. "Sort of," I hedge. "It's complicated."

"What isn't?" Mom laughs. "I've been married to your father for forty-one years, and it's still complicated. Is it another police officer?"

"It is."

"You don't sound happy about it."

I sigh. "We fought yesterday."

Mom takes a minute to reply to that, and when she does, she says, "You know, sometimes your father and I worry about how we raised you. The... impressions...we might have left, without meaning to, and I just worry that it's made things harder for you now that you're grown."

"You're going to have to be less vague," I tell her, "because I don't understand." And I mean it. My parents were the ideal parents. One a judge, one a doctor. They doted on me, their only child, and while there were certain expectations of etiquette and demeanor required of me, I never doubted their love. Or their respect, once I reached adulthood.

"I'm afraid we've raised you to be, well, *picky*," she says carefully.

"Oh, Mom."

"We really did adore Frazer," she forges on quickly, "but maybe your father and I didn't tell you enough that we didn't mind that he was, you know, *poor*." She whispers this last word as if it's not a word for polite company, and I lean my head against the doorway I'm standing in.

"Mom."

"We're so proud of what you do and that you do it for not very much money. It's so honorable, and we would extend the same perception to any police officer you wanted to date."

I'm suddenly and fiercely grateful I never told them about Kenneth, because I know with a deep, regretful certainty that dating Kenneth wouldn't have required this conversation. They would have been overjoyed with Kenneth's background and career in law, especially my retired judge of a father, and we never would have had this talk about them *not minding* someone I loved.

It's both exasperating and sweet, I suppose, that Mom feels these things must be said to me now. Exasperating because, generally, when someone goes out of their way to tell you they don't mind something, it's indicative that they *do* mind, on some level. And sweet because I can tell she means well, in her own privileged way.

"That's thoughtful of you," I say because I'm truly not sure how to respond.

"I know," Mom says with benign obliviousness. And then she adds, "And we just really, really want to have some grandchildren before we die!"

I manufacture an excuse to get off the phone very quickly after that, but her words find their mark. Not because her guilt finds any real home in me but because her words echo the fleeting, forbidden fantasies that have been chasing through my own mind. Feeling my belly swell with Jace's baby. Watching his big, strong hands cradle our child. Seeing him play on the floor and roughhouse and carry our child on his shoulders.

Fantasies that would rob him of his youth and the rest of his life.

Fantasies that can never come true.

Monday morning finds me at my desk two hours earlier than normal.

Without Jace laid out behind me in a wall of warm male, I find it hard to sleep, and then I also find myself intensely irritated because I shouldn't miss him so damn much after such a short time. After repeatedly telling myself nothing can ever come of our ill-advised liaison. After doing my goddamn best to guard my heart.

But I do miss him. I do.

After tossing and turning and barely skimming under the surface of consciousness into bleak dreams, I finally gave up and decided to start the day. So here I am, poring back over the license plate data from the last burglary. Last week, I had Jace run the plates through our system to see if anything came back flagged as linked to a criminal record, and we got a few hits. All dead ends.

Now I'm back to the beginning, narrowing the list down to the plates caught in the hour before the alarm was triggered and then seeing if I can find any patterns. It stands to reason that any burglar worth their salt would have done reconnaissance before—at least driven by once or twice—so I go back to the larger data pool to see if I can find any matches.

Ah, the glory of detective work. Spreadsheet-driven analysis and data tabulation. No wonder there's so many TV shows about us.

After getting a fresh mug of hot water for tea—tea that I get endless taunting for drinking in a station full of coffee addicts—I pull up emails from the different office managers listing the plates of employee cars so I can eliminate them from any potential patterns I find. I highlight all of those and then cross-reference them with information from the burglary sites.

I find something.

I roll out my shoulders and take a sip of tea as I consider the screen, and then I pull up our informational system and run a plate through. Since it's a cop system, it takes a long minute to load, and I click back to the spreadsheet while it searches, tapping my fingers against my lips.

The same plate number pops up at four of the five burglaries within an hour of the alarms being triggered. And at scene number five? The car passed through the closest intersection at 7:48 that morning and didn't pass back through until 10:23 at night. Three minutes after the alarm had been triggered.

Drywall, I think. *The stupid drywall.*

I click back to the database to see the car is registered to a woman in her late forties named Debbie Pisani.

I scribble a quick note to Jace about where I'm going, grab the keys to a squad car, and head out the door, calling a patrol captain as I go.

CHAPTER TWELVE

JACE

I nearly jerk my dick raw that weekend, being away from Cat. Three weeks of her in my bed and I've turned into something insatiable and ravenous. I've always had a healthy appetite before, but now with Cat, my need to fuck has exploded into a ceaseless, throbbing ache. An ache only she can ease, and she's not here to do it.

I could call. I know I could. I could show up at her doorstep right now, and she'd let me inside and we'd fuck until this awful thing between us tucked its tail and hid. We could lose ourselves and our hurt in each other's bodies, and maybe things would go back to how they were.

But I don't want that.

I don't want things to be how they were. I want *more*, and I'm not going to cheat us out of something better simply because a day and a half without Cat is agony.

No.

I love her. I need her forever. And I know I'm going to need every tool in the box to woo her away from these superstitions about age and occupation.

The most important tool: time.

Time for both of us to cool down. To miss each other. Time for the argument to recede enough that we can see all the unspoken fears underneath the words we said to each other.

So I settled for my hand as my body demanded its woman, and I made plans. Of what to say, what proofs to give, of when I'd concede her points and when I'd kiss the arguments right off her perfect mouth. We just have to get through work today, and then I'll take her home and tell her about my love over and over again until she realizes that love is strong enough to swallow up everything else. What are some years between us when I love her so much? What is a *job*? Nothing at all.

But she's not at her desk when I get there, even though I'm easily fifteen minutes early. I set down the cup of tea and donut I got for her—despite all the silk blouses and high school dressage trophies, Cat likes donuts just as much as any other cop, although she prefers the gourmet honey-and-sea-salt-type flavors to the glazed ones we usually have at the station—and then read over the note she left by her desk.

Ran out to reinterview Gia Pisani. Back by lunch.

I'm reading it over a second and third time when the phone at her desk rings. I answer it, in case it's her.

"Sutton."

"Um, hi," comes a hesitant voice. "This is Shelley Abadinksy, from the Mastin Cancer Center office? I'm calling for Detective Day?"

"She's away from her desk at the moment," I say, glancing at her note. Conclusions are fitting together in my mind, and there's a sharp bite of worry in my chest. The itch to go find her is difficult to think through. "I'm one of the officers assisting her on the case. I can take a message and make sure she gets it."

"Sure," Shelley says, sounding relieved. "And actually you might be able to help me anyway. I had our office manager, Gia Pisani, send in an updated inventory of all the missing items, but I just realized we might have to contact some federal authority, and I thought maybe Detective Day would know which one."

I'm standing and my body is already angled toward the cubicle opening, I'm that desperate to get to Cat right now. So I say hurriedly, "No need to report the televisions to anybody federal, ma'am. We'll handle it all here at HGPD," and make to hang up.

"Oh, I'm not talking about the televisions," she says, surprised. "Did Gia not tell you? Our cobalt therapy machine has been damaged, and the cobalt inside was stolen."

"Cobalt?"

"Nuclear material? It's used for radiation therapy."

Cobalt. It rings a bell from my army days, and my already tight hand practically cracks the phone receiver in half.

Cobalt. It's used for radiation therapy...*and dirty bombs.*

"And you didn't notice it was missing until now?"

She sounds defensive when she answers. "Look, we just refitted a new therapy room with a LINAC machine, so we haven't used the cobalt machine in over a month. It was scheduled to be removed next week. I went in there Friday to take a few measurements for the disposal company. That's when I noticed it had been pried open."

And Gia Pisani is the office manager. Cat is interviewing her right now.

Things come together in a horrible rush.

"And I just wasn't sure if *we* needed to contact someone like the Nuclear Regulatory Commission or if you did that," she goes, oblivious to the fact that I'm splitting apart with panic on my end.

"Shelley, I'm going to call you back, but I have to go right now."

"Okay, but—"

"We didn't know about the nuclear material," I tell her, already reaching up to click on my radio. "And I have to tell a lot of people about it right now so no one gets hurt."

"Oh," she says faintly, the gravity of it finally seeming to sink in. "Oh, of course. I should have—yes, of course."

"Goodbye, ma'am." And then I'm hanging up the phone and calling for a captain on the radio.

☩

"Day's got two uniforms with her," Captain Kim tells me as I'm speeding south to the medical office. "More are on the way."

"And the NRC?"

"Notified." A pause. "And the KBI and the FBI."

"Is she with Pisani now?"

"They're in the staff breakroom at the back of the building. The uniforms are just outside the door. Pisani doesn't know they're there. Everything's under control, Sutton."

Funny how hard that is to believe when the woman I love is alone with a criminal who is apparently selling nuclear material on the black market. I click off the radio and focus on driving, pushing the low-profile detective car to its limits. It roars into the parking lot before any of the supervisors arrive, which is good. I don't need them forbidding me from going in, because I'm going in no matter what.

I park and push my way into the building. There's an unfamiliar woman at the desk who looks puzzled at my appearance, so I assume she doesn't know about the other cops in the building.

"Where's your staff room?" I ask through gritted teeth, trying to keep my voice low.

"Back by the lab," she says, still puzzled. "First left. Hey, are you with that one lady—"

377

I don't stay to chat. I move down the hallway as quick as I can, pressing the hood of my holster down and forward in preparation for drawing my weapon. I pray I don't have to, because if I have to, it means Cat's in danger...

I round the corner and see a door marked *Employees Only*. Taking a risk, I open it with wary, slow caution, making sure I can slide into the restricted area without being seen or creating any noise. After I'm in, I close the door with a barely audible *click* and enter a fluorescent-lit hallway to see two patrol officers outside a windowed room. One of them puts a finger to her lips, indicating I need to be silent, and I creep up to join them.

Through the window of the staff room, I see Cat sitting across a cheap table from Gia Pisani, two disposable cups of coffee between them. Gia is agitated but trying to hide it under a veneer of friendly confusion.

Cat is unreadable—save for the occasional twitch of her lips as Gia talks. The Ice Queen's signature cool amusement. It seems to piss Gia off.

For a moment, I relax. It's just an interview in a forgettably bland staff room—a tense interview, maybe, but nothing more. No weapons, no open containers of nuclear waste, no anonymous men here to protect their supply. Cat doesn't know about the nuclear material yet, which means she won't question Pisani about it, which means the interview probably won't escalate into—

Gia stands abruptly, her chair knocking back behind her, her cheeks glowing as she says something heated to Cat.

Cat merely crosses her arms and arches a perfect brow, as if to make the point that the young woman is embarrassing herself with this outburst. Like most cops, Cat has the gift of complete reticence—that is, refraining from reacting to another person until she's good and ready—and her lack of response only provokes Gia to say more. Which was probably Cat's intention the entire time.

Hardly any sound makes it through the window, and at this angle, it's hard to attempt any kind of interpretation to what Gia says, but Cat tilts her head and murmurs something in an unperturbed tone.

Gia blanches, and I know whatever Cat said hit home. Hard.

She's so fucking good at this.

Weird how I *feel* that thought in the pit of my stomach—not with lust but with fear.

Because she's so good, she's more than good—she's sharply perceptive, intelligent beyond measure, fierce as hell, and that's not even taking into account all that sophistication and beauty. She's so far out of my league that we've never even played on the same field, and with a sudden, gripping terror, I wonder if *that* was what our fight was about. If she's not truly worried about our age difference or my job, but if she's trying to let me down easy because I'm not good enough for her.

And shit—she'd be right. I'm not.

I have to glance down to take a breath—a big, deep one to try to stave off panic I've never known before, and right at that moment, something happens that blows even that panic right out of the water. Gia shrieks something and, in a clumsy but quick movement, fumbles a gun from behind her back where it was tucked in her waistband.

She aims it right at Cat.

I'm moving before I can think, my gun out and my shoulder ramming the flimsy interior door open, and it's like all sound and feeling are gone, all extraneous sensation. There's only the gun in my hand and the palpable presence of the woman I love who's about to die.

She can't die.

Oh God. She can't die.

Reality comes back in with a vicious, adrenaline-laced flood.

The explosion of me through the door draws Gia's attention, and I hear myself yell for her to drop her weapon. I hear the two other cops behind me shouting for Gia to get on the ground.

Cat says something in a low, soothing tone as she gets to her feet and gracefully gestures for everyone to lower their weapons, and for a moment I think Gia is going to do it. I think she's going to drop her gun and give up this pointless resistance.

But then the officer behind me speaks again, his voice jangling with sheer human panic, and it jars Gia free from thoughts of surrender.

She swings the gun.

She shoots.

And pain, big and stark, swallows me whole.

Then darkness.

CHAPTER THIRTEEN

CAT

I've died. I've died and I've gone to hell.

And I'm not even the one who was shot.

A cup of coffee appears in my vision. Black, slightly oily, tiny bubbles rimming the edge of the liquid where it sloshed gently against the paper cup. I take it, although the idea of drinking or eating anything while my stomach is still twisted up into my throat is laughable. I don't bother to look over as Russo settles next to me, her own cup of coffee in hand.

"How is he?" she asks.

"Stable, last I heard. The bullet caught an artery in his arm and he lost a lot of—" My voice catches, and I suck in a breath, forcing myself to face tonight's events with the usual blunt, cold honesty I face everything else with. "He lost a lot of blood," I manage after a moment. "They closed the wound and did a transfusion, and he's recovering now. I should be able to see him soon."

Russo reaches out, touches my hand with her rough, unmanicured fingers. I know she sees the dried blood still trapped along the lines of my cuticles. "You saved his life," she says quietly.

"Maybe," I say, because at no point during those frantic, bloody moments after the gun went off did I allow myself to hope. At no point when I stanched his wound with my bare hands, the scene cruelly overlaid with my memories of trying to save Frazer, did I let myself believe it could end any differently.

Instead, I felt his hot, wet blood against my skin, sticky and slick all at once, and I thought *it's happening again.*

It's happening.

Again.

The uniforms cuffed Gia while she was frozen in horror at what she'd done—we arrested her without any one of us firing a weapon or using any kind of force. Good police work any way you slice it, and the paramedics were a credit to the city. They arrived as fast as humanly possible and took charge of

Jace's life with expert competence.

Someone had to peel me away while they worked. Another paramedic? Captain Kim, maybe? But I was allowed to ride in the ambulance with him. Allowed to hold the hand on his good arm while I frantically searched for all the prayers from my Catholic upbringing.

I could only remember fragments, and finally my thoughts disintegrated into vague, broken pleas as the ambulance raced to the hospital.

Please don't let him die.

Please.

Don't let him die.

"There was nothing else you could have done," Russo points out in the here and now. "The other officers told me what happened. You had the interview under control, and from what it sounds like, you might have been able to talk her down even without Sutton crashing in."

"I should have searched her first," I murmur.

"You wouldn't have been able to—not without cause—and what you had on her going into the interview would have been pretty weak grounds for a body search from a court's perspective."

She's right, and I know she's right, and it's almost worse that way. It's almost worse to know I did everything right and *still.*

Still.

I take a drink of the coffee. Not because I like it or because I need time to think, but just because it's something to do. Some new input that isn't self-recrimination and terror and misery.

"He did what Frazer did," I say after a minute and mostly out of nowhere.

"Yeah," Russo sighs. "I know."

"Why do they do that?"

Russo gives a dry laugh. "Who? Cops? Men? Men who are in love with you?"

I don't want to answer that, and I can't anyway.

"I know he's in love, Day," Russo adds gently. "All anyone has to do is look at him and know he's gone for you."

"He's young," I say, trying to sound dismissive. It only comes out as sad. "He doesn't know what he wants."

"I disagree," Russo says. "I think you're the one who doesn't know what she wants."

"He did what Frazer did," I repeat softly, and she gives me a rueful look.

"Is that so unforgivable?"

I look down at my fingers, still stained with Jace's blood. "It might be."

An hour later, with Russo gone and Jace's family camped all around me, a nurse comes in to say we can go in to see him—but we can't go all at once.

I'm desperate to get to him, desperate to trace his lips with my fingers and reassure myself that they're still warm. Anxious to see the rise and fall of his chest and know he's here. Still here. Still alive.

But Jace's parents are here, and they have the right to go first. I lace my fingers around the cup of tepid coffee and give Jace's mother a look I hope she'll interpret as a signal that I won't protest her going first...no matter how much I want to.

She walks up to me. "You're Cat Day?" she asks. Her voice is fractured from crying, and tear tracks have dried in streaks along her cheeks. She's very pretty—gray-eyed and full-lipped like Jace, and as tall and broad as he is too.

"I am," I say quietly. "Please, you go in first."

She gives me a watery smile. "Jace told us about you," she says, tucking a gray-salted lock of hair behind her ear. "That you two were dating, and he couldn't wait—" Her chin trembles. "He couldn't wait for us to meet."

Jace told his mother about me? Wanted us to meet? My heart flips over at the discovery, at the proof that his declarations weren't just the lust-fueled blurtings I'd suspected. That he not only wanted more with me but was actively laying the foundation for more.

Telling his parents. Wanting me to meet them.

The same things my illicit fantasies have been showing me for the last three weeks: a real life together.

My flattered joy is tempered with something unpleasant. I look up at his mother and realize she can't be more than ten years older than me. I realize she's looking down at me and seeing...

Seeing what?

A predator? A peer?

Both options are depressing.

"What you must think of me," I manage with a weak smile, and she shakes her head.

She reaches out and touches my shoulder. Not as a gesture of comfort but to draw my attention. I look at her hands, rough and calloused like Russo's, and remember that she was a firefighter. That her son's bravery and dedication to hard work comes from her.

She's touching stiffened patches of garnet splattered on my blouse. There's dried blood all over me; I look like I've emerged from some kind of abattoir.

"I think you're a hero," she pronounces. "You saved his life."

And then she and her husband follow the nurse into the ICU.

⟐

It's another hour before they leave, and finally I get to go in.

Jace is still unconscious, his face pale and his huge frame dwarfed by the massive mechanical bed, and I cover my mouth with my hand so my unhappy gasp doesn't wake him. As if anything could wake him up after all that blood loss and morphine.

There's a chair pulled up beside his bed, but I ignore it, dropping my things on the floor and crawling right into bed with him, careful not to tug on any cords or tubes as I do. He's warm but not as warm as I'm used to, and I'm just as cold as I press my body along his and lay my head on his good shoulder.

"Jace," I mumble. "Why? Why are we here?"

Tears are leaking now—the fast, uncontrollable kind and the first I've cried since Gia fired that gun. "I love you," I finally admit, hating myself that I never told him before. That I never told him when it mattered. "I love you, and it scares me. It scares me because you love me back and you love me back so much that you'd get yourself killed trying to protect me."

Just like Frazer.

Beneath my cheek, I feel Jace's steady if shallow breathing. All around us, various machines and monitors beep and glow with reassuring consistency, as if to say *he's doing okay, he's doing okay.*

But how can I ever be reassured of his safety ever again? After I've been spattered with coppery, vibrant blood as I begged and begged him to stay alive?

Maybe he didn't die today, but he came close enough to prove every point I've ever made about us. He is blessed enough to live and have this second chance, and surely he doesn't want to waste it on a woman so much older than him. Surely he deserves more tomcat years before he even has to think about settling down.

And most importantly...

He's too young and he's too heroic.

I've loved those young heroes before. I know what happens. I know how it ends.

I cry for a long time into his big, muscled shoulder, leaving streaks of mascara on his hospital gown. I slide my hand over his chest to feel the thump of his heart, and I listen to the machines, and I tell him, "I love you, I love you,

I love you."

And before I leave, I kiss his stubbled jaw and say, "And I'm so fucking sorry for what I have to do."

CHAPTER FOURTEEN

JACE

I'm too dizzy to open my eyes.

Sounds bleed through the haze of strange dreams—sounds I don't recognize—and I can't open my eyes to see what they are because the world is spinning, spinning, spinning.

I smell something familiar. A delicate, French perfume, and the smell conjures a face in my mind.

Cat...

But before I can manage to speak her name, heavy, drugged unconsciousness pulls at me, the sounds receding as I disappear back into the spinning dark.

&

When I wake again, the dizziness isn't so bad, but Cat's scent has disappeared into a miasma of cleaning chemicals and fast food. I manage to pry open my bleary eyes to find my parents sitting next to me, McDonald's cups in hands, talking in low tones about replacing the fence in their backyard.

"Mom?" I rasp.

"Oh!" she says, setting her cup down and rushing to lean over me. "Oh God, Jace, you're awake!"

She sounds happy and sad all at once, and even in my groggy state of mind, I can see the drawn lines around her mouth and eyes, the ashen cast to her face. Whatever I've been through, she's suffered more watching me go through it. My dad joins her on the other side of the bed, taking my hand.

I'm so glad to see them, although the reasons why are hazy...

"Where's Cat?" I whisper. "She was here, I know she was..."

Mom and Dad exchange a look over me. Mom's look distinctly says *I told you so.*

"She's been here constantly," Mom says as she looks back at me. "We sent her home today to get a change of clothes and a nap. She hasn't been taking care of herself since you came in."

I close my eyes, pained that Cat has been suffering but hopeful too—hopeful that if she's been here and had to be forced to leave that it means something for us. For our future.

"How long?" I ask. My voice is dry and raspy. "How long have I been here?"

"Three days," Dad says. "The first day was the hardest—"

His voice cracks, and he clears his throat in a manly sort of way. "You got moved down from the ICU yesterday. They say you're in good shape—no sign of infection so far. They'll be in to assess potential nerve damage later."

Infection.

Damage.

The haze clears a bit around what I'm feeling in my body—like my right arm is on fire—and *why* I'm feeling it. Gia's face, florid and angry, her hand shaking around the gun so hard that she could barely keep it still.

Cat, slender and cool, eyebrow arched as she stared down the barrel without so much as flinching.

The barb of real, primal terror that lodged in my heart when I realized Cat was about to die. I've never felt fear like that. Not even in Afghanistan.

Funnily enough, I was also never actually wounded in Afghanistan. It was here, on these mean suburban streets, by a Vassar grad with a flair for supplying terrorists with rare metals. Who would've guessed?

With my parents' help, I sit up and manage to chew some ice chips, and then I fall back asleep, the seductive pull of the pain medicine too strong to resist. I don't dream much, but what I do dream is strange and warped and distressing. And always, always about Cat.

When I wake up again, it's dark outside the window and the nearby highway is mostly drained of traffic. The lights in the room are dimmed, and a television is playing a rerun of a sitcom I normally hate. But I'm too tired and out of it to bother trying to find a way to change the channel.

Most importantly, there's someone in bed with me. Someone warm and sweet-smelling. My arm wraps around her instinctively, pressing her tight against me as my heart squeezes in a familiar, achy way.

The monitor next to me reflects that, and Cat shoots upright in alarm.

"Jace," she says urgently, searching my face. "Are you okay?"

"Yes," I murmur. "Just awake. Just holding you."

The panic recedes from her expression slowly. "Does your arm hurt? Do you need the nurse?"

"Cat," I say, reaching for her again. "I only need you."

With a huff of disbelief, she nestles back into me, and I savor the feeling of her close to me. My body gives a faint pulse of aroused response—muffled by the pain meds—and I ignore it for now, simply enjoying the contact. Enjoying the weight of her against me and the spill of her hair, messy and tousled as it hardly ever is, cascading over my shoulder. She's in something surprisingly casual too—jeans torn at the knees and cuffed at the ankles—and an old army shirt that I left at her house once.

For some reason, seeing her in my shirt makes me want to cry. I fight off the urge by burying my face in her hair and breathing her in.

She's here.

She's safe.

I kept her safe.

A few more days pass like this. Russo comes by and tells me I'm on medical leave until I'm cleared by the doctor to come back to light duty. Cat comes in at night, after my parents leave and always wearing my shirts, and snuggles in the bed with me, much to the nurses' amusement. She doesn't say much, which begins to worry me, and every time I bring up the case or my injury, she shuts down completely.

I'm not sure what to do about it. I want her to know how happy I am she's safe. How few fucks I give about getting shot when it means that she's here now, unharmed and whole. Even if I have lingering impairment in my arm that means I can't wear the badge anymore...

Worth. It.

I'd do it again and again if it meant Cat left that staff room alive.

But the more I try to tell her that, the more closed off she gets. I'm desperate to get out of this hospital bed and into a real bed with her so we can extinguish all this pent-up frustration and fear in a frenzy of touch and sweat. If I could just get her underneath me...

She's in bed with me now. The lights are dimmed and the nurse just checked on me, giving me a conspiratorial wink when she shut the door, and I know we have at least an hour or more before she returns. Without giving myself time to doubt the wisdom of this, I tuck Cat close to my side and roll us so that she's underneath me and I'm covering my body with hers. I have to grit my teeth a bit as I settle my weight on my injured arm along with my good one, but the stitches hold and the Demerol blunts the worst of the bite.

"Jace!" Cat says breathlessly, blinking over at the door and then to my injured arm. "You'll hurt yourself. You'll—"

I cut her off with a fierce, hard kiss—the first real one I've been able to give her since the shooting. I silently thank God that I've been able to walk around the past two days and shower and brush my teeth and all that, because I don't have to hold back. I lick at her lips until she parts them for me, and then I lick inside her mouth, tasting her and teasing her until her wary body begins to melt under mine. Until she's moaning and her hands wander to the back of my hospital gown to clutch at my ass.

"The only way I'll hurt," I breathe against her lips, "is if you don't let me taste you right now."

"Taste me? But—"

It's too late. I'm already working my way down her body, careful of my IV and monitor wires, and rucking up her borrowed T-shirt to kiss around her navel as I unbutton her jeans.

"You can't," she says, "you can't, but oh God, you are, *you are...*"

I yank the jeans down past her cunt, ignoring the sharp pain in my arm as I shove the denim to her knees and expose her silk-clad mound to my stare. The silk goes down to her knees too, and then I push her legs up to her chest so that she's available to my mouth.

I lick her slit, and the sweet, earthy flavor explodes on my tongue. She cries out at the same time my heart monitor pings its alarm.

"Shh," I pant, "or the nurse might come in."

She presses the back of her hand to her mouth and turns her head to the side, as if that's going to make my onslaught any easier to bear. I highly doubt that, since it's been nearly a week since I've eaten her pussy and I'm hungry as hell.

It's hard work to service her properly, with her legs bound together by her jeans and her knees shoved up to her chest, and with my body hanging off the bottom of the bed and my ass hanging out of my gown.

But I don't care—it's like heaven to me. Burying my face, getting my lips and chin wet, seeking out her swollen little clit with my tongue and stroking it. Lapping at her entrance like it's the only real medicine I need.

I have to force myself to breathe, to be calm, because I know there's only so much I can push that heart monitor before the nurse feels compelled to check on me, no matter how much she wants to be my wingwoman.

But it's nearly impossible to slow it down. I can't keep my heart from pounding in anticipation. Can't keep blood from going right to the throbbing weight between my legs.

Although judging from the way my balls have drawn up tight to my body, I'm guessing I won't be making the heart monitor go off for long. After so many days without her, her taste alone is enough to send me to the edge. And then she comes against my tongue with a muffled cry, her sweet little well contracting in rhythmic flutters, her hand reaching around and twisting in my hair to keep my mouth right where she needs it.

I can't last.

With a quick move that has my arm screaming, I'm back on the bed and rolling her to her side as I get behind her. I manage to plunge in right at the end of her orgasm, and I have to clap my hand over her mouth as she starts coming all over again at the fresh invasion.

It only takes three thrusts and the feeling of her moaning against my palm before I'm there, emptying everything I have inside her, pumping her full of a week's worth of need, and all to the beeping consternation of the heart monitor. Its insistent tones underscore my final few thrusts as I give Cat every last drop of what I have, and then it finally begins to settle down as I slide out of her and pull her snug against me.

We're both wet and messy and her pants are still around her legs, but I don't want to move. I just want to hold her tight and relish the sensation of having her here and close and safe.

My woman.

Mine.

Cat wriggles free, though, not saying anything as she reaches for a tissue to clean up. Not meeting my eyes as she pulls up her panties and jeans.

A slow curl of unease blooms in my chest. "Cat? Baby?"

She doesn't answer at first, still buttoning herself and smoothing back her hair, until finally and with a long swallow, she meets my stare.

Oh God.

I don't know what's happening or why, and I don't know what she's about to say—but I'm certain she's about to leave me. There's something about the hollow pain in her gaze and the unhappiness around the lines of her plush mouth...something about her posture that looks defensive and determined all at once.

"Cat," I say again, sitting up. The heart monitor, which was calming down, starts beeping faster. "Don't do this. Don't do this to me."

She takes a breath, like she's steeling herself. "Jace."

"No." The beeping makes it hard to think, but the more frantic I feel, the faster it gets. "No, Cat. I don't know what you're thinking, but *no*."

"I held off doing this," she whispers. "I thought I'd wait until you woke up...and then I thought I'd wait until you were discharged, but I was just fooling myself because I don't want to leave..."

"Then why do it?" I demand. "Why put us through this when I love you?"

She lifts her eyes to the ceiling, ignoring my plea. "I thought you were going to die. I felt your blood on my hands, and there was so much, and I thought how can anyone lose this much blood and still—" She pauses, steadies her voice. "I can't go through that again. I used to think I couldn't go through it for anyone after Frazer, but it's *you*... I can't go through it with *you*. I love you too damn much."

I'm off the bed in an instant, but my IV and monitor wires mean I can't get close to her. I want to rip them all off and go and gather her into my arms. Crush her against my chest and kiss her hair until she stops this madness.

"If you love me," I try to reason with her, "then everything else will work out." I reach out my hand, knowing that I must look ridiculous in my bare feet and my hospital gown, but I don't even care. I just want her to come closer. I just want her to stay.

"No," she says, and her chin is trembling. She still won't look at me. "I wish that were true, I really do, but loving each other doesn't erase who we are. You'll always be in danger—"

"I'll stop," I interrupt her. "I'll quit. If quitting is what it takes, I'd do it in a heartbeat for you."

"No!" she cries. "That's not what I want at all! I don't want you to change who you are or what you love to do."

"It's just a *job*, Cat. I can find another one."

"Can you?" she whispers. "Can you tell me you don't miss the action from when you were deployed? Can you really tell me you won't be bored doing something else, something safe?"

I open my mouth.

Close it.

I can't lie to her.

"And you're a hero, Jace," she adds, blinking fast at the ceiling. "You're a good cop. We need more of those. *I* need more of those, because I'm not planning on giving up this job either, and I want cops like you by my side. I just can't *love* them."

"It's too late for that," I say roughly. "You already do."

She finally meets my eyes, and what I see there shreds me. Those aren't the eyes of someone about to fall on a sword—they are the eyes of someone who's already fallen.

"I love you enough to know that I'll ruin your life," she says in a broken voice. "Thirteen years is too big of a hurdle. You might think it's not now, but what about in twenty years? When I'm close to sixty and you're still in your forties? When you've felt forced into deciding whether or not to have children because it's not going to be possible for me to do it much longer? You deserve to spend your years free of all that. Free of responsibility until you *choose* it."

"I'm choosing it now," I rumble, trying to pull closer and feeling the IV in my hand protest. "Why is that so hard to believe? I don't want to spend those years being 'free.' I don't want to spend any years without you at all."

"It's been three weeks," she says. "It all feels real now, but it's not, Jace. It can't be."

"It *is*."

Goddammit, it is.

"I'm sorry I couldn't let you go sooner," she whispers. "It was selfish of me to wait, to want to be with you one last time..."

She takes a step back, and I know if she walks out that door, I'll lose her forever. It really will be the end. I make to yank off the monitor wires, and her eyes flare in panic.

"Stop it," she pleads, and I don't care. I'm not letting her leave. I'm not letting her finish us when I know she loves me, when I love her, when she's mine.

I tear them off my chest, not even feeling the sting, and then I start on my IV, trying to peel back the clear bandage they put on top.

"*Stop it*," she says more desperately now, and then, "I didn't want to say the real reason I need to leave." These last words come out in a rush.

"And what's that?" I say, looking up with a scowl.

She bites her lip, blinks twice, and then says, "You're not enough for me, Jace."

It takes a minute for her words to truly register, for their meaning to unfold in my mind. And when they do, I freeze. "I'm sorry?"

"I meant what I said about everything else," she explains, "but the real reason we can't be together is that we just don't fit. I'm sorry. I don't make the rules about these things, but there it is. You're too young, too coarse. Too reckless."

Her words hurt worse than that fucking bullet ever did, digging into the same fear that plagued me watching her question Gia through the window.

She's too good for me.

"Reckless," I echo. "I thought you said I was a hero."

"It's a kind word for a stupid waste," she snaps. "If you're that careless with your own life, how the hell can I trust you with my heart?"

Behind me, the heart monitor is making all the noises I can't seem to.

"I could never spend the rest of my life with you," she says coolly. "And now that you're well, I can tell you."

"Cat...*baby*. Please."

She takes in a sharp breath at the endearment, and I'm not sure what I see on her face. Confusion? Cruelty? Regret?

Pain?

But it disappears in an instant, leaving only the familiar face of the Ice Queen behind.

"Goodbye, Jace," she says and starts for the door. "I'm looking forward to your return to duty."

I don't rip out the IV after all.

I watch her leave. I watch her leave in my army shirt with her hair still tangled from our impromptu fuck. I watch her leave, and I can still taste her on my lips.

And for the first time since I was shot, I feel like I might die.

CHAPTER FIFTEEN

CAT

I have a meeting with the FBI, and it takes over nine hours.

Nine hours to detail all the evidence against Pisani, sift through her statement, and apply it to what we know. She used her mother's car as a way to deflect visibility, and she robbed all those other doctors' offices as a way to keep suspicion on the stolen televisions and not on the decommissioned medical equipment in her own place of work. The FBI is tracking down a boyfriend they think helped her with the physical aspects of the burglary, and they're also attempting to track down the cobalt itself.

Why a Vassar grad became a criminal is still a question the FBI will have to answer, although I think I saw a hint of the reason in Pisani's statement.

I couldn't find a job after graduation, not a single one. And then I finally found this office job, and it barely paid any of my bills, and it was so boring I wanted to die...

Very smart and very bored. Add in some money problems and a healthy dose of anger, and that's all it takes.

By the time the meeting is over, I feel ready for an entire bottle of wine. Maybe even two.

It's the first time since I transferred into investigations in the weeks after Frazer's death that I've missed being a patrol officer. Missed being spared the interminable meetings, missed the clean-burning energy of working hard and then burning off steam at a bar or in someone's bed after.

Of course, right now there's only one bed I want to be in, and I made damn sure I'd never be invited back.

It was for his own good, I tell myself for the millionth time since I broke Jace's heart a week ago. He wasn't listening to reason, he wasn't letting me do this *for him*, so I had to *make* him let me go. I had to find the things I knew would make him flinch and make him doubt. I had to hurt him so he'd accept that we had to end.

One day he'll thank me. One day he'll realize that I was the one mature and sacrificing enough to protect his chance at having a full life.

That it killed me in the process is inconsequential. What's important is that he has his future back, full of all the opportunities and new women he deserves. Full of time for him to meet his real soul mate and do things at the pace they're supposed to be done.

What's important is that I won't have to wait up at night for him anymore. I won't ever have to watch someone hand a folded flag to his mother. I won't have to miss him so much it feels like the muscles of my heart are tearing themselves in half.

Except.

That's exactly how I feel right now.

And when the FBI finally has everything they need from me to formally assume responsibility for the case, I go home so my heart can tear itself open in peace. I curl up in one of Jace's shirts, smelling the achingly familiar scent of tea tree oil and leather.

It was for his own good.

But I think I may have shattered any hope of *good* being a part of my own life now, and even though it was worth it, I still have to mourn the cost.

I gave him his future...

And now mine is empty without him.

Captain Kim calls me a few days later to tell me that both Jace and I will receive commendations from the chief at a special ceremony next week. He also tells me that since the case is no longer ours, Jace will return to Russo's squad whenever he gets off medical leave.

I should be happy about this—I know I should—but I hang up the phone and stare at my suddenly-too-big desk and feel like I've been hit in the chest.

He'll probably be relieved that we'll be back to never seeing each other at work, but I'm not. I can't be. I've only just now realized it, but I was counting on having at least *this* with him. At least the perfunctory *hellos* and *goodbyes* and accidental brushes of elbows and feet as we jostled for space at the same desk.

It's selfish to want it. I broke a good man's heart, and I don't get to have him close to me anymore. The sooner he moves on, the better it is for him, but I can't stop the ache of grief that comes with it all. The gnaw of bitter loss. I just want him near me, even if I can't have him, even if it's better for him to meet other women and go live his life... The idea of not seeing those flashing gray eyes and that stern mouth, of not hearing that deep, rough voice...

Ah, fuck, it hurts.

It hurts so much I don't know how I'll survive it.

But survive it I must, and survive it I do for the next week. I bury my pain in work, coming in early and staying up late in an attempt to exhaust my body and my mind. In an attempt to keep the sadness at bay and make myself too tired to miss Jace at night. It doesn't work on either count, so I only succeed in making myself tired *and* miserable, which I feel like I deserve.

I resist the urge to call.

I resist the urge to visit, even after I hear he's been released from the hospital.

I resist the urge to throw myself at his feet and beg, beg, beg his forgiveness.

It's for his own good.

It's unfair that I have to be the strong one right now—the wise one—when all I want to do is curl up in his lap and have him play with my hair. When all I want to do is marry him and have lots of gray-eyed babies and spend the rest of our lives making each other breakfast and sharing the job we love.

Because, yes, I see that now. I thought I hated that he was a cop as well. I thought I could never live with it, but now that we're apart...I miss it. I miss having someone to talk over a case with, someone who understands the uniquely exhausting and exhilarating parts of the job. I miss having someone to share it with.

All this tired unhappiness makes me jittery and anxious on the evening of the commendation ceremony. I pull on my dress uniform and pin on my brass with trembling fingers, and I don't bother to apply lipstick because I know I'll make a mess of it. And all because the man I love and had to push away will be there too.

Get it together, Cat.

But I can't. My stomach is hollowed out and my pulse is pounding when I get to the central station and walk inside. It's like every beat of my heart is saying *Jace, Jace, Jace.*

I'm sorry, I'm sorry, I'm sorry.

I detest these ceremonies anyway. They're anemic and bureaucratic and pointless. I already have several commendations on my wall. I've already gone to this same small reception room six times in my career and shaken the chief's hand and received a signed piece of paper I'll never look at again.

And now I'll have to go and do all this for the case that both brought me to Jace and also nearly got him killed?

It's very tempting to take this heavy dress hat off and go back to my car.

Tempting just to walk away from it all—the ceremony and the memories and the inevitable agony I'll feel when I finally lay eyes on the man I love.

The man I hurt.

But it's not in my nature to shirk my duties, even if I think the duty pointless, so I keep the hat on and enter the reception hall, not surprised to see that it's only half full, and that half is all Jace's family.

His mom looks over her shoulder at me as I walk in, and a flush rises to my cheeks, wondering if she hates me now that I've hurt Jace. Wondering if she now sees me as the predator I initially feared she would.

Her face opens in a smile, and she gives me a small wave, her husband doing the same, and I manage a nod back as my heart squeezes. Even still, I want his family to like me. How foolish is that?

There is, of course, nobody here for me. It's much too trivial to ask my parents to come over from France, and I don't have anyone else. No siblings. No close friends.

A bolt of loneliness hits me so hard that I can barely keep my back straight... and that's before I see him standing in front of me. Because when I see him, I think I might drop to my knees.

He's shaved for the ceremony, exposing fully that bladed jaw and that solemn, sensual mouth, but his hair is longer than he normally keeps it, dark and just a little messy, practically begging for my fingers to sift through it. The long-sleeved dress shirt stretches across his broad shoulders, testing the seams, and then the fitted fabric hugs the lean lines of his torso and waist. The tailored pants fit him almost indecently well, showing off narrow hips and long, powerful thighs, and even with his wounded arm up in a sling, he's still all potent, dominant male.

And when his fierce gray eyes lock on me, I know exactly whom he wants to dominate.

My body answers immediately, obedient to his silent command, and my nipples harden against the silk of my bra. I hope the thick fabric of the uniform is enough to conceal my response, but I know there's no hope for the blush on my cheekbones or the dilation of my pupils. He owns even the automatic responses of my body. He owns everything. So much so that even in front of this small crowd, I want to drag him off by his uniform tie and mount him in the first empty room we find.

No, Cat.

For his own good, remember?

And anyway, his desire is fueled by his palpable anger with me. I can feel it radiating off him, seething, lustful hurt, and God help me, it makes me want him more than ever. I want all of that possessive, revengeful man over me and underneath me. Claiming me. Destroying all my fears that he'll one day want a younger woman, obliterating my fear for his safety with the primal, urgent proof of his life.

I want to surrender the responsibility of doing the right thing. I want him to be the one to make all the hard choices now, and I want him to choose me.

I want to tell him I love him and that I'm sorry.

It hurts to tear my eyes from his, but I manage, approaching my chair and sitting without acknowledging him, which he scowls at. He also takes his seat, his long legs making it so our thighs brush briefly as he sits, and I can feel the shudder run through him as we touch. See his entire body quiver in ferocious restraint as the chief begins talking to the crowd.

Minute by minute, my resolve lessens and my famous ice thaws. I can smell that masculine scent of clean leather and tea tree oil. I can see his clenched thigh next to my own and those huge hands white-knuckled where they rest in his lap.

I'm weak, I'm so weak, because I want to beg his forgiveness and beg him to make me atone with my body, but I can't. *I can't.*

Dammit, Cat, you can't.

"...and that's why we're proud to present Officer Jace Sutton and Detective Catherine Day with these commendations. Let's give them a round of applause, shall we?"

We stand up, and then there's handshakes and pictures with the chief formally presenting us our commendation, and then finally, thankfully, it's over.

I bolt out of the reception room as fast as I can because I don't trust myself around Jace a moment longer. If I so much as look at him, speak to him, I'm going to crumble. I'm going to beg him to *make* me crumble, and if I'm going to survive losing him, I have to hold on to my pride somehow.

So I leave while he's talking to his family and take a shortcut through the employee-only hallway back to the parking lot, breathing a sigh of relief when the door closes behind me. This is the hallway where most of the civilian employees and administrative personnel work, and since it's evening, they've all left and I'm alone.

I need to get home. I need to get home where I'm safe from my own weaknesses, where I can burn off this need for Jace Sutton with a long run and a good toy and not by finding him and fucking myself on his angry erection until we're both too exhausted to move.

A door creaks; I stop and turn.

Jace is framed in the doorway like a wrathful god, striding toward me with a look on his face that would signal to any other woman to take cover.

It only makes me ready for him, so ready that I ache. I'd do anything right now to ease that ache, any undignified thing, oh God oh God—

"We're going to talk now," Jace says, reaching me and yanking me into him with his good arm. Every curve of mine presses against his hard body, and the unmistakable proof of his wanting to "talk" digs into my belly. "We're going to talk until I fucking understand why you said the things you said that night."

I close my eyes in regret, in uncertainty. If I tell him I hated the things I said, that they were lies I chose for the plain fact that I *needed* to hurt him, then everything else will tumble out after it. How much I love him, how much I want him and want him to be mine.

And if he knew that? If he knew he had permission to claim me forever?

Then all of this would have been for nothing, and I wouldn't have saved him or myself from all the pain waiting for us in the future.

It's remembering the awaiting pain—inevitable, unavoidable—that gives me strength. I open my eyes and gaze up at his face.

"I said them because I had to," I say, which is not a lie.

Jace's eyes narrow. "You said them to hurt me. Every day, I thought you'd call to explain more, to tell me you were lying. To tell me I wasn't just..."

"Just what?" I whisper.

He exhales forcefully. "Just a young, dumb fuck. Just a good body for you to ride until you got bored."

I want to close my eyes again. I hate myself for giving him this doubt, this *wound*, but what else could I have done?

His face changes when I don't deny it right away, his defensive expression pulling into a dark scowl. "If that's all you want," he says roughly, "I can give it to you. You want me to fuck you like I did that first night, hmm? Bend you over the table and take what I need? Or what about the night I found you with Kenneth? What about the night I tore up your pretty silk blouse and tied you up with it so I could fuck your virgin ass?"

Despite all my regret and torment, his words stir up my already primed body, and I can't help the little moan that leaves my lips. His eyes flare, and suddenly I'm spun around, my hands pinned to the wall and my ass yanked back to his lap.

"I knew it," he breathes in my ear as his hand works at the belt to my dress pants. "Knew you wanted me."

I recognize distantly that I need to stop this, that I need to tell him my decision still stands no matter what, but dammit, I don't *want* my decision to stand! And how can I deny my neglected body what it's been keening for since I left him in that hospital room?

Instead, I grind back against his cock and whimper the moment his hand slides into my panties, his middle finger finding my clit with unerring accuracy and rubbing me so perfectly that I feel the climax already pulling tight in my belly.

"Yeah," he grunts behind me, rocking his clothed erection against me as he fingers me with that blunt male prerogative that gets me so hot. "That's it. Remind me how wet and tight that pussy gets for me. Remind me how hard I make it come."

I've been too long denied, too desperate, and his words eradicate any barrier between me and what he demands of my body. In a sharp, vicious instant, I come so hard my knees buckle and it's his hand on my cunt keeping me upright.

"Need to fuck you," he mumbles into my hair. "Need it."

"Yes," I breathe, still riding it out on his hand. "Yes, please, yes."

He pulls his hand free, and then I hear the unmistakable noise of him sucking his finger clean. It's so carnal and raw that I think I might pass out from craving alone, from needing that massive cock stroking inside me—and then he uses his damp fingers to gently brush my hair away from my neck so he can kiss the sensitive skin there. That combination of dirty and tender that undoes me, every single time.

I can feel him reaching for his belt, unfastening it one-handed and then tugging at his zipper. I arch my back, thinking I'll yank my own pants down around my hips just so I'll be ready when he is—and then he stops. Hand on his zipper, his lips against my nape, he goes completely still.

"Please," I whimper. I'll die if he doesn't give it to me. "Jace."

He shivers at my plea, but then the ragged inhale he sucks in tells me his shiver wasn't one of pleasure.

"I can't," he says after a moment. "I won't."

He's there behind me, erect and unzipped, and I'm wet from the frantic, heated orgasm he just gave me in the hallway of a police station...

...and it's not going to happen.

He's not going to fuck me. There's not going to be some kind of electric connection that fixes everything between us. No frenzy of sweat and need that absolves us of past sins and leaves us clean and ready for a new future on the other side.

I'm frozen in place, my hands still spread against the wall like I'm being frisked, and I don't know what to say or what to do. I don't know what he needs or what I need. I don't know how to make this okay between us, how to get back to where we were before I defaced it with my fears.

Oh God. *I want things to go back to the way they were?*
What does that even mean?

His hand fists at my shirt near my shoulder, keeping me close to him. "I want to," he murmurs against my neck. "*Fuck*, I want to. And I thought maybe... maybe if this was the only way you'd take me, then I'd give it to you, because that's how much I want you in my arms. But I—" He takes a determined breath, his chest swelling against my back. "But I can't do that to us, and I won't cheapen what I feel for you."

God, how is he so *good*? So good even now, after I've hurt him? After I've shut him out? Maybe I've been wrong about which one of us is the mature one, the wise one. Maybe I should have trusted Jace's faith in us from the beginning...

He lets me go with a finality that makes me wince, zipping up and buckling his belt all before I can manage to turn to face him.

Fix this! my heart demands, but I don't know how. I don't know if I can.

And it doesn't matter because Jace is right in front of me, but he may as well already be out the door. His silver gaze is filled with pained resignation.

"It was never something tawdry or transactional on my end," he says quietly. "In fact, I always believed you were the best thing to have ever happened to me."

A choked noise echoes in the hallway, and I only realize it came from me when I feel a hot tear trace down my cheek to my jaw.

"And now I know," he continues, just as quietly, "that you never believed the reverse."

"Jace," I say, more tears coming now. "Stop. Please, that's not—"

"It's okay," he says, running his hand over his face. "It's okay. I can't make you love me like I love you, and you know what? I don't want to *make* you. I thought I could prove to you that you were mine. I thought I could possess you with my body, and that would be enough—but I don't want to possess you if you don't want to be possessed, you know? It's only worth calling you mine if you say it right back to me. And I know what happened with Frazer was fucked up, I know me getting shot was terrifying, but there's got to be a time when you choose to move forward, no matter how scary it is."

He leans forward and kisses my forehead, and my mind—normally the sharp, focused tool I prize—fails me. I'm searching through his words for an answer, searching through my own thoughts, and it's so hard because I'm crying and I can't see, and all I can do is slump back against the wall and try to breathe. Try to live.

Because what is he really asking me?

For the truth and an apology, almost certainly, but I think he's asking me for more. I think he's asking me to take a risk, to relinquish control...to be vulnerable.

To thaw.

Ever since Frazer died, I've been doing everything I can to keep myself as frozen as possible. Deep down, I never really minded being called Officer Ice Queen. I was a little proud of it, in fact, because it meant I did what I needed to. It meant I succeeded in keeping myself safe and my heart protected.

It meant I was strong.

But now?

Is this the kind of strong I want to be? The kind of strong that hurts other people "for their own good"? The kind of strong that would rather push someone away than do the hard work of loving through fear?

God, no. Maybe I needed these last twelve years of control. Maybe being an island has served me in the past, but not anymore. Not anymore because I have Jace and I have the knowledge I've had all along but somehow still couldn't believe until now: surviving isn't living.

And I'd rather be vulnerable with Jace than strong without him.

My breath catches, my heart pounding with this epiphany and my fingers already flexing to grab him back to me, to pull him close and tell him everything.

To tell him I love him and I want to move forward with him, even though, yes, I'm scared.

But when I wipe the tears from my eyes, I see something awful. I see that I'm alone.

Jace is gone.

CHAPTER SIXTEEN

JACE

My instincts have never failed me.

Not in a war zone, not on the beat. Not even when I took a bullet in a medical building staff room, because taking that bullet meant Cat was safe. Which means I'd do it a thousand times over again if I had to, even knowing how the shooting unraveled into pain and heartbreak. I'd still choose it because keeping her safe is the priority.

No, my instincts have never failed.

Except for right now.

I walk out to my car with fast, jerky strides, desperate to avoid anyone lingering after the ceremony or the usual flow of evening-shift cops dropping off in-custodies or hopping into the report room to catch up on paperwork. I smell like Cat and my uniform is rumpled, and I can't decide if I need to cry or smash something with my fists. So yeah, avoidance seems like the right strategy.

And as I go, I question myself over and over again. How could I have been so wrong about us? How could my instincts have let me down?

From the moment I first saw that woman, I knew she was mine. Knew we fit together in some important way I didn't entirely understand yet. And truly, through the next near month we shared, I saw our fit become better and better. She laughed more, played more. She trusted me, shared that keen mind with me, shared moments of genuine, unfiltered joy.

I knew she was good for me in every measurable way. But hell, I thought I was good for her too. I *needed* to be good for her. Not because of my male ego— well, okay, not *only* because of my male ego—but because she deserved it. She deserved someone to be good for her. Because it felt wrong to sponge up all that intelligence and determination without giving her something in return.

All of that came crashing down that awful night in the hospital, of course, but there'd been some stubborn part of me that refused to believe she really meant the things she said. This silly, fragile hope that she would confess she'd pushed me away out of fear and wanted to make it right.

Too young, too coarse.

A stupid waste.

Even now, the words rake over an unhealed wound, but even in my pain and shock that night, even through her cruel tone, I heard something almost sad in her voice when she accused me of being reckless.

If you're that careless with your own life, how the hell can I trust you with my heart?

Yes, I'm young, and yes, I'm probably coarse and reckless and everything else she said—but I know the woman I love. I know she's afraid and afraid with good reason. I know she's kept herself safe for a long time by keeping everyone else away.

And I thought tonight when I chased after her...

It doesn't matter. You were wrong. She didn't confess to any of that. She didn't apologize. She simply offered me her body. As if that were any kind of substitute for her heart. So now, here I am, alone and torn up and forced to acknowledge I was wrong about all of it.

She's not mine, and she never was.

When I get in my car, I'm not even sure where I want to go. My apartment is still haunted by her. By the few odds and ends she left there. By the tea I bought for her and by the memories of her presence. I don't feel like seeing any of my family or friends, and I don't really feel like getting a drink at the Dirty Nickel and watching whatever sports thing is on the television there. Every place I can think of feels wrong because every place I can think of is a place without her.

I finally decide to hit the gym. It's attached to my duty station up north, and I've got a change of gym clothes in my locker. Better yet, since it's only for cops, it's usually only got one or two other people in it, and I'll have a chance at some privacy while I try to burn out these feelings.

I try not to let myself think too much as I drive from the main station to my station. I try not to think about Cat's silence when I laid myself bare for her or about how she didn't correct me when I told her I knew she didn't love me like I loved her.

I try not to think about her at all.

And fail miserably.

An hour later, I'm sweaty and ragged, having set the treadmill to a dead sprint and then pounding out a run like I was being chased by ghosts, my arm wound screaming like hell the whole time. I grab my reusable water bottle and start chugging as I leave the gym and walk down the short hall to the locker room. Even though my body is thirsty and beat, my mind is still chewing on itself, wondering where I went wrong, and my chest still feels like it's been cracked wide open.

I strip off my clothes—miserably, tugging on the waterproof sleeve over my bicep to protect the bandage there—and then I shower—also miserably, too messed up to even touch the swelling erection my starved cock is offering up against the water. Even fatigued, my body remembers that just ninety minutes ago I had Cat pressed against me, ready and whimpering for me to slide inside her. Even heartbroken, my flesh still aches for hers.

With a long, weary sigh, I shut off the shower and wrap a towel around my waist. I slide the curtain aside with a vicious gesture, scowling down at my unrepentant cock.

"Jace. Look at me."

My heart stops. The air turns to concrete in my lungs. I look up and see the woman I love in front of me, still in her dress uniform, her aqua eyes like oceans of feeling and her Hollywood hair still tousled from where I kissed it earlier. Despite everything, my stomach flips over with an idiotic, naïve flip. I still want to see her. I still *want* her even though I know better, and it's frustrating as hell.

"What do you want?" I ask, irritated that the words come out husky and curious when they should come out cold and flat. But I can't help it. I can't help anything about how I feel about Cat. She could rip out my heart with her bare fingers and eat it in front of me, and I'd still want to pull her into my arms.

But she doesn't look like she's come here to eat my heart. Instead, she's sinking her teeth into her bottom lip and twisting her slender fingers in the department-issue necktie she's wearing with her dress uniform.

She looks...well, *nervous.*

But every second she doesn't speak reminds me that I'm damp and wearing nothing but a towel—and that towel has an oblivious erection twitching underneath it—and I finally say, "Look, we can talk later—"

"I haven't told you everything about Frazer's death," she blurts out before I can finish.

Her eyes widen fractionally, as if she can't believe she really just said those words, but then she takes a deep breath and forges on while I stand frozen in my towel. "That night—that call—I got there first. The dispatch notes said someone heard a woman screaming inside. Now we know it was the perp screaming, but then we thought it was someone else he was hurting..."

She trails off, and I nod because I know. Lots of situations require

SIERRA SIMONE

backup—but sometimes they require an officer's immediate intervention more. If she thought someone was in danger, of course she would have gone in alone. I would have too.

But that doesn't stop my pulse from spiking with worry, no matter how long ago this happened, and I think I possibly understand how Frazer felt when he realized she'd gone in there without him.

"The power had been turned off. I told you that, but did I tell you how hard it was raining that night? Flash floods all over town. The streets were like rivers. Every other step I took, there was a clap of thunder or a fresh gust of wind. Scared even me, and when I found the perp, he was huddled in the back room, crying and frightened. Abject, utter terror. Hearing him cry like that was... bone-chilling."

Cat takes another deep breath and looks at the ceiling to gather herself. "I started talking to him. It took a minute or two, but he began to settle down. He told me it wasn't a storm at all but people trying to kill him, and he was so, so scared. Had a kitchen knife with him in case 'the people' made it into the house. But I managed to get him to set it down, managed to get him to make eye contact, was able to say over the radio that the subject was alone and compliant and that we were in the back bedroom."

"But then Frazer..."

A tear spills over Cat's eye, and she wipes furiously at it as she nods. "He kicked in the back door—maybe because he thought it would be closer to the bedroom? If he'd just entered through the front door, which I'd already broken open, or if he'd just trusted that I'd call out on the radio if I needed help..."

"Cat, it was the suspect he didn't trust, not you."

She shrugs, and I know she thinks the distinction doesn't matter. And maybe it doesn't. The outcome was the same, after all.

"It startled the suspect. He grabbed his knife and pushed past me and went down the hall toward the noise. It was so dark, so fucking dark, and I tried to follow him, but I was tripping over all the trash in the hallway, and I—" Another tear, but she doesn't flinch away from her next sentence. "I was too late."

Her words hang in the cool, damp air of the locker room. I give her time to find her next words.

"He didn't have to die," she finally whispers. "Nobody had to. If only he'd waited or taken a minute to think and come through the front...he might still be here with me."

Oh God. Suddenly I see exactly where this is going. "I'm not Frazer."

She shakes her head. "No. No, I know you're not. I can't fault Frazer for trying to keep me safe, and I can't fault anything you did with Pisani either. But

I'm just trying to explain...why..."

I soften. "I know *why*, baby. It's never been a secret to me."

She looks down at her hands, still twisting in her tie. "I just thought if I didn't let anyone in, then they'd be safe. And I let you in...and you got shot. You did the same thing he did, and you rushed in and you almost got killed. You can see why that's hard for me."

I wince. I hate how this is between us, this mountain of causality. This reality of our job, jagged and insurmountable. "Cat."

She doesn't let me cut in; she keeps going. "But you know what? I'm tired of the hard things keeping me from what I really want. I'm tired of the walls and the precautions and the ice. I was wrong, Jace. Wrong about what I wanted."

Her words hit me good and hard, like a cold shot of top-shelf vodka. I think I feel those words buzzing in my veins.

"What do you mean?" I ask, voice rough. "Say what you mean."

Her eyes are the sweetest sea color, and she gives me a sad, pleading smile that makes me want to slay monsters for her, even if the monsters are the sins between us.

"I mean I'm sorry for the things I said," she says. "They were lies, Jace. The worst lies I could think of to make you let me go. I'm too selfish to want you to find a better, younger woman. I want you with *me*. I want to be your woman, age be damned."

I can't help the hope swelling in my chest like a balloon, and I take a step forward, reaching for her. She lets me. She lets me pull her into my chest with my good arm, and then she tilts her head back to look up into my face.

"I mean I love you," she says softly, her hand coming up to cup my jaw. "You're too young and too brave and so very caveman—and I love you. I love you so much that I'm willing to be scared. I'm willing to be vulnerable. I love you so much that nothing else matters."

"Babe," I rumble, burying my face in her hair as I squeeze her even closer to me. "Babe. Nothing else does matter. It never did to me."

"Oh, Jace. Can you forgive me? The terrible things I said?"

"I already have," I say, and I mean it. It's the truth.

"And pushing you away? Leaving?"

"You're here now, and that's all that matters to me." I kiss her hair again, never able to get enough of that delicate silk against my lips, of that exquisite, expensive scent of hers. "Fuck, I love you. And yes, I was hurt and angry and all the things when you left, but if you're willing to be open with me, then I'll be open with you. I don't see what we can't figure out if we have love and honesty."

I feel her smile against my chest. "So wise for one so young."

"Well, I stole that line from my PTSD counselor, but I still mean it."

She laughs. "Good."

She kisses my chest, and my cock responds, surging again under the towel and brushing against her. She purrs a little. "Young man."

And then she reaches under the towel to give me a firm, urgent stroke. My eyes flutter closed. "What happens next?" I manage to ask. "Do I get to take you home?"

"Every day for the rest of forever. But first..." Another stroke.

I groan.

"First," she whispers, "we're going to see how fast you can make this ice queen melt."

Game. On.

EPILOGUE

JACE

A year later...

"At some point, you're going to have to let me sleep, caveman," Cat teases, but she parts her pretty thighs for me all the same as I walk toward the bed.

"We'll sleep in tomorrow," I promise, giving my already primed cock a few slow strokes. Even though I just came back from putting away the warm cloth I used to clean her, I'm ready again. It's our third fuck of the night because I can't fucking get enough of her right now. I mean, I never have anyway, but right now, with my ring glinting on her finger and her belly heavy with our first child, I'm more caveman than ever.

"We have to work on the nursery tomorrow," she reminds me, idly plucking at her nipple as she watches me approach. "We should rest..."

But her sensible words are canceled out by the hungry way she watches my cock bob up and down as I climb onto the bed.

"No rest for the wicked, babe," I say, even though she is right about the nursery. I moved into her house when we got married half a year ago, and we've only just now finished integrating my things and turned to making the baby's room ready for his entrance in four more months.

"I suppose we have time," she muses, her free hand going between her legs to toy with the place I've already thoroughly pleasured tonight...and plan on pleasuring again.

I grunt in agreement as I mount between her thighs and take myself in hand.

"*Young* man," she sighs happily, petting my hard abs and sliding her palms up the flexed lengths of my quads. "My young stud."

And then her sigh turns into a broken moan as I slide on inside. She's wet and swollen from all our earlier play, which makes her slick as hell and tight as a fist. She cradles her own breasts as I give her a second, deeper thrust, and the sight of her hands plumping and squeezing her own tits is almost too much.

"Shit, babe," I mutter. "Gonna go fast if you do that."

She just gives me a sly smile and continues the show, driving me to a state of indecent desperation and making my own palms itch to feel her. With a growl, I pull out and move us so I'm lying behind her, my chest to her back and my cock prodding at her sweet pussy from behind. I nip at her neck as I flex my hips and search out her tits with my own hands.

"Mine," I grunt.

"Yes," Cat gasps, arching so that her ass is pressed against my lap and her breasts press even harder into my hands. "All yours."

Her curves are irresistible like this, and my hands can't stop their possessive roaming as I take my time fucking her. I love the heavy weight of her tits now that they're growing full for our baby. I adore the swell of her belly that I helped create. I love them all so much that I tell her I'm going to have five more babies with her, maybe seven or eight even, because I just love it so much.

Funny how she was afraid that I'd balk at having to choose a family too soon. If she'd asked me, I would have told her the truth.

Nothing with her is ever too soon.

She's been horny as hell since I knocked her up, and it takes her almost no time to come again, writhing back against me and working my cock inside her to wring out every last bit of pleasure. When she finally settles, limp and satisfied, I wrap her tight in my arms, pull her ass flush to my lap, and rock into her with slow, grinding slides, feeling my shaft thicken with the inevitable.

"Give it to me, Officer," she whispers. "Every last drop."

She doesn't have to tell me twice. With another ferocious growl, I release all my love and passion into her, spurting hot and thick and wet inside her channel and flexing my hips to get deeper as I do.

I've come enough already tonight that this climax has a bite to it—a sharp ache with every dizzying pulse, and I love it. I love knowing the ache comes from making her mine over and over again. From claiming her body so thoroughly that we're both spent and sweaty. And I finish my claim now with a bite on her neck. Not enough to truly hurt but enough so she feels her caveman marking her on her skin and inside her body at the same time.

It feels so fucking good to empty inside her with my arms holding her tight, so good that my orgasm goes on and on and on, until finally I'm completely drained and not a little sore. I slide free with a kiss to her shoulder and go to get a fresh rag. When I come back, she's got her hand on her stomach and her aqua eyes are wide with delight.

"Jace," she murmurs. "I think you might be able to feel him from the outside now."

I practically sprint to the bed, touching where she is. I've been dying to feel the baby move, to feel all the little kicks and rolls that she's already been able to feel. And sure enough, after a long, quiet moment, I feel the slightest, faintest movement against my palm. And then again. And then again.

I'm smiling like an idiot, I know, but I don't even care. That balloon of hope I felt on the day Cat came back to me is so big in my chest, I think I might float away. I think I might already be floating.

"That's our baby," I say in awe.

"That's our baby," she says. "Still want to have seven or eight?"

"More," I tease, nipping at her ear and finally cleaning her. "I want you pregnant all the time."

She rolls her eyes, but her little smile tells me she's in on the joke. I want us to have the right size family for us, whatever that looks like and however we can balance it with both of us wearing badges. And while I jest that I want as many babies as she'll give me, she also knows I'm content with any future of any kind. More than content, I'm ecstatic. I'm married to the smartest, bravest, strongest woman in the world. Why wouldn't I be?

Cat likes it when I exercise my "male prerogative," as she calls it, so when I finish cleaning her, I tuck her close to me and kiss her head and make all sorts of primal promises about what I'm going to do with her body as soon as we've rested up a little. And then she falls asleep, snoring sweetly on my bicep with my other arm cradling her pregnant belly and her strong heartbeat thrumming under my palm.

No, this could never happen too soon. In fact, when it comes to this stunning, clever woman, nothing can ever happen fast enough.

ACKNOWLEDGMENTS

This book is forged out of fourteen years of marriage to a cop, and to that cop, I owe a tremendous debt for almost anything you can imagine goes into the writing of a story. From everything to how multiagency investigation works to how quickly a duty belt can come off, and then of course with all the life essentials like solo parenting and making sure the cats get fed, my husband made sure the family, the house, and the book all came out the other side of the writing process ready for inspection. Thank you, Sergeant Karate, for literally everything.

Thank you to my amazing editor, Scott Saunders, who not only kept my burglaries separate from my robberies but also kept the words clear and sensical and pretty. And a huge thank you to the incredible Waterhouse team that's shepherded Misadventures in Blue out into the wild: Meredith Wild, Robyn Lee, Haley Byrd, Jonathan Mac, and Amber Maxwell.

Thank you to my agent, Rebecca Friedman, for being a tireless champion, and to all the usual suspects who help me pull a book together: Ashley Lindemann, Candi Kane, Melissa Gaston, and Serena McDonald. Julie, Tess, NCP, Nana, Sarah—your friendship, advice, and beer fridges (some beer fridges more metaphorical than others) are the reasons why I can keep going in this wacky world of ours.

And finally, thank you to whoever dressed Gillian Anderson in those amazing silk blouses in the three seasons of *The Fall*. One of these days, I'm going to write a book of hymns dedicated to her wardrobe, but for now, I've written a romance novel.

ABOUT SIERRA SIMONE

Sierra Simone is a *USA Today* and *Wall Street Journal* bestselling former librarian (who spent too much time reading romance novels at the information desk). Her notable works include *Priest, American Queen,* and *Misadventures of a Curvy Girl,* and her books have been featured in *Marie Claire, Cosmopolitan, Entertainment Weekly,* and *Buzzfeed.* She lives with her husband and family in Kansas City.

VISIT HER AT THESIERRASIMONE.COM!

MORE MISADVENTURES

VISIT MISADVENTURES.COM FOR MORE INFORMATION!